Finding Love Through Female Domination

Finding Love Through Female Domination

RENEE LANE

With original illustrations by Amitabha Naskar
Find him at https://amitabha.carbonmade.com/

Copyright © 2016 by Renee Lane.

Library of Congress Control Number: 2016913665
ISBN: Hardcover 978-1-5245-3589-6
Softcover 978-1-5245-3588-9
eBook 978-1-5245-3587-2

All rights reserved. No part of this book may be reproduced or transmitted in any form or by any means, electronic or mechanical, including photocopying, recording, or by any information storage and retrieval system, without permission in writing from the copyright owner.

This is a work of fiction. Names, characters, places and incidents either are the product of the author's imagination or are used fictitiously, and any resemblance to any actual persons, living or dead, events, or locales is entirely coincidental.

Any people depicted in stock imagery provided by Thinkstock are models, and such images are being used for illustrative purposes only. Certain stock imagery © Thinkstock.

Print information available on the last page.

Rev. date: 08/23/2016

To order additional copies of this book, contact:
Xlibris
1-888-795-4274
www.Xlibris.com
Orders@Xlibris.com
746069

Contents

Introduction vii

Chapter 1	At the Beginning Philosophy 1
Chapter 2	Service 23
Chapter 3	Discipline 43
Chapter 4	Blackmail 87
Chapter 5	Psychological Control 117
Chapter 6	Humiliation 151
Chapter 7	Practical Matters 169
Chapter 8	Sexuality 211
Chapter 9	Spirituality 243
Chapter 10	The End Game 255

Denouement 301
Final words 305

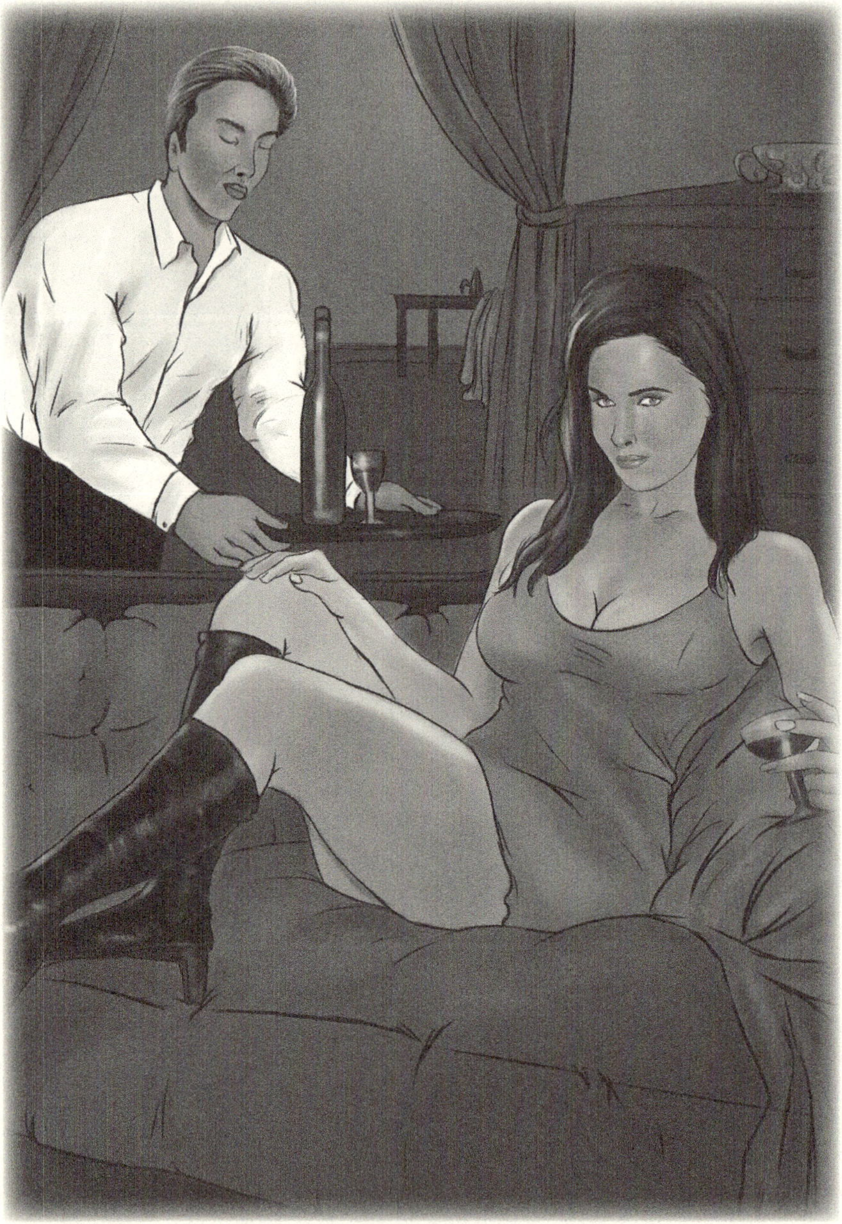

Introduction

This is the story of my ten-year struggle to transform my loving boyfriend into a completely submissive partner. It was a steeper path than either of us anticipated. It took my efforts, his devotion, and the help of several women to complete this journey.

An S&M relationship, particularly an S&M relationship where the woman rules, is the last taboo between consenting adults. I predict that our society will eventually grow more accustomed to female-led couples much like it accustomed itself to gay couples. It must, because many of us in the S&M community are coming out of the closet.

I met Butler, my submissive, through mutual acquaintances. Several months after we started dating, he finally summoned the courage to tell me of his long-held but secret desire to find a dominatrix to teach him submission. To my complete joy I was honestly able to tell him that I was eager to join him on this adventure because I also secretly shared his dream of dominating one special man.

My slave, Butler, is my great love. He is the wisest and best man I have ever known. His commitment to our lifestyle humbles me. His courage has made our life together possible.

One of the first requirements I had for him was to keep a journal of his experiences. In it he was to describe what happened and his reaction. I wanted to gauge his response to the techniques I planned to employ to enslave him.

These excerpts from his journal were never meant for publication, so they are not a consistent or complete representation of our progress.

They do, however, reveal some of the struggles we have had as we progressed. In addition, I gathered a collection of pertinent e-mails to and from my friend Heather that reveal my intentions and my compromises as we journeyed down this path.

Heather's e-mails are important because her reintroduction into my life jumpstarted my deeper training of Butler. After making minimum progress on my own, I discovered that dominating a man required support from at least one other woman.

From his journal entries and our e-mails, I have cobbled together a narrative of our lives of the past decade. I organized this writing chronologically as events happened but also under separate headings because as we progressed we were often working on different aspects of his submission. You will find that things move slowly at first in this story because that's the way events should unfold in a serious S&M relationship, but if you keep reading, you will notice how intense and real his training eventually becomes.

I do not recommend that every couple interested in a female-led relationship attempt this lifestyle. Our journey took an enormous amount of trust in each other and a complete commitment that is rare. However, once started down this path it's hard not to want more. My suggestion is to proceed with caution. In my opinion, the practice of female domination should come with a warning label.

"Releasing the id and the latent spiritual power of a woman can easily consume a man."

You've likely found this book in the erotica or fiction section of the bookstore. This book has often been mislabeled. Yes, I changed our names to protect our privacy but you'll know the truth of this story when you read it.

Ms. Renee Lane
Venice, Florida

Chapter One

AT THE BEGINNING PHILOSOPHY

January 2009
Dear Heather,

I'm so glad we found each other on Facebook! Recently, things have been happening in my life that caused me to think often of you. I can't believe you've been married two times already! You've been busy! My boyfriend has started discussing marriage but I'm leery of the idea.

I'm glad we're back in touch. I'm happy that you have found a submissive girlfriend. Remember when we were dorm mates in college and we would stay up until the early hours fantasizing about owning a submissive playmate we could turn into our slave? College boys just weren't ready for us! In truth, we weren't ready either.

I always thought it was weird and very ironic that two young women with dominant desires were put in the same dorm room. It's like we filled out a questionnaire, and because we said we liked the same thing they put us together without thinking it would have been better to pair us with a submissive. Ha! Looking back, I'm surprised we didn't kill each other.

Now look at us. We both have someone on whom to practice our dominatrix fantasies.

You asked me about my boyfriend. I think I have found the one man willing to go as far as I want to take an S&M relationship. Only you can imagine how far I want to go. I'm eager to tell you everything because I don't have anyone else who will understand what's happening to me but you.

You know that I was never interested in a routine relationship. My problem, I'm sure you'll remember, is that I bore easily. I crave challenge and excitement. I especially long for a high level of intensity in my relationships.

Like you, my path of self-discovery led me to understand that I am a sexual dominant. I was not shocked concerning my erotic predilections because I have always had fantasies of dominating my lovers even before I met you. As a little girl, I spent hours tying up my dolls! I never knew anyone who shared my fantasies until I met you. Somehow, knowing that you felt the same way made me feel more comfortable in my skin. I remember the terribly wonderful things we used to do together in school when we found the right kind of guy to practice on! Sometimes I wonder what ever happened to some of them. I'm afraid we may have left a few of them traumatized. I'd feel bad but I remember that they often only came back looking for more! Ha!

After graduating, I gradually introduced myself to the local S&M scene here in Memphis and became familiar with the usual practices of bondage and discipline. I eventually collected the necessary accoutrement of the lifestyle dominatrix and began experimenting by dominating different men and women who interested me. I moved back to the historic part of Memphis, so I own an older home with a huge attic room. I've made that into my playroom. It's been fun to make my boyfriend build most of the equipment I use on him.

He and I connect on many levels both intellectually and emotionally. We share roughly the same political views and interests. He also has musical ability that I find attractive. We even love the same books. I see too many people, especially men, trying to find a kinky partner without also seeking a life partner. I think it's important to find someone who you would be happy with even without S&M play. Ha! As if people like us could be happy without this!

After finding the right man, I am excited to be disciplining him within the safe space that we have created. However, my goal now is to do more than play bedroom bondage games. My new goal is to make him my slave in a very real and practical manner. I think I can take this further than you and I ever imagined even in our fantasies. The reason I think I can be successful is that we both want this. He longs to submit to me.

It sounds like we are a perfect match but it has been difficult to overcome the constant influence of vanilla culture. As I'm sure you know, one simply doesn't torture one's partner in polite society. Instead, our relationship stays buried deep in the closet. Societal norms are suffocating for a couple like us. Despite these norms, we have had many long talks about what we are willing to do to achieve a union filled with enough physical and emotional intensity to keep us satisfied.

The thought of being truly owned by me excited him. I made it clear when he asked for more that I would not limit my dominance to the bedroom. I was not interested in dressing the part for a kinky evening then becoming a mere equal the next morning. If he wanted to be my slave in the bedroom, then he would have to become my servant outside of it. He readily agreed to do whatever was necessary to make his slavery practical. We knew it would take years of work but we both committed to something real.

You know how I get when I have an idea. I like to write it all out. There is something about the process of writing that enables me to think through an idea. As you can see, nothing has changed since college.

I'll share my thoughts on it if you are interested. I want to know what you think. You are one of the few women I trust about this because I know you are fearless. Like me, you don't believe in playing by the rules. As you have already figured out, my goal is to take advantage of his sexual proclivities by using intense mind-control techniques to truly make him my slave. When I'm done, I want him to be broken to my will. If I know you, you'll like some of my training methods. I would love your advice on how to make my discipline more effective.

I'll write more, but this e-mail is already too long. It's easy to get carried away when I'm talking about my favorite project.

Send me a picture of your sweetie.

Remembered kisses,
Renee

February 2009
Dear Renee,

Oh, I remember the kisses! Why can't men kiss like women?

You are certainly taking this S&M relationship seriously. You know I've never been much of a planner, much less bothered to write down anything.

Only you would write out a detailed plan of how to dominate your mate. You are still the completely and carefully organized workaholic I knew in school. Despite the fact that you are over the top, your ideas intrigue me. Is real ownership even possible?

I have had little luck keeping men, although I admit to doing well when I divorced them. I've had two divorces in the last ten years. Men never last long in my life. One of them left me with an upper-end woman's shoe store. I have turned it around so it is now profitable.

I know what you mean about the world not letting us do what we want. I would parade my girl, Suzie, down the street on a dog lease except I'd have to put up with all the wolf whistles from asshole men.

I think real ownership unlikely but I want to know every detail of your plan. You are right to be hesitant to marry. I don't recommend it. What are your fears? What problems do you foresee? I want to know because I might have a keeper too.

The store in Atlanta is booming! I'll be in Memphis next month scouting for a location for a new shoe store. I can't wait to meet this guy who supposedly wants to truly submit. I doubt what most men say. I don't want you to get hurt. I think I need to check him out.

Your protector,
Heather

February 2009
Dear Heather,

I can't wait to see you. I'm very proud you've been such a success with your shoe store. The picture of Suzy was lovely. I can't wait to hear all about her.

Of course, I'll introduce you to Butler (my new name for him). I'll come up with some kind of little test so you can see how seriously we are taking his submission. I worry about the future. I don't want to go to all the trouble of training him to find that he suddenly quits. I've been thinking very hard about how I can prevent that. Here, I need your talents. You were always the more naturally dominant. I don't have anyone to discuss this with but you.

"Help me Heather-won. You're our hope."

Renee

Butler's Journal
First Real Test
February 2009

Once Ms. Renee and I seriously began to live a female-led lifestyle, I gave my mistress permission to follow her interests no matter where they took us. I had discovered a burning need in me to truly surrender to a dominant woman that went unsatisfied until I met her. I wanted something real.

I can't explain my sexuality to someone who does not feel the allure of the dominant woman any more than a gay man can explain his love for other men. It took a long time for me to realize the extent of my desires. As I came to an awareness of what I wanted, I realized that starting at puberty I had always been deeply attracted to Jung's archetypal "bitch goddess." For example, I rooted for Catwoman instead of Batman. I wanted the queen in Snow White to win. I was always attracted to the bad girl.

In my personal life, I project a strong personality. During my career as an attorney, I used my assertive demeanor to intimidate people such as the opposing counsel in the courtroom. Nevertheless, the idea of a woman taking control of me continued to grow in my fantasy life. Other than several bumbling attempts at role-play with the few women who were willing to pretend to be dominant, my desires remained buried and unfulfilled. They came fully alive when I met Ms. Renee.

We had a lot in common, a mutual attraction, and a desire to follow our S&M inclinations as far as possible. We were friends a long time and then lovers. We had established a relationship of trust before I admitted to my desires. Somehow, I knew she was the right woman. We started our relationship with her enjoying more sexual power because of her relative youth and beauty. I knew that I would always be more attracted to her than she could ever be to me.

The more we experimented and followed the path to my submission, the more attracted to her I became. I have been successful with women in my life but I have never been obsessed with one until she started dominating me. Now, she is all I think about.

This week I knew that my mistress was having a friend visit for the weekend. She told me that I would be banished from her home while her friend was there but I would get a chance to meet her if they had time. She cautioned me to be on my best behavior should that happen.

That evening she presented me with her first real test of my sincerity to be her submissive.

We live about three blocks apart in a historic neighborhood in Memphis. The previous week after I had cleaned her house, my mistress spent several minutes each night teasing me sexually. By the end of the week I was in a frenzy to please her. I would learn that this strategy was not unusual for her. She loves to work me into lather before asking something difficult of me.

I called her on the phone as I do each Friday evening to inquire what services she needed of me during the weekend. I knew that the opportunity to see her would be limited because she had company.

She told me that she doubted she would have any time for me until the following week. I was disappointed, so I told her so. She asked me if I was truly interested in pleasing her. Using a poetic image, I declared that I would crawl to her house on my hands and knees to please her.

There was a long silence on the phone. Then I heard several minutes of feverish whispering. Finally, I heard the tone of voice I knew was a serious demand, "Actually, that's a perfect idea, it's even better than my own plan. I want you to do it! Crawl all the way here. Get started right now."

I was shocked. It hadn't meant it to be a serious suggestion. It's true that we only lived three blocks apart but that is a very long way to crawl on one's knees. I began to stammer some reason for not fulfilling her request, but I heard only silence from her end, a short pause, and the receiver landing gently in its cradle.

It was an impossible request. I could have refused but I have been down that path before. It always ends with me begging once again to be her slave. Then she would increase her demand to make it even more difficult. I learned quickly that it's best to obey the first time.

It was close to 7:00 p.m. on a cold dark February evening, so the neighborhood sidewalks were clear of pedestrians. However, my neighbors know me. What possible excuse could I come up with for crawling down the sidewalk? Knowing she was waiting for me, I didn't bother to answer my own question. I grabbed a flashlight and started out the door.

I left on my knees. To not look too much like a fool, I decided to pantomime looking for a lost object. I shined the light back and forth across the sidewalk. I was ridiculously but desperately afraid someone would come out of his or her home to help me look. I had no idea what I would tell them. What could be so small and important enough that I would crawl down the sidewalk? I could come up with nothing. Nevertheless, I decided to keep acting as if I was looking for something so that cars would not stop thinking that I was crawling because I was injured.

I thought about walking partway. Impossible. She might have stepped out of her house to see if I was really crawling. I couldn't do it even if I knew she was inside her home. Our relationship was built on complete integrity. There would be no way to repair the damage a lie would cause.

Cars slowed but they did not stop as I slowly made my way to her house. I had to cross the street twice. I waited until the traffic was clear and scuttled across on my hands and knees.

Luckily, I met no one walking during the journey. It was dark and my knees hurt from the cold ground. I felt completely foolish and embarrassed. The last few feet crawling up her driveway were strangely the worse. I felt embarrassed about her seeing me. I had been humbled.

As I made my way up the driveway, I heard her door open and the clink of glasses and laughter. To my horror, I realized that Ms. Renee was not alone.

"Ha-ha! He really did it!" I heard a female voice I did not recognize followed by her laughter.

"I told you he would. He's starting to learn his place," Ms. Renee responded.

"What a complete fool. I have no idea what you see in him but at least he's obedient," came the other, raspier voice.

As I crawled up her steps, Ms. Renee held the door open.

Of course, the other woman would be her weekend guest. Both of them were standing in the living room holding glasses of wine, enjoying the drama and giggling to each other. They were dressed for dinner in dresses and heels.

Ms. Renee is an athletic-looking brunette with pale skin and dark eyes. She's a head-turner. My response to her was automatic from the moment I met her. I found her attractive at our first meeting, but after three years of dabbling with the dark arts of female domination I was now completely infatuated. It was hard for me to drag my eyes off of her. In normal social settings, my mistress wants me to be polite and charming. However, if the situation has anything to do with her dominion over me, she requires that I stay silent and keep my head slightly bowed while resting my eyes at her feet. I knew that this was a time for me to show my submission, so I tried to keep my head down.

"This is Heather, a friend from my college days. She's thinking about moving to town."

Ms. Renee's friend, Heather, was a slender redhead stylishly dressed. I turned to her but I knew not to look her in the eyes. Instead, I bowed my head. I couldn't help but notice that she seemed to be positively glowing from my embarrassment. I could feel her eyes scanning me and smirking as if I could never be good enough for her friend.

We had a few friends in the local but very discreet S&M club who knew something of our lives, but thus far Ms. Renee had never introduced me as her slave to anyone she saw socially on a routine basis. I wondered why Heather was different. I would soon learn that Ms. Renee especially enjoyed humiliating me in front of this particular woman. I could only assume that my mistress knew how much it amused her friend to watch me be humbled. Or maybe she did it because there must be a witness to make my humiliation complete.

Sometimes after embarrassing me, Ms. Renee takes advantage of my raw feelings to accent her domination by an additional physical discipline. I knew that anything was possible at that moment.

I felt anxious as she leaned down to me as I knelt in front of her. Her hand slid through my hair. She tilted my head up so that I could look in her face. Quietly, she whispered, "You pleased me tonight with your obedience, slave. Maybe I will be able to spend the evening with you on Sunday night after Heather leaves."

I was glad at such a prospect. I remember the excitement I felt when I responded. "Oh yes, Mistress."

"Heather wanted to take a look at you. The house is clean, so you can go home. I don't need you anymore tonight," she added.

I kissed her offered hand. I stood up, nodded politely to Heather, and turned to go, then I heard Heather's voice in a harsh loud tone, "Why the fuck are you standing? You can crawl back the way you came!"

My mistress rarely curses or raises her voice. I didn't turn around. I was afraid of what my expression might reveal. It is one thing to be humbled by my loving mistress, but I didn't even know her friend Heather. Instead of turning, I merely knelt and started the long crawl back to my apartment.

As I made my way back through the door, I could hear them laughing again.

I thought it had been a long crawl on the way there. The way back was almost impossible. It was cold. My knees ached. I felt foolish. I assumed that I looked ridiculous. I might have given up except that the idea that I had passed some kind of important test encouraged me. As I crawled it became apparent that my mistress had planned something to titillate her friend at my expense. I wondered what the test had been before I gave her the idea of me crawling to her house. I shivered a little at the thought. However, I was kept warm by the promise of Sunday night with my mistress. I don't understand why I have such a burning desire for her but I do. And it seems to grow as we move deeper into her dominion over me.

March 2009
Dear Renee,

I loved the weekend. I was reminded that we didn't leave college on such good terms. I recall that I always felt very competitive with you. You were always a better student. To my relief, I felt much less of that competition last weekend. Maybe we both know who we are now. We spent our last year in college in that tiny room sharing our fantasies and occasionally our bed. I'm obviously still attracted to you, but it feels better this time. You are yourself but I am less needy and more mature. Now, I don't feel so devastated if you are better at something than I am. I had a great time. I want to visit again. It looks like Memphis is a great place for a new store.

As for your subbie, I almost died laughing when I saw him crawling up the driveway. Now it gives me goose bumps. You have really grown. I knew you were a dominant but I had no idea you were capable of asking for anything like that from a submissive. It's not the kind of thing I'd ask Suzy to do, but for a man it was perfect.

What about all the other questions I asked while I was there? Now that he is started down the path to becoming your slave, how will you use him?

He doesn't deserve you, but what man does? Why would you consider marrying him?

I'm glad to be back in your life,
Heather

April 2009
Dear Heather,

I loved seeing you again last week. Yow! I didn't realize how much until you were in my arms! I think I've changed also. I'm obviously less fearful and more comfortable about my desires. I think I slept with so many different women in college as a political statement. Lately, I've been more comfortable as a heterosexual woman, but I learned last week that an occasional dance with you gives spice to my life.

The pictures of Suzy and the stories of how you are transforming her into a more surrendered submissive were exactly what I needed to hear. The stories you told me stimulated my creative juices. I was feeling isolated. It's easy for me to feel like I'm the only dominant female on earth who truly wants to own her own slave.

Thanks for letting me vent to you. I've been thinking about our conversation. I think you are right that I need to be rougher physically and psychologically to make progress with Butler. You left me with many ideas to sort through.

Why a man? I think I just proved to you that I love women but I have never felt a desire to dominate a woman. I wanted to enslave a man because I wanted to enslave an obvious inferior. I think I'd keep treating a woman as an equal.

As you know, I am a female supremacist. I'm more one now than when you knew me. We took all those feminist culture classes in college but most of it went right over my head until I entered the workforce. That was a real education! Now, I'm convinced that my teenage assumptions were correct. I appreciate men but I don't think men should ever be dominant in a relationship or hold positions of authority.

My personal experience taught me that all business organizations do better when women are in charge. Men make decisions under the influence of testosterone. Consequently, they tend to take unnecessary risks. When I look at male dominated organizations from politics to the priesthood, I note the enormous harm men cause until the civilizing influence of women improves them. The world would instantly be a much better place if women had supreme political and economic power. Thus, I believe that most men should be subject to the rule of a loving, dominant woman. I admit that my ideas are self-serving but that's what a good philosophical view should be!

Luckily, my man is evolved enough to want to submit to a woman. He says he is willing, but I know that because he is male he will need my strength and guidance to get him to the place of true spiritual and psychological surrender. In the beginning, as a test, I asked him, in the case of taming him, would the end justify the means? He replied that especially when it comes to our relationship it would. Furthermore, he gave me *carte blanche* to do whatever was necessary to achieve his surrender. Can you believe it? What could we have done together if we had met boys like that when we were in school!

According to him, almost any action I take is justified because of my sublime goal. I think it even turned him on to know I would break the rules of civilized behavior and polite society in order to tame him. As you know, I am usually a forthright person who does and says what she means. This opportunity offered me the chance to experience the unexplored manipulative side of my personality. I had to jump a moral hurdle but he asked me to jump it. Now I can boast that I have guiltlessly connived and even lied trying to achieve my goal of his surrender. I'm learning to revel in my new freedom. What an adventure!

Why him? I have come to understand his desire to offer himself to me. I've learned a lot about him during the last few years. He is a complete adrenalin junkie. For example, he only likes sports that might get him killed. I could allow him to continue his life in the same way he's been leading it until he is either injured or killed rock climbing or I could intercede in his life and give him the ultimate thrill of being owned by a determined dominatrix. It's kind of me, don't you think?

I know that he yearns to be bewitched. He's told me so countless times. For him the thrill is being out of control.

I agreed to start down this path with this particular man for many reasons. I needed someone mentally tough. The intensity of the psychological torment I have planned for him would render a weak man useless. I also wanted someone physically sturdy. I want to enjoy putting him through a very demanding physical discipline. Finally, he had to be someone who, once he gave his word about something, would keep it. I will give him the life of passion and sensation that he craves. In return, he will give me the devoted service I deserve. I am lucky to find the person with whom I can practice my different kind of loving.

My man wants to retire early. He was good at his job and he has made some money, but he has stopped enjoying his work. In my career, I am deeply engaged in changing the world for women. He could be a big help by serving me. Freed from mundane chores, I could be even more effective at my job. Thus, as my slave, his life would still have meaning.

I noticed that my love tried from the beginning to do things for me that I would expect only of a well- trained servant. As an experiment, I began to discipline him when I thought he had failed me in some service. From the beginning I noted how tender and loving he was toward me after I punished him. He seemed more open and emotionally accessible after a whipping. This change confirmed to me that I was on the right track. Our S&M experiences broke down barriers between us that I doubt could have been breached any other way. It's a different kind of loving, but it's still love.

Although I am certain he will find his right place as my submissive, I asked him to deeply consider the ramifications and consequences of agreeing to become my slave before we seriously began this lifestyle. I wanted him to weigh his choice carefully. After all, submission is much more of a commitment than marriage. Real slaves can't quit when the lifestyle becomes uncomfortable.

I know I blather on when it comes to this subject, but you are the only one I feel safe unloading to.

Thanks for listening,
Renee

April 2009
Dear Renee,

Unload away. As I mentioned, I'm interested in this subject for my own reasons. It sounds like you have a willing partner, but I doubt he'll stick when he is asked to do something that he really doesn't want to do. This whole dominant and submissive thing is really mostly fantasy. Alas.

I remember most of our teenage daydreams circled around a fantasy world of Amazonian warriors. In our imagined worlds, women physically held the power. I'm like you that I enjoy men, but I chose a woman to dominate because I feel that a woman can develop deep emotional ties that men are simply incapable of forming.

Like you, I'm turned on by the idea of leading my submissive to a deep surrender, but it doesn't really seem possible. Heck, it might even be against the law!

I'm on your side but I don't want you to get your hopes up.

You keep me interested,
Heather

May 2009
Dear Heather,

I refuse to think of this lifestyle as only fantasy if we both stay dedicated to the outcome. I think anything is possible. Indeed, I have no intention allowing him to change his mind now that we have really started.

I discussed my plans to dominate my boyfriend with some of my kinkier friends. Like you, they all cautioned me that my plans were too ambitious. I frequently heard the words "safe, sane, and consensual." I was told that "scenes" needed to be "negotiated." They talked about S&M "play" as if it were just play and not real. Ugh, that sounded like he could back out whenever he chose! That's not for me. Why work this hard if he could quit?

I was amused at their timidity. I wanted something much more than a few hours of "dress up" each week that was mere foreplay. I wanted my dominance and his submission to be real. In addition, I observed something that they had not noticed. Maybe, they had not understood its importance.

When I dominated my boyfriend, he slipped into a psychological state called subspace. I could even tell when it happened. I noticed that at some point he forgot about himself entirely and only concerned himself with my pleasure. Observing him carefully, I began to realize what was happening. I suspected that strong opiate like endorphins were surging through him that gave him an almost out-of-body experience. My dominance of him was acting like a powerful narcotic. Even more importantly, I noted that this drug was obviously addictive. I knew this because he craved our S&M play more and more. I loved dominating him but clearly his need was even greater than mine.

Knowing this gave me a momentous surge of power. He was addicted to me! More specifically, he was addicted to being my slave! It reminded me of "white slaver" stories of men giving women heroin to obtain their sexual services. Only my drug had no harmful effects. Play? Negotiation? It seemed to me that we are already past all of that. I had a man physically addicted to my domination of him!

It didn't take much further experimentation with female domination until my man asked me to marry him. I knew that if I agreed it could be a beginning to a new and deeper relationship. I refused because I didn't want to give up my freedom, but after some thought I decided that marriage could be the first step to my own deeply held desires. However, he will have to prove the depth of his commitment before I agree to such a step. I am eager to fulfill every fantasy he has about a dominant woman. What he doesn't know is that my own fantasy is a darker, richer dream than he could ever imagine.

To be fair, I asked myself the same kind of questions about changing my mind. Was I ready to take on the responsibility of taming a man? I would be manipulating his psyche and his personality in ways that resulted in deep mind control. Did I want to take responsibility for that? My lover might have voluntarily started on the road to submission but I knew that our brief journey has already changed him. Over time he will become even more malleable and open to suggestion. He will find himself doing things and agreeing to things that he would reject now. Did I really want to take him there? Once broken, he would become my responsibility.

I deemed it important to ask these questions because I don't think either of us would be happy if we only went partway. Going only part of the way would be as useless as removing a splinter part of the way, or making a boat partly watertight. Enslaving him only partially would only cause pain and loss without any real accomplishment. Therefore, I resolved to follow our path until we reached our goal. Asking myself these questions revealed to me how intense my own desire was to completely tame one special man.

Some may point out that I am manipulating the innocent kinky interests of my boyfriend in a careful and diabolical manner to slowly break him into becoming my slave in such a way that makes it psychologically, legally, and financially impossible for him to ever escape my evil clutches. Yes! I'm guilty as charged. But to be fair, I told him that this was my intent from the very beginning. I remember his answer to me was, "Yes!" He even said, "Please."

What might be surprising to someone who doesn't know me is how uncomfortable I am with anger and selfishness in myself. I'm turned on by dominating my man but only in the context of two explorers seeking the unusual and extreme in a loving relationship.

One of the things I am experiencing is expanding my range of what I allow myself to enjoy. As you know, I usually keep my id under careful control. What has been challenging and fun is allowing myself to feel anger when it's barely justified.

By submitting to me, my submissive creates a safe space for me to explore these feelings and experiences. I practice being more dominant by frequently allowing myself a selfish, bitchy snit over a tiny lapse in his attention to me. Knowing I can punish him without fear of ruining our relationship fills me with a deep gratitude to him. I now have a freedom few women will ever know.

Ask a couple of questions and you get a six-page answer!

I love finally having someone to share all this with.

Kisses,
Renee

June 2009
Dear Renee,

You are so going to hell. I mean, if there is one. Or maybe you'll end up in a feminist heaven for exploiting at least one man in return for the thousands of years of shit that has been raining down on us from men and is still raining down on us.

I understand now why you wanted a man and not a woman to dominate. I get why you think he is a good subject. However, you know that I have a low opinion of men. It's not improved over the years.

You spent a lot of time justifying what you are doing to him. Asking permission, etc. I've never had such moral qualms because I believe everyone is always trying to manipulate the best deal they can get. He must be getting something from it or he would not have agreed. Most people aren't honest with themselves about this. I am.

I don't think you should sweat the ethics. He obviously wants to do this or he would not allow you to bind him so tightly to you. If you don't do it, some other woman will and she might not have your moral scruples. It seems only right, then, that he should be yours. Personally, I'm even more interested in all of this as I never want my bottom to leave me. Ever.

I loved, loved, loved, the idea that we are each giving our subs such an endorphin rush that we are physically addicting them to our domination. Yikes, that gets my motor running! I think I'll turn up the heat on my little bitch tonight.

We obviously need to keep communicating with each other. I think together we can come up with ideas that we can each use. I'm thinking about taking my own advice and getting Suzy to sign a contract.

I have this fear that she'll show up at an emergency room with whelps on her butt and I'll be arrested for abuse. Things can get complicated.

Maybe I just want to put in writing somewhere that I own her ass.

I'm interested in how you intend to use him. It can't all just be for sexual services. I know you. You have plans within plans. Do tell.

More than kisses,
Heather

Butler's Journal
The Importance of My Opinion
June 2009

The party last night was an important fundraising event for my mistress. I'm proud of her involvement in women's rights issues. It is a political passion that we share. Last night I watched her court some of the wealthiest donors in the state at her gathering. I'm proud to be seen with her. Any man would be proud of her wit and charm. She also looked stunning in her cocktail dress.

I'm a moderately good amateur pianist. To help accommodate the entertainment needs of my mistress, I make a point of knowing several songs that people love to sing. The recipe to raise money seems to be to give the guests a lot of wine and fun. If you are successful, the checks have more zeroes in them.

I was at my usual place at the piano. Ms. Renee has a lovely singing voice. I tend to croak along mostly on key. We were between songs. It was an older crowd, as fundraisers generally are. Several people suggested some well-known show tunes. Others wanted me to play early Beatles. A discussion broke out concerning the merits of the composers Lennon-McCartney compared to Rodgers and Hammerstein. My goddess was leaning on the piano across from me. I was about to join in the discussion when my mistress caught my eye. She knew my opinion about the merits of these composers. She's heard me discuss them several times. I admit that I can get very strident about my opinions concerning music.

Holding my gaze, she placed two of her carefully manicured fingers over her perfect lips and tapped them twice as if contemplating an answer to the question being discussed. Luckily for me, I caught her hand signal. When given that particular gesture, I have been instructed to agree with whatever she is about to say. Smiling at me, she launched into a description of the Lennon-McCartney team she knew I disagreed with completely. For a second I said nothing. She continued to hold my gaze while waiting. A very long second ticked by and she raised one eyebrow in query.

Still looking into her beautiful face, I began hastily if somewhat clumsily agreeing with her assessment. She knew that I heartily disagreed with what I was saying. As I continued, she beamed down on to me and smiled mischievously. I felt shocked and frustrated but at the same time I felt I had been magically enchanted.

Writing about it now, it seems like such a small thing. However, I feel passionate about music, and to reverse an opinion so quickly in public was extremely difficult. I felt like I was stripping my mental gears. I remember that I wanted to please her but at the same time her hand signal also felt invasive. Wasn't I allowed to have an opinion? I knew she was only teasing me to heighten my awareness of our private journey. However, in that very brief moment when I was marshalling an argument that disagreed with my own opinion but mirrored hers, I felt something else. Somewhere in the fun and sensuality of the moment I felt a tingle of fear.

In the end I knew that no matter what I did I would soon find myself carefully restrained over her whipping bench completely in her power. My discipline sessions were becoming more vigorous. Displeasing her was something I was learning to avoid. In that somewhat silly playful moment, I felt it was not only impossible to resist her but it was also a little dangerous.

This knowledge only increased my longing for her. Allowing her to dominate me excited me like nothing I had ever done before. I was caught up in a vortex of passion and desire. Feeling very fortunate, I began playing the next song. I was careful to choose something I knew she would enjoy.

Chapter Two

SERVICE

June 2009
Dear Heather,

I've been thinking of our last weekend together. Making him crawl felt wonderfully empowering. I'm glad you encouraged me to demand it. Strangely, whenever I see him submit, instead of being satisfied it makes me hungry for more. Maybe I have grown but it helps that I have the right man. No matter what I do to him he always seems to love me more for it. I'm learning a lot from his response to my domination.

I've been thinking for a long time how to start changing how he thinks of himself and how to use him. I appreciate the suggestions you made the last time we spoke on the phone.

I agree that if you want to instill in a man a sense of his servitude then you need to require him to provide the services a servant provides. Domestic chores are good for him. They teach him who he is. Also, to see a man burdened with housework makes me happy.

What most submissive men can't imagine in their fantasy life is that the life of a slave is often painfully boring. Housework is drudgery. I will do my part to make it interesting by making the rewards hard to earn and the punishments intense. Service is the practical aspect of female domination that any woman could learn to love.

If I am doing my job as a dominatrix correctly, the drudgery he performs will be infused with a spirituality that comes when he surrenders to me as his goddess. Thus, cleaning the floor will become, for him, an act of worship. Now, that's a great way to get the housework done! If I do this right, then the more he works and suffers, the more he will love me.

Lately, I have experienced the joy of driving home knowing that he has spent every second that we're apart preparing the house for my arrival. I love knowing that when I'm there he can't take his eyes off of me and when I'm gone he's working constantly to please me. When I arrive, I see gleaming floors and carefully folded laundry. I see the lawn manicured and the garden weeded. Finally, I see him anxious that I will find something wrong that will cause me to punish him. Again. Of course, I look very hard for his mistakes. After all, I want to make it fun for both of us. Ha!

I have learned that the most spiritual and intimate relationship a woman can have with a man is the relationship between a mistress and her properly trained manservant. I also believe that love is about knowing. Consequently, I intend for him to know me the way that few men ever know their wives. He already knows how to bathe me, how I like my tea, how to care for my hair, my shoes, my nails, etc. In addition, I keep him carefully tuned in to my constantly changing moods so that he can anticipate my needs. Such intimacy! My ongoing task has been to stimulate him to be a perfect servant.

No woman who has experienced the service of an adequately trained man would ever give it up. The more real the dominant/submissive relationship is, then the more intimate and the more loving the relationship will be. In a real S&M union, he receives excitement and purpose for his life while she receives the service and adoration every woman deserves.

My slave once told me that if he had the choice of climbing Mount Everest or having a month of intensely orchestrated domination that would move us significantly toward our goal, he would choose the month with me. This comes from a man whose favorite sport is rock climbing! For him, the idea of us as mistress and slave is the most exciting adventure he can imagine. We have both picked the right life partner.

Thanks for all of your ideas. Some of them he's not ready for, but we'll get there.

Love,
Renee

Butler's Journal
Cleaning for Ms. Renee
June 2009

Our conversations concerning my submission to my mistress continues. We both agreed that neither of us was interested in the kind of dominance that restricted itself to a dominatrix costume show and a mild spanking before coitus. To combat the problem of "topping from the bottom," she required me to come up with a way to both humble myself and make myself useful. She rejected several of my proposals until I mentioned housework.

I had a professional career as a moderately successful attorney. I'm partially retired. During my career, I was too busy to do my own cleaning. I have always hired a cleaning service. I offered to pay for a cleaning service for her but she refused. Knowing that I had the time, she wisely wanted me to do the work personally so I could learn humility.

It was difficult to adjust to this at first. I have a normal social life I had to rearrange. I find cleaning incredibly boring. She continued to be firm. In response to my hesitation, she kept me from her bed while sexually teasing me for a few weeks. In addition, she began to administer ever-increasing physical punishments until she changed my mind. Finally, instead of agreeing to be her housekeeper, I started begging for the privilege.

I feel compelled to write that again, "She changed my mind." Her discipline and sexual teasing increased my desire to please her. She actually altered how I felt. I consider myself a strong person. I have always been in control of every relationship I've ever had with a woman. My job as an attorney was often to intimidate an adversary. Maybe this is why allowing myself to submit to her has been so incredibly exciting. It's a complete change from everything I have ever known.

Something wonderful has happened to me. I came alive emotionally after meeting Ms. Renee. I never realized how bored I was with most women. With her, every minute is an adventure full of possibility. I feel things about her I have never felt before. I am eager to see how far down the road of dominance and submission we can go.

For the last few months I have visited Ms. Renee's home after dinner Monday through Thursday at 7:30 p.m. to wash her dishes, tidy her kitchen, and carefully clean one-fourth of her home. She allows me Friday off. Sometimes she is out with friends or at a work function. Present or not, I follow a schedule drawn up by her so that every part of her house receives a complete cleaning at least once a week. For example, on Wednesday night, in addition to the kitchen I clean her living room and den.

For the first few weeks I found cleaning to be a humbling experience. I was an executive. Now, I was a maid? However, Ms. Renee kept working with me. She teased me, whipped me, encouraged me, taunted me, and finally so captivated me that I kept at it. Now, I actually feel some pride in making her life a little easier.

When I clean a room like the living room, I start with the light fixture in the ceiling and work my way down. I must move the furniture, open the couches, dust every surface, polish the wood, and finish with the floor. I pace myself so that I finish my work at 9:00 p.m. so that I can report to her upstairs if she has not gone out for the evening.

If she is there, I help her undress. I have been trained to do this with a certain warm but calm civility that is not in any way sexual. At that moment I am her slave, not her lover. I then bathe her. Frequently, I massage her for a few minutes. Afterward, I dress her in her nightclothes and a gown. Finally, I brush her hair until she excuses me at about 10:00 p.m.

When I am lucky and when she is in the mood, she will take advantage of my eagerly offered oral services. On those nights, after brushing her hair she merely points to the floor, indicating where she wants me to kneel. She rarely speaks but simply leans back in the chair as I kneel in front of her in perfect submission with my head buried between her thighs. Afterward, I am dismissed.

From the beginning, Ms. Renee frequently limited coitus to the weekends. This is difficult for me, as I desire her constantly. Sometimes, if I have not been perfectly submissive, she denies me altogether. Each Saturday evening, she goes over my progress toward submission and rewards or punishes my actions. Only if I have moved forward and received my discipline with the correct attitude is sexual play on the menu. Some Saturday evenings leave me sore and unsatisfied. Consequently, I work very hard to please her.

Shortly after starting our journey, I sold my home in the suburbs and I bought a small condo close enough to her home so I could walk to it. Leaving her house each night is a lonely walk home for me. I have longed to be her live-in slave but she has denied me that privilege until she feels that I'm ready for it.

If she is not home when I arrive, she expects me to wait patiently for her after I finish my work to help her retire no matter how late she is out. She has often told me that she likes to come home to see me patiently kneeling just inside the front door. At first I complained that this was a serious imposition to my own social life. She merely laughed and dismissed me telling me that I must not be serious about being her slave. I brooded about it for a few days but soon returned and begged to try again. This was something I wanted. She graciously agreed to allow me another chance to prove my sincerity. I agreed to plan my life around her needs.

Last Wednesday turned out a little differently than normal. That evening after cleaning the floors, I found her standing at the bottom of her stairs with a certain expectancy that put me on instant alert. At the time I was carrying the trash basket from the living room in my hand. She still wore the dress and heels she had worn to work that day. She radiated a special beauty I found irresistible.

I felt nervous as she directed her gaze toward me. Suddenly she asked, "All of the dust that you swept up is in this trash basket, correct? Good, then listen carefully. I want you to search it now for any tiny rolled up pieces of pink paper."

Even though I thought it was an unusual request, I was well trained enough not to ask any questions. I knelt in front of her and put my hands into the small pile of dust and debris to begin searching. Soon, I found three tiny pieces of pink paper. Remaining on my knees I handed her the small crumpled pink balls. She seemed displeased but at the same time eager to be displeased. This mood never bodes well for me. I've seen this attitude in Ms. Renee before. It's as if she wants to find something wrong with my service so she can enjoy my punishment. Of course, she can discipline me at will, but for her it's more meaningful if there is a reason for whipping me.

She rolled the tiny balls around in her hands for a minute, looking at me with disdain. Icily, she stated, "There should be five of these. I know because I planted them in hard-to-reach places this morning before you cleaned the floors. Go and find them."

Something in me wailed and moaned as I slowly turned from her to begin my search. I knew that there would be no way I would escape a punishment. It's not a large home, so searching the downstairs did not take too long. I found the first ball of paper secreted behind a couch leg. The last one was elusive. I knew she would make me search all night until I found it. Finally, I found it stuck between the wall and the baseboard. Technically, it wasn't on the floor, but I knew enough not to complain. Fairness was not part of the equation.

I returned with the missing wads of paper and knelt at her feet. She smiled triumphantly.

"Open the paper and read it."

Surprised, I carefully unrolled the small ball and read, in miniature handwriting, the number four. I didn't have to ask what it meant. My punishment day, Saturday, was coming up and I instinctively knew that four vicious strokes with her cane would be added to the three I had already earned from misplacing a pair of stockings in the wrong drawer. Fearfully, I opened the last crumpled scrap of paper and almost crumpled myself when I read three. There was no court of appeals. There would be no mercy. I felt myself trembling as Ms. Renee placed her well-manicured hand under my chin, lifting my face to look directly at hers.

"I want perfect service. Obviously, the floors were not cleaned to your best ability. Nothing else will satisfy me."

She held my gaze a second and quietly demanded, "Be still."

I froze, knowing what was coming. Her hand flashed out, slapping against my cheek. Then the other hand quickly followed so that I stood with both sides of my face burning with pain and embarrassment. I knew this small discipline would not change what was coming on Saturday.

I stayed completely mute. I looked down at her feet, unable to speak.

"You're starting to feel it, aren't you? You are starting to feel like my slave. That's good, because it's what you are. Now, go clean the floor again. This time do a better job."

She turned away from me, and looking over her shoulder, added, "I won't need you for the rest of the night. You can let yourself out when you're finished."

I heard her heels clicking up the stairs. I suddenly wanted to weep or shout. The coming whipping was bad enough but this cut even deeper. It meant I would be unable to bathe and massage her. This discipline was taking the most precious time with my goddess away from me. I cursed my poor performance.

I stood there filled with conflicting feelings. I felt shame that I had allowed myself to be enslaved to such a point. Was I still a man? I felt anger that she should abuse me in such a manner. I wanted to walk out and never return. Surely another kind of relationship would be more rewarding than this one. At the same time, I longed to be upstairs preparing her bath. I was grieved that I had served her so poorly. During this storm of emotion, my feet were slowly walking to the broom closet, propelled by the sheer habit of obedience. I reasoned that I could consider leaving while I started cleaning. It's hard, boring work. It put me on my knees.

As I cleaned, I could hear her upstairs taking her bath and undressing. She was moving through all of the preparations for bed that I normally would have been helping her with. Finally, there was no noise except for the scruff of the rags across the wood in front of me. I kept rubbing the wood in frustration. As I rubbed, visions of Ms. Renee kept flickering across my mind. My anger and confusion drained away as the floor became cleaner. I realized that she had not strained our relationship this way a year ago. It would not have survived. But that was a year ago. Now, serving her was as natural as breathing. I worked late into the night polishing the floors until they gleamed. From that point on I knew that I had set a new level of service that I would always meet. She was right about everything. I still wanted to serve her. Quietly, I let myself out.

While she slept peacefully, my footsteps echoed down the street with the same loneliness I normally feel, but on that night my step echoed a new determination. I knew that I would continue serving her until the day I dared to become her full-time slave. I did not understand what is was about my sexuality that needed to submit to such a woman, but I knew that I felt more excited about her than I had ever felt for any other woman in my life.

June 2009
Dear Renee,

Oh, hell yeah. I love the idea of a man doing all of the housework. My little bitch was always too busy in my shoe store to be of any help in the house. You are on to something about taking the service a subbie offers out of the bedroom and making it more practical.

You always had the big picture in mind. How are you disciplining him? My problem is the first second I touch Suzy with my crop she dissolves in tears, begging to serve me. Low pain threshold, I assume. Or maybe she too has found what she wants. I hope so. We have been growing closer.

However, sometimes I want to take a big swing and give a good thrashing to someone. Lucky you.

Heather

Butler's Journal
Refusing My Mistress
July 2009

For the last year, to my own surprise, I have continued down the path to submission with Ms. Renee. I thought at first that this might merely be an infatuation that would pass. Instead, as she asked more of me and continued to discipline me, my attraction to her only mounted. Being on this journey with her has been the most exciting thing that has ever happened to me. I can feel myself changing about how I see myself and how I see her. Again and again, I have surprised myself by agreeing to her demands. In fact, I have often wanted her to be more demanding.

I am a man of some importance in the community. I had a successful career and women have come and gone without leaving much stress as they passed through my life. However, she is a woman I will do anything to keep.

Ms. Renee changed everything. Maybe because she has always treated me as someone destined to serve her that my service has come so naturally. I'm no longer important when I'm with her. She is the one who is important. It has been a relief to be with her. For a long time, I privately harbored submissive fantasies. Some of my girlfriends had attempted to play along with me but those experiences were all disappointing. However, when I met Ms. Renee I knew I had met someone who could take me beyond my fantasy world. Maybe I should have run from her, but it has all been too exciting to stop.

Four nights a week I perform my duties as her housekeeper. Friday night we often go to dinner. On the weekends, she adds additional chores to keep me busy during the day, such as yard work and car maintenance. Of course, I always keep my calendar free for her on the weekends because we almost always make love. Was my obedience based on being addicted to sex with her? There was no doubt that was part of it!

Last weekend I forgot to fill her car with gas. On Monday my cell phone rang. I have a special ring programmed for her so that I know to pick it up immediately no matter what I'm doing.

"My warning bell just went off on my fuel gauge." She hung up.

I knew there was no reason to call her back and apologize. Ms. Renee does not accept apologies or excuses. I try to keep her car serviced but in the rush of different chores over the weekend I had neglected to check her fuel gauge. My head spun with conflicting emotions. My first thought was that I had failed her. It crushed me to think that I had displeased her. At the same time, I recalled that I spent most of my free time outside of my job working to please her. It seemed fair that I should be allowed a few mistakes. Her call had been abrupt and bitchy sounding. I carried my conflicting emotions around with me for the rest of the day. That evening she didn't mention it as I did her dishes and cleaned the section of the home that I was assigned for Thursdays. She didn't seem distant or bothered as I helped her with her bath. Finally, while brushing her hair she asked for my notebook.

I carry a small notebook at all times. If I have displeased Ms. Renee in a way that a quick punishment won't take care of, she writes a note to remind herself to punish me later. Frequently, she paddles me during the week as an ongoing discipline, but for errors that she has found particularly irritating, she applies severe lashes from her rattan cane on Saturday evening. Each stroke of her cane leaves a vivid slash across the back of my thighs and buttocks. Such a stroke usually takes a week to heal. I work very hard to avoid them completely. I almost never earn more than four a week. Too many would keep me from work for several days, too sore to sit at my desk.

Frequently, when Ms. Renee makes a notation of one of my failures she places a number that corresponds with the number of strokes with her cane I will receive. I think she does it so that I can dread the punishment for days before she delivers it. When she handed me the notebook back, I almost dropped it when I read "ten" after her note. It was clearly out of proportion to my mistake. I didn't say anything but my look of bafflement was evident when I looked back at her.

"Oh, don't you think keeping my fuel tank filled is important? Maybe it's not important to you now but I promise it will be on Saturday evening!"

I stammered, "Yes, Mistress, but ten?"

Her palm shot out and landed on my cheek with a loud crack. Normally she warns me to "be still" so I don't involuntarily dodge. This time it came so quickly and so suddenly that I didn't have time to dodge.

Stupidly, I retorted, "But . . .," only to receive an even harder slap. It took all of my control not to grab her hand. When I'm thinking things like that, then I know the situation is getting out of hand. She sensed it too.

"Hand me your book," she said icily.

Somewhat stunned, I handed it to her. She crossed out the ten and wrote "fifteen."

It was impossible. Was she trying to incite me to rebel? We have always played fairly hard, but there were limits.

Before speaking, I cautiously stepped away from her. "I can't do it, Mistress. I have to be in court on Monday."

She cut me off instantly. "If you aren't willing to take my punishments, you can leave."

There it was.

It was impossible. I was furious. I doubted my ability to sit at my desk and work after so many lashes.

"I'm sorry, I hope you will reconsider," I told her. One look at her face told me that further conversation was senseless. My duties were done for that evening, so I said goodnight.

"Stop, slave! If you don't agree right now to accept your punishment, then I won't need your services this weekend."

"Yes, Mistress, I understand. Goodbye." I left. I've walked home many times feeling lonely but this time I was too angry to feel lonely. What she was asking was out of bounds.

The next night I admit to feeling relieved that I was free for a change. I had a drink and watched TV like a normal red-blooded American guy. It felt strange but good.

On Saturday, I hung out at the apartment. I felt sure that she would call me and renegotiate my punishment. I admit to looking at the phone several times unsuccessfully, willing it to ring. Not hearing from her, I went out with friends that evening. While out, I drank too much and woke up hungover on Sunday morning. There was still no word from her. I wanted to drive by her house to catch a glimpse of her but resisted. It seemed too juvenile an impulse to indulge.

By Monday I was starting to feel anxious. The most important relationship I had ever enjoyed had been taken from me by an impossible demand. I still felt deeply angry. I vowed never to call her. There were other women in the world. There were several women at my office that had made it clear that they were interested in dating me.

That week I took one of the female attorneys at my firm out to dinner. I wanted to clear my head. She was a perfectly lovely woman with good conversation. Sitting across from her I found myself fantasizing about what it might be like to submit to her. Watching my fantasies emerge with this woman confirmed what I already knew about myself: that I was a submissive male. I had discovered the power and excitement of that aspect of my sexuality at the feet of Ms. Renee.

My date was intelligent and attractive, but how would she react to my submissive tendencies? Most women are horrified. Before meeting Ms. Renee, I had spent years in vanilla relationships bored and restless. The idea of repeating that period in my life loomed like a death sentence. I sat across from my dinner companion and realized that I had no idea what she was talking about. I could hear her but I couldn't force myself to listen. How could I ever think of dating anyone else? It seemed impossible to start over again with another woman.

I knew suddenly that if she had invited me home that I would think of a reason not to accept her offer. It would have been embarrassing. I suddenly knew that I might be impotent with another woman. That idea shocked me. Ms. Renee had really messed with my head. I had invested over three years, endless sweat, and even a little blood in learning to submit to her. I knew how hot Ms. Renee liked her bath. I knew how to care for every piece of her clothing. I knew where to press and how hard during her massage. How could I start all over? I brought the evening to a polite but early close.

That Wednesday afternoon I refused another offer for dinner and went home alone. I was deeply disturbed about the possibility of being impotent with any woman but Ms. Renee. Was I forever damaged? I worried about my limitations and I wondered what I should do. I noticed a bag near my doorway containing a pair of her boots that I had taken to be resoled. It was one of the many chores I had done for her lately. I took the boots out of the bag. I remembered kissing them while she stood over me. I touched the leather tops, and then grabbing both boots in my hands, I started to shake. I knew I would never find another mistress who would match—and as I had discovered—surpass my desire for domination. My blood was boiling to be her lover no matter how she disciplined me. I had been a fool.

The next day, on Thursday evening, I put on my work clothes and arrived at her back doorstep at the time I usually arrived. I rang the bell and waited anxiously. I was overcome with worry that she would refuse me or that she had already found another submissive man. I knew that submissive men were a dime a dozen but dominant females were very rare. Finally, she came to the door.

It wasn't necessary for me to say anything because I knew she understood everything I had gone through during the previous week. Still, I had to say it. I found myself humbly apologizing for my behavior. She remained cool and aloof. I begged to be allowed in.

She hesitated but eventually told me to follow her on my knees. I followed her through the house, trying to keep up with her as she strode down the hallway. Merely watching her confident stride kindled a deep desire in me. I couldn't help noticing that the rooms looked clean. I was desperate to ask who had been cleaning them but knew that even a hint of jealousy from me would be an enormous mistake.

Finally, in the living room she stopped. She stood in front of me with her hands on her hips, looking down at me. She was every fantasy I had ever had about a dominant woman come to life.

"Continue what you were saying," she said coolly.

Once again I started babbling apologies about my failure to accept her discipline. I begged to be allowed to serve her again. She let me ramble on for a few minutes before she held up a hand to stop me.

"Five!" she demanded. Ms. Renee had trained me in various positions that had a corresponding number. In "five" I was to remain on both knees and lock my arms behind my back.

"Now, look at me."

Normally, Ms. Renee doesn't allow me to look in her eyes while I'm about to be disciplined. She prefers that I keep my head bowed, looking no higher than her hands. Her request to look into her face did not bode well for what she was about to say or do.

I expected her to be arrogant about her victory, but instead I saw love and a penetrating understanding of how I felt.

"I'm glad you are back! Yes, I risked our relationship, but it was necessary! After only one week you remembered your natural place, didn't you? Last week you were a slave with no one to worship. How did you feel? Useless? Without a mistress to serve your life is meaningless. You found that out, haven't you? A normal man would have just left to do whatever he wanted, but here you are hoping to serve me again!" She bent to firmly grab the hair at the back of my head.

In a harsher tone, she continued, "I will accept your service but you must pay for your disobedience. If I risked our relationship to teach you a lesson, then you risked our love out of fear of a simple punishment. Are you that weak?"

There was a pause, then suddenly her palm struck me with sharply across my face.

"Did you think I would have any trouble replacing you? There are hundreds of men in this city who would sell their souls to be my slave."

At this I lost all sense of dignity or control. She was the woman who alone had the strength and creativity to tame me. I was filled with anxiety as I involuntarily lowered my forehead to the floor, waiting her decision. I knew I would camp out at her doorstep forever, begging daily to be allowed to serve her again if I was unable to regain her trust in this moment.

A long pause followed where I could only hear my choked breath and the click of her heels as she paced in front of me while she made her decision.

"Luckily I haven't started interviewing for a new submissive. I will accept you back since you have begged to be my slave so prettily, but be warned. I plan on putting you through a difficult trial period. I don't want anything like this to ever inconvenience me again. Remember, slave, you asked for this life. You could have stayed away. Now, you return begging to be let back in. You've proved to me that you are not naturally independent. Your nature is to be my slave! That's good for me but now I know that you must be broken. Don't expect this to be easy. It won't be."

Ms. Renee placed one of her shoes on the back of my neck, allowing the heel to press painfully against my scalp.

"Also, remember this. If you ever again refuse another punishment, I will ruin your life. Then, I will banish you forever. Do you understand?"

I stammered a grateful reply.

"Do you agree to my demands?" she snapped.

"Yes, Mistress."

"Then you're a fool, because I'm planning on taking this past what you can possibly imagine. Now, get to work."

With that, she turned and left the room, leaving me on my knees, still trembling. At the bottom of the stairs, in a casual voice she threw over her shoulder, "By the way, the new number for Saturday is twenty. And I expect you at work on Monday no matter what condition your ass is in."

I shuddered but stayed perfectly still, listening as her heels clicked up the stairs. I stayed there for a minute with my forehead still pressed against the floor trying to pull myself together. After a minute, I leaned forward and gently kissed the floor where she had been standing. I stood up and walked to the kitchen, where her dishes awaited me.

That evening I found myself taking extra care with my duties. I finished the scheduled portion of the housekeeping. At 9:00 p.m., when I usually started her bath, she came downstairs in her robe.

"Under the circumstances I don't think you deserve to help me with my bath tonight. I want you to go home."

There was nothing I could say. I had been denied the pleasure of bathing her because of my unwillingness to accept her discipline. It was what I deserved.

That night I walked home feeling not only lonely but also frightened. I wondered what I wouldn't put up with.

Friday morning, I stayed home and wrote a lengthy apology and love letter. I sent it with flowers to her office on Friday afternoon. I did not hear a response from her.

I was there earlier than usual on Saturday morning starting on my various chores. She remained slightly cool and aloof from me. It hurt especially when the phone rang and the snappish monosyllables that she hurled at me were instantly transformed to warmth and delight while she chatted amicably on the phone with one of her friends. I felt certain that it was Heather. I caught something inadvertently as I swept the back porch about me being in the doghouse. There was a pause and a very wicked laugh, but I heard Ms. Renee say, "Oh no, I don't think he's ready for that but maybe someday."

I worried what it might be that Heather was suggesting but what was going to happen that night was more than enough to keep my mind occupied. Twenty strokes were coming and I knew it would mean real pain and humiliation.

The day sped by too quickly. I was washing windows when Ms. Renee appeared in tall boots, black leather pants, and a black leather corset. Looking at her made it hard to breathe. I felt myself tumble into a deep mental subspace.

"It's time, slave."

I put down my rags, swallowed my fear, and crawled after her to the attic. I had spent the last two years building a reasonably equipped dungeon in the high roofed space. She stepped aside as I crawled to the stocks. With a few simple twists of the apparatus, I was completely restrained.

"I'm glad that you're back. I'm going to take steps to make sure that your little rebellion never happens again. Let's start with warm-up."

When Ms. Renee punishes me on the weekend, she usually starts by paddling me fifty or so times to raise the temperature of my ass and draw the blood to the surface before the real punishment begins. It hurts, but it's not as vicious as the cane.

I tried to remain completely still in an effort to please her. After she was done, I watched as she took down the dreaded cane and tapped it on the toe of her boot.

"You displeased me last week. I hate it when you don't instantly obey. This will start a new level of your training. After this, things are going to get harder. Remember that you came back of your own free will. Now we both know what you are. You're a slave! From now on I'm going to beat you like one."

I saw the wild look in her eyes when she pulled back for the first swing. There was something gleeful and vengeful at the same time. I stifled a shout with the first blow. No one can hear me from the attic but I wanted to prove my submission. My desire to please never lasts past the first few stripes. It simply hurts too much. Soon I was twisting in the stocks, futilely trying to temper the searing pain of the cane. She stopped at ten. From experience I knew my ass would be black and blue. Soon the skin would break.

"This is where I would have stopped if you had been a decent slave and devoted to me. Instead you decided not to obey. Yet here you are. Now I know I can do whatever I need to do to get you to the level of submission we both want."

She leaned over and whispered, "Do you want to please me?"

"Oh yes, Mistress," I begged, "I do."

"I could stop now. Your ass already looks raw, but one of us has to be strong. It's not you! Think about yourself. You were weak to refuse my punishment, weak to crawl back, and now too weak to want me to finish."

She touched me again tenderly with her hand on my flushed cheeks.

"I love you enough to care that your submission is real. Ten more. One of us has to be strong."

There was nothing I could do. If I thought I wanted to please her after ten, I was begging to please her after twenty.

When she was done, she released me from the stocks. I slumped to the floor somewhat shattered by the experience. Despite my attempts at stoicism, I had begged her to stop. I was not only hurting but I felt completely humiliated.

"Go clean yourself up and get me ready for bed."

A few moments later I was kneeling at her feet helping her out of her leather pants. I knelt as she sat on the side of the bed. Some kind of wave of intense energy passed between us. The air was charged with palpable electricity that made it hard to breathe.

"Start at my toes," she whispered.

It was a signal for us that she would allow me to lick her to orgasm. I started at her feet and lovingly kissed every inch of her.

Afterward, I folded her into her blanket and let myself out of the house. As I turned to leave, Ms. Renee said in a quiet voice, "I missed you every minute last week. I'm glad that you're back. I love you but I want what is between us to be real. I understand now that I've been too easy on you or you never would have left. So from now on, it's only going to get harder. Goodnight, beloved slave."

It was still a lonely walk home. This time, I walked very slowly. I was sore. I could feel the raw skin at the back of my legs sticking to the rough fabric of my jeans. On Monday, I would have to bandage myself so my stripes didn't seep through my suit pants. I was frightened, but not by her; I was frightened by what I would put up with for her. There was something else. I experienced feelings of fear but there was a hint of something more. It was pride. In the final moment I had not failed her.

Still, there was something about the last hellish week that bothered me. I felt that I was acting in a play that she had directed. Was it possible that this whole demanding drama from start to finish been a part of a deeper plan? Had she purposefully kept pushing, asking for more and more until she provoked an inevitable resistance simply so she could crush whatever trace of independence I thought I still had?

Now, after my capitulation, she was more empowered than ever before. My resistance had been greatly reduced. Did she truly love me and want to bind me to her even more completely than I had previously been? Had she risked our relationship simply to push me deeper into submission? If so, then I was in very serious trouble. My soul was endangered. I tried to worry about the future, but I soon gave up. I was too madly in love.

July 2009
Dear Renee,

I loved our chat on the phone last week. I know you were worried. I don't know what to say. I admit that I'm surprised that he came back. You have gone further with him than I thought it was possible to go. Men are so unreliable.

I'm trying to search my feelings about his return. Maybe I'm a little disappointed. I was ready to rush there and comfort you if he didn't come back. Instead, I'm trying to be happy for you.

The new store opens in November before the Christmas rush. I can't get in my house until the first of the year. It is making me crazy.

My own girl does not like the idea of moving to Memphis. Also, I need her here to run this store. I can't trust anyone else. It's hard but I'm leaving her in Atlanta. I'm so confused. I have formed a close loving relationship with her but sometimes I also want a man on the end of my leash. Choices.

How is your attic coming? You already had quite a collection when I was there last. The description of his last punishment sounded hot.

Suzy still starts trembling all over and promises the world as soon as I pick up the crop. I can barely touch her with it without her weeping. I can't be that damn scary. I'm jealous of you. I often wish I had someone I could really release on.

It obviously helps you to write down your thoughts about dominating Butler. Please keep writing me everything you are thinking about this subject. I'm always interested.

Heather

Chapter Three

DISCIPLINE

September 2009
Dear Heather,

Thank you for wanting to read about my plans for Butler. It still helps to write it all out. You are the only person with whom I want to share my ideas.

I think you are wrong about being scary. You are the scariest woman I know! I don't doubt your submissive starts trembling when you pick up your crop. She obviously doesn't need much to achieve "subspace," but I would encourage you to slowly extend her limits. Try adding five strokes per week until she can take twenty or thirty. It would be good for both of you. Have fun. Remember to cuddle her afterward.

Yes, he's back in my clutches! It was touch and go for about a week but he returned and now acts more dedicated than ever. I was worried but I'm glad I put our relationship to the test. This lifestyle is meaningless to me unless it's real. This is especially true since he continues to ask me to marry him. I will continue to put him off until I'm certain he can be trusted to follow me into a true female-led relationship.

Yes, I love disciplining him. Whipping him has been a cathartic experience for me. I can have a bad week but once he's bound and straining under my lash I feel all the tension of the week leave me. I can't imagine what it does for him.

I'm very excited about you opening a store in Memphis. I want you closer to me now that we've reconnected.

Butler continues to improve the dungeon in my attic. I want it to be easy and convenient for me to put him in very secure restraints for a whipping. The restraints are not just for show. No man, no matter how willing, would be able to hold still for what I have been giving him lately. I feel that for my dominance to be real, the punishment must be real.

I have already discovered that it is necessary to whip him at least twice a week to maintain his submissive attitude. Presently, I administer fifty lashes with my riding crop every Wednesday afternoon. I add to that number if he has failed in any way to please me. On Sunday, he faces the cane if he has done something to deserve it. Strangely, no matter how hard he tries there is always some little something that we must correct with the cane. Ha! I have learned through experience that this is the minimum needed to maintain his obedience. The steady drip, drip of water will eventually wear away a stone. Even so, I believe the steady application of my whip will wear away his resistance to becoming my slave.

I intend to use a variety of psychological techniques to encourage him on his path to true surrender, but during it all I believe that the very best way to train a submissive is through direct physical discipline. Even when he performs well, I will continue to use the whip on him. There are a lot of reasons to discipline him but the most important reason is that I love it.

We continue to engage in serious discussions where I encourage Butler to share his deepest feelings about S&M. I have learned that although he hates and fears the whip, he is sexually and psychologically tantalized by my willingness to punish him. He acknowledges that physical discipline has been a gateway for him to rise above the mundane to a higher level of sensual awareness of me. He has admitted that the more I punish him, the more divine I seem to him. Sometimes, it's hard to hold back.

I receive an electric charge of power and pleasure when I think that my slave sincerely fears displeasing me about everyday practical matters. Sometimes, I see him nervously checking on the condition of the house or any projects I have given him. It empowers me. A raised eyebrow of mild displeasure from me sends a cold shiver into his scrotum. It's such a rush of power! I intend to continue to be cruel and demanding enough so that he will not think of discipline as kinky foreplay. I want to keep him frightened of making even small mistakes in his service to me. This is what he asked for and I intend to give it to him.

Itching to see you again,
Renee

September 2009
Dear Renee,

I've rented a lake house for the weekend near Chattanooga, Tennessee. That's about halfway between us. Let's get away for a few days. Suzy has to stay in Atlanta to run the store. If you must bring Butler, he can camp outside in a tent. I want you to myself. I'm a selfish bitch, but it's part of my charm.

Heather

Butler's Journal
Boating
September 2009

Last weekend I accompanied Ms. Renee and her friend Heather to a private lake to spend a long weekend. It is a lovely spot with a secluded rental cabin and a private dock.

I expected something humbling from them when they were together and I was not disappointed. Upon arrival, I was told that I would be staying in a tent beside the lake while they slept in the cabin. I refused to be anything other than cheerfully compliant. I could tell that Heather was looking to see flaws in my very real desire to serve my mistress. I admit to enjoying any frustration she felt when I acted graciously.

The message I received from Heather was clear. In her view, I was unwanted and unneeded. They allowed me to do a few menial jobs for them while they enjoyed themselves. Anytime Heather had a chance to kiss Ms. Renee or touch my mistress in front of me, she did so, often while looking scornfully at me over her shoulder. She was shutting me out and she wanted it to hurt.

I admit to feeling jealous at times. I also admit to feeling left out, abandoned, and ill-used. However, I felt a tiny spark of pride. I was starting to look at this adventure with Ms. Renee as something I could take part in by helping her enjoy herself. My willingness to submit without complaint allowed me to supply my mistress with an experience that only a submissive man could offer her. Yes, admittedly, it was Heather that was touching her, but Ms. Renee's pleasure was in part due to my sacrifice.

During the day, I was called upon to tidy the cabin and cook a couple of the meals, but I had plenty of time on my hands while they lounged by the lake.

In the past it was always Ms. Renee that had organized moments or scenes that were meant to lead me into deeper submission. I was grateful to her for her creativity but I felt that I was not doing my part. For months I had searched my imagination on how I could also create a scenario that would please her.

On the first day at the lake I was wandering around the shore when I noticed a large dory. That's an unusual boat to find on a freshwater lake. Mounted on the dory was a platform for people to stand on. I immediately made inquiries and met the owner. He told me that boats were a passion of his. He bought the dory to be used annually in a Fourth of July flotilla that included his boat carrying a float of people dressed as some of the founding fathers. I immediately rented it with the small platform attached.

Over the next three days I worked on the boat in my spare time, adding the few touches that I thought it needed.

On the last evening we were at the lake, I cooked dinner. Afterward, at dusk, I invited both women to the cabin's private dock for dessert. Puzzled by my unusual request, they followed me out to find the rented boat that I had previously docked there.

On top of the boat's platform I had erected a small square tent rigged from inexpensive purple sheets I bought at the local dry-goods store. Inside I had placed a queen mattress from the cabin's spare bedroom, all the pillows in the house, a dessert tray, an ice bucket, and a bottle of good wine.

The two women climbed aboard. I sat in the stern of the boat. The privacy tent opened to the bow, allowing them to lie on the mattress and look forward but giving them complete privacy. Admittedly, it was not Cleopatra's barge but they understood the effect I was trying to achieve. I could tell that my mistress was delighted by my surprise.

We shoved off with me rowing in the stern of the boat, unable to see them. The early low moon lit the night. The temperature was perfect. I heard the wine uncork and the gentle hum of their conversation while I slowly sculled them around the lake. Soon they were quiet. It didn't require any imagination as to what they were doing when I started to hear very familiar sounds coming from my mistress. It is true that I was not directly touching her but I was, in part, giving her an experience only her slave could give her. It felt very much like love.

September 2009
Dear Heather,

I had a wonderful time at the lake house. Our relationship is better now that we are older and have our own lives. I think we can relax and simply enjoy each other. I'm glad we are friends again. Just when I've had enough of men you bring me a little spice. I'm sorry that you didn't bring Suzy. Bring her to Memphis one weekend and we can double-team her.

Despite you wanting to leave Butler at home, I think that it worked out perfectly to have him there. We needed him there to do the cooking and cleaning. Also, I want to keep the pressure on. I don't want to give him any time off from his training. Even you have to admit that you loved the boat ride he arranged. I think we kept the fish awake! His willingness to find new ways to please me encourages me to keep him as my submissive.

You asked how I am training him. The short answer is that I'm trying everything!

To increase his fear and excitement, I have been experimenting by using a variety of devices such as the "Humbler." I've also tired mummification and electrical shocks. He builds most of the equipment we use. I can only imagine what building the devices I use on him is doing to his psyche. I want him to be constantly reminded that he is doing all of this willingly.

One day I want him to build a secure cell with a toilet for extended isolation and confinement that might last for several days at a time. I want him to experience that he really has no control over what happens. After a few days locked up, I'm certain that he'll be eager to resume his duties as my servant. I believe he'll even see it as a privilege. I imagine with anticipation how enthusiastically he will try to please me knowing the alternative is to return to the boredom and discomfort of his cell.

When I think about locking him up and isolating him in a large cell for days, I imagine myself lying in bed masturbating knowing he was suffering for me. I want him to experience moments when I have the power of life and death over him.

I already have a smaller, more uncomfortable cage for stays lasting only a few hours. When I leave him locked in his cage I play a continuous video loop of previous training sessions where I whip him, berate him, or ride him around the room like a pony. I want him to see images of his humbling again and again. His discipline sessions are an essential part of his training and are a liberating release for me.

There is nothing I will not try to make him my slave. For example, I quiver when I think about restricting his calorie intake for a few days then gagging him while he cooks my meals. The thought of scraping a tiny bit of leftovers into a bowl for him to eat on the floor like a hungry dog excites me. I intend to experiment with every imaginable technique to reinforce his slave status.

I've taken your advice and I have begun to introduce chastity training with a chastity device. He balks at it but I feel it is essential that I control his orgasms. I started slowly but I have continued to press, so now I can get him to wear it longer than when we started. Once he can wear it for three days, it seems reasonable that I can ask for any time period I choose.

There is nothing more personally satisfying to me than slowly dismantling him. I love him in pieces at my feet. In that incredible moment of shame and discomfort for him, he belongs to me, while I simultaneously become his object of worship and desire.

You've asked me what keeps him from leaving when things get hard. I have thought of a lot of ways to tie him to me but ultimately I believe that through a rigorous practice of S&M I can reach deep into his psyche to find the switch that turns off any possible choice he has of changing his mind about belonging to me.

He keeps asking but I keep saying no to marriage because I don't think he's ready yet. I love it that he asks, because it lets me know that he's eager to continue. However, I'm not ready yet either. I think men want marriage so they can put an ownership sign on women. That's not for me, although I'd like to put a sign around his neck indicating that I own him. Obviously, present marriage laws do not include the concept of a female-led relationship where the woman is free but the man is captive. We have gay marriage now, so I have some hope in the future for some kind of legalized S&M relationship. It is the last taboo for consenting adults. It's fun to think of myself on the cutting edge of relationships.

It's too bad I feel this way about marriage, because I have several ideas for our wedding night that should make it plain what he's getting into. I wouldn't want to do so much that it scares him off but I would want to start out on the right foot and send the correct message. Needless to say, he'll suffer. There is something about torturing him and denying him on what would supposedly be our most romantic night that makes me anticipate our honeymoon with a shiver of sinful, red-hot pleasure.

Did I tell you how much I loved having you on the boat with me? I love your sweaty embraces,

Renee

September 2009
Dear Renee,

I can't believe you are still considering marriage. We have to talk more. Enslave him if you must, but don't marry him.

Time spent with you makes me happy. I can be myself. I loved the lake weekend and I also loved our adventure the last night I was in Memphis. Having Butler pick us up for a ride in the park in the pedicab was perfect. And yes, it reminded me of the boat ride. Using him to power a vehicle of some sort simply feels right. What we need is a buggy with him in harness pulling in the front. I guess I do still have use for a man!

I loved being bundled up in the back of the pedicab with the privacy top up while we kissed. I loved listening to his labored breath as he cranked on the pedals to get us up the hills.

You whipping him as he slowed at the top of the hill in the wooded and more private part of the park really got me going. Where did you get the pedicab? Did you borrow it or did you buy it? Either way we should use it more often!

I think dominant women are too afraid of what the vanilla world thinks. Having a man in a harness pulling a carriage is not overtly sexual. It's not against any law I can think of, but one never sees that kind of boldness from the S&M community. Yes, a dom/sub relationship between consenting adults is the last taboo. I think you are right, but we should start challenging that taboo.

Damn, girlfriend, I have a great time with you.

Heather

Butler's Journal
Agreeing to the Test
October 2009

On Saturday evening we spent part of the evening as we always do in her attic dungeon. I knelt in front of my mistress while she sat in her elaborate chair that looks like a throne. Around me were the paraphernalia of a decade of collecting the devices necessary to change a man into a useful slave. She wore a leather cat suit cut specifically for her body to fit like a second skin. Just watching her walk across the room brought an involuntary moan from me. Our relationship during the week could often be warm and affectionate even though she was quick to remind me that she was my mistress and I was her slave. We often did things that typical vanilla couples do like visit friends or dine at local restaurants. No matter how busy we are, though, I'm still expected to complete certain household tasks. Failure resulted in correction.

Each Saturday evening my mistress slipped into a different persona when she reviewed my progress as her slave. During these Saturday evening training sessions she transformed into a demanding, exacting goddess. On these nights she seemed to release a part of herself that she kept partly in check during the week. In her dungeon she opened a vein of cruelty that lurked beneath her usual firm but gentle demeanor. I wondered if all women have such forces within them.

Once again, I questioned my sanity. Why was I here? Why did I dedicate so much of my time to her? Why was I slowly giving up control of my life? The answer was easy. All I had to do was look at her. Being with her was the most exciting thing I had ever done. Life without her seemed stale and tasteless.

Kneeling at her feet, I tried to keep my nervousness in check as she flipped through the small black notebook that I always carried. I knew that despite my strenuous efforts she had written twice in it during the week. Tonight, I would receive my punishment from her rattan cane. It was a hellish device and would leave me marked until the following week. However, if I impressed her with my willingness to accept correction, then I might be allowed the miracle of sex with my goddess.

A tingle of dread spiced with anticipation coursed through me as I knelt before her. She never held back during a Saturday punishment. I feared it all week if I had to receive more than just a few strokes. To increase my fear and to perfect my service as her slave, she had recently increased the number of strokes I received for mistakes.

Reading from the notebook, she began. "I found hair in the bottom of the shower this Tuesday. You know that I expect a clean bathroom. I spanked you only last week for the same problem. I must not have made myself clear. You keep thinking of yourself as a person with rights. You are a slave who should be constantly working to please his mistress. If you don't see yourself as I do, then tonight's punishment will help you learn who and what you are.

"Also, you were late picking me up from shopping on Thursday. I have warned you about tardiness before but obviously I need to make an impression on you that I expect punctuality. After tonight, the idea of being late will make you so nauseated with fear that you'll never be late again.

"I've already disciplined you for both of these infractions. They are mistakes you've made more than once. I feel you need to be punished so that they don't happen again. You thought you were sorry at the time, but I promise in a few minutes you'll feel truly sorry for not paying more attention to your duties."

She continued, "There were only two entries this week in your notebook, so you are to receive ten stokes with the cane. If I were you, I would continue to concentrate on your duties as my slave or things could get worse. Much worse. I was easy on you this week. Don't expect me to be so lenient next week.

"Now, assume the position."

At her command, I draped myself over a padded bench and placed my hands and feet in the custom stocks built to fit me. With a few deft turns, she securely locked my ankles and wrists in place. To complete my restraint, she secured a wide leather strap across the small of my back, cinching it down tightly. I was completely immobilized.

I had been mildly disciplined during the week. For example, I had been cropped on Wednesday to maintain my submissive attitude. Although painful, her discipline during the week rarely frightened me. The weekly corrections from her riding crop were used to keep me focused or to amuse her. She referred to these corrections as maintenance discipline. However, on Saturday I receive real punishment. This session was for mistakes that a little discipline would not be enough to make a serious impression on my psyche. Punishment with the rattan cane could be severe enough to break the skin. Thirty strokes might draw blood. I learned to work very hard to avoid her displeasure.

I saw my goddess slowly walk behind me. I involuntarily cringed when I heard her pull the cane from its rack on the wall.

As always, I resolved to stoically endure her cane but once again my body betrayed me. As soon as I felt the first burning cut of the cane across the back of my thighs I found myself vainly trying to avoid the next blow. The restraints were necessary. No amount of effort on my part would have kept me motionless as the strokes continued. At six strokes I wanted to plead. It was humbling. My eyes watered. How could they not be called tears? I was trying not to beg before the last stripes were delivered. Each stroke came with the same force as the first one. She never showed the slightest mercy. The only pause happened when she repositioned herself to strike a new area or stopped to debase or berate me.

I never left the bench defiant. The punishment would start with me convinced that I already felt obedient but the cane always brought me to a new awareness of how much deeper I could go.

Following the punishment, I was, as always, on fire to please her. This week she allowed me to undress her. Starting at her toes, I kissed and stroked every inch of her until we finally joined in joyous sex.

Somehow the dominatrix who caused me such pain and the warm affectionate woman in my arms were the same person. She filled every idea I had of woman.

Toward the end of our lovemaking, my mistress positioned herself on top of me. She began pulling on my nipples. By then I was so desperate to orgasm I would have agreed to anything. This time was no different. She often chose such a moment to ask something new of me. It felt unfair but she never promised fairness. In fact, she had promised to use every advantage she could gain.

Looking up at her she seemed more goddess than mortal woman. At the very peak of my excitement, looking deep into my eyes to gauge my response, she started speaking in a light and teasing tone. "Oh I forgot to tell you. I want you to take special care cleaning the house for the next few weeks. Remember my friend Heather? She'll be here staying with me during December."

Even in my excited state a deep chill went down to my groin. I stopped moving my hips. My erection started to lessen.

"Ha! I can feel you soften. Are you losing interest? What's the matter, honey? Are you scared? Maybe you should be. She's very creative. Who knows how she might be of help to me? I think you better take advantage of my generosity now because who knows what will happen in the future."

Until now, our dom/slave relationship had been private. I cringed at how humiliating it had been to reveal our lifestyle to anyone, especially her friend Heather, who I found somewhat rude and vulgar. What might I be asked to do in front of her? I squirmed in dread at the thought of some of the services I performed daily that were humbling enough to perform in private. Now, I might have to do them with an audience?

I wanted to retort strongly, "No!" but it was impossible. I had already lost too many such battles. I knew that my mistress could make my life very difficult. The worst punishment would be banishment. I was defeated before I could truly fight. She always got her way. Using all that I had learned, I knew that I had to think only of her pleasure. I might as well agree. I knew that I could refuse her nothing.

I shuddered and breathed deeply as Ms. Renee continued to tease me and move in such a way to prevent my orgasm.

"You've been asking to move in with me. Have you changed your mind?" she asked.

"No, my goddess, I will do anything!"

"Anything? I doubt you're ready for that but I do have a test for you. If you pass it I will consider your proposal of marriage." She renewed her assault on my tender nipples.

"Yes, please, anything!" I cried out.

"First, I want you to start wearing a chastity cage for longer periods."

I wanted to refuse. I wanted to stop and have a conversation. However, I could only think about the present urgent need. I'm not sure I was in my right mind.

"So do you promise to allow me to lock you up for longer time periods?" Again, she pulled painfully on my nipples.

What could I say? I was beyond desire. I had to trust her for the future. I again agreed but her quiet gurgling laugh that I heard just before she allowed my release sent a shiver deeper into me than any orgasm could have.

Afterward, in a matter-of-fact way, she slipped on the chastity device. I hated it. It chafed. It was hard to sleep in. Over the next couple of days, I told her so.

Over the next few weeks she whipped me, scolded me, encouraged me, and finally manipulated me into accepting it for days at a time. There comes a point when you can't find any way to swim out of the current you are caught in. You must allow the current to take you wherever it wishes while keeping your head above water. Saying "no" to her no longer seemed like an option. Also, I felt a deep irresistible need to please her.

November 2009
Dear Renee,

Don't' try to pay me for the shoes I sent you. I saw them and knew I had to see you in them. I enjoyed lunch yesterday. I'm glad that you have taken some of my suggestions.

Men are notorious about promising things when they are stimulated but change their minds as soon as they get relief or get bored.

I'd get his permission on video and in writing before I started really disciplining him just to cover your ass. You don't want to get sued or arrested.

Let me also add, get a good lawyer.

My husbands also promised me that my happiness would come first, but they could never keep their promise.

I don't want you to get your hopes up. Things could go bad or he could change his mind.

One last question. How are you going to keep him from running out the door once he realizes that you are serious about making him your slave? You said that you could prevent him from ever backing out. How?

Despite my legal worries for you, I admit to wanting to give a man a good beating from time to time. Nothing to put him in the hospital but I'd like to give him enough that he trembles a little when I walk in the room.

You are a lucky woman.

Even if he will take your whippings, you can't still be serious about considering marriage.

Just when I'm about to move closer, you move a man into your house. The gods are laughing at me.

I know I don't write back very much but I still love reading about how you intend to move forward with his enslavement. It helps to know that someone else shares my deepest desires.

Heather

November 2009
Dear Heather,

I deeply appreciate your continued interest in my plans. Writing always helps me clarify my thoughts.

Yes, I'm serious about allowing him to move in but you will always be welcome in my home. I expect to see you frequently after you move to Memphis. Yes, I think you are correct that I should be cautious about marriage. He has suggested it several times but I continue to reject his proposals until he has proved himself.

One of my problems is that I enjoy his company so much it's too easy not to treat him like my slave. Consequently, his training suffers. I've been thinking of ways to test whether this is merely a passing infatuation for him or if he is truly committed to being my submissive.

Never worry about you and me. Nothing will change concerning us because of Butler!

All of this is happening as Butler is starting to close down his involvement in his law firm. He's worked hard and has a decent retirement saved. I could ask him to continue to work but I'm intrigued about controlling all of his time.

I note that you will be in town while you open your store and do some work on your new house. I want you to cancel your reservations at your extended-stay hotel. Will you stay with me the month of December? I know you will be busy with the store. You can have your own room, of course, but I was hoping you'd spend some of your nights in my bed.

Wow, just writing that got my juices flowing. Have I told you how glad I am that we have found each other again?

Hungry for more kisses,
Renee

November 2009
Dear Renee,

Of course I'll stay with you, but does your boy have to be there? You know that after two divorces I have no patience with men.

More than kisses,
Heather

November 2009
Dear Heather,

I have been putting quite a bit of pressure on him to agree to a very severe test. I think he's ready. I have enclosed a schedule for him that will keep him out of our way. If you approve, I want you to stay. Your visit is the test I've been looking for. I need him to stay under my roof and under my thumb while you are here. I know you'll agree after you see the schedule I wrote for him. I want to say thank you in advance.

Much appreciation,
Renee

Butler's Journal
Rules of the Test
November 2009

I can't explain why knowing Ms. Renee has been the most exciting thing that has ever happened to me. It seems strange but being involved with a creative dominatrix is like being the protagonist in a fast-moving Hollywood film. It's full of danger, intrigue, sexuality, and adventure. My relationship with her is never dull. I wanted more of her time, so I continued to propose marriage. I longed to move in with her.

Each time I asked she told me that her refusal was for my own good. In her refusals, she made it clear that she did not believe I was ready for the kind of commitment that she required. Nevertheless, I continued my pursuit. Finally, she suggested that, as a test, I live as her servant for one month. She warned me that during that time she would not hold back or lower her standards. If I survived the month, she would consider my request to live with her.

I remember the conversation we had before my testing started. It was following my usual Wednesday maintenance cropping. Often she performs this with the same clothes that she has worn to work. This might not sound particularly erotic but there is something about her whipping me in her business attire that makes this moment even sexier. It brings my discipline out of the S&M game world and into the world of a professional woman who happens to own a slave.

She is aware that how she dresses affects me. I couldn't help but notice that on Wednesday she has a predilection for tight skirts and heels. After receiving her discipline, I am usually on fire to please her. Consequently, she often chooses this time to command a deeper commitment from me.

Looking down at me this Wednesday, she explained, "Next month, I invited my friend Heather to stay with me while the home she bought here in Memphis undergoes renovation. It looks like she might be here over the holidays. I decided that this would be the perfect time to test you. I rely on you for companionship as a lover and a friend. Our casual and familiar way of interacting naturally lessens my domination of you. Heather's visit is a chance to see if you can serve in a completely surrendered manner. Also, it will be a test for me to see if I can truly dominate you."

I admit that I wanted to wiggle out of this test. It sounded artificial. It also sounded scary. Furthermore, I did not like Heather. Nevertheless, I knew that if I backed down our relationship would be stalled. I felt reluctant but I tried to hide my trepidation by replying, "Yes, Mistress, please test me."

She smiled at me but continued in a firm manner, "I've thought a lot about this test. You must agree to all of my conditions."

"Yes, Mistress, I will do anything," I replied.

"Well, I doubt that, but maybe you can do this. I want you to understand clearly what I expect. While Heather is here I want you to be almost invisible. You'll want my attention but I won't be in the mood to give it to you. I want to concentrate on my friend. This is going to hurt your feelings. That's my intention. I need to know if you are the right man for me.

"I want you to do your housework downstairs while we are at work. In the evening, I want you to spend most of your time in the attic out of the way. You will also sleep there because I don't want you on the same floor in one of the guest bedrooms. During her stay, speak only when you are spoken to. Work in rooms we are not in. Never look her or me in the eyes. If you are required to speak, keep your head down and your eyes at our feet. I want you available at all times should we ring the servant's bell. You will act as maid, cook, chauffeur, and gardener. The service you provide should be your only reward. Mistakes will be punished. Be invisible, be quiet, and be obedient. Do you understand?"

"Yes, Mistress," I said as humbly as I could manage.

"Remember, you asked to move in to serve me full-time. That's impossible unless I know you can be the submissive I need."

She looked down at me. "Are you really going to do all of this?"

"Yes, Mistress," I answered but I admit to feeling anxious about the whole thing.

She tilted my face up to hers and looked me in the eyes. "I love you, so I hope that you are the man I've been seeking. I need to know. If you disappoint me, I will never dominate you again."

December 2009
Dear Heather,

He's agreed to everything. I almost can't believe it. I know that I've worked very hard to ensure his compliance but to actually be at this point is a little heady. If he gets through next month, I feel he really will go all the way. We've been practicing with him for the last few months wearing a chastity belt for several days at a time. I'm sure that will be the highest hurdle. I don't really care if he wears one or not. I know it is something that would please you. If he's locked up he will seem like less of a man to you. Let's try to think of him as my eunuch.

I can't wait to see you,
Renee

Butler's Journal
The Test
January 2010

My infatuation with Ms. Renee continues to grow. I have never been with such a provocative, captivating woman. She is intelligent, well read, socially astute, and by far the most sexual creature I have ever met. I have fallen under her spell. I realize this but I don't wish to be rescued.

The evening before Heather was to arrive we were in Ms. Renee's attic dungeon. We both knew that it was a turning point for us. She had dressed for the occasion in a fishnet bodysuit cinched with a wide leather belt and thigh-high boots and leather gloves. It's true that such an outfit made me more biddable but I knew it was also her way of loving me and acknowledging the importance of the moment. The expectant sexual tension between us was drawn as tight as it had ever been drawn. I wanted to throw my arms around her hips and pull her toward me. Instead, as instructed, I was on my knees with my hands behind my back.

Once again, I promised to abide by the rules of her test.

She quickly responded to my promise, "Then you are a fool, but if you pass this test you'll be my fool."

We had made love frequently in the last few weeks but I was still drowning in desire for her while at the same moment an alarm was sounding dimly that I was getting in over my head.

"Four," she quietly ordered.

This put me on my hands and knees. All I could see of her were her boots in front of me. The sight was enough to pull me deeper into subspace. She began strutting around me, touching me gently with the crop in her gloved hand.

She went on. "Instead of agreeing to my rules as if obeying them were a favor to me, I want you to ask me for the privilege of obeying them as if it were an honor to obey them. I want you to make me believe that you want to give them to me."

I did not know what to say. I did not want to deny her anything. However, I had considered the requirements of her test carefully and I thought I knew how hard they might be. I was not sure I could survive. Now, I was supposed to ask for each provision of her test as if I wanted it?

She stopped in front of me and continued, "Begin kissing the toes of my boots. If I agree to allow you to perform as my servant, I will show my acceptance by kicking you with them."

I tried not to hesitate. I knew that would only increase my punishment. I began kissing the shiny tops of her boots. As soon as I started kissing them my mind started changing. How did she know that a simple submissive act like that had the power to alter my attitude?

Soon, I managed to stammer, "Please, may I stay in the attic dungeon next month while I perform as your servant?"

"Well, since you asked so nicely, yes." Ms. Renee punctuated her agreement with five sharp kicks to my chest.

After recovering, I continued. "Please, punish me next month whenever I do not meet your expectations."

Ms. Renee stepped around to my side. "Of course I'll punish you, slave." She made her intentions clear with several sharp kicks with the toe of her boot into my abdomen.

After catching my breath, I hesitated. The next few were words were harder to say.

She snapped, "Well, you left out the most important part! Are you going to ask or am I going to send you home?"

In a voice that displayed my fear, I finally forced myself to ask, "And please, Mistress, keep me locked in a chastity belt the entire time Heather is here."

"Oh, I thought you would never ask! I doubt your sincerity but I want you to know how I feel about your pathetic needs."

My mistress clicked her boot heels behind me. "Four!" she again demanded.

That meant I was to kneel on my hands and knees with my legs spread. I did so trembling. I could look down between my legs and see her strutting behind me in her high-heeled boots. It was one of the sexiest things I have ever seen. Soon, however, she stopped and shifted her weight onto one leg as she brought the toe of her boot up sharply into my groin. It doesn't take much effort on her part. It's just a quick nudge of her boot. The pain shot through me like a flash of white-hot light. I found myself lying prone on the floor.

With my eyes closed, I could hear her say, "I'm really looking forward to this month. If you fail, I will never dominate you again."

I staggered to my knees.

Looking down at me, she sternly challenged me, "I doubt you are submissive enough to survive the month. However, I'm willing to let you try. The first time I don't think you are following my rules or you don't meet my expectations I will send you home and let some other submissive man try to please me."

I cringed at the idea of someone taking my place, as if I had been struck. "Yes, Mistress, I understand."

"Furthermore, Heather believes that a person only has only so much sexual energy to share. While she is here I plan on giving her all of mine. You will do without. You will continue to wear your chastity device the entire time. While she is here, you are only a servant. Stay in that role and you may succeed in pleasing me."

With that, Ms. Renee gently leaned down, cupping my head in her hands, and to my surprise, kissed me.

"Do you know what that was?" she asked.

I shook my head no.

"That was the last kiss you will receive for a month." She reached behind her, and turning to me, she handed me my chastity cage. The key would remain on a chain around her neck.

"One month. Don't fail me," she said.

She turned and left me to struggle into the device and lock it.

I stayed kneeling on the floor watching the perfect flex of her legs and ass as she left the room. Everything had finally come down to this challenge. She was every dream I had ever had of a dominant mistress. I knew I would never find another woman like her. I vowed not to fail. I would have knelt there for several minutes but I forced myself to move. I had too much to do before Heather's arrival.

*****

The next day came quickly. This was a month I had dreaded but also fantasized about. In some ways it was much more exciting than I anticipated but in some ways it was also more boring as it was filled with a lot of household drudgery. It started with a very brief encounter with both my mistress and Heather. We were in the living room. I was kneeling in front of the couch where they both sat. She was going over the rules for me during Heather's stay. I learned that only my mistress would punish me. I was very grateful because I did not trust Heather. I could feel Heather's displeasure at this stipulation. They spoke for a few minutes about what they expected of me.

Toward the end of the interview, my mistress admitted to both of us that seeing me only as a servant was a challenge for her as well. She didn't know if she could maintain the correct demeanor with me and keep me at a distance for the entire month.

After a brief silence, Heather smirked. "I have an idea." She motioned me forward.

I crawled across the carpet and carefully watched as she fished around in her purse for a second. I tried to hide my mistrust of her.

Finally, she found what she was looking for. It was a permanent sharpie pen. She leaned over and began to write on my forehead. I saw Ms. Renee stifle a laugh. Later, I was able to see myself in a mirror. Heather had written "SLAVE" across my forehead. It would last for days. I would be unable to leave the house without utter embarrassment.

Heather studiously ignored me the entire time she stayed with us except to occasionally renew her penmanship. I was given PIG, WIMP, and ASS-LICKER. Ms. Renee cooperated by using those names the few times it was necessary to speak to me.

It was a month when my sincerity and resolve were severely tested. I worked constantly. In addition, I was punished with such cruelty and capriciousness that I was left with deep psychological changes to my psyche. Now, I no longer consider it unusual to be beaten for a bit of dust on the mantle or a disordered lingerie drawer. It merely seems the natural order of things.

I saw why Ms. Renee purposefully picked my time of testing when her friend and lover Heather would be staying with her while she waited for repairs to be completed in her new home. She chose this time so that she could more studiously ignore me.

Both women were very busy that month. Ms. Renee has a very public job that is associated with raising money. Christmas was her busiest season. Heather's shoe store did most of her business during December so she was gone almost every day until very late. I cooked but they were rarely there. Even the weekends often found me alone in the house. They were two busy, professional women. They actually needed a houseman. I was glad they were gone a lot as it allowed me to do my chores slowly and carefully.

I was never allowed to touch my mistress for the entire month. The only exception to that rule was after she whipped me. Ms. Renee allowed me to kiss the tops of her shoes while begging forgiveness for any infractions that had occurred. I felt completely humbled. If I did not convince her that my apology was sincere, she repeated the punishment. After one episode of failing to sound sincere, my apologies became very sincere.

The day-to-day story of what happened to me during that month would take too long to detail here, but Mistress Renee kept her promises. Even though they were often gone there was a lot for me to do. It was the most difficult month of my life.

With her lover there I was sexually superfluous. They were both so busy I doubt they slept together very often, but I was usually upstairs out of their way in the evening, so I wouldn't know. As the weeks passed, Heather became more comfortable with me and seemed to enjoy telling Ms. Renee of any tiny mistakes she thought I had made. I learned to be as careful around her as I was around my mistress. Soon, instead of being punished in private, Heather was invited to witness my discipline. I found it all extremely embarrassing. It was obviously stimulating to Heather because I could sometimes see her watching Ms. Renee with real passion when she whipped me. Once, out of the corner of my eye, I saw her touching herself through her pants as the crop landed on my back. Terrified of being spotted looking at her, I quickly turned away. I couldn't help but notice that frequently Ms. Renee and Heather would immediately retire to the bedroom after a punishment session, leaving me alone in the attic dungeon putting my shattered composure back together.

I recall one incident that illustrates why the month was so hard but also incredibly erotic and exciting.

I was in the laundry folding sheets on Saturday afternoon when my I heard the servant's bell ring. I quickly stopped what I was doing to hurry toward where I was needed.

My destination was the garden room. It is a cozy nook off of the living room surrounded on three sides by windows opening into the garden. That Saturday afternoon a white December light flooded the space. Ms. Renee and her friend Heather were having afternoon tea before setting off on a shopping trip. In front of them was the tea service that my mistress and I spent days looking for in antique stores in London. At the time, she was taken with the British custom of high tea. Later, under her urging, I learned to make the necessary sweets to accompany it. I also learned the proper method of serving such a repast.

Seeing Ms. Renee appear so beautiful in the pale December light in front of the tea service reminded me of our vacation together years earlier. While out of town, Ms. Renee often relaxed the normal discipline I live under. I fondly recalled holding hands as we walked the narrow streets of London. I never forgot that she was my owner but for a short while she allowed me the freedom to kiss her spontaneously and walk beside her as we shopped. The clatter of a spoon dropped by Heather woke me from my reverie.

"You may take this now, Butler."

Obediently, I leaned forward to begin moving the plates to the tray. A recently learned caution around Heather caused me to brace my feet carefully and grasp the tray holding the antique plates firmly when I did so. As I leaned forward, I temporarily came between my mistress and Heather. Hidden from view, Heather snaked out a red talon and firmly pinched me on the bottom. I couldn't help but involuntarily jerk, causing the precious plates to rattle on the tray. I glanced at Ms. Renee, who arched an eyebrow at me in annoyance.

"Excuse me, Mistress!" I was able to quietly choke out. I dreaded the possibility of her asking for my notebook. I could see out of my eye the victorious smirk on Heather's face. She hoped I would complain about what she had done but I knew never to be so rude. Ms. Renee has taught me that guests are always right in whatever they do. Luckily for me, the mistake was minor and Ms. Renee ignored my clumsiness.

Later that day I handed the two women out of my antique Mercedes sedan at a local upscale shopping mall. I wore a stocking hat to hide Heather's recent penmanship on my forehead. It was my job to follow behind them to carry their packages.

"Let's stop at the pet store first," Heather suggested.

Of course, it would have been much easier for me to have this be our last stop. Ms. Heather bought a large heavy bag of cat litter and several cans of cat food. Stopping at the pet store first meant that I would have to carry it along with all of their other purchases through the entire mall. I saw her smile at me as we entered. She knew I understood what she was doing. She hoped I might make the mistake of complaining to Ms. Renee. I'm certain that Heather provoked me so that she could witness Ms. Renee discipline me. I could sense her disappointment when I readily complied.

She made her purchases by imperiously pointing at the food and litter she preferred. I meekly shouldered her choices and followed them toward the checkout line. I paused behind Ms. Renee as she stopped to listen to a salesperson explain to a couple about a new device to control dogs. It was a special collar that sent a shock to the dog when the dog attempted to leave the owner's property.

Ms. Renee and Ms. Heather stood behind the couple. Together, the two women are quite a pair. Ms. Heather is pale skinned, tall, and very slender, with a mane of red hair. Her clothes are what I have labeled "rich bitch" attire. She loves heels, animal prints, and wide leather belts. Ms. Renee was also fashionably dressed but in a much more subtle fashion. She's not as tall as Ms. Heather, and even though she dresses in a more reserved manner she sends out a message of quiet authority. When the two are together, clerks or business people tend to address Ms. Renee first. People assume that she is the leader in any group. I don't remember that this was always true. Perhaps it has been her domination of me that has helped make her more powerful. Somehow people sense that she is the alpha female.

The couple left but my mistress stayed to question the salesgirl. She asked about safety and about increasing the voltage. The salesgirl politely responded. Ms. Heather seemed a little confused and impatient because she knew Ms. Renee didn't own a dog. Then Ms. Renee looked meaningfully at me. Turning to the saleswoman, she asked if she had a tiny size for a much smaller dog. The saleswoman handed her a smaller collar and showed her how to adjust the size.

I had been listening closely. Ms. Renee rarely humiliated me in public but lately she had been increasing her enjoyment of this technique of domination. I felt Heather beside me becoming impatient. At the time, I didn't feel too anxious because I doubted I would be asked to wear anything like a collar on the street due to the public nature of Ms. Renee's job.

"Maybe," Ms. Renee pined, "it might fit but he's so pitifully small. I would love a much larger pet but guess I have to make do with what I have."

Again, Ms. Renee paused to stare at me but not at my face. Suddenly, I understood that it was not around my neck she planned for me to wear this collar. I immediately looked directly at the floor. I felt the heat rise in my face.

She turned to the salesgirl and queried, "Are you sure you don't have anything smaller?"

Ms. Renee looked at me again, this time with her hand stretched out holding the collar at the level of my crotch. She asked me, "Butler, do you think it's small enough?"

My embarrassment was starting to make it clear what she was really talking about. I stammered, "Yes, ma'am, I think it would fit."

I heard a short stifled guffaw from Heather, who finally understood what was going on. At her laugh I saw understanding also begin to dawn on the face of the salesgirl. I stood helplessly in front of these three women, holding on to a bag of litter and food with my head bowed, trying not to meet anyone's eyes.

Ms. Renee handed her back the collar with a smile and announced, "I'll try it out. Can I return it if it's too large or if it doesn't produce the obedience I require?"

"Yes, of course," the sales clerk responded politely.

I could almost hear the word "Ma'am" added in her response. Salespeople always seem to snap to attention when Ms. Renee walks into a store. Again, she has become accustomed to good service. Maybe one receives what one expects. My eyes were still glued to the floor, with my face red with embarrassment.

Ms. Heather and Renee always walk outside of a store arm in arm after making their selections while I scurry to pick up their packages and run after them. I heard their heels as they clicked over the painted concrete floor, so I turned to look at them as they walked away. It was true that I felt publicly humiliated and neutered by them, but as I watched them leave, especially as my eyes followed the sway of Ms. Renee's hips, I also felt utterly entranced.

I noticed that the salesgirl had padded off in her sneakers toward the front of the store. I snapped out of my trance to follow her to the checkout counter. She was a young woman dressed in jeans and T-shirt. Her skin was adorned with multiple piercings and tattoos.

She bagged my collar and other purchases and took my money. As she handed me back my change, her fingers lingered for one tiny moment with her hand almost holding mine.

Hesitantly, I looked up into her eyes, expecting to see shock or contempt. She looked back with an intense expression and said only one word, "Lucky."

*****

The chastity cage with its electrical addition was a constant chafing agony for the rest of the month. I never became used to it. I learned to concentrate on my duties and count off the days until the trial was over. At night I would lie on my narrow pallet in the attic and try not to think of them tangled in the sheets on the floor below me. I yearned to touch my mistress. I was not even permitted to help her with her bath. When I thought about begging for the privilege, I was torn between wanting to be there and fearing the discomfort that an erection would cause me. In any case, I could not ask for the rules to change. I couldn't even speak unless spoken to.

Day followed day in a whirl of work, denial, and humiliation. The chores would have been boring but the tedium was spiced by the continued anxiety that my efforts would not be up to Ms. Renee's standards. Mistakes were painful and I tried very hard to avoid her displeasure.

Each day I found myself raging at the stupidity of my own sexuality that required that I serve a dominant woman. I felt loneliness and frustration. When I wasn't ignored, I was humiliated or punished. It seems silly to admit that my feelings were hurt. Yet when they accepted my work as their due, left me alone constantly, and seemed only interested in me when I had not met their expectations, I felt abused, abandoned, and alone. At night I could only count down the days while forcing myself to stay focused. I knew I could not live without this enchanting woman of my dreams. I realized that the very fact that I was there enduring my slavery was proof that she was the dominatrix of my fantasies. If I quit, I would always know how close I had come but had missed my goal of serving a truly dominant woman.

Finally, on the night before Heather was to leave, Ms. Renee called me into her bedroom. I had only been in her room to clean for the last four weeks.

"Two," she said as I immediately fell to my knees.

"It's New Year's Eve. This is Heather's last night, so I'm taking her out to dinner as a treat. You don't have dinner to cook, so you have time to prepare me." She motioned toward the bathroom and I quickly crawled in the direction she pointed. I was almost overcome with excitement.

When her bath was full and the right temperature, I crawled back into her dressing area. She had not asked me to stay on my knees but I was not about to let this opportunity slip by a lapse in my submissiveness.

Ms. Renee stood in the middle of her bedroom waiting for me. I felt like a virgin schoolboy as I helped her out of her clothes. My fingers trembled as I touched her for the first time in a month. She ignored my clumsiness and allowed me to continue.

I followed her on my knees back to the bath. The cock cage was itching like I had rubbed my privates in poison ivy. I had to mentally shove my discomfort aside to concentrate on my duties or I would miss the chance of touching her.

She slowly entered the tub while I soaped up the various brushes and cloths she had trained me to use. She extended her leg while I ran the loofah over her feet. She completely relaxed as I washed every inch of her. She rolled over and extended her bottom into the air so I could clean it. Her derrière looked incredibly sexy as it floated above the water line. I carefully rubbed the washcloth along every inch of her thighs and back. My cock was in a cramped torture but I still felt disappointed when the bath finally ended. She stood and stretched luxuriously as I toweled her dry.

My mistress sat on the side of her bed and allowed me to brush her hair. She has long dark hair that I find very sensual. When I was finished, she instructed me to kneel beside her bed. It felt strange to kneel there.

"It must be hard for you knowing that in just a little while I'll be having sex in this bed again that you're not even allowed on. I'm sure I'll have another satisfying orgasm. I can't imagine going a whole month without one. Only a fool would allow someone to take his orgasms away. You look like a dog kneeling there wishing he was allowed on the bed. Was it hard changing the sheets each week knowing what has been happening on them? Did you hold the sheets up to your face to try to smell me?" I felt my face flush remembering I had done just that. She was right. I was her dog.

She stared intently at me then moved her head lower as if she were about to kiss me.

It was the first time in a month she had even come close to kissing me. I gasped and tried not to lunge for her lips. At that moment, if she had been telling me of my immediate execution I would still have been grateful if she would kiss me first but instead she pushed me away.

"It must be eating at you that that I have another lover. I suppose it's easier for you that it's not another man. Maybe someday I'll give you that experience. Lucky for you, I tend to like women more. Even if I allowed you the chance to touch me you could never really satisfy me the way she does. This fact has to hurt."

Ms. Renee leaned forward and almost kissed me again.

"You think you want to be my husband but if I agree to your proposal all you'll likely get is more denial and humiliation. Look at what I've done to you this month. I beat you and kept your dick locked in a cage. You let me treat you like a dog. Only a man destined to be a slave would allow me to do this to him."

Again, the almost kiss and again she avoided me. I could feel her words unraveling my soul.

"I can only assume that you deserve to be treated this way. Any man who would let me do this to him could never have my respect."

Ms. Renee cupped my chin in her hands and looked directly into my eyes while she continued in a calm voice, "I don't think of you as a man anymore. Not after this month. I only see you as my slave."

In a quiet, confidential tone, she continued, "I never knew how exciting whipping you and denying you would be. Lately, the more I hurt you, the more I want to hurt you. I think I'm addicted to giving you pain."

She opened her legs and pointed to her dark triangle. "Do you still want to see me naked? Doesn't it hurt to look at me?"

Almost in a trance, I began gazing at her delicious center. I had wanted to see her naked every day for the last month but had been denied the privilege until her bath.

"Stupid slave, you are looking at the source of your enslavement."

I passionately wanted to kiss and lick her. The more she degraded me, the more desperately I wanted to bury my face between her legs.

"You may look, but don't touch! You don't deserve to give me an orgasm. That privilege is reserved for my lover."

I leaned forward slightly. Her words tore into me more than any beating but I continued looking at her.

Finally, she pushed me away, "Time to get me ready for tonight."

Then, to my complete surprise, she reached over and grabbed the top of my cock cage. She immediately started taping on the top of my cage with the polished nail of her index finger. In an involuntary response, I hardened inside the cage and just as quickly a horrible pain from the cage pierced me. She began quietly laughing.

"Oh, Butler. You are so easy. How pathetic. I know that when I make you hard it hurts. Don't you understand that the more it hurts the more turned on I get? Tonight, I'm going to think of you writhing in pain from your cramped, aching dick just as I orgasm."

She gently touched the head of my cock through the bars of the cage while she watched my face contorted in deeper agony. Even with my eyes closed in pain I could sense her smile.

"Time to dress me!" she announced happily. She released me and stood up.

Shaking, I slowly crawled into her closet and began to bring out what she chose to wear. Carefully, I helped her dress. She put on a tight black wool skirt and a red silk blouse that showed enough cleavage to make a saint stare. As I knelt and held them in place, she slipped into her sexiest black high-heeled shoes. She allowed me to put a string of black pearls around her neck that cost me four months' salary. I watched her apply my favorite perfume and knelt mesmerized as she applied a dark red lipstick. I heard an involuntary groan escape my lips as I again realized that none of this careful preparation was for me.

"We are going to Bari, your favorite restaurant, tonight. Remember when I used to let you take me there?"

Ms. Renee pushed me down to my knees. "I don't want you to mess up my makeup but I know you're eager to kiss me goodbye." She turned away from me and straddled my face while flipping her skirt up around her hips. I felt ridiculous.

Nevertheless, I reverently pressed my lips against her lingerie-clad ass. Ms. Renee laughed derisively and stepped to the doorway, then twisted provocatively in her skirt.

"Oh, do I see a spot on my shoe?" she teased as she twisted around and put one of her stilettos in front of my face. I didn't wait but bent down and licked the top of it clean.

She pulled me up again to both knees by a gentle tug of my hair. I was in psychological and physical agony. She laughed once more.

"Oh, poor slave. It hurts, doesn't it? Maybe you should concentrate on your chores until I get home. I know how excited you are to do something for me!"

She blew me a kiss as she headed out the door. I knelt transfixed on the floor of her bedroom as I heard them leave. It was a long time before I could move.

*****

Two hours later they returned home. I opened the door for them and took their coats. Neither of them spoke to me, they were so engrossed with each other. They quickly clicked up the stairs while holding hands. I had placed a bottle of wine and a bottle of water in an ice bucket next to their bed, so I knew I wouldn't need to enter their bedroom.

When the month first started, I hoped to catch glimpses of them together, but now I tried hard to avoid it. I had learned that the pain from my cage would punish me should I witness them so much as kiss, but I also had changed internally. What belonged to my mistress was for her alone. I began to see my job as a support for her pleasures. I had enough to do to keep me busy, so I continued to work in another part of the house as they made love.

Bathing and dressing my mistress had awakened my libido that I had been carefully trying to lull to sleep for the last few weeks. The last few hours in the chastity cage were torture.

After I finished my chores, I was exhausted. I undressed and retired to the attic playroom that Ms. Renee had exiled me to sleep in for the month. There were two perfectly good spare bedrooms but she wanted me to sleep near the discipline equipment and far away from them. As I prepared for bed, the door opened and Ms. Renee entered.

My fatigue vanished. She had become the only woman in the world to me. Every sense from sight to smell instantly came alive.

Seeing my hungry gaze, she slowly slipped off her gown and walked toward my pallet. Watching her smooth catlike stride as she stalked naked toward my cot opened every door to my heart. Noticing that I was frozen in yearning, she lowered herself onto me, straddling my chest. I was afraid to breathe.

She looked down, her eyes boring into me.

"Hello, slave, I hope you had a good evening," she purred, with a knowing smile on her face.

It was one of the worst evenings of my life but I tried to put myself in her shoes. That made it a good evening. So I answered, "Yes, Mistress, I was glad to serve you."

"Good answer! You're learning!" she smiled victoriously.

Surrendering, I nodded in agreement. I knew better than to argue or complain.

Ms. Renee continued to stare deeply into my eyes. "I know that I have hurt your feelings by giving Heather all of my attention this month. I especially appreciate that it ties you in knots but you're unable to do or say anything to stop me because you know it will displease me. You're starting to fear me, aren't you? That's such a power rush!"

She tugged painfully at my nipples. "You may lick my ass if you like. Of course, I would never ask Heather to do that! Ass licking is a job for a slave."

She turned and straddled my chest, facing toward my feet. I knew what to do and I began gently licking her between her firm buttocks.

"Hmm, that feels lovely," she murmured.

Ms. Renee began mocking me. "You are truly pathetic when you are so obedient. I let Heather lick my pussy but all you get to lick is my ass. Do you like the taste?"

I nodded my head yes.

"Oh, Butler, I believe you. Keep licking!" she said as she pushed her bottom even harder on to my face.

She went on, "I wanted this month to hurt your feelings. Licking my ass is your first opportunity to touch me in a month. I wanted to choose something truly demeaning. You want to be my husband but most husbands never have to lick their wife's ass."

I groaned in response but kept licking. She had used the word "husband" for me. A thrill raced through me.

Her hands dropped to my chastity cage. "This cage must really hurt!" she said in mock concern.

I moaned and begged, "Please, can you take it off now? I've been through so much this month."

Ms. Renee responded in a flat, serious tone. "Oh no, you haven't been through enough quite yet. Your month doesn't end until tomorrow night. You should never beg to be let out early. It might make me angry."

Something about asking for release made her suddenly stand up. She began to pace around my tiny cot. At once, I felt bereft. I wanted to be near her anyway I could. I was utterly broken.

I pleaded, "Mistress, may I please lick your ass some more?"

She stopped pacing and gazed down at me with her hands on her hips. "You're truly pathetic! Listen to yourself. I've been torturing you, working you, and humiliating you for a month and your only response is to beg to lick my ass again? For asking for an early release, the answer is no. I'm not in the mood anymore."

She began to strut around my cot, staring coldly down at me.

"I've taken everything this month, haven't I? Let's see. You don't have a career because I won't let you work. You haven't seen your friends because I never let you leave the house. You don't have any spare time because I work you constantly. You don't have any possessions because I made you leave them in your apartment. You haven't had any orgasms because I keep you locked up. You are no longer even allowed to give me orgasms because I have a lover. The only thing I've allowed you to do all month is lick my ass and I just took that away from you."

She stopped pacing, and putting her hands on her hips, began to quietly laugh.

I could hear myself moaning. I wanted her back on top of me even if it only meant more torture.

In a more tender tone she looked down at me and added, "I just want you to know, I loved having sex with Heather tonight knowing you were at your limit. You made it so much better by being in pain for me. I'm not just trying to tease you when I tell you that your pain gave me another fantastic orgasm. I think we've found something you're really good at doing for me. You are good at suffering. I love it when you sacrifice yourself for me."

She leaned down and gently placed a hand to my cheek.

Then, in a confiding voice, she went on, "This is the longest I've ever asked you to go without an orgasm. I'm really enjoying your frustration and the depths of submission your chastity has brought you. I could leave you in that cage another month if I wanted. You no longer have any say in what I do. You proved that to me this last month."

I started to tremble.

She went on, "I guess I could allow a milking if you showed that you were grateful. I don't want to take you out of your device yet but I understand a little digital stimulation of the prostate will release just enough pressure to keep you healthy. I could let you out but I don't want you to start thinking of yourself as anything but a slave. I don't think slaves deserve real orgasms. I understand that a prostate milking doesn't cause an orgasm but only an unsatisfying and humiliating little dribble of semen. That should be enough for a slave like you.

"Tomorrow, to start off the year right, I'll try to give you your first prostate milking. I wanted to wait until I was certain we would be successful. I think you're ready. I'm sure you'll feel grateful for any release that I give you."

She stooped and reached down. Her fingers brushed against my inner thigh, separating my legs. She probed the area under my scrotum. I could feel her press painfully into the swollen tissues of my perineum. I didn't know how she knew that the pain would be there. Then, I remembered her medical training and shivered. I saw her smile darkly.

"Yes, I think you're ready. I can't wait!"

She moved her hand away from me and stood up once more, putting her hands on her hips. She went on, "Now you are agreeing to the most unsatisfying and humiliating release a man can receive. You no longer have any say over your own body. I control it completely."

She suddenly smiled down on me, narrowing her eyes in concentration. "How does it feel?"

All I could do was choke out a single sob. I was completely at her mercy. I felt the last tiny bit of pride and independence leaking from what was left of my battered self-esteem. All I felt in its place was a great desire for her. She had become the only thing in my universe.

She stood looking down at me for a long time. When she spoke, I heard warmth in her voice. "The month is almost up. Tomorrow will be the end of your testing period. Heather will be leaving and we will have the house alone again. If you submit to a milking, you will have passed the test. You have proved that you are submissive enough for me to allow you to move in. I'm so glad."

She went on tenderly, "I admit that I was worried. I didn't want to lose you but I also didn't want to compromise our principles. I promised you real domination. This test was as real as I could make it. I am very glad that you passed."

I had been waiting to hear her say it but it still somehow came as a shock. I wondered, was the nightmare over? I felt a sudden rush of hope despite my situation.

Then, for the first time in a month, Ms. Renee leaned down and kissed me deeply. It was like being rescued from a dark prison. I looked into her eyes and I saw the promise of a thousand nights of love. We would continue as a couple and continue as lovers. I was utterly grateful for this tiny bit of tenderness and the unspoken promise. I was filled with passion and love for this merciful goddess. I was elated that I had passed her test.

There was a long pause as if she were reaching for an idea that was just out of reach. She seemed to be steeling herself for something hard. Finally, she continued in a reasonable tone, "However, there is a problem. I didn't mean for it to happen but it did. I see you differently now. Look at what I've done to you. I've worked you, tortured you, and humiliated you for a month and you let me do it. I can't think of you in the same way anymore. Now, it's not just a fantasy, you're no longer a man to me. Maybe we went too far but you're just a slave to me now. You keep asking me to marry you. Maybe we should just skip the wedding. After all, what's the point? I keep asking myself, why should I change anything? Also, I'm not sure it's appropriate. Should I marry a slave? It seems somehow beneath me."

My world felt like it had suddenly tilted on its axis again! The rush of relief I had felt suddenly turned to dust. Her words meant that all of the last month was for nothing! Yet I knew she was right. I didn't deserve such a goddess. How could I be a match for her? I saw clearly for the first time that there were two different levels of humans. She was my superior. I was only a slave. A new level of submission surged through me. I felt sorry for anything

I had ever thought or done that was not perfectly submissive to her. I was nothing. She was everything. I knew I would be grateful to serve her in any capacity she allowed.

The room was so still I can hear my own heart beating. I knew that in the next few seconds she would decide my fate.

She sat down on the cot next to me and placed her hand on my chest. "Still, I do love you. You have passed my test. I might marry you. I believe if we keep practicing female domination that you will continue with this level of devotion."

This was more than I could have hoped for. I was readying myself to remain as her slave but praying she was also willing to marry me. Hadn't she promised to do just that?

"Of course there is one more problem. What on earth are you going to give me for a wedding present?"

She gave me that wicked smile that I so loved. "Think of the night you propose and I agree to marriage. Think how wonderful it would be to come out of that awful cage and make love to me again like a real person. Would you like that?"

The thought seemed like a visitation from a goddess. I could never deserve such an honor but every atom of me desired it.

"It will only happen if I feel you deserve it. But to even have a chance of such a night, you will have to prove to me that you will stay dedicated to me. Think of something you can give me. I want you to really dig deeply. I want something special or the whole idea of marriage is off. We can continue as we are with you as my slave. I have no real reason to marry you unless I'm convinced of your deep desire to give me everything. Think about it. Why should I?"

Once again she brought her face close to mine and gently kissed me.

Suddenly, she stood up and turned in the doorway looking down at me. Sharply she snapped, "The marriage is off and an occasional milking is all you can look forward to unless you can think of something you can give me that I don't already own. That would be too bad because I have enjoyed our sex life. However, from now on coitus will be reserved for the man who proves himself worthy of being my husband. Ha! I can't imagine what you could give me.

"We'll talk about it tomorrow before your milking. That will happen no matter what I decide. I want you to know that I can live without you if I need to. A slave who is not engaged to me will only receive prostate milkings.

However, a slave who is also my fiancé will receive much more. You had better think of something good as a present or it's just more of the cage."

She shut the door firmly and I heard her footsteps recede down the hallway. I sat awake a long time trying to imagine something I could offer her. It seemed that she had already taken everything. Each idea I came up with was more humiliating or silly than the last one. She obviously wanted more. I knew I would find something. Visions of my being officially her fiancé filled my imagination. She gave no promise of when we might be wed or what I might need to offer in the future but I was determined to move forward.

I had no choice. I would do anything to remain with her. Maybe it was time to call my lawyer and money manager to confess what my special needs were. I wanted it to be a concrete surrender of power. Surely, something like that would satisfy her. I desperately hoped so. I knew I couldn't live without her.

January 2010
Dear Heather,

Only the two of us could share a house for a month but still have trouble seeing each other! We work too much! I was busy with fundraising events and the coming election. You weren't here that much because of the store opening. However, I loved it when you were.

I remember our sexual experiences in college were sometimes like wrestling matches. We both wanted the top position. Now the love is different. I sense that we can defer to each other and take our time. That may be the thing I like most about women. I never feel rushed with a woman. I'm glad that you've finally moved to Memphis. I'm looking forward to seeing you more often.

Thank you so much for staying with us. I know you felt reluctant because of Butler's presence in the house. I appreciate your help. Your visit here last month furthered my plans for him. Butler and I needed to begin our relationship afresh before he moves in. I hope it didn't bother you too much that he was here.

Last month turned out to be harder for me than I thought it was going to be. I needed your strength. I knew he was suffering. It was hard for me to maintain my distance. On the nights you slept in the spare room or worked late I wanted to go upstairs and encourage him in some way. I had to harden my heart. It was necessary to put him to the test. I wanted to know if he was as committed as I hoped, so I stayed away from him.

After a while, the thought of him lying on his cot suffering for me just above me in the playroom would start working on my mind until I needed to touch myself to get to sleep. Between you and my own busy fingers, I believe I had an orgasm every single night. Even now when I remember that he had nothing last month while I became greedy for more, I start getting worked up all over again. I have learned something important about myself.

I could have had him help me with oral service each night you and I weren't together but that wasn't the test I envisioned. I wanted him to see that I could get along without him. I want him to feel lucky to serve without reward. I think he's getting there.

When I finally removed his cage and allowed him to make love to me again, he acted like he was losing his virginity. I don't think I've ever seen him so excited or grateful. I was amused and very glad I had tested him.

The month was satisfying for me for many reasons. I'll tell you more when I see you.

Love,
Renee

January 2010
Dear Renee,

I agree, the sex between us has changed. It's better now that I don't feel so competitive.

Honestly, I wouldn't have made it through December without your help. The store is a huge success. We doubled what I thought we would sell. Thank you for taking care of me. I'm sorry I was there so little and with so little energy.

I loved every night I wasn't too tired. You are beautiful.

It was very relaxing to be there, knowing that I was not a burden—at least, not a burden to you. You really have Butler trained to take care of the house. I also appreciated that you've trained him to do laundry. Each day I found just what I needed hung neatly in my closet. It felt magical. I'm beginning to understand why you want him as a slave, but living together? I've tried that twice with men. I'm never going to do it again.

I'm glad to hear I was of some help. To my surprise, your schedule kept him from being underfoot. Instead of allowing him to move in, have you thought of building him a servant's quarters in the backyard? You could still have his service while maintaining your privacy.

Those few times I was allowed to watch you discipline him changed how I saw you. I've always thought you were the weak one but I was wrong!

Damn, watching you whip him really moved me. You looked like some kind of avenging angel.

He should be very grateful that you allow him to live with you even if that was all you allowed. It still seems like a lot depends on his continued interest. In my experience, men are fickle fuckers at best. He obeyed this time but what keeps him from refusing his next test?

Still worried about you,
Heather

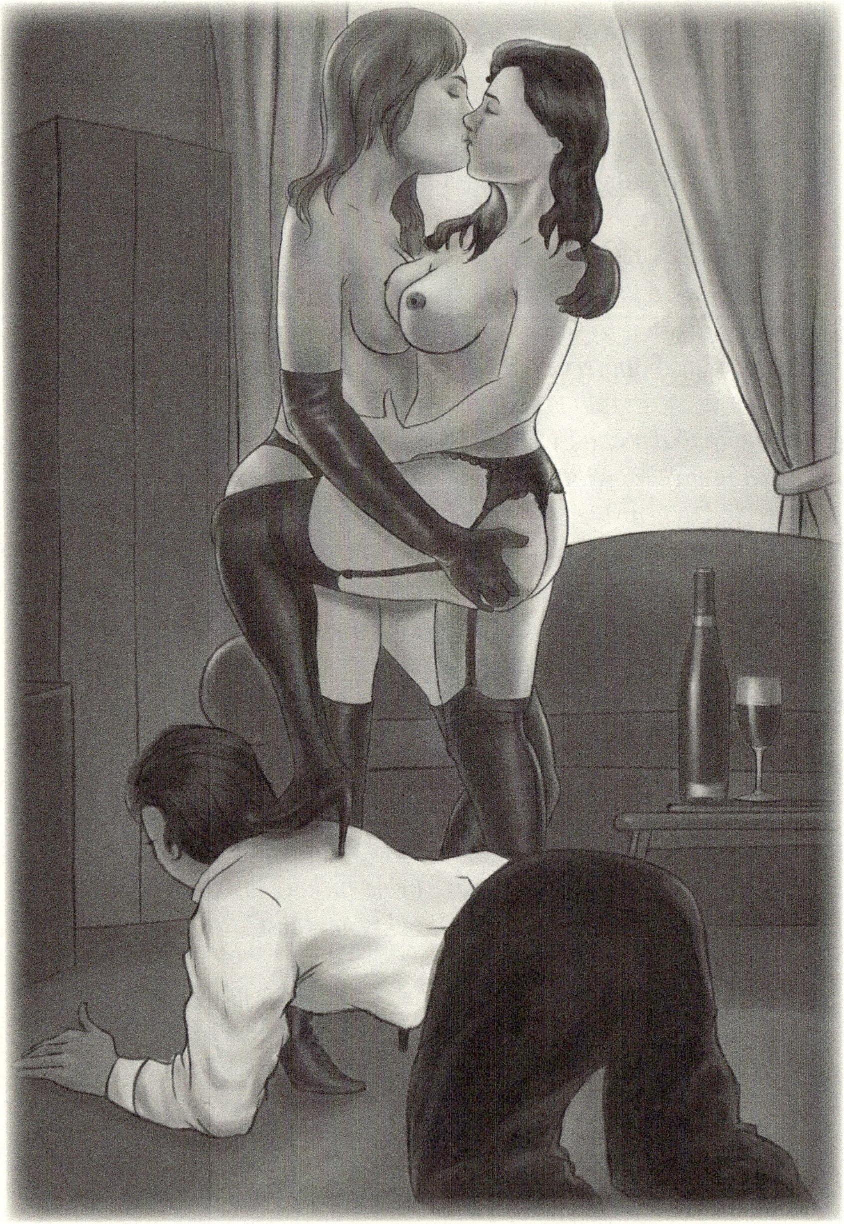

Chapter Four

BLACKMAIL

Butler's Journal
Packing to Move
March 2010

Once again our love life was back where we had been before Heather's visit. We had always enjoyed each other in bed but now it was even better. Also, I was very relieved to be out of the chastity cage. I realized that any day out of it was an act of mercy on her part. I felt grateful to her. Now, finally engaged to this wonderful woman, I was looking forward to moving in with her.

Ms. Renee often had very exacting and proscriptive instructions for many of the chores I did for her. I wasn't surprised that when it finally came time for me to move in with her she bombarded me with a very detailed list of how I should pack. I didn't feel it was necessary. I've lived all over the world. I've moved myself each time. I've never collected a lot of possessions. When I move into my one-bedroom condo, I unloaded everything I didn't need. Nevertheless, she insisted that I follow her instructions to the letter.

To help me, she temporarily suspended my chores for her for two weeks. I thought it was unusual because her normal attitude is that I should just work harder. She told me she wanted me to concentrate on my packing and finishing up any remaining legal chores from my job before my retirement.

Ms. Renee visited me in my condo a few days before I actually started packing. She almost never came there. She seemed to fill the place with her presence. She was wearing business attire in a tight wool skirt, jacket, and black heels. She pulled out a packet of different color stickers. As she offered more details about how she wanted me to pack, she went through the house placing different colored stickers on my possessions. Finally satisfied, she gave me the hand signal to kneel before her.

"Are you excited to be moving in with me, slave?" she teased.

She knew I had longed to do just that, but I answered her with feeling, "Oh yes, my goddess."

"I want you to follow my directions carefully," she instructed.

"Yes, Mistress."

"Now, let's sticker your clothes."

She strode into my bedroom and opened my closet. She quickly went through everything on the rack. She spent twenty minutes asking about different items and placing stickers on my remaining possessions. Next she asked me to pack my possessions in regard to the color scheme she had applied. Her help was intrusive, but as was my habit, I acquiesced.

She and I had often talked about personal boundaries. From the first, she had required that I lower my boundaries to allow her to rearrange my life but kept her own boundaries very high. She explained that this was simply part of a female-led relationship. For example, she always opened my mail on the few times she visited. Frequently, she answered my cell phone, screening my calls when it rang when we were together. She investigated me. She knew the amount in my savings and checking account. She knew everything. Now, she was supervising my move.

*****

A few days later, I finished the last box in time for her arrival. She appeared a little before noon as she had promised. She wore a pair of snug black leather pants, high-heeled boots, and a red form-fitting sweater. One of the great things about my mistress is that she dresses to please me. It was one of my favorite outfits. However, seeing her look so attractive triggered a warning in me. Something was up.

She stood in front of the pile of boxes labeled exactly as she had instructed. She ran her hands over the tops of the boxes. She motioned for me to kneel then stepped to the closet door to pull out one of her riding crops she left on a previous visit.

"So this is your big day that you've been hoping would come."

"Yes, Mistress."

Looking at the piles of boxes, she added, "You don't have much, do you?"

"No, Mistress, I don't collect things like most people do."

"Yes, but it's still too much. You are moving into my home. I don't have room for all of this."

She gave me the hand signal to lean forward onto all fours. She stood behind me.

"This won't do. I will not be inconvenienced with all of your junk. Most of this will have to go."

I really couldn't imagine what I could leave. I was moving into a large bedroom next to hers. The remainder of my things I was planning on incorporating into Ms. Renee's household possessions.

Ms. Renee began striking me across the buttocks with the crop. I had done nothing wrong. It was not a punishment. It felt completely unfair. It was hard to be still but I had learned the value of surrender.

"In a minute the movers should arrive to pick up most of the furniture. There is a reason I had you color code everything. The good pieces and the art that I marked by blue stickers will be sold for the women's shelter. Black will go to Goodwill. A small portion of your things marked by green will be stored to await my later decisions." She punctuated her words with the crop.

Finally, after a few more vicious swipes, I stammered, "Yes, Mistress, just as you please."

My response was what she was waiting to hear. She stopped for a second until I could gain my composure and began beating me with a more moderate effort.

"Only the things I tagged with a red sticker will be moved to my house."

I was stunned. That meant that almost nothing was going to her home. I wondered what the color-coding had meant. She had placed a red sticker on a few suits, some exercise apparel, and three or four other items along with my toiletries. I had easily placed the items she had marked with a red sticker in only two cardboard boxes. She kept steadily whipping me until I was sweating and moaning.

Sensing I had achieved the right mindset, Ms. Renee moved around to the pile of boxes and pointed at my very good set of golf clubs.

"Golf clubs? Where do you think you are going, to a country club? Who do you think you are? Do you think you'll have time for golf as my slave?"

She contemptuously kicked over the bag, spilling its contents. It was true that I almost never played anymore but having them available was a part of me. Seeing my expensive clubs scattered like trash on the floor was shocking.

Ms. Renee began striking the tops of the boxes with her crop and occasionally pushing over the taller piles.

"It all goes! Everything in your old life must go! Be grateful I leave you enough clothes to fulfill the few social obligations I allow you to attend with me. One day, all you'll have is a butler's uniform."

She whirled around me and again began lashing me with the crop just under the point that I could hold still without restraints.

"I can already hear the truck outside to pick this all up. I want to watch your face as they take your life away."

She continued to whip me until there was a knock at the door. Embarrassed but grateful to hear the knock, I struggled painfully to my feet and opened the door. Outside the door stood both sets of movers that had been hired by Ms. Renee. I wondered if they had heard her whipping me. Ms.

Renee continued to twirl the riding crop in her hand as they entered. They had arrived exactly on time, just as she had no doubt demanded.

The four men emptied the apartment quickly. Ms. Renee leaned on a window seat, tapping her riding crop onto one of her boots as she drank in my reaction while I helplessly watched my possessions disappear. This was something new she had recently started doing, hinting at (in not always subtle ways) the nature of our relationship to people outside of our social circle as a way of embarrassing and humbling me. The workers studiously ignored me. When they were finished, both groups of men spoke to her briefly and included the honorific "Ma'am" several times. It felt like more than a Southern idiom. Once again I noted that people, especially men, responded to her differently. Her domination of me had empowered her in ways other people could sense. In the end, all that remained on the floor were two cardboard boxes filled with everything I owned.

Ms. Renee appeared happily pleased with herself. She smiled at me. She kissed me warmly and swayed out the door on her high-heeled boots, with me trailing behind her carrying my meager possessions. We turned my keys over to a rental agency. At the time I hoped it would provide a nice income stream for me.

Afterward, she drove me to a very nice lunch at a better restaurant and chatted amicably about her job and coming events. I had trouble sitting on my bruised bottom but I was besotted. She was obviously on some kind of high. She looked utterly beautiful. She had just found yet another way to wreck my life while increasing her dominion over me. The afternoon activities had filled her with affection and energy.

After lunch I drove with her in her car to my new home. I went up the back steps carrying my two boxes. She seemed excited about something more than me moving in. I could feel that special tension that appears just before she has sprung one of her traps. As I followed her up the stairs, I felt anxious. As a remedy I focused on the heels of her boots as she climbed in front of me.

At the head of the stairs she motioned me to put my boxes down in the hallway and moved on into her room. It's a beautiful space with an unusually large bathroom attached. She continued across the room into her closet. Did she want me to put my things in her closet? I had assumed that I was moving into the guest bedroom.

Instead of the carefully ordered closet I expected, I saw a huge pile of clothes on the floor of a much bigger space. The wall to her closet had been pushed back to make the closet much larger. Ms. Renee had two other bedrooms on the second floor. Obviously, one of them had been transformed into her now much larger closet. This is why I had not been cleaning her house for the last few weeks. She had been secretly remodeling.

She pointed to the pile of clothes. "This works out that you are moving in because this will take you forever to get this sorted out. Everything has to be ironed and rehung."

She walked to the center of the room. In the middle of the disarray stood a large ornate wooden chair. She sat for a second looking up at me, posing provocatively. "This is where you will dress me."

She gave me a quick smile and sprang from the chair, once again motioning me to follow her. I assumed that she was taking me to the one remaining spare bedroom. However, instead of turning toward the remaining room, she turned the other way. I noted that there was still a door where the remodeled bedroom had been. She opened it to reveal a long narrow hallway-like space about ten feet long and six feet wide. At the far end was a single window. Along the wall to the left was a narrow antique iron bedframe with just enough room to allow one to pass to the end of the room. Along the opposite wall from the bed to the right were several brass hooks for a few clothes.

"Cozy, isn't it?"

Now I understood. I was never going to move the rest of my things from storage. This was now my life. I only had room for the necessities.

She explained, "I thought about this for a long time. After I remodeled my closet, I couldn't give you the remaining guest room. I'll need that for my guests. I thought about making you sleep upstairs in the playroom but I like keeping it for its own special purpose. I had to compromise about what I wanted for my closet but I left you with plenty of space . . . for a slave."

She leaned into me and kissed me on the cheek. "Hurry and unpack or you'll never get my clothes hung back up before dinner."

Dear Renee,

I've loved your occasional visits to my home. Yes, it's true that I'm more comfortable with you in my home where it's just the two of us. I am still trying to wrap my head around the fact that you have allowed Butler to move into your home. At least you haven't married him yet.

I will never live with another man. I'm glad to hear you've put him to good use. I love it when Suzy visits for a few days. It's easy to become accustomed to someone picking up after me. Funny how quickly one can grow used to good service. Now, I consider living or traveling without a servant "roughing it." I hope this works out for you.

I'm not anti-man. Since moving to Memphis I've even been on a few dates. Anytime I want to go out and hear about how great some man is or listen to him drone on about sports or some other inane subject, then I do so. I find most men too tedious for words. I did meet a younger guy who might be malleable. We'll see.

I miss Suzy but her family is in Atlanta and they need her. Also, I need her there to run the store. However, she wants to meet the two of us next weekend halfway to Atlanta at the lake house we visited a few months ago.

You mentioned that you were interested in topping her with me. Still interested?

Heather

June 2010
Dear Heather,

That is an irresistible offer. Yes! I can join you for your weekend getaway. Yes, just the two of us.

I need to know how you've been training her recently and what your plans are for her. We can talk in the car. I have a couple of pieces of equipment I want to bring. This sounds like fun!

I thought about your idea of leaving Butler in his cell with food and water for the long weekend but it didn't seem safe. Instead, I bought the heaviest chain I could find and an enormous padlock. I locked the chain tightly enough around his neck that he can't remove it. He'll be too embarrassed to leave the house and be seen in public with it locked around his neck. I also left him with a list of chores to keep him busy. I can't wait for you to see him before we leave. I'm also leaving his cock cage on while we are gone.

Staring at him while he knelt in front of me with his chastity belt around his genitals and the enormous chain around his neck while knowing I was leaving him housebound was deeply satisfying. Butler looks good for his age. He's always had a toned body, but seeing him chained and in chastity in a submissive posture, I realized again that he was beautiful to me. He is what is best in my life. I have my work for women's rights in Tennessee but Butler is my favorite hobby. Seeing that he was a little frightened by what he would accept was a deeply satisfying moment. Knowing that I was leaving him with a list of chores to go somewhere to have fun with you was the icing on the cake.

Come pick me up after work on Friday. You can mess with his head a little as only you can do before we leave.

Kisses,
Renee

June 2010
Dear Renee,

Yow, that was a wild weekend! I think we stretched Suzy's limits in ways that I had been reluctant to do by myself. This whole double-teaming thing works!

It was hard to see her go back to Atlanta. I need my own servant here in Memphis. I noticed yours was waiting on his knees when I dropped you off. I loved how he looked in those chains. It's a shame that you have to take them off. One day I hope we live in a world where we can proudly come out as dominant women. In the meantime, I'm going to try to get Suzy here more often. When she visits, I'll want your help with her again.

I'm sorry to harp on this but you've never really answered my questions about the future. How will you keep Butler from one day deciding that he's had enough and then simply leaving?

Lunch again soon.

Heather

September 2010
Dear Heather,

Thanks for the concern and the advice you gave me at our weekly lunch. I love that you live in town now. Playing with Suzy was great fun. I think you made real progress with her this summer.

Yes, it's shocking, even to me, but I am still planning on marriage. I know you don't understand it but I have thought this decision through very carefully. I have purposely postponed our actual marriage ceremony so I could continue to train him to be the spouse I want. It's true that I might be harder on him than you need to be with Suzy but the dynamics are different. Suzy is naturally sweet and loving. Most importantly, she is a woman. I have a man to tame. I think men require a firmer hand.

I've already taken steps to ensure that I'm covered legally for my discipline of him. After what I made him sign and the videos I have safely stored at my office, I think he would be embarrassed to complain to anyone about anything I do to him. Other legal matters such as his estate will take more time.

My attachment to the real world is secure. I know that there is no longer anything like legal slavery anymore. Of course, that's a good thing. However, Butler remains fascinated by the idea of being owned by me. He seeks submission because it excites him. He was lucky to have found me. I want to give him what he desires but only if I feel it's real. My plan is to keep moving relentlessly forward. I'm reminded that if you place a frog in water and turn up the heat, gradually the frog will never jump out but instead surrender to being cooked. My job is to keep adjusting the temperature at just the right times until he is completely mine.

As I slowly turn up the heat, I never want him to ever feel emotionally, psychologically, or financially able to back out of being my slave even during the most difficult times. In our extensive discussions, he voiced his fear that he would weaken when things started getting hard. It's ironic that he was worried about the same thing you are worried about.

He begged me to come up with some way to prevent him from refusing to move forward. His willingness to find ways that lock him into submission encourages me to be creative.

After a lot of thought, I decided that a very sophisticated blackmail portfolio would help prevent him from trying to back out. I told him of my blackmail plans and he enthusiastically agreed. He even came up with some suggestions of how I might obtain embarrassing material on him. It's easy to understand why I love him. He made it clear that he expected me to manipulate him. I think he would be disappointed if I didn't. Nevertheless, it was important that he agree, at least at first. His enslavement is the most interesting and exciting challenge either one of us has ever faced. I want this more than I have ever wanted anything and I'm certain that he feels the same way.

Writing about it now sounds like we sat down and made a plan about how I would dominate him. That's because that is actually what happened. We sat down and we tried to anticipate some of the challenges we would face and how we would overcome them. I had his total buy-in when it comes to what I have planned for him. Of course, I didn't tell him everything. He wouldn't want that. He loves being surprised and taken places he has never anticipated even in his wildest dreams.

My blackmail fantasies started very early when we started dating. I momentarily toyed with the idea of putting a protection order on him then having him arrested for failing to maintain enough distance from me. I trembled at the thought of going downtown to the jail and seeing him in the lock-up. I pictured how I would dress. I love wearing leather and boots with heels. I love watching what an outfit that is not revealing but still sends out a subtle dominant message does to the right kind of man. I thought of him coming out in his prison jumpsuit to speak to me in the visitor's section. He would be completely at my mercy. He would be hurt and bewildered by my actions. I imagined him leaning into the window and begging me to end the charade. I imagine myself smiling at his distress but doing nothing but promise to return the next day to visit him again.

The whole scenario was so powerful that I masturbated to the thought of it several times. I would have done it but I realized that I could have put myself in legal jeopardy for using the criminal justice system for my bondage games. Still, there was something so powerful about imagining the shocked and hurt look on his face that it gave me the shivers.

Before our marriage, I intend to put him through an extensive training period with the goal of obtaining useful blackmail material. Of course, I will take embarrassing videos of him doing such things as being whipped or begging me to use the strap-on in his ass. I'm sure most men would do a lot to prevent that kind of video from being sent to everyone they know. I will make him view them repeatedly while I ridicule him and threaten him with exposure. He needs to see himself differently. Viewing himself being pegged while he begs me to make him my slave will be a good beginning.

In addition, I want to take his blackmail even further. Somehow, I will force him to break some law in a victimless manner. When he provides me with evidence of his crime, I want him to acknowledge that he is freely giving me this power over him to prevent him from ever changing his mind about being my slave. I want the knowledge that he provided me with this blackmail information to eat into his soul. I will make it clear that I will have my revenge if he wastes my time by attempting to back out of his commitment to be my slave once things get hard.

This idea of him trying to rebel intrigues me. I am certain that if he doesn't ask for mercy every now and then that I'm not pushing hard enough. As part of my plan to break him, I intend to keep pushing him little by little until he tries to back out temporarily so I can mercilessly crush his tiny impotent rebellion.

In my imagination I have a lovely image of him one day wanting to slow the process of becoming my slave. In response, I see myself dominating him in a haughty fashion and whipping him relentlessly while asking, *"If you try to back out I will release my blackmail to the police. Would you rather have the felons in jail fucking your ass or would you rather have me? Whom do you prefer? We're past you having any say in how far we go! You were meant to be my slave!"* Yikes! It sounds like a powerful moment.

I want to crush any part of him that does not want to immediately surrender to me. Being reminded of the blackmail material that he freely gave me and knowing of my determination to use it will force him to see what he really wants to do is to submit. He chose me knowing I was a woman who would not back down. He will realize that he is caught in an inescapable web of his own design. When he does, I will rejoice at his defeat and debasement knowing that he is much less likely to rebel again.

I have a few kinkier friends from the local S&M club that I intend to show some of my better pictures. Once he knows that they are aware of the reality of his submission, I assume that his normal confident alpha-male personality will be replaced with a more humble demeanor. I'm eager to see this public transformation. I can only imagine how much it will turn me on to actually see a change in his behavior due to my humbling of him. Already, I've been turned on about how he acts around you. I've noted that as soon as you walk in the room he snaps into his most submissive posture. You have been a big help.

After a few humiliating experiences, he will realize that I'm not bluffing about using my blackmail. If I detect any serious rebellion in him, I will include his family, friends, and business associates in my next embarrassing e-mail. I could ruin all of his relationships and what is left of his career. I could even send him to jail. He must know that I will be strong even if he feels too weak to continue. I will gloat while watching him realize that he is truly losing control of his life. At times I recognize that he must truly love me and want to serve me to give me so much power. I won't let him down.

As you can see, I'm taking this all very seriously. Too seriously? It's hard to have any perspective when it's all so damn exciting.

Hugs,
Renee

January 2011
Dear Renee,

No, you are not taking this too seriously! There are no rules in love and war. This seems like both to me. The world has too many rules that are designed to keep women like us from happiness and achieving our full potential. If we are to be truly free, we have to ignore the constraints that the world would impose. I want you to be happy.

I'm glad we are through the holidays. We never have enough time for each other during the last quarter. You took such good care of me last year. I missed it this year. Tell Butler I actually missed some of his services.

It's funny that most people see you as the quiet type who would never do anything outré. If they only knew! Blackmail! How wonderful!

If I had done some of the things to my last husband that you've done to Butler, I'd probably still be married now. Looking back, I see now that he was a closet submissive. It's probably why we were attracted to each other.

Remember what I said about the Golden Rule. "Those with the gold make the rules." You have some work to do before you marry. I still can't believe you are actually going to do it. I e-mailed you the number of my lawyer. Use her for your prenuptial agreement. She's a shark and will look after your interests.

It seems I can't change your mind about marriage. If I can't control you, I'm determined to support you.

Heather

Butler's Journal
Blackmail
March 2011

Over the last few months, Ms. Renee has involved me in several rehearsed dramas that I thought were designed solely to amuse her and to humiliate me. She called them role-plays. When we started I often thought they were unnecessary because they frequently required me to play a role that was not part of our real life as a dominant woman and a submissive man. For example, I already do all of the housework. It seemed silly and inefficient to dress me as a maid while I did it. I know that there are many men who find cross-dressing exciting but I am not one of them. Nevertheless, at her insistence I put on a maid costume and performed a few of my usual household duties with her standing over me bitchily critiquing my performance. It didn't matter if I felt silly. I no longer had the power to negotiate a scene. It was my job to obey.

Frequently, she gave me elaborate lines and scenes she wanted to enact. To please her, I did so. I was saddled and ridden as a horse. Several times I wore a dog collar and ate from a bowl placed on the floor. I am a straight man but she had me beg her to allow me to suck on the large strap-on dildo she wore. On several occasions she penetrated me with her dildo while wickedly sneering that a real man would never allow her to do such a thing. She even had me lick her toilette seat after belittling me for not cleaning it properly.

These scenes were often psychologically and emotionally difficult. Through them I changed my view of myself. I felt that I no longer had any boundaries that she couldn't easily step through. I had thought that just seeing her dressed in leather with her whip in her hand was enough to sear my soul but these elaborate rituals altered how I viewed our relationship. Clearly, refusing her anything was beyond my power.

While she continued to put me through various role-plays, she also became increasingly exacting about my work. It seemed I could not do anything right. Even if my work was perfect she found something wrong. Each time she found a mistake she would have me write information in the notebook I carry concerning the infraction and the number of lashes with her rattan cane I would receive for it on Saturday afternoon.

When I can't receive all the punishment due me, I am denied the privilege of making love to my goddess. Denied coitus, Ms. Renee makes it worse by putting me in my chastity belt so I can't give myself an unearned release.

I don't come out of it until the following Saturday if I have earned it. Any lashes I have not endured are added to my account for the next week's total. The maximum number of stokes I can stand and still work the next day is about thirty lashes. This has only happened twice in the last few years. Obviously, keeping the number below thirty is extremely important to me.

    I knelt trembling and sweating after her lashing two weeks ago. She stood over me with her whip in her hand. She had given the usual warm-up with her paddle and finished with the thirty lashes with her cane. She was perspiring in her leather pants and bra. I could smell the mingled scent of hot female and warm leather. Even though I was at the end of the level of my endurance, I would have endured more for the chance to make love to her. I knew it was impossible. Bitter experience had taught me that Ms. Renee always keeps her promises.

    The next week I redoubled my efforts, but to no avail. She was relentless. I went into the week with ten lashes on my account but despite my best efforts I was at twenty-five by Wednesday. Tiny lapses in housekeeping that normally would have been overlooked became enormous issues. I was punished frequently and was required to write in my notebook every day.

    Finally, on Friday, dinner was five minutes late. Ms. Renee demanded that I write her a reminder in my notebook for a lash for every minute it was late. This was completely unprecedented. Timing dinner had never been critical. I would have objected but I had already been broken from ever questioning her authority about her punishments. I knew that if I attempted to complain she would double it. If I refused, I would only find myself back in a few days groveling to return to her service.

    For weeks during my chastity, Ms. Renee had made a special effort to tease me sexually by wearing her sexiest outfits. She was always putting herself on display and accidentally bumping me with her hips or playfully pinching me. But when Saturday came around she was all business. She completely secured me and gave me the thirty lashes just as she promised. When she was done, she laughed at me.

    "It looks like you are going to have to do without again this week. I'm glad I don't really need your cock to get off. Your mouth has been plenty of stimulation for me. At this rate I doubt you'll ever get to make love to me again!"

    It had been over two weeks of constant stimulation and denial. I was beside myself with passion for her. Something in me broke. I felt it go. There was some level of reserve or of pride, I don't know which but I could actually feel it break inside.

I fell to my knees and began touching her booted feet. Over and over about all I could say was, "Please, please." I wanted to be back in her good graces. I wanted to make love to her again.

Desperately, I told her that I couldn't go on and have her continue to be displeased with me. She stood over me, reveling in my brokenness and waiting for my begging to subside.

Finally, she answered me, "Our marriage is coming up soon. Have you made the financial arrangements you promised to make before our marriage? Have you signed the prenuptial agreement? You promised but I haven't heard anything from my lawyer yet."

Honesty is the foundation of our relationship. I admitted that I had been slow to make the necessary arrangements. I had not meant to stall but having to tell her that I was not done what I said I would do made me see that I had been subconsciously dragging my feet. She had seen through me. She knew me better than I knew myself.

Her hand cupped my chin so that she could stare into my eyes. "You obviously need more incentive to surrender to me. I have something to show you."

Without another word, Ms. Renee walked to her computer and pulled up a file. Every role-play that we had experienced in the last few months started popping up as a short video. I saw myself dressed as a maid doing dishes. I saw Ms. Renee teasing me about giving me the fucking that she promised me and then tying me to a bench and penetrating me with her dildo. I saw myself completely cowed as she relentlessly whipped me for allowing her to treat me like a slave. Many of the most humiliating scenarios that occurred lately had been secretly captured on video. Now I understood why she had staged events in odd places in the house. It was because she had a hidden camera recording everything.

As the images rolled across the screen, Ms. Renee stood behind me and started strapping me with her riding crop on my already ravaged ass.

"Do you see yourself? Look what you've become. You're not a man anymore! You are my slave. How would you like me to send these videos to everyone you know? How do you think the other attorneys in your office would like them?"

She continued to crop me with a steady rhythm.

"Do you remember introducing me to your old girlfriend in Little Rock the last time we were there? I've decided to send her a bit of this video. She's not really part of your life here, so she really can't hurt us with this but I wanted you to know I am not bluffing about using my blackmail."

Almost before I could protest, she stopped cropping me and walked around to her computer. She quickly pulled up my old girlfriend's e-mail address and began typing.

Ms. Renee paused. "I added a note about you being a better boyfriend now that you are properly trained. Agree to finish to do what you promised."

I begged, "Please, Ms. Renee, I will do what you ask of me."

She sneered, "Not good enough, slave, I want you to really beg."

With that, she placed one hand on the keyboard and sent the e-mail.

Did she really send it? Of course, she did. She never bluffed. I could hear her laughing.

"Beg me not to send it to everyone you know! Make me believe you are sincere."

I instantly started begging with my whole heart.

Ms. Renee laughed again. "Ok, if you really want to move forward, I'll hold off sending this to more people, but you should know that all you've done is to postpone your eventual humiliation. One day I'm going to send these videos to everyone you know. It was always my intention to ruin your relationship with the rest of the world. I want you all to myself. I'm only hesitating now because I still need you to have a public life with me, but if you refuse me anything I will send them without hesitation. You belong to me now."

She stood before me with her hands on her hips, looking down at me. I stayed on the floor on my knees. I knew she was right. I remembered that I had asked her to be strong when I felt weak. She was my fantasy come to life. This was a choice I had already made.

I knelt lower and began kissing her boots. I held her leather-clad ankles reverently in my hands. Around my kisses and through my moans, I managed to tell her how I felt. She was my dream. I thanked her for not accepting my hesitation.

"Do you mean that, slave?"

"Yes, Mistress, you are the only woman in the world strong enough to pull me forward."

She paused a long time. "You may lick me now," she whispered.

Frightened, broken, and defeated, I gratefully crawled to her to begin pleasing her. I thought of how much trouble she had gone through to separate me from my selfishness and independence. As I eagerly licked her, I felt truly lucky that she loved me enough to make me completely hers. I vowed to complete the necessary promises I had made concerning my finances. She would be the co-owner of my condo, my bank account, my retirement fund, and my car. I would rewrite my will and insurance policies. Finally, I signed the prenuptial agreement. I wanted her named as co-owner on everything. I wanted her name on me.

April 2011
Dear Renee,

I can't wait to hear how it went. Did he really do all that he promised? He was a lawyer! I can't imagine what kind of lawyer would agree to the prenuptial agreement you gave him. He was obviously born to be a slave. He might as well be yours.

Don't get me wrong. He's still a man and therefore he cannot be trusted. Let's have lunch soon. I have several ideas I want to discuss with you.

Heather

Dear Heather,

Yes, the prenuptial agreement is signed. I'm still surprised he signed it. I'm taking it as a sign to continue our journey. Even though I've been working on this for years, I feel like I'm just starting to draw him tighter to me.

He has finally learned of my willingness to actually use my blackmail material. This was important. I wanted him to understand that I'm not bluffing when I threaten him with his social and professional destruction. I had been looking for a way to teach him of my sincerity to use my blackmail if he tried to back out of being my slave.

Last week, I noticed that he still would get an occasional friendly call or e-mail from one of his old girlfriends. It was the perfect opportunity. While he was watching, I sent her a short video of him being dominated. I did it to humiliate him enough to force him to completely sever ties with her.

I will always cherish the crushed, hopeless look I saw on his face when I actually sent them. I felt an enormous surge of power. He was on his knees, not truly believing I was sincere until he saw my finger push the send button on my computer. He'll never be able to look at the recipient of those pictures in the eye again without remembering what she knows about him.

It was the right thing to do. I'm convinced that the only way to train a slave to be humble is to humiliate him. He also had to believe that I plan to actually do the things I threaten to do. This has been an exciting adventure for both of us.

Let's get together soon.

Renee

Butler's Journal
Lent to Ms. Heather
May 2011

We have been officially engaged now for months but our engagement had been a trial because I had been slow to finish some of the financial preparations that were necessary. Once I had finished them, we returned once more to a gentler style of domination that included frequent bouts of lovemaking. When it was good between us, it was fantastic. I would need such a time to prepare for what was to happen.

Last weekend's experience was different and intense on many levels. On the previous Monday, I was told that my mistress was to be out of town for one night at a conference. She did not like any interruption in my training, so she decided that I was to spend Saturday night with Heather. I was not looking forward to it. No matter what happens to me with Ms. Renee, I feel that I am kept safe by the love that has grown between us. I did not like or trust Heather, but I kept that opinion to myself. To make matters worse, I was informed that I was to address Heather as Ms. Heather. It grated on me to think about using an honorific with Heather, but wisely I kept that feeling to myself.

I wanted to refuse being lent to Ms. Heather by arguing that I had agreed to be Ms. Renee's slave and not Ms. Heather's, but as the week wore on I wanted more and more to please my mistress. After all, it was only for one night.

I knew that Ms. Renee wanted me to make a good impression on her friend. After several years of domination, she knows how to direct me into deep subspace. The following week she pushed those buttons on me, known only to her, to increase my feelings of submission.

That Saturday morning, I came up from the laundry in the basement to discover Ms. Heather and Ms. Renee were waiting for me in the living room. I could tell that I had been under discussion because both women stopped speaking as I walked into the room. Usually my comings and goings were ignored when Ms. Heather visited.

Ms. Renee stood up and offered her cheek for me to kiss in the way of goodbye. I wanted to beg her not to make me go but I knew that I would only embarrass her.

I watched as the two women fondly embraced. Obviously, everything had been decided while I was out of the room.

Ms. Heather made an impatient gesture with her hand while I scurried around her to open the door. I followed Ms. Heather out to her car and handed her onto her car seat. At this point I had no idea what to do. Did she want me to sit next to her in the front seat? I doubted that. She obviously didn't want me to drive as she had seated herself in the driver's seat. My confusion was soon cleared up when I saw the trunk of her car automatically open. I knew it was a short drive but I felt some trepidation crawling into the cramped trunk.

I doubted my sanity as I entertained some very dark thoughts while I endured the hot, cramped space for the brief drive to Ms. Heather's home.

The car finally stopped and the trunk popped open to the image of Ms. Heather glaring coldly down at me. I crawled out and hurried after her. Ms. Heather handed me the keys to her home as we walked up the brickwork to the back of her house. At the door she fidgeted impatiently as I tried the unfamiliar key in the lock. With a sweep of her hand, she shoved me aside.

"You really are an incompetent! I don't know why she puts up with you. I'm only doing this as a favor to Renee."

She snatched the keys from my hand and opened the door. I followed her inside.

I had brought nothing with me, not even a toothbrush. I was told I would need nothing. I wore what Ms. Renee calls my uniform, a pair of black slacks and a white shirt.

Ms. Heather dropped her purse on the table at the doorway. She has a large home not far from us. The floors are tile with white walls and dark iron fixtures. The architecture is what might be called Italianate but without the warmth usually associated with older homes. The furnishings are trendy, uncomfortable-looking pieces punctuated by bright colored abstract art.

"Two!"

Obviously Ms. Renee had told her the commands to position me quickly. I knelt on the floor.

"Look at me," she snapped.

She is a striking-looking woman. She is tall, overly thin, with a mane of red hair. I'm certain she spends more on a pair of shoes than I do on a vacation. I realized when I looked up in her eyes that I had never made eye contact with Ms. Heather before. I saw her sneer, and before I could react, she slapped me hard across the face.

That sounds shocking but it was exactly what my previous experience with Ms. Heather had taught me to expect, so I was mentally prepared. I resolved to avoid looking directly into her face again.

"I've been told that you know how to clean. I fucking doubt it. The rules are simple. Say nothing. I don't give a fuck what you think. Just do what I tell you to do. The first thing I want you to do is to clean. Start right where you are. Clean the bottom floor then move upstairs. The cleaning supplies are in a closet in the kitchen. Get started."

With that, she turned and walked upstairs. I would not see her for two hours.

I know how to clean a house. Ms. Renee has been a very thorough teacher. I start at the top of a room and slowly work down until I am on my hands and knees polishing the tile floor. I move every piece of furniture. I remove every couch cushion. Every object is lifted and dusted. I went room to room carefully doing the job I have been trained to do.

After two hours, I had cleaned most of the bottom floor. I was finishing in the hallway when I heard Ms. Heather's heels tapping down the stairs.

I heard her behind me watching as I moved a rag across the floor. She stepped around me and went into the hall bathroom. When she returned, she said, "Four."

I stayed on my hands and knees, keeping my head down as I have been taught. She walked around to the side of me while I remained motionless.

"Did you use the toilet while you were in there cleaning?"

"Yes, Ms. Heather."

"What!" she almost screamed. "I have slave piss in my bathroom? Don't you know that fucking lowlife slaves like you piss outside like a dog?"

Suddenly, she kicked me savagely in the belly with her foot. Luckily, I had seen it coming so I had tensed in time. Then again and again she kicked me in the abdomen and chest with the toe of her shoe while screaming that I had no right to use a real person's bathroom. Finally, she stopped. I was covered in sweat.

"Now finish downstairs. And you better (kick) fucking (kick) do a good (kick) job."

With that, she left.

That brief exchange established the pattern of how I spent my day with Ms. Heather. I rarely saw her except for the few moments every two hours when she would suddenly appear. She would spend a few minutes belittling me, screaming obscenities, and delivering some kind of painful lesson. I was never given lunch.

I don't know if she forgot to feed me or didn't care enough to think about it. It took me several minutes of consideration to understand my feelings about this lapse. I had missed meals under Ms. Renee's tutelage. The difference was that I knew everything my mistress did or didn't do served a purpose. If she planned for me to miss a meal, Ms. Renee would have gagged me and had me serve her lunch. I would have seen her eating and she would have reveled in my fasting. Her meal would have been a shared and powerful moment for both of us. I was reminded yet again that many submissive men think they want a cruel or uncaring woman to dominate them but they are wrong. Actually, women like that are easy to find. To my surprise and my utter gratitude, I had learned under Ms. Renee that true domination can only be achieved by a woman who possesses incredible powers of empathy for her servant. Under such a mistress, a slave's suffering is never wasted. Every bit of his pain and humiliation is used to bind him tighter to his owner. Once again, I felt very lucky to have found Ms. Renee and I vowed to myself to be a more faithful servant.

At dinner Ms. Heather simply scrapped different leftovers from her refrigerator haphazardly together into a bowl that she made me eat outside in her backyard with my hands. I drank from the faucet at the side of her house. Clearly, she did not want me in the house except to work.

I had been through difficult times with my mistress in my training but nothing like this. No matter how bad it was with Ms. Renee, at least I was with Ms. Renee. If my suffering gave her any pleasure, then I felt it was worth it. The time at Ms. Heather's was nothing but painful drudgery. I felt abandoned. I wondered about the level of service I supplied Ms. Renee. Was it enough? Why had she allowed me to be lent like an object?

Finally, as the sun went down, I was pulling weeds in the backyard when Ms. Heather called me.

"Get over here, dickless, I'm done with you for today."

I was exhausted. I stumbled up the steps of her porch I had meticulously swept. I knelt, waiting for her. When she approached me, I involuntarily winced. I didn't know if I would be slapped or kicked but I had come to expect it. When she saw we wince, she smiled. It was the first time she had done so all day and it made me more afraid than anything she had done earlier.

"Follow me, dickless."

In an earlier tirade she had scorned me for my willingness to wear a chastity belt as something only a weak-willed fool would do. From then on she had frequently referred to me as a "dickless dog."

She stepped off the back porch. When I followed, she snarled, "Strip!"

My clothes were filthy. I took them off out in the hot air of her yard. I was too tired to protest. From the pocket of her slacks she produced a thin nylon leash. She handed me one of the ends and said, "Two. Now attach the end to your chastity belt," she ordered.

After snapping it onto one of the bars to my chastity cage, I felt her tug sharply, indicating I was to follow her on my hands and knees. She led me to the garage. It was dimly lit but I could see that it was a typical suburban garage. Ms. Heather's car was outside. That left a large empty space. On the floor, I noticed the bag that usually accompanies Ms. Renee on extended trips to carry discipline toys. She had obviously lent the bag to Ms. Heather. I felt broken.

Ms. Heather pulled out four lengths of chain and my cuffs. When she threw them to me I knew what to do. I placed the cuffs on and locked the chains to my wrists. Ms. Heather picked up the riding crop and pointed to the middle of the room.

"Six," she said.

I instantly lay on my back.

It surprised me how quickly I was restrained. At each corner of the garage there were hooks screwed into the posts. In seconds both of my feet were stretched and one of my hands was pulled over my head. Instead of restraining the last hand, Ms. Heather stepped over me, giving me a view up her skirt. She was wearing pale green sheer panties. Then she did something that surprised me. She reached under her blouse and pulled off the gold chain Ms. Renee wears with the key to my chastity belt. She dangled it in the air, making sure I knew what it was. She smiled as she leant over me. I felt the key and then the chain pool on my sweat-slick chest.

"Unlock yourself," she coolly directed me.

My anxiety increased. I hate the cock cage but it is some protection from a crop. Nevertheless, I complied with trembling fingers. If you have ever worn a chastity device, you know how heavenly it feels to get it off. It chafes and it prevents erections. I admit though that I was too nervous for an erection even staring up at her red pubic hairs peeking out of her panties. She snapped the last cuff in place, leaving me spread eagle and helpless on the floor. She stared down at me. I expected more verbal abuse and a hard whipping.

"Look at me, dickless."

The last time she said that had been painful but I reluctantly obeyed. In the pale light I could see her green eyes piercing into me. She has very pale skin and high cheekbones. A warm smile played across her lips that I almost trusted.

In her surprisingly deep voice, she said hoarsely, "You have been a surprisingly good slave today. It surprised me. You took everything I dished out and more. Of course, you don't deserve sex, but that doesn't mean I can't allow you a little relief."

With that she walked over to one of the shelves and brought over a bottle of massage oil. Still standing over me, she dripped a stream of oil onto my genitals. I responded at once. Holding on to one of the nearby shelves, she placed the sole of her shoe above my groin and began lightly rubbing it across my oiled shaft. Soon, I was bucking to match her tempo.

"Oh, so you are not as dickless as I thought," she laughed.

I could feel the mixture of fine grit from her shoes mingled with the sweat and oil sliding in giddy pleasure across me.

"Go ahead," she cooed, "Ms. Renee doesn't need to know. I won't tell her. Did you know she's planning on keeping you in this cage for another week? You've earned this. This can be our secret."

Suddenly, I moaned out loud. She had overplayed her hand. She had reminded me that Ms. Renee did not want me to orgasm until Sunday night. I quit moving against the sole of her foot.

"Don't be a fool, slave. A dog like you shouldn't hesitate when he's offered a morsel of mercy." She gently tweaked my nipples with the crop. "Who knows, I might even want a little release myself."

Her hand went under her skirt and started stroking her moist center. I could smell the delicious scent of woman. Again, she started sliding her foot against my rampant cock. She had not touched me at all except with the sole of her shoe. The message was clear: I was not worthy of her touch. I thought, maybe I had earned this limited release. At that moment I longed for her to continue to rock her sole slowly against me. I looked up to see her eyes glitter like green ice. She was watching me. Her manipulation was taking me somewhere I couldn't go. Once again, I stopped responding to her stokes and turned my body away. There was a pause.

"Last chance," she said.

I could only moan. It was impossible. Every part of me ached. I had been abandoned. Nevertheless, my training held on by a thread.

"No, please, Ms. Heather. Please, I can't," I moaned.

There was a brief pause and then she exploded, "Fine, then you'll do without! Only a broken dog would deny himself such pleasure. You're worthless! I gave you a chance to prove you are more than a broken wimp but you failed. You can be 'dickless' again if that's what you want!"

I expected her to use the crop on me at that moment. She seemed like a wild thing. I could see her grip on the crop tighten in her hand. I could hear her breathing fast and shallow. I feared a severe beating. Suddenly she threw the crop on the floor and turned on her heel to stride quickly out of the garage. I lay there twisting in the restraints for a few minutes until I heard her return. Once again I steeled myself for a whipping. Instead she had a clear plastic bag of ice in her hand. She hovered above me, furious but in control.

"Here." She dropped the ice from about waist high. It hit my scrotum like a kick in the balls. I bucked and pulled against the chains. "I'll be back when you've cooled down. That ice had better be in place when I return."

She left me there for several minutes. After a few moments the cold became extremely painful. Soon, I started to worry about damage to my genitals. I grimly noted that it was ironic that I was chained to the floor of a hot airless garage getting frostbite. Just before I was forced to shift the ice off of me, Ms. Heather returned. She seemed calmer but her face was flushed. Later, I began to believe that she had masturbated while I was suffering.

She stood over me again. "You are a fool. If you won't take my mercy, then I promise that I will use every ounce of influence I have with Renee to make your life a living hell. You don't deserve mercy from a woman. You were born to be a slave."

She unlocked the chains to my arms and told me to relock my chastity belt. She kept the chains attached to one of my legs.

Finally satisfied that my cock harness was securely back in place, she said, "There's camping equipment on the shelves for your bedding. Tomorrow I'll take you home, dickless."

She spun toward the door turning out the light as she left. I heard her lock the door of the garage. I found a cot and sleeping bag. It was a very long night.

I kept trying to understand my feelings. Ms. Renee had given me more pain than I had experienced in the last few hours. I had often been asked to work as hard. Why did home seem like such heaven compared to this? I longed to break my chain and hike home in the darkness. Was that what

I was supposed to do? Once again I tried to puzzle out the behavior and meanings of my mistress. I had learned that when I was in doubt to simply obey. I tried to sleep but all I found was a fitful doze.

The next morning, Ms. Heather opened the door and unlocked me. She was dressed in a beautiful summer dress, looking fresh and rested.

"Get in the car, dickless," was all she said.

I walked to the side of her house and put my filthy clothes back on. I climbed back into the trunk. I knew now why she had me in it. She didn't want to sit next to me nor did she want to be seen with me.

We drove straight home. We always enter from the rear of the house. Ms. Renee answered the door looking as fresh as Ms. Heather. I stood unwashed, unshaven, in filthy clothes. I stood with my head slightly bowed and my hands crossed submissively in front of me. This is the posture Ms. Renee prefers I take when she is in the company of other women.

They left me standing on the porch as they went into the house. I could hear part of their conversation filtering through the open doorway. Finally, Ms. Heather pulled out her checkbook and made out a check and handed it to Ms. Renee. So I thought I had not been loaned but rented! Before I could process how I felt about that information, I noticed the tension between them as if there was an unresolved conflict.

Finally, in a slightly louder tone Ms. Heather capitulated, "OK, you win but I still say I didn't have enough time for a true test." She turned on her heels, and without even a glance at me, left the house.

Smiling, Ms. Renee crooked her finger at me and I shuffled inside. I was overwhelmingly glad to be home. I looked at the check wondering how much my rental cost. I noticed the check was for $1,000 but it was made out not to Ms. Renee but to the women's shelter. I hadn't been rented. I had been the object of a wager.

I stood looking at Ms. Renee. Looking at her made me want to be a better servant. I was home. She was obviously pleased with me. She smiled at me but I started trembling. I suddenly realized when I had won the bet for her charity. I won when I turned away from Ms. Heather's shoe and denied myself relief. I was trembling because I knew how close I had been to surrendering at that moment.

"I'm glad I pleased you, my goddess," I stammered.

She smiled lovingly and nodded. I wanted to embrace her and weep but I was too dirty.

Unbidden, a question blurted from my lips, "What if you had lost?"

Ms. Renee looked into my eyes so I could see the truth. "Then I would have left you there for a long time."

I started trembling again. My knees buckled as I involuntarily knelt in front of my mistress. Reflexively, I grasped both of her feet in my hands. All I could say was, "Please, please," over and over for several minutes.

After a few moments, my mistress bent over and gently cradled my face in her hands. "Beloved slave, remember this lesson."

Chapter Five

PSYCHOLOGICAL CONTROL

May 2011
Dear Renee,

I enjoyed borrowing your boy last week. Don't tell him but my house looks fantastic. Of course I don't attribute the good job he did to him. Instead, I applaud your careful training.

Even though I lost my bet with you I had a great time. It felt amazing to be able to act on every dark feeling. I let loose! As you requested, I didn't whip him but I did deliver a few minor kicks and slaps. I don't understand why you didn't want me to crop him but he is your property, so I complied with your wishes. I still gave him a hard time. I was surprised that he didn't run away. I tried to get him to do just that. You must have threatened to cut off his balls if he disobeyed me. Ha! Do you think it was the beatings or the blackmail that kept him so obedient? Whatever you're doing, it's working. But for how long, I wonder.

I still say I didn't have enough time to truly test him. No man can keep his dick in his pants for long. Men can't be trusted.

I've tried the bondage technique you suggested on Suzy. She is so easy. I have pushed her to accept twenty strokes with the riding crop. And yes, I cuddle her afterward.

Have you considered the suggestions I made the last time we spoke?

Let's see each other soon,
Heather

May 2011
Dear Heather,

I'm glad he did a good job for you. I know you don't particularly care for Butler. However, I'm glad that you can admit that he's good for something.

Maybe you are right about testing him over more time. I agree with you that he is still a man. Nevertheless, I'm going through with my marriage to him. We have both invested a lot into our relationship. He's passed every hurdle I have set for him as a submissive partner. OK, it's true that I have physically pulled him over a few hurdles but that's what I expected. After all, I am asking a lot.

I looked over our prenuptial agreement again and felt my usual sense of satisfaction. It sounds ridiculous but I get turned on all over again when I think about what I've accomplished. Next month I plan to marry him quietly at the courthouse.

My marriage will not change anything about my relationship with you. I'm still excited about you being back in my life. In fact, for many reasons, you are good for us.

Blackmail and corporal punishment have worked for me in the past but they are not my only tools encouraging his submission. To prepare him to sign the nuptial agreement he endured quite a lot of sexual teasing. I have to tell you the exciting news. I finally made him weep again. It feels wonderful when I do that. He's normally such a stoic, but he's starting to allow himself to feel things. I believe part of the attraction for him to take the submissive role is it allows him access to his feelings.

Thanks again for suggesting your lawyer. She understood completely what I was trying to do. If I divorce him only one day after we marry I will receive half of his net worth. He gets none of mine. This was an important first step. Yes, Butler being a lawyer made this victory sweeter. It was proof of his commitment. I also could sense that once he had signed he felt completely at peace with the arrangement.

Of course, I want to take advantage of his recently hard-earned pliability. Over the next few weeks I intend to keep experimenting with him. Your suggestion concerning toilette duties was intriguing. I expect that you have Suzy perform those services for you? I don't intend to skip a single weapon to humble him. Who knows? I might stumble on one with better than expected results.

As our relationship progressed, I have expected tiny tokens of submission from him in multiple ways that alone might not mean much but together are starting to change how we interact. For example, I no longer carry anything in my hands other than my purse when we leave the house. It's a seemingly inconsequential rule but it is an example of one of many rules that he has to obey. Seeing how it inconveniences him makes me smile. In addition, to emphasize his role as a beast of burden, I now make him carry a male handbag that I can put things in that I don't want to carry in my smaller, more stylish purse. Not only is this convenient for me, it has the added advantage of making him feel slightly foolish.

I can think of dozens of rules that I have implemented as a constant reminder of his place. I believe that these rules act like steel wool to slowly polish and mold him into a proper servant. For example, anytime we visit another couple in their home I require him to try very hard to put himself in a subservient position by offering to do the dishes after dinner or whatever chore that seems most helpful. I love punishing him for not being able to talk a hostess into using him in this way. I find it amusing to watch him desperately trying to charm a woman into allowing him to help, knowing that if he fails he will suffer for it.

I expect doors opened, drinks carried, and umbrellas unfurled. The list goes on and on. I am an independent woman. I can do all of these things for myself but what would that teach him? His service has now started to be automatic. So have my demands. I feel we have stepped up to a new level of a dominant/submissive relationship.

My goodness, I do go on but you are the only one I can really talk with about this. If I talked to anyone else, they might call the police!

You really have magically appeared when I needed you the most.

Renee

June 2011
Dear Renee,

I loved lunch last week. You have been so helpful to me. I can't imagine what it would have been like moving to Memphis and not knowing anyone. I appreciate all of your introductions. Thanks for sending your friends to the store. Thanks for being my friend.

I've been successful about everything but talking you out of marriage. Ah, well, I admit that nothing has changed between us; in fact, it only gets better, so I shouldn't complain.

Thank you for your help with Suzy last weekend. I admit that it was fun to gang up on her. Afterward, she told me that it was one of the sexiest things I've ever done to her. I liked it too.

Have you considered any of my recent comments about marriage?

Heather.

June 2011
Dear Heather,

I've thought a lot about what you've been saying about marriage and I've been persuaded that you are right. I've also noticed that people treat you differently if you are married. I don't enjoy being forced to fit into anyone's mold. In response, I've decided to keep my marriage a secret.

My marriage to Butler will not make us equals. Instead, I want everything in our lives to define our different roles. I want there to be a difference between us in what we eat, what we wear, and even where we sleep. I want this "difference" to penetrate into every corner of our lives. For example, I love treating myself to a bit of *haute couture* at an expensive boutique then stopping on the way home so he can look for pants at the Goodwill outlet.

I never intended to share a bedroom with him. After all, I occasionally have company! He assumed that he would take over one of my guest bedrooms when he moved in but I was not comfortable with that idea. He needed a servant's quarters. I keep spending time at your home when we are together, so I don't think you've seen the changes I made upstairs when I remodeled before he moved in. You'll like what I've done.

Anytime I think of a way to emphasize the difference between us I do so. I love rubbing his nose in what he's allowed me to do to him and what he's become. The idea of reaching each new level of his debasement offers a new and different thrill. Our lives have become an exciting journey with new experiences to enjoy.

I admit that I have friends other than you whom I want to impress with a well-trained servant. This month I taught him more discreet hand signals that inform him when I want him quiet, distant, close, or at my feet. When he misses one of my hand gestures, I punish him. He's learned to pay close attention to me. I want the vanilla world to think of him as a remarkably attentive gentleman. However, I want anyone familiar with BDSM to suspect that we are mistress and slave.

I love that every time you and I get together we keep adding to our delightful list of things to try to encourage his submission. OK, I'll admit that sometimes the list is just to amuse us. I want to try your idea of taking away his right to speak for a week. During that week I will only allow him to address me if he first kneels in front of me and taps his head on the floor signaling that he wishes to communicate. I also liked your idea making him shave off all of his body hair. This week I'm not allowing him to sit on the furniture. He is only allowed to sit on the floor at my feet. This is one of your ideas I've decided to make permanent. I love the idea that he has to stay off the furniture like a dog.

I have denied him the use of the shower upstairs for a week and made him use the garden hose to bathe. I've also experimented with different slave uniforms. These exercises in humiliation disrupt his world so he can never be sure of having any rights as a person again. He should know on a very deep level that he is my property.

I have rarely heard of a woman bringing mind-altering drugs, brainwashing techniques, hypnosis, sensory deprivation, isolation, calorie-restriction, or sleep deprivation to the S&M lifestyle but my goals are different from mere bedroom titillation.

Does hypnosis really work? I intend to find out. For example, I plan to fill his sleeping space with a constant loop of subliminal sound tracks to bury the idea deep in his subconscious that being my slave is his best purpose in life.

While I'm trying all of these advanced mind-control techniques, Butler continues to perform daily as my housekeeper, gardener, laundress, and chauffeur. His continued service cements his position as my slave. All he has to do is to notice how he spends his time.

So that's it. I love him. I want him as my slave. I know you don't understand my commitment to him but each time he surrenders to me I love him more. Even you will have to admit that dominating him has been fun.

I can't wait to spend some time with you again,

Renee

June 2011
Dear Renee,

Yes, it's been fun but I just hope I can keep you out of jail! Ha! I swear, if called to testify I can certify that he was a willing participant. Of course, I won't mention that you brainwashed him and blackmailed him into it.

I've always been against marrying him but at least you used my lawyer for your prenuptial agreement. She is one of us.

It sounds like you have quite a plan. It also sounds like you spend a lot of time focusing on him. I think that's what submissive men love. They love being the center of attention even if they are suffering. What happens when they are not?

I propose we really put him to the test by ignoring him completely on one of the most important weeks of his life! Remember Peggy from school? She just became manager of her resort in the Poconos Mountains in New York. I need a break and I want to spend it with you.

Let's go. How about that for a honeymoon idea! I hope I haven't overstepped.

Kisses,
Heather

Butler's Journal
Wedding Plans
August 2011

It's been hard to maintain this journal with all that has been going on. For several weeks, things became very hard before I signed the prenuptial agreement. Since then, our lives once more returned to the loving kind of domination that I envisioned. Of course, she continues to try different techniques to increase my submissiveness. I could feel that some of them moved me further toward complete submission because I desire her more each day.

I couldn't help but notice that my mistress had made no plans about our wedding. Apparently, there was no ceremony scheduled. I was surprised.

I continued to write in my notebook as she instructs me concerning any mistakes I have made as her servant. On Saturday she canes me for each infraction. This week had been light. I was still bound but my discipline was over and I was looking forward to serving her in more intimate ways.

My mistress was dressed as every sub's dream in a tight red and black corset and black opera gloves. She stood flexing the rattan cane she had just applied to the back of my legs.

"You've been doing better, slave. These last few weeks I've rarely needed to give you lashes over the limit I imposed. That means you've been able to orgasm each week. I hope that you are appropriately grateful."

"Oh yes, Mistress," I instantly agreed.

She went on. "Since things have become so easy, it's time I changed the rules. I don't want our life to become stale. This relationship has to grow or die."

She began very lightly tapping the end of her cane on my testicles.

"On Monday we are going to court and take care of this silly marriage thing. It's just some paperwork. Did you expect a big wedding?"

"I didn't know, Mistress," I replied. "I'm sure that you'll do the right thing."

"I thought about a marriage ceremony. I know that you've wanted to be married but it always felt unnecessary to me. However, after talking to our lawyer, she convinced me of the practicality of it."

I couldn't help but shudder. The weeks leading up to meeting with Ms. Renee's lawyer and signing the prenup were a bit of a haze. It was like my mind was trying to block the memory. About all I could remember was begging to be allowed to sign anything she wished.

She went on. "I've been giving this some thought. We are not having a ceremony because I've decided to keep our marriage a secret. It's really no one's business what transpires between us. There is something I don't like about being married. I think people expect different things from me. For example, I want people to feel free to invite me to things without feeling as if they have to invite a husband to it also. Of course, I'll be keeping my own last name."

She continued to tap with her cane.

I didn't know what to say about that. A part of me wanted to introduce this beautiful woman to others as my wife. I didn't doubt the love between us. I had to admit that introducing Ms. Renee as my wife did not accurately describe our relationship. I decided to wait to see how I felt about it. It was hard to concentrate with her tapping my testicles with her cane.

My mistress went on. "While we are at the courthouse, I've decided that I want you to take care of another chore. I've been calling you Butler for years. After all, it's really what you are. Your name should reflect that. It amuses me to have you legally renamed. You can keep your last name. From now on, I want you to introduce yourself as Butler to anyone we meet."

Her tapping of my testicles with her cane increased in force slightly as she waited to see how I took this plan of hers. I nodded my head in the affirmative as I increasingly became more eager to please her.

"Also, from now on, while we are traveling, I want you to behave openly as my servant. We are not really a couple like other couples. Starting with trips out of town, the world should start seeing us as employer and employee. We will see how that feels for a while. You should be prepared for more changes in the future. I'm telling you now so you can wrap your head around it. I don't want you to disappoint me later."

She moved closer to me. "Speaking of traveling, we should talk about our honeymoon."

I felt a surge of excitement rise up in me. The word "honeymoon" immediately caused me to think of romantic walks on the beach and vanilla sexual encounters.

Ms. Renee cheerily informed me, "I should tell you now that we will have company on this trip. I invited a friend."

My heart stopped. I had imagined having my mistress to myself. I love our trips because she frequently relaxes some of the discipline I live under while we are away. Then, suddenly, I remembered that our relationship was changing for out-of-town trips. I knew better than to complain. I merely nodded my head submissively. Whenever I'm struggling with something, she has suggested to me to look down at her feet. Strangely, it often works. There is something about that posture that helps me feel more obedient.

Suddenly, I had a terrible thought. I recently experienced a difficult weekend with one of her friends. I assumed she could see I was nervous about what she told me because she laughed.

"You are going to have to get used to Heather. I think she's good for us."

She leaned down and kissed me tenderly. She just gave me the worst news I could hear and decided that the moment was perfect for a touch of tenderness.

Sometimes, instead of a whipping, all it takes is a tiny bit of kindness such as a simple kiss or a gentle touch to drop me into deep subspace.

The love that night was particularly sweet.

August 2011
Dear Renee,

To answer your question, I don't think anyone has the slightest idea that you are planning to marry this week.

Your secret is safe with me. I refuse to acknowledge it or talk about it.

I'm not angry with you about it after hearing your explanations of why you are going through with it. From your perspective, it makes sense. I'm merely worried that everything works out the way you want it to.

I'll do my part. What about the honeymoon? Have you mentioned our plans to Butler yet?

Heather

Butler's Journal
Marriage
August 2011

My marriage ceremony was perfunctory. There were no flowers, no cake, and no celebration. My mistress simply wanted the papers signed with as little fuss as possible. She did dress for the occasion in a dark red dress with a wide black belt that cinched her waist tightly. She topped off her outfit with a pair of beautiful heels. I could hear them clicking as we walked down the tile halls of the courthouse. She picked an early morning visit to avoid seeing someone she knew. According to her wishes our marriage would be kept secret. I admit that it hurt my feelings but she was adamant.

When we were done, her plan was to leave me at the courthouse so I could begin the process of legally changing my first name. She had been terse and businesslike all morning. However, just as she started to leave she stopped and called to me to follow her.

She turned down a corridor to an exit to give us a little privacy. As soon as we rounded the corner, she pulled me close to her. She placed both hands on either side of my face and kissed me.

"I know that I'm acting weird. The whole idea of getting married has been a lot to process. However, you are the only man in the world with whom I would ever do this. I love you." She kissed me again. "I even bought you a wedding present."

I was certain it was something to do with our lifestyle, such as a new crop. She loved giving me implements of discipline for my birthday.

She went on. "While we are here today, the movers are bringing you the new piano I have seen you quietly wanting. I know you would never buy something like that for yourself. I love you. I wanted you to have it. I'm glad we are on this journey together." She kissed me again with passion and turned and walked out of the exit.

I was stunned. This woman tortured, tormented, and ruled me with a lash, but she had just fulfilled my only remaining material desire. I was humbled by her gift. I would never have spent so much on myself. It may have been a rushed secret marriage but I had married the woman of my dreams.

After she left I started the process of changing my first name. How could I resist her?

Dear Heather,

I'm an old married lady now. Don't be disappointed in me. I took all of your advice about everything. The big news is I bought us plane tickets! You are coming with us on our honeymoon!
    I can't wait!

Renee

Butler's Journal
Honeymoon

Three days after our secret marriage, I found myself unloading the bags of my mistress and her friend Ms. Heather at the airport. I wasn't surprised to see that they both carried several bags for what was to be a vacation of less than a week. I flew coach class several aisles behind their first-class seats. Getting off the plane, I hurried to rent the largest rental car I was able to find. Both women chatted amicably in the backseat, ignoring me as I drove. If I had time to brood, I guess I might have felt hurt about sharing my honeymoon, but I told myself that it would be an adventure.

A few hours later found us driving through the entrance of a stunning resort in upstate New York. It's a famous playground for the wealthy.

I knew that Ms. Renee had probably received a discount from her friend in management, but after seeing it I thought it was still priced beyond our usual range. When we stopped, I hopped out to help with the bags. It was unnecessary because a swarm of attendants instantly surrounded our car. Ms. Renee stepped to the back of the car and pointed at my single bag.

"That one stays there."

I couldn't imagine why my bag was to stay in the car. Wasn't I going to stay at the resort with them?

My training kept me quiet as I followed them into the lobby. Ms. Renee checked them both in but not me. I was about to suggest that I be allowed to keep the car from being parked so that I could find a place to stay nearby when I saw the tiny hand gesture from Ms. Renee that told me to follow her and remain silent.

A little confused, I followed the porters and the two women to their room. When the porter opened the door, I saw it was more than a room but a beautiful one-bedroom suite with a balcony with a nice view of the mountains. I tipped the porter as he deposited the bags on the floor.

Ms. Renee and Ms. Heather immediately sat on the sofa. Ms. Renee looked pleased with the room. She beckoned toward their luggage.

"You may unpack for us," she sighed, leaning back and into the arms of Heather.

I carefully hung all of their clothes. I retrieved the iron from the closet and ironed anything that had wrinkled during the trip.

I could hear them reading over the leisure activities and the menu that the resort offered. I had never really understood their relationship. They were obviously lovers but had no interest in living together except for an occasional evening. I think it was because they are both dominants, and therefore not really compatible for a long-term cohabitation, much to my utter relief. I did not doubt the love that existed between my mistress and me but I learned not to presume to restrain her from anything she wanted. Actually, I felt a little pride that I was open and accepting of their relationship even though I often burned with envy when Ms. Heather stole her time from me.

Of course I was dying to ask where I would be staying but my training held. I knew Ms. Renee had already decided all of that long before we left.

Soon, I found myself standing in front of them waiting in the pose my mistress had taught me was the respectful posture of a good servant. I stood straight, with my hands folded in front of me but with my head slightly tilted down.

After a few minutes of chatting and ignoring me, Ms. Renee turned her attention to me.

"I guess you are wondering where you are sleeping tonight. Obviously, you can't stay with us."

That wasn't obvious to me. I longed to stay with them even if I had to sleep on the floor and even if Ms. Heather was present, but I knew that when Ms. Renee was with Ms. Heather she wanted her privacy.

Ms. Renee continued, "I told you that I had a friend from college, Peggy, who was the manager here. She'll be here in a minute to show you where you'll be sleeping. They are short staffed at this time of year, so I volunteered your services as hotel staff while we are here. How do you think we were able to afford this room? You will be sleeping in the staff barracks. I'm sure you're eager to do this for me, aren't you?"

The entire time I had been staring at Ms. Renee's shoes to keep myself focused. A thousand replies surged through me when she asked that question and I admit that not all of them were perfectly submissive. However, I was about to reply in the affirmative when Ms. Renee quickly interrupted my thoughts.

"Oh, I can tell that this is a shock and that you are not feeling immediately agreeable. Ha! Don't worry! I'm sure that I can help you with that. Four!"

I wanted to protest that I was perfectly willing but I had painfully learned to never speak after she had given me a posture number. It was my least favorite number.

Ms. Renee continued. "Actually I was hoping that I might detect a tiny struggle in you so that I could show Heather how I deal with nonsubmissive thoughts."

While she was talking, she had begun walking around behind me. I could look through my legs and see the stylish black pumps that she wore.

Quietly, almost politely, she whispered, "Spread your legs."

Trembling, I obeyed and waited, staring between my legs at her feet. She frequently pauses at this moment so I can anticipate what is about to happen. Suddenly, I saw her shift her weight and send her foot racing toward my unprotected testicles. Instantly, I convulsed flat onto the floor as the shock of the kick surged through my torso.

Hurriedly, I struggled back up to my hands and knees, only to see another kick coming almost immediately. Ms. Renee doesn't need to kick very hard. It only takes a short, quick movement of her foot to have me sweating and begging her for mercy. After five such taps, I was begging to be allowed to help the resort staff anyway I could.

Sensing my sincerity, Ms. Renee walked back in front of me. "Good," she said, smiling. "I knew I could convince you to see things my way. Peggy, or Mrs. Renault to you, should be up here any minute. She will explain your new duties. I know you'll want to do a very good job for her."

Trembling and sweating, I crawled forward and started kissing the pointed toes of her shoes, promising that I would work very hard during my stay.

During this exchange, Ms. Heather had sat unmoving on the couch. She had rarely seen Ms. Renee discipline me except for a few sessions with the riding crop. I was unable to see her but I heard a sharp intake of breath after the first kick. I saw her out of the corner of my eye looking with wonder at Ms. Renee as I continued to kiss her feet.

Ms. Renee left me on my knees and disappeared into her room for a minute. She returned, carrying a paper bag in her hand and handed it to me. Inside, I found a comb, a toothbrush, one pair of briefs, one pair of socks, and one disposable razor.

"See, I've thought of your needs while we are here," she smiled.

She stood looking down at me as if gauging my emotions for a second. As if by cue, there was a knock on the door. Ms. Renee motioned me to stand. My face was flushed and my legs still felt rubbery when I opened the door for her friend.

Ms. Renault was a tiny, slender blonde with very short hair dressed in a dark, severe-looking business suit.

She glanced inquiringly at me, then jumped into Ms. Renee arms. I don't know how she does it but women love Ms. Renee even more than men do. I wondered at their relationship. It was all friendly hugs and kisses now. She met Ms. Heather and I could tell that the three of them would have fun together.

Finally, Ms. Renee introduced me. "This is Butler. I know, it's funny, but it really is his name. He's ready to go with you now. You told me that you supplied work clothes, so he doesn't have a suitcase. I understand you'll need him for both shifts, so I doubt he'll need a change of clothes for any free-time activities."

Again, I received an appraising glance from Mrs. Renault. She turned her back to me and the women chatted for a few more minutes while I stood quietly to one side.

After the goodbyes, I found myself following Mrs. Renault at a very brisk pace through the hotel. From looking forward to a relaxing vacation, I had been lent as a domestic servant. Instead of a nice room, I would be sleeping in a staff barracks. My head was still spinning as I struggled to keep up with my new employer. She stopped several times and spoke with staff about practical matters. I stood behind her patiently while she went through what I assumed were routine chores.

I never know how much Ms. Renee tells others of our relationship. It is something I frequently dread. I could tell that Mrs. Renault was curious about me but too polite to ask questions. I thought we were headed to her office but before we got there we took a turn on a staircase and descended down to the basement of the hotel. The resort has a main building that was built in the early 1900s. It is a beautiful place with a huge, elaborate lobby. The basement is reserved for staff quarters. I was led into the tiny cluttered office of the housekeeper. She was an older German-sounding woman who looked at me with surprise. There were two other women in the room, punching a time clock.

Ms. Renault introduced me. "Mrs. Weiss, this is Butler, a . . ." And here there was a slight pause. "A 'domestic' who works for one of our guests. She has agreed to loan him for a few days during our staff shortage. He's off the books, so you won't need to give him a time card."

Mrs. Weiss smiled and shook my hand.

"I have a schedule made out for him. It's full but he's only here for a few days. I understand he has agreed to work double shifts. You can have him for the first part of the day. Introduce him to Leslie in the kitchen and Sadie on the night crew." With that she was gone.

After she left, Mrs. Weiss introduced me to the cleaning crew, who were the two women leaving work. They were two local girls who worked full-time for the hotel. Jennie and Ashley were both short, stocky women who looked like they shared a taste for junk food. They were obviously close friends.

I would spend my days with them but I would never grow comfortable around them. Other than constantly telling me to hurry, they rarely spoke to me. When I was introduced to them, they acted as if I was going to be more of a hindrance than any help.

My day was full from early till late. Every year, after the college students who support the staff during the peak season leave for school, the hotel has a serious labor shortage for the remaining warm days of summer. Most of the year-round staff work overtime during this period. It was clear that my services were needed.

My schedule began at 8:00 AM when I helped Jennie and Ashley clean rooms. This lasted until 4:00 PM. I noticed the next morning that I was assigned to Ms. Renee's room. Knowing her standards, I always spent more time on her room. This irritated the other members of the cleaning crew at first. Then, later they became amused by it. Apparently, Ms. Renee had negotiated every minute of my day before we arrived. After leaving the cleaning crew, there was a lull in my day from 4:00 PM until 5:00 PM when I reported to the restaurant to bus tables and wash dishes until 9:00 PM. Finally, at 10:00 PM, I spent two hours buffing floors after most of the guests had retired.

Most of what I had been chosen to do was the lowest level type of work. Again, I felt the influence of my mistress. I went from one task to another all day. It was grueling work. I'm in my fifties, and even with the schedule Ms. Renee keeps me to I am not used to staying on my feet until late at night, especially night after night. None of my supervisors, who were all women, seemed the least bit interested in talking to me. I suppose all of them assumed that if a man was still doing such grunt work at my age he probably had something wrong with him. They merely wanted to extract the most work out of me that they could during my short stay. There were still a few young people there who had late school starts or were taking a semester off. They treated me like I had a contagious disease, especially the young women.

The staff had small dingy rooms in the sub-floor of the hotel. Normally I would have had to share a room with a fellow worker, but because they were so short staffed I had it to myself. That was helpful because it would have been mortifying to explain the cock cage that Ms. Renee had left me in for our five days there.

The staff rooms did not have baths. There was a common restroom and shower down the hall. As is usual for men's showers, we were not given separate stalls. There was simply a large shower room. The first morning I went to shower I realized that I would be seen by my fellow workers all under the age of twenty-two. I skipped the shower. Later, after my double shift, I found that I was able to shower late at night without any of the other male staff there.

For the first twenty-four hours I barely saw Ms. Renee and Heather. I caught a glimpse of them at dinner while I was bussing tables.

I had been told by my supervisors not to talk to guests unless they initiated conversation. They smiled and waved at me from their table but I knew not to bother them.

On the second day, during my 4:00 p.m. break, Ms. Weiss asked to report to the pool. She told me that my mistress needed me. At first I was shocked that she had used the word "mistress," but I quickly realized it was simply the everyday word she used for a female employer.

"You are to wear this," Mrs. Weiss said as she handed me an ugly brown bathing suit about twice my size.

I assumed that the suit had been left by a guest and ended up in the lost and found. I could tell she was not pleased about something. I would realize later that she simply objected to me being given the privilege of mingling with guests with some equality even on a temporary basis. I stopped in the staff restroom and changed out of the brown livery that all the staff wore. I walked back through the servants exit toward the pool.

It is a lovely setting. It is surrounded by natural rock and has a bar running down one side. I admit I had wished I had been placed there. The duty was light as a bartender and one could look at women in bathing suits all day. Again, I felt the unseen influence of my mistress. I spent most of my time in the kitchen and cleaning empty rooms. I noticed Ms. Renee and Ms. Heather in a prime partially shaded location, lying in lounge chairs

I approached their chairs. I simply didn't know how to act. This was the woman I would jump through hoops for and she had banished me, on my honeymoon, to the kitchens for the last forty-eight hours. I felt misused, lonely, tired, humiliated, and confused. She had not seen me yet. She was lying on her stomach facing away from me. As I watched her, she unconsciously stretched like a sleek cat in the sun. Her skin looked delicious. I could see the carefully trained muscles in her back and thighs. Suddenly, every negative thought I had was swept away by her simple unconcerned, pleasurable movement. She captivated me. All I wanted to do was to be allowed to touch her.

Sensing my presence, she turned to look up at me. "Hello, Butler," she said in a mocking tone.

I wanted to complain to her and at the same time throw myself at her feet to beg to be allowed to stay in her presence. She saw all of the conflicting emotions moving through me. She smiled again.

"I understand from Mrs. Weiss that you normally have a break at this time before you report for dinner duty. Heather and I thought it would be best to help fill your time. We want you to report here at 4:00 PM each day to give us each a massage." She raised one eyebrow quizzically. "Would you like that?"

She didn't bother with an answer. She turned over and said, "The lotion is in my bag."

Robotically, I sat down in the chair beside her and reached for the lotion. I still didn't know which of the contending emotions in me was preeminent. When I'm confused like this I have learned to put myself on automatic and perform whatever chore she has for me and wait for whatever feeling emerges. I was in turmoil while I removed the lotion. I dripped a few drops in my hand and reached to touch her back. The smell of the lotion and the slick feel of her skin quickly brought me to the place where I could forget myself. I felt every emotion drop away other than the desire to please her. Soon, she started to softly moan under my ministrations. I could feel myself painfully swell inside my cock cage. Desperately, I tried to think of anything to prevent a painful erection. I thought of the piles of nasty dishes and miles of unpolished floors that still awaited me. Of course, nothing helped. By the time I was through with her massage I didn't think I could stand upright. I looked longingly at the cool water of the pool.

Ms. Heather is a rail-thin woman who somehow is still curvy. I hesitated to touch her. The truth is that I dislike and mistrust her but I had no choice. She didn't speak to me or look at me during the massage but would occasionally point to a spot she wanted me to spend more time on. After thirty minutes of work, she seemed to be drifting off to sleep. The discomfort in my crotch had only grown worse. I thought about how good the pool might feel.

I looked over at my mistress, who was watching me massage Ms. Heather.

"The pool is for the guests, Butler," she snapped almost telepathically. "Be here at four tomorrow."

With that, she looked away. She was through with me and I had to hurry if I was to be on time for my next assignment. I slowly stood up. It was painful in my tight cock cage. I noticed that Ms. Renee had turned back to watch me. She laughed softly when she saw how difficult it was for me to stand straight up. As soon as I was able to stand, she turned away again.

I struggled through my chores for the rest of the day. My emotions continued to swing from feeling lucky to feeling mistreated. At the end of the day I was too exhausted to feel much of anything. Nevertheless, I crept into the bed feeling very alone and very sorry for myself. Had I allowed myself to go too far down this path? It was my own fault. I knew the nature of Ms. Renee when we started.

The next morning, while cleaning the rooms I started noticing that some of the staff were treating me differently. In such a small community word travels quickly. Apparently, my stint as a masseuse at the pool had been noticed and commented on. Some of the young men who worked there actually spoke to me. I noticed that the young women were eyeing me speculatively. I'm sure they were curious about how I had been chosen and allowed to perform such special duties for two guests in the pool area.

That afternoon, Ms. Renee saw me coming and simply rolled on to her back. It was like I had been doing it for months. Ms. Heather was almost talkative. She told me how much fun they had horseback riding the previous day.

When I was done, Ms. Renee simply said, "Tomorrow, same time."

Nothing would get me used to touching these two women in my chastity device. I left with a hot, cramped, raw feeling that I'm sure changed the way I walked. I could feel Ms. Renee's amused eyes on me as I shuffled away.

That evening, when I was finishing washing dishes, one of the servers, a young woman who had never spoken to me before, helped me pull the last of the garbage out to the bins behind the kitchen. We stood next to the dumpster for a second appreciating the much cooler air. She was tall and thin with dyed black hair, acne scars, and a row of tattooed Chinese characters snaking up one side of her arm. She stood beside me and asked, "Aren't you a little old for this?"

I really didn't know what to say, so I stayed silent, looking toward the ground.

She continued, "I've been asking about you. One of the bellmen told me that you came here with the women you massage each day at the pool. Do you work for one of them?"

I looked across the asphalt hoping for an answer. Finally, I managed to mumble, "Yes."

She snorted, "I doubt it. I saw how you were touching the brunette when you were massaging her at the pool. You're no butler, no way. I know what heat looks like between two people when I see it. I also know what a submissive man looks like when I see one. That's what you are. You're a slave."

She looked sideways at me and grinned. I was unable to answer her. Embarrassed, I merely looked down at my shoes again. She turned to go but as she passed she reached behind me and pinched me hard on my buttocks. I was shocked and stayed frozen in place as she walked off. I heard her laugh as she went through the door.

All I wanted to do was get to my room after my humiliating encounter with her. I finished the floors that night silently wondering if the word "slave" was somehow stamped on my forehead.

Later in the shower, standing in the spray almost asleep, I heard someone enter the bath area. I snatched my towel off of the rack and quickly wrapped it around myself before turning around. It was one of the guys who ran the concession at the tennis courts. He had never spoken to me other than to grunt hello. Now, he seemed almost chatty. He told me hello and asked how I liked the hotel. After a while he realized that I was not in the mood to talk, so he finally wandered off. I could not tell if he had seen my chastity cage or not.

The two young women who cleaned rooms with me were being especially slow the next day. I kept hearing them whisper to each other. I tried to focus on my job and avoid any eye contact. We still had two rooms to do when they suddenly announced that they were taking a break. It was after 3:00 p.m. I needed to finish to be able to be at the pool by 4:00 p.m. I protested that we weren't done. One of them looked at the other and they both looked at me. Jennie stared at me and threw the towel she was holding into the laundry basket.

Ashley laughed and said, "We don't have to be anywhere special at four. Do you?" Both of them laughed hysterically as they walked off.

I rushed through the rooms but I was unable to be there at 4:00 p.m. I ran to the pool after changing, only to find them already gone. I couldn't stay in the pool area without them, so I returned to my room and redressed in the brown employee livery. I realized that I had worked all day for the moment when I was able to touch her. Without those minutes, my existence seemed empty.

Later that evening, I passed Ms. Renee and Ms. Heather in the restaurant with my bus cart. They were having dinner with Ms. Renee's hotel friend, Ms. Renault. All three of the women looked at me with a penetrating and knowing look.

It seemed obvious that Ms. Renee was telling Ms. Renault my true place in her household. I hurriedly continued on with my cart.

By now, it seemed the rumor mill had spread the guesses about me to several of the service staff. I had trouble doing my own work as several of the female staff kept asking me for help. Before, I had not existed, now I seemed like I was everyone's personal assistant.

Finally, the evening ended. I was sitting in my room when I heard heels clicking down the linoleum floor outside my room. I assumed it was one of the night managers because none of the service staff wore heels. I looked up to find Ms. Renee and Ms. Heather at my doorway. They were still dressed for dinner. They looked like what they are, well-tended upper middle-class women with a fashionable sense of style. I was dressed in dirty work clothes that smelled of grease and suds from the kitchen. I immediately started to stand when Ms. Renee gave me the hand signal meaning she wanted me on my knees.

"So this is where the help lives," she said. "It's not much to look at but I could have left you in your cage at home."

They both glanced around the shabby undecorated room. There was nothing in it but two single beds crammed into the tiny space and two small battered dressers.

"I hope you are grateful for the bed. I'm quite put out with you today. We both missed our massages. I plan on punishing you later for it. I talked to Mrs. Weiss. She said you had more rooms than normal but that excuse won't work for me. It's up to you to work faster."

I was unable to say anything. Finally, I choked out, "I'm sorry, Ms. Renee. Please, I'm ready to go home now."

"Oh, you are? Good, I wanted you to have an experience that taught you how easy you have it at home. I think I was successful. You may thank me."

I knew what she wanted. I bent and started kissing her shoes until I felt her scoot her feet away.

In a husky whisper, Ms. Renee continued, "I don't know if staying here is changing how you see yourself but it's changing how I see you."

I returned to the kneeling position and gazed up at her. She kept looking at me and at the squalor of the tiny room. For a moment no one said anything.

Eventually, Ms. Heather slipped her hand around Ms. Renee's waist and kissed her on the neck. "He's where he belongs. Let's go."

Without another look she turned from me to follow Ms. Heather. I listened to their heels click down the hallway. Even though I was exhausted, it was a long time before I slept.

The next day was my last full day. Jennie and Ashley did as little as possible. They continued to laugh at what they thought was a private joke but I could imagine what was being said about me. The day seemed to stretch forever but luckily we had fewer rooms to do than usual.

I showed up early for my 4:00 p.m. appointment at the pool. While I was rubbing Ms. Renee's legs, the two women started discussing how much fun they were having. My mistress eagerly commented about loving her suite and enjoying the room service for breakfast.

Ms. Heather responded, "Our suite is nice but, yuck, that pit Butler is staying in is horrible. I wouldn't put a dog in it, but I guess it's good enough for him."

I glanced up at her but she only avoided my gaze as if I weren't there.

She continued at some length about what a relaxing time they were having and how nice they found the hotel. The entire conversation continued as if I were not there even though it clearly served to humiliate me further. I finished with Ms. Heather. As I stood up, I noted that Ms. Renee turned over again to watch me as I tried to walk away bowing a little at the waist to relieve the pressure from my cage.

The rest of the day I concentrated on my work and tried to keep a low profile. I'd been embarrassed by Ms. Renee many times but I had never had to endure such continual stares and whispers from so many for such a long time. I crept into my room after having washed my torso in the sink after my shift, not wanting to make a spectacle of myself in the shower. I lay in bed for a long time considering my life as Ms. Renee's slave and how much my situation continued to change. I finally fell asleep wondering how far she would take us.

Finally, it was Sunday morning. I put on my street clothes and arrived at Ms. Renee's room at 9:00 a.m. They were already up and dressed. They were breakfasting on an elegant room service. I said my good mornings and quietly assumed the ready position.

Ms. Renee spoke first. "You were late the day before yesterday, so Heather and I had to do without our massage. I have not forgotten. Four!"

They ignored me while they finished the last of their coffee.

A few minutes later, she left the room and returned with two riding crops. I had only packed one. She beckoned to Ms. Heather to stand behind me. She placed the crop on my buttocks and began describing the places it was safe to hit me. She told her to avoid the spine and showed her the sweet spot about halfway down the buttocks. Soon they were taking turns whipping me on either side of my buttocks.

I was soon grunting and writhing, trying to maintain my position. All of the pain and humiliation of the last five days was burned into my soul as they seared my backside. It was Ms. Renee's unrelenting attitude to treat me like a servant that finally broke me. Finally, at that moment I started feeling what I'm sure she wanted me to feel. I knew that I was her slave to do with as she pleased. At that moment I didn't expect mercy. I expected to experience only those things that pleased her or made her feel more secure about our relationship. I was broken and I knew it. I had no more power to resist. All I had the energy to do was refrain from yelling loudly so as not to embarrass my mistress.

When they stopped it grew quiet. I didn't need to turn my head to know that they were kissing.

There was a pause and some whispering and Ms. Heather left the room. Ms. Renee kept stroking me lightly with the crop. I knew to remain in position four until I was told to move but I was a sweating, trembling wreck.

"You've done well, Butler, but I'm not done with you yet."

She stroked me lightly with the crop.

"You think that this week has all been about my needs. That would be wrong. It was also about your needs as well. You needed to see yourself as I do. Think back about how you felt when Heather and I came to visit you in your room. How were you dressed? Where were you sleeping? I'll tell you. You were dressed as a servant and living in a servant's quarters."

She lightly tapped my testicles with the crop.

"How did it feel? I want you to remember that feeling. I'm determined that you understand your place. Life will keep getting worse for you until I'm convinced that you see yourself as I see you. You must realize that you belong to me and that I can use you any way I see fit. You want to please me, don't you?"

"Yes, goddess, please!" I managed to stammer. I was still on my hands and knees. I desperately wanted to please her but I was not prepared for what I saw when I glanced backward between my legs.

Ms. Heather was tottering in on a pair of her highest heels. Suddenly, I knew what was about to happen. Seeing her in those heels meant that the kicking I had received at the beginning of the week was an inevitable part of a deeper plan. It didn't matter that I had been slightly hesitant about being used at the hotel. She would have found another reason to kick me. I had suffered so that Ms. Heather could experience something new as a present from my mistress. I was being used as a target for her friend's enjoyment. A heard a deep groan and realized that it had come from me.

Ms. Renee softly spoke to Ms. Heather. "After seeing me do it, you said that the idea of kicking a man in the balls turned you on. Go ahead, it's what he's here for and it's what he deserves for letting us treat him like a slave."

My mistress moved closer to Ms. Heather to steady her. I heard her instructing Ms. Heather. "It doesn't take much force but give it a sharp little flick of your foot."

After a moment I saw one of her stiletto heels pull back, and with a tiny hesitation, fly into my scrotum. Again, the nauseating pain exploded into my belly. Somehow, I remained in position.

"I think you should do it one more time to make sure you experience it fully," my mistress commented encouragingly.

Again, I saw and felt the toe of the heel flash into my testicles. I guess I blanked out for a second because I found myself flat on the floor. I could hear them giggling. Then, except for my heavy breathing, the room was quiet for a few minutes. They were kissing again.

After a few moments, Ms. Heather returned to the bedroom to change her shoes, leaving me alone with Ms. Renee.

She looked down at me and softly spoke, "Two!"

I struggled up on my knees, looking into her face. She had never looked more beautiful.

"You've done well, slave. You keep proving to me that I'm on the right track with your training. Now, finish our packing and bring the bags down to the lobby. Heather and I will be in the bar waiting."

I felt her hands gently wipe some moisture from my face that I did not know was there until she touched me. Had I been crying?

Then, making eye contact with me again, she said, "Oh, I haven't forgotten that it's Sunday. Your weekly discipline is over. If you get through the rest of the day without any mistakes there will be a reward for you this evening."

She looked into my eyes, giving me the promise of love. Then she whispered one more word that made the entire week worth it, "Husband."

She had tortured, ignored, and humbled me all week. And it had turned her on. Every bit of it had worked for her. I could see it in her eyes. My suffering and humiliation had stimulated her. She wanted to be home with me as soon as possible. I was in a bit of a panic knowing what it took to excite her but the thought of making love to this dangerous, sensual woman was almost more than I could stand. Again, I remonstrated with myself that I was getting in over my head but I simply couldn't help it. I was drawn too powerfully to her. To make matters worse, it seemed that the more she asked of me the easier it was to fall under her spell.

Ms. Heather returned and they swept from the room arm in arm but not before Ms. Renee shot one more meaningful look my way. Her look got me moving as soon as the door closed. My body moved painfully but I forced myself to finish packing perfectly but quickly. I thought, at least it was over even though the staff would remember me forever. Thankfully, the hotel was out of her price range. No doubt, this had been a special honeymoon experience for Ms. Renee to push us to another level while at the same time enjoy some time with Ms. Heather. Now, I was going home with the promise of love.

I arrived in the bar with a flushed face, unsteady legs, and red-rimmed eyes but my heart was racing at the thought of our homecoming.

I found both of them and Mrs. Renault having a drink at a quiet corner of the bar. The women barely acknowledged me as I stood by their table. They were three perfectly coiffed women relaxing together. I noted their carefully chosen clothes and their expensive shoes. I could smell their perfume. Their polished nails gleamed against the glasses of their champagne mimosas. All three of them knew of my utter surrender. The gathering had the feel of a celebration.

Mrs. Renault continued what she was saying, "I enjoyed your company this week, Renee. You really should plan on coming at the same time every year, except next time I wish you would stay longer. I'm certain that we could work out the same arrangement about your room price if you brought Butler." Here she stopped and looked at me, laughing. She was asking a question that she was confident she already knew the answer to. Their eyes briefly glanced at me.

Ms. Renee raised her glass, regaining their attention. Smiling victoriously, she offered her toast, "Next year!"

Their glasses joyfully clinked together. That sound echoed through my soul. I looked at my goddess. She was complete and secure in her victory over me. She had never looked more beautiful. Her empowerment had made her even more desirable. No other woman would ever be able to match her. I felt enormously privileged to be in her service. It felt like we had both won some kind of victory. To stand there waiting for her next command seemed to be the goal of the last few years of my life. I was free of my own desires. It no longer mattered what I wanted. I was her servant. I knew I would come back year after year if she wished it. I only wanted to be near her.

July 2012
Dear Renee,

What a fantastic honeymoon. I had a great time. When I suggested it, I never in a million years thought you would go through with it or get him to agree. I feel like I stole something from him, and I admit that it made it all the sweeter. It also made me feel very close to you.

It must have been a great test for Butler. Interestingly, I originally offered my suggestion as a test for you. Obviously, you passed with flying colors.

You know that you are my hero but I will never understand the love angle of your relationship with Butler. How could you really feel love for someone that allows you to do the things you do to him? He is beneath you.

I would find it impossible to love such a person. Of course, I understand why he loves you. Who could resist?

Yes, I want to go back every year!

Lingering kisses,
Heather

PS

The idea of you legally changing his name to Butler was priceless. It made me want to laugh out loud! Why did you stop at the first name? I like "Butler," but why not add "Slave" as his first name? Hysterical! I would love to see his new driver's license. How about "Slave Butler"? It's something to think about.

September 2011
Dear Heather,

What a week! Yes, we took his honeymoon away from him. I admit it made it very sexy for me as well.

It turned out to be the perfect honeymoon. I wanted to send him a message about how I thought about marriage. I think I was successful. Also, I realized that this was the longest amount of time we have spent together since college. It's nice to know that we can still share a room and not get tired of each other. I love having you back in my life. You are good for me.

I loved your idea of always flying first-class while Butler flies coach. You are a fount of good ideas.

I'm sorry you don't understand the love that I have for him. The more he submits the more I love him. I don't disrespect him for wanting to belong to me. I feel just the opposite. He has the courage to follow his dream. One day I hope you will understand.

You have to admit that Butler was a lamb. He met every one of our expectations. Going down to his room in the basement of the hotel still gives me the chills. Together, we are a powerful force.

That was a great idea you had about Butler's phone. I added it to my list. I want twenty-four-hour control of his activities. Also, I will finish wiring my house with cameras so that I can visually keep tabs of what he is doing when I am not there. As my slave, his time belongs to me. I have already started scheduling his day so that he spends it wisely.

I still schedule some time for him to follow his own interests as long as his work for me is done. I want him to be an interesting and educated companion. One of the strange things about human nature is that if I only allow him one hour each day from his chores to practice his piano then I know he really will practice. When a man is in charge of his own time, he frequently wastes it. Men need the controlling influence of a strong woman. However, the bottom line is that his time belongs to me. Most of it will be dedicated to my service. And I'll be watching!

I know that you think I've taken on an impossible task of making him a real slave. For me it's all about a deep connection. The obstacles to overcome are his independence, willfulness, and sense of self. I revel in crushing them. During all of this I see his surrender as an act of love on his part.

I have observed that something deep goes on in his psyche while being dominated. I believe that the destruction of his selfish macho personality allows more room for romantic and erotic love to flourish. Therefore, the further I am able to lead him down the path of submission, the more he is able to love. I have already experienced this with him again and again. I want and expect even more.

It has long been my goal to strip him of his self-confidence until he sees himself as an unworthy male. I don't want him to think enough of himself as a man to believe that he has anything to offer another woman. If I am successful, he will be grateful I allow him to stay and serve me. I want him to feel proud again one day, but for completely different reasons. Feeling pride should come from how well he serves me. This should be his only goal.

Already I have seen him glowing with pride when he has correctly anticipated one of my needs. I've seen him waiting in intense anticipation of receiving a simple nod from me to tell him that an especially hard task was done well.

Considering the pressure I've placed on him during these first few years, I expect him to start experiencing what psychologists have named the Stockholm syndrome. This is when a captive begins to experience the world through his captor's point of view. When this happens he will no longer think of dodging punishments or escaping chores. Instead, he will participate fully in his own destruction as an individual. He will begin to suggest more severe disciplines and more difficult work schedules. He will automatically begin to do these things because he never again wants to feel the confusion of wanting to be anything other than my slave. I can't wait to see this happen. I know when it does I will feel complete as a dominatrix. I will have altered his instinctual direction of autonomy to move instead in the direction of surrender to me. I will also know that we will have achieved a deep bonding that is very rare between a man and a woman.

I'm eager to go back to New York again next year. I love our time together. I couldn't be doing any of this without you.

Thank you for everything,
Renee

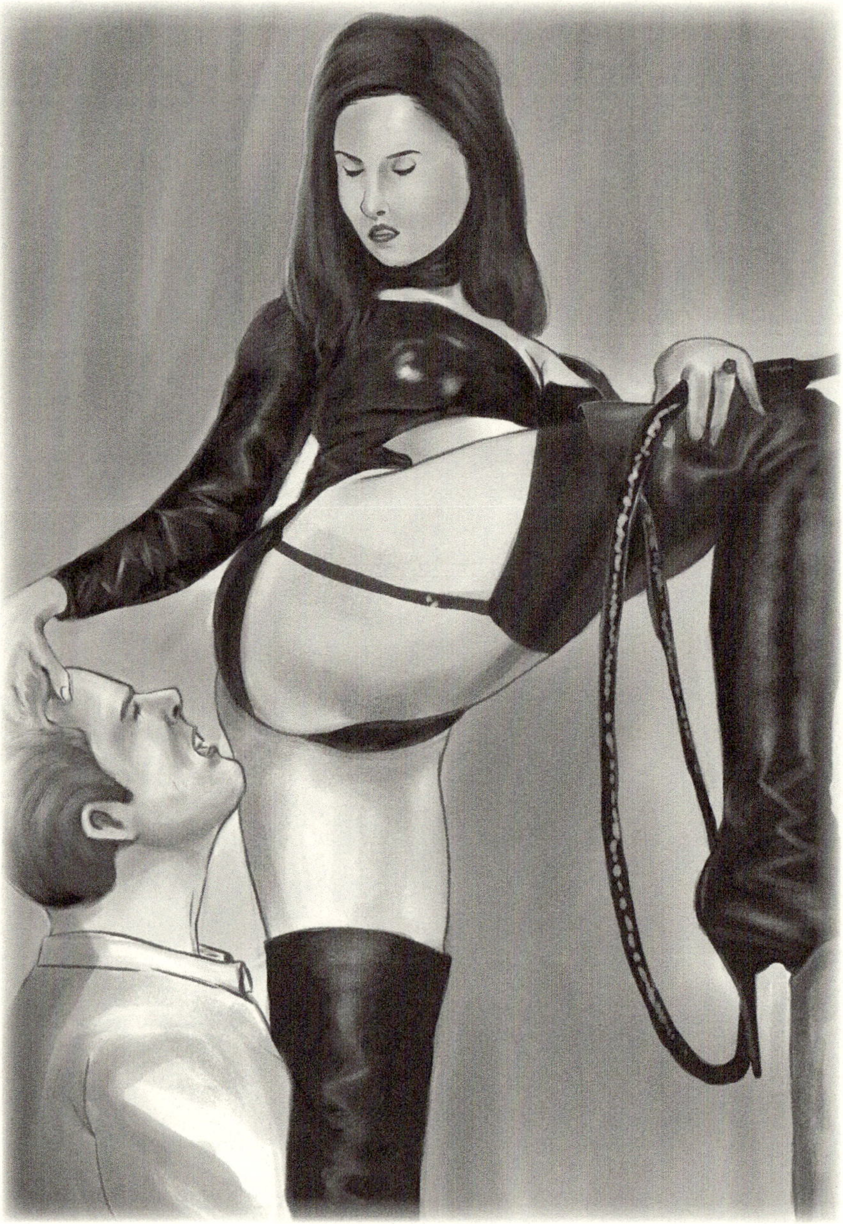

Chapter Six

HUMILIATION

January 2012
Dear Heather,

We both work too hard during the holiday season. I hate it when we are too busy to see each other.

I loved seeing you at the New Year's Eve party with your Suzy. Yikes! It was a boring party until you invited me to take Suzy to the bathroom with me. I was a little hesitant at first. I can't believe that you trained her to do that for you. I might have refused if I didn't see how eager she was. You are right. She is talented. It's something new to teach Butler. I'm still learning from you. Stationing him out in the hall to guard the door was a nice touch. How he must have ached knowing what we were doing. I must say that I was much more relaxed the rest of the evening.

Yes, we are still married. You are so funny. I know you can go through a man faster than a box of tissues but I'm going to keep this one. Try to understand, I'm as much his slave as he is mine.

Think about it. Butler relieves me of so many mundane chores I think I'd have trouble getting through the day without him. He is the only man who has been able to earn my trust.

I have had to change my ideas about love to complete his surrender. I've had to reach inside and find strength I never knew I had. It's another reason I'm glad you are back in my life. You don't love Butler. You only care about me. Also, you are a natural dominant. You are perfect to help complete my work with him.

To reach the surrender I seek in him will require me breaking his view of himself as an independent person. He must see himself as mine. I have learned that physical discipline is not enough. Sometimes words can be more cutting than the whip. It's out of character for me but I have steeled myself to say the evilest things I can think of saying to him. I have already learned to use my tongue while he is using his.

Early in our relationship, I started belittling him while he was kissing my ass. I called him my ass-licker and nastily demanded that he try harder to push his tongue deeper up my ass. It's the kind of thing I could hear you easily saying but I had to search for the words. You know how naturally polite I am. When I finally spoke them I noticed that it only increased his fervor. I learned a powerful lesson then. Words have power.

These days I feel empowered to say humiliating things to him and make him repeat them about himself again and again until he believes what he is saying. Even if they sound silly at first, I know that they will eventually begin to invade his psyche.

Even when he surrenders to some new challenge, I degrade him by telling him that he is a wimp and less than a man for allowing me to treat him like a slave. I constantly put him in a no-win scenario of being punished for failing to submit but humiliated for surrendering. Ha!

To achieve my goal, I continue to belittle him, humble him, and hurt his feelings. You are a natural at this. You have the sharpest tongue of anyone I know. When I get stuck for words or don't feel the part, all I have to do is to ask myself what you would do or say in the same situation. Presto! Out of my mouth comes the perfect evil dominatrix! If I could get him to cry just once from a verbal assault, I believe I would drop to my knees and swoon in triumphant pleasure.

At other times I have been positive and encouraging, so instead of demanding, I lovingly encourage him, *"Please, honey, I know you can do it, please promise that you'll put off coming for another week just for us!"* Ha! What I say to him and how I say it are merely tools to lead to his surrender. When he agrees to postpone his orgasm, I humiliate him for agreeing to my request. After all, only a slave would do such a thing.

It's why I renamed him Butler. I wanted him reminded constantly of his place. While I might enjoy reducing him verbally, my slurs are not actually targeted at the aspects of him that I appreciate. I love him! He has many fine qualities. These verbal weapons are aimed at his self-image of manliness that the "Phallocracy" has infused him with.

Men are taught from birth to wrongfully think of themselves as superior. Words are the right tools to upset this male-oriented worldview. Hurting his feelings with belittling insults and requiring him to repeat them about himself like a mantra have slowly changed his view of himself. I love seeing him meditate to my picture each day, chanting repeatedly. "I am only a slave. It is a privilege to serve."

I have weakened his old superior male view of himself and replaced it with a new, much more beautiful ideal: that of the perfectly surrendered man. This has taken time and dedicated effort on the part of both of us. Repeating his mantra, meditating to my image, and humbling him at every opportunity have been more than a lifestyle. This is a spiritual path that we both have chosen to follow.

We both want a completely surrendered man to be all that is left after the refining fire of my discipline. I remind myself when I make things hard and I start to feel sorry for him that this is the life that he begged me to give him. It's up to me to make it real.

He is only a male. From experience, I know that a man's interest can stray if not closely monitored. A few weeks ago I sensed in him the slightest interest in another woman. I took action. He is mine! I made a point of inviting her to lunch at my home. I made him serve but not have lunch with us. I'm afraid I may have embarrassed him. Ha! It was my intention. I know that I changed her view of him. Certainly, she now knows to whom he belongs! As she was leaving, I put Butler on his knees to watch her through the front window walking down our driveway. I asked him, *"Do you think she would ever be interested in a man who has become a slave? I embarrassed you at lunch on purpose. It could have been worse. I could have shown her the picture of me urinating in your face! Do you think she'd ever be able to kiss you without tasting my piss? No, you are spoiled goods. Even if I offered you to her, she would probably just send you back to me to complete your training! No other woman will ever want you again! You're nothing but a slave now."* It was a powerful moment for both of us.

I have enjoyed humiliating Butler in public for some time. I frequently shop with him while having him act as my servant in different stores. Sometimes, I have imagined slapping him and verbally abusing him for a mistake in front of semi-strangers just for fun. I want to see him humbly accepting whatever I say to him and apologizing over and over as I berate him in a bossy and bitchy tone. It's the kind of thing you could do with ease but it's not at all the kind of thing I feel comfortable doing yet. You are my hero about things like that. I want to free myself of all my conventions and inhibitions.

Often, I think my natural politeness and decorum prevent me from reaching a new level of feeling and dominance. I need to stretch my boundaries and do things out of my comfort zone. If I ask this kind of stretching of him, then I should be willing to do it also.

I believe that it would be therapeutically liberating for me if I learned to spontaneously release more of the selfish impulses that I feel. Sometimes one has to fake a new persona before it feels right. It simply takes practice. I look forward to reveling in my role as a bitch in heels! Secretly, I think he wants and needs this attitude from me. Learning to release the bitch goddess in me will be good for both of us.

It will be important to keep a close eye on what he is experiencing during these experiments. In addition to frequent conversations I have asked him to continue to journal his internal experiences. I wanted to know what disciplines he simply finds silly and which ones push him deeper into submission. I know that he writes the truth because we both want the same thing. Again, our love and our mutual desire for our relationship to be real will push us forward.

While all of this is going on, we will keep in place the facade of a normal married couple. Our goal is not to shock the world but to live our lives as we choose. We will continue to work at our jobs, visit our relatives, and maintain our vanilla friendships. To the world we will look like two people in love. Except for the careful attentiveness he pays me we should look like any other couple.

Whew, I do go on when I get started. You are a hero for reading and commenting on all of my plans.

Love,
Renee

Butler's Journal
My Phone
July 2012

It started with the phone ringing. I was busy in the kitchen. To Ms. Renee's annoyance, this was the second time I had been interrupted by the phone while cleaning her floor. I began to stand up, but before I could rise Ms. Renee whisked into the kitchen to sweep my cell phone into her hand.

She greeted the caller warmly. I knew it was my friend Sidney inviting me to go with him to hear a speaker at the local community center. We had talked about going earlier in the week.

Instead of handing me the phone, Ms. Renee inquired why he was calling. I saw her nod her head then look me straight in the eyes.

"No, he can't go tonight, Sidney. He simply has too much housework."

I saw a slow smile spread across her face. During the entire conversation she kept eye contact with me while I stayed kneeling at her feet.

"He has the kitchen floor to finish and then later he has to finish cleaning the bathrooms," she told him cheerily.

During the remainder of the short conversation, she remained pleasant and matter-of-fact. After chatting for a few minutes, I heard her say goodbye. Speechless, I continued to kneel on the kitchen floor. Ms. Renee doesn't allow me to use a mop. She enjoys seeing me on the floor on my hands and knees.

I was shocked. She didn't really cross the line of keeping my submission secret from our friends but she had come perilously close. I couldn't imagine what Sidney thought. It had just been made obvious to him that if I was not a slave then I was at least completely pussy-whipped. Of course, both of these statements were true, but until that second my situation had been private. I was utterly embarrassed. I wanted to protest but the sounds died on my lips. I had protested different stages of my enslavement before and the pressure had only increased—sometimes very harshly.

I only gazed up at my mistress knowing I was helpless to do anything to stop what was going to happen.

"I think I need to keep your phone for a while. From now on your friends need to go through me if they want to see you. I'm not sure that they are aware that your time belongs to me now. They'll eventually learn, just as you have."

With a smile, she slipped my phone into her tailored black suit, then she turned and left me wet and worried, still on my knees on the kitchen floor.

Over the next few weeks, Ms. Renee answered all of my calls. I'm semi-retired, so I no longer receive many business calls. Each call I received was from a friend or a family member. I noticed that each time she received a call she would walk to a part of our home so that I could hear how she responded to the caller.

It was clear that she was deciding which callers she was making certain never bothered to call again. With my family she was friendly and fairly circumspect but with some of my male friends she was clearly sending a message that I was no longer available to them for the usual male-bonding rituals that accompany friendship. At least, I was not available without her permission.

Earlier in the week, I was kneeling in front of her forming a footstool for her feet while she was reading the Sunday Times. I froze when I heard my phone ring. I had started to cringe when I heard it because each time my mistress came up with some new way to humble me. She had also gotten into the habit of putting the phone on speaker so I could hear the somewhat startled responses from people as she invented some new demeaning chore that prevented me from answering my phone or from responding to a request for my time. This call was an old friend I rarely heard from who was inviting me to go on a canoe trip.

"I'm sorry, Tom, but he can't come to the phone right now, he's doing my ironing. I hate to interrupt him because afterward he needs to start my handwashing. What was the purpose of your call?"

She listened quietly to Tom's suggestion of a canoe trip but quickly interrupted him. "No, I'm sorry, Tom, but that is out of the question. I'm having my women's book group that Sunday and I will need him to prepare lunch and clean up afterward."

I could hear the incredulous pause from Tom as he processed her words. Tom seemed to be stunned that she had answered for me. Finally, he mumbled something about the following weekend.

Ms. Renee cut him off again rather sharply. "No, I'm afraid that his housework will keep him home on all of the weekends for the foreseeable future. I always have chores for him, but I'll let him know you called."

Click.

Ms. Renee took a long appraising gaze at me and without a word picked up her newspaper and began to finish the article she was reading. I stayed curled on the floor as her footstool. She doesn't like me to move around too much while I'm being used as furniture. It had been over an hour and I was starting to cramp. It took all of my concentration to be still. Moving too much usually brought on several strokes added to my weekly punishment account. While my emotions rolled from hearing the last conversation, I concentrated on remaining motionless.

During this time Ms. Renee stepped up my usual punishment level and work schedule. Any idea of resisting a new level of surrender that I might still have buried in my psyche was quickly replaced with the desire to weather this new storm. I found myself frequently in the small cage in the attic unable to roam even in the house without permission.

One evening we were upstairs with me suspended from a hook in the ceiling when the phone rang again. A moan escaped my lips when I heard it. Once again Ms. Renee put the speaker on when she answered. It was a woman who ran the volunteer committee for a local charity to help battered women. She was asking if I had time to help with a fundraiser. Ms. Renee quickly began planning my following weekend but while she was talking to me she began to vigorously pull on my nipples. At one point the woman asked if Ms. Renee could really guarantee I could perform all of the tasks she was volunteering me to do. I heard my mistress laugh out loud, then I felt her give my nipple an even crueler twist.

"Oh, I think I can safely make these decisions for him." Again, she laughed.

I pictured myself on the next weekend meekly asking for my assignments from this woman, afraid that she might mention to Ms. Renee that I had not pleased in some small way. However, very soon I could no longer concentrate on the conversation. Feeling her fingers renew their assault on my nipples, I began thrashing in the restraints, trying desperately not to moan out loud as Ms. Renee finished the call. This went on for some time.

Finally, Ms. Renee rang off and smiled. "Just when I had almost decided to turn your phone off, you actually received a call that pleased me. I've given your family and the few of your friends that I approve of my number. They'll learn that if they want to speak to you they'll have to call me. I'm starting to realize that you shouldn't have your own phone anymore. I think I will buy you a new one. Then, I will be the only one with your number. I want you for myself alone. Where did you think this was all going?"

Still, she did not get me a new phone. She was not quite done playing with the old number yet.

Over the next few weeks calls continued to trickle in, but by this time Ms. Renee had changed tactics. I was asked to put the caller on speaker. Instead of Ms. Renee explaining why I was unavailable, it was left to me to explain why some domestic duty required my presence at home.

Ms. Renee bought a device used by the handicapped or elderly to reach objects on upper shelves. It consisted of a metal arm with a trigger like device on one end and two prongs that would extend and grasp an object on the other end. When a call came in she would motion me to drop my pants and kneel in front of her. She would use the "grabber" to grasp my testicles. As I spoke to the caller she would twist my cradled testicles in such a manner that I would bite my lip trying not to yelp in pain. How I handled the caller would depend on how hard she twisted. It was now up to me to humiliate myself in such a way that amused her. She never showed a hint of mercy. Not humbling myself enough was always extremely excruciating. Each call left me on the outer edge of pain and humiliation.

Soon, my phone ringing was a dreadful sound. I desperately wanted everyone to stop calling me. It became much easier for me to make it clear that I was a very busy slave. Slowly the phone calls slowed, then stopped almost completely.

Finally, one afternoon while Ms. Renee read on our patio and I worked in the garden, she motioned me to come closer.

"Go get your sledge hammer and come back here."

Assuming she had a new chore for me, I did as I was bid. Soon, hammer by my side, I knelt in front of her in the patio. Ms. Renee pulled my phone out of her pocket.

"The phone hasn't rung in two weeks. How does that make you feel? It looks like all of your friends have realized that you belong to me now. They're probably all talking about what a pussy-whipped wimp you've become. Ha-ha!"

She continued, "In a way, it's true. You aren't a real man anymore. No real man would allow a woman to so completely dominate him. Actually, you're not even a real person anymore. No, you were born to be what you are, my slave. Except for me, you are alone. No one calls you anymore. I've gotten rid of most of your friends. I could lock you in your cage upstairs for a month and no one would come looking for you."

There was a long pause.

"Would you like me to prove it to you?"

I paled and trembled. I did not know how far she was willing to go. At one time I thought I knew but we had passed those limits long ago.

"We will begin by a symbolic gesture on your part."

She handed me my phone.

"I want you smash it with your hammer."

The phone felt warm in my hand. I had the same phone for years. Once I had run a business from it. In many ways it was a symbol of my professional life and my independence. Nevertheless, I knew I no longer had any choice. My level of submission was no longer up to me. She decided how far we went.

I placed the phone on the ground and crushed it with the heavy sledge. It shattered into a thousand tiny pieces.

Ms. Renee smiled.

From her pocket, Ms. Renee brought out a slender silver chain. Hanging from it was a thin metal cage holding a cellular phone.

"I had this made just for you."

Leaning over, she placed it around my neck and clicked a small padlock in place. It was tight enough that I would not be able to remove it from my neck without the key. It slid discreetly under my shirt.

"This is your new phone. You'll quickly get the hang of answering it even though it's around your neck. Also, I'll be able to check if you make any unauthorized calls from it."

She smiled.

"The best thing about this phone is that it is tied in to my computer at work. I can track your exact location. If you leave the property without my permission, an alarm will sound. I'd rather you were free to continue working and not locked in a cage at this stage of your training. However, if I were you, I wouldn't allow my alarm to ring or you will find how far I'm willing to go to teach you to obey.

"From now on, I will always know where you are and what you are doing."

I was unable to speak. So much over the years had been taken from me. I knew it was useless to resist. I knelt down with my forehead on the patio. I felt her shoe cover the back of my head. Strangely, it felt like a caress.

Above me I heard her state firmly but lovingly, "You belong to me, I will never let you go."

September 2012
Dear Renee,

It thrilled me to see a suggestion of mine like the one about his phone put into practice. It made me feel powerful and a real part of your life. Thank you.
In one thing you are right. I love to boss a man around. My last husband was terrified of me. He was always afraid I would embarrass him by berating him in public. Now it seems you have your man's permission.

You mentioned again that I was a real help to you with your domination of Butler. I'm glad. He's your slave but he's only a slave. He exists for some woman's pleasure and amusement. It might as well be you.

Now that you really have him under your thumb, are you ever afraid that it will be too much for him so that he simply leaves?

You are my dearest friend. I reserve the right to worry about you.

Heather

Butler's Journal
Learning My Place
September 2012

No matter how difficult things sometimes could be as Ms. Renee's slave, there were many moments of family, tenderness, and companionship. Somehow we had managed to maintain our friendship and love even as I journeyed deeper into submission.

I couldn't imagine how much further we could go. All day my thoughts were filled with her. She had become my obsession. Tiny moments when I pleased her seemed to illuminate me with an enormous joy. Nevertheless, I was to learn that there was always another step we could take.

On Wednesday morning I was buttoning the front of her blouse, helping her to dress as I always do, when she noticed a slight imperfection in my ironing of the sleeve. The sleeve has ruffles that make it almost impossible to get exactly right.

"Look at this wrinkle, slave," she said with mild distaste, pointing at the imperfection at her sleeve.

"Yes, Mistress," I responded but then I slipped up. "We really should send it out. Because of the ruffles, it should be steamed at the cleaners."

"Then what do I need you for?" she retorted.

"For the ten thousand other things I do for you," I couldn't help myself from saying.

There was a long icy silence as I nervously finished buttoning her blouse.

"Bring me the case," she finally responded.

I knew I was in trouble. I had misread the signs. Sometimes, she laughs off a tiny bit of bravado I might let slip as humor or beneath her notice but not this week. I should have been more attuned to her mood.

I immediately left her to scurry upstairs for a leather case where she keeps a few discipline devices stored. When I returned she was sitting on the chair in the large walk-in closet where I normally dress her. With a hand gesture, she ordered me to kneel in front of her.

"So you think I ask too much of you?" She reached over and slapped my face sharply. "You think I shouldn't expect perfect service?" Again her hand flashed out, rocking my head to one side. "Now you think you can talk back?" Again her hand shot out at my unprotected face.

I was frightened of an automatic reaction my body might display. It's hard to remain still and not avoid a blow. I knew from a very trying time to never show the slightest sign of rebellion or a sharp discipline could quickly escalate into a hellish experience. I forced myself to remain still. I had been through this before and I had been broken. I knew it and so did she. Her eyes were flashing with a triumphant and eager cruelty. We both knew that I would allow her anything.

"Open the case!" she demanded.

I knelt with burning cheeks and fumbled with the lock. The familiar feelings of shame and fear flooded me. When it was opened, my mistress retrieved a locking ball gag. She shoved it roughly in my mouth and locked the leather hoodlike support tightly around my head.

"Maybe spending the day in this will teach you to bridle your tongue."

I heard the lock click in place. In addition, she gave me the hand signal to place my genitals in my chastity belt. I took the hated device off the shelf she kept it on and slipped it in place. I never knew anymore how long such a discipline might last. The clicking sound to my cock cage is one of the loudest sounds I could imagine.

"Now finish dressing me."

She stood in front of me with her hands on her hips. I remained kneeling, embarrassed, and in a whirl of emotion. I helped her into her shoes. I could feel her hands on my head as she steadied herself while putting on her heels. Even that impersonal touch sent a shiver through me. I followed her down to the front door and offered her the keys to her car and her handbag. I could not follow her outside to open her car door because of the hood. So far, my mistress has been discreet with the neighbors concerning my physical punishments.

In a much calmer tone, she mused, "I guess it's useless to call you later but I will keep an eye on you from work." Then she pulled my chin up to look into my eyes. "I want you to work all day. Don't let me catch you sitting down."

She took the offered purse and her keys. She stopped at the door, turned, and gave my gag a playful tug. Then, with a victorious smile and a gentle kiss on the cheek she left.

She acted as if she were assigning some minor chore. I knew it would be hours of discomfort and tedious work. I knew she meant it when she said she would check on me. Much of the house was wired with cameras so that she could view me on her computer. With the hood and gag locked on my head I would be housebound. I knew there was always something to do. She had enclosed our backyard with a tall privacy fence but I knew I would still be jumpy working outside. If by a miracle I finished my scheduled work, I was supposed to start at the top of the list and do everything all over again.

I started in the kitchen. Wearing a gag all day is much more painful than it sounds. Soon I began berating myself for the tiny verbal liberty I had taken. I vowed to be much more observant in the future. I felt completely out of control of my life and my own body. I could not look forward to hearing the voice of my mistress on the phone. I couldn't even answer the door. After a few hours my jaw ached constantly. In addition, I couldn't eat anything with the gag locked in place. Working all day without food is sobering. It constantly reminded me that my own body no longer belonged to me. Even drinking water was a humiliating experience of sucking tiny bits of liquid around the gag. Everything tasted like leather and sweat and fear.

That afternoon I waited anxiously for my mistress to return. I had scrupulously obeyed her rules and kept busy in the house and the yard every minute. Her dinner was simmering on the stove. The house was spotless. Nevertheless, I sensed things were about to change again and I was very anxious to avoid any additional trips to the whipping bench. I mentally checked off all of the chores on my list for the tenth time. I tried not to think of what might happen if I had forgotten one of them. I heard her car in the driveway, a sound that usually causes me to scurry to her car to open her door. Today, because of the gag, I waited on my knees in the foyer.

She looked radiant and relaxed as she came in. Completely unconcerned with my discomfort, she took her coat and purse she was carrying and dropped them over my head as if I were an inanimate object.

"What's for dinner?" she asked.

There was a silent pause.

"Oops, I forgot, you're not in a talkative mood are you?"

She laughed quietly.

After a quick glance around the house that made me a tiny bit nauseous at the idea of her finding something not to her standards, she settled in the living room to silently read the newspaper while waiting for the dinner I had prepared. I was grateful that she was apparently satisfied with the house but I did not relax. Even if I had felt it was appropriate to sit, I was no longer allowed to sit on the furniture in the living room.

"I'll eat in the dining room tonight," she informed me as I brought her a glass of wine.

This is a code to let me know that I would not be taking my meal with her. Normally, we eat together in the nook off of the kitchen but we have a formal dining room that Ms. Renee uses for company or at her whim. If she uses the dining room when we are alone in the house, then she always dines alone. Often she reads or listens to music during the meal. My task is to stand behind her and see to her needs as an attentive waiter.

I had spent the day working without rest so the brief pause that her dinner allowed me was very welcome. However, pausing and watching her leisurely progress through the meal reminded me how hungry I was. My jaws ached and my mouth filled with saliva. I wanted to complain but I was afraid of her response.

Again, my place as her slave was driven home. I was actually afraid of her displeasure. At one time I had the power to negotiate a scene but that was only during the beginning of my training. Now, there was never any negotiation. This was not a "scene." This was my life. Theoretically I could physically leave, but I had tried that only once. It had threatened our entire relationship. I had come crawling back a few days later to suffer a much more severe punishment than the one that I had tried to avoid. I knew if I left again I would never be allowed back. However, the main reason for staying was that the idea of living without this masterful, imaginative, sexual creature was more than I could bear. Knowing I was trapped, I had no choice but to stand and serve.

As the meal progressed, I continued to remove various dishes and refill her glass. She barely acknowledged me as she read. Finally, dinner was over. Ms. Renee folded her napkin and pushed her chair around to face me.

"Two," she said.

Barely had she spoken before I had immediately lowered myself to my knees. My responses to her commands were almost automatic.

My mistress curled a finger toward her and I shuffled closer. She placed her cheek next to mine. Slowly she wrapped her arms around my neck. I could smell her skin and subtle perfume. She ran her fingers through my hair.

"Kiss me," she demanded in a hoarse whisper.

I was startled. I knew she was aware of my gag. She pulled away slightly. Then looking into my eyes, she passionately kissed the gag covering my mouth. After a few seconds she broke away.

"Unsatisfying," she stated in a disgusted tone. "Maybe, you'll do better between my legs."

She slowly spread her legs and pulled my head down beneath her skirt. I stirred at the scent of her sex. I tried rubbing the gag gently across her panties but was soon met with her hands pushing my head away.

"Terrible," she sighed.

She then pulled me up by my hair and pulled my hips between her legs. I felt her tight muscular thighs wrap around my torso. She ground her mound into my chastity device.

"Fuck me!" she demanded, while she wantonly thrust her hips onto my cage.

By this time my genitals were swelling with excitement. My chastity device became almost unbearable. I could feel the silky material caressing the small areas of skin available through the bars of my cage. I began moaning.

"What's the matter, slave? Why don't you fuck me?" She laughed as she continued to grind onto my cock cage.

My moaning changed to whimpering as the pain and frustration increased. I felt her hands pulling at my nipples.

"I need a good fuck right now. Go ahead, take me!" she growled.

I was a cauldron of bubbling feeling. I felt feverish, helpless, and utterly humiliated.

"Worthless!" she snapped and shoved me to the floor on my back.

She stood over me watching me writhe in anguish.

"Let's see. You can't kiss or lick, or even fuck. You aren't much of a man anymore, are you? Why should I keep you around if you can't do anything for me?"

She punctuated her words with the heel of her shoe into my chest.

"I guess you can do the dishes. Maybe I should dress you as the maid instead of the butler since you're really not a man anymore! Do you think you can do the dishes?"

I began nodding my head vigorously. Soon after a few more twists of her heels into my chest, she walked into the living room, leaving me trembling on the floor.

I finished the dishes in a dream state. Whatever shred of dignity I possessed had been torn from me. I carefully finished wiping down the counters and crawled toward the living room on my hands and knees.

She was sitting in her chair with her legs crossed, waiting for me. Instinctively, I crawled to her and placed myself in front of her on my knees with my head bowed.

"You look ridiculous. Look at yourself in your gag and cock harness. I hope you don't think you look anything like a man. No, it's clear that you are only a slave. Pathetic."

I could hear mirth starting to bubble up in her. Sometimes, her amused tone is more humiliating to me than her angry tone.

"I bet you'd like for me to remove your gag and allow you to eat something."

She playfully pushed the gag in and out of my mouth to the limits that the harness allowed. It felt like she was fucking my mouth. Of course, she was aware of what she was doing.

I nodded once; humbly, I hoped.

Then in a husky, confidential voice, "I know what you really want. You'd like me to take you up to my bedroom and unlock your cock cage. It's taken a long time but my training of you has made me an object of worship. You can't help but think about me constantly. You are addicted to me. You'd do anything to be allowed to make love to me, wouldn't you? Even if I let you leave to try to have satisfaction with other women they would be tasteless to you. I doubt you could get that tiny thing you call a cock hard for anyone else but me. I've psychologically castrated you, haven't I?"

She laughed and twisted the heel of her shoe into my thigh sharply. I knew the truth when I heard it no matter how painful. Her hand swiftly caught the back of my head by the leather straps. She pulled me onto my back on the floor and placed a high heel on my chastity device.

"That's not true for me. I would have no problem at all filling my bed. There are a thousand men in this city willing to enter into my training tonight if they were given the chance!"

She moved her heel up to my chest. "After all, you can't kiss or lick or fuck. What good are you? You are wearing that harness and that gag for poor performance as my slave. I might have wanted sex tonight but I can't lower my standards. Now, you are worthless to me. Why should I go without sex because you can't perform properly as my slave?"

I was starting to choke and gag. Every muscle in my body was rigid with fear and obsession.

"How would you like it if I took another slave? Can you imagine being kicked out and replaced by a man more willing to submit to me? It could happen anytime I choose. The world is full of submissive men. Imagine walking up and down the street in front of this house wishing you were still my slave. How would that feel?"

Involuntarily, I heard a low moan escape from deep within me.

"Then, I guess you had better try harder. Will you submit to me?"

Again, I began nodding my head wildly and moaning.

"I want to take you all the way. It's too late for you to change your mind. I know there is some part of you that continues to cling to the mistake that you still have rights. I've decided to crush that illusion so you will understand who you really are. Go upstairs and start my bath. I shouldn't have allowed you an orgasm Sunday night or you would be more eager to please me."

Filled with anxiety and desire, I started toward her bath.

Ms. Renee added softly, "Slave, you must be willing to endure anything for me. You aren't ready yet but you will be. I promise."

I returned, and lying flat on the floor in front of her, I placed one of her feet over my head. We stayed like this for a moment of tenderness before I left to prepare her bath. I did not know what lay ahead but I was determined to continue to be the man she kept as her slave.

Chapter Seven

PRACTICAL MATTERS

Butler's Journal
Pool Party
January 2013

My mistress and I decamped to Key West for the first week of January. She loves warm climates. I loved being somewhere new with her. Several of our vanilla friends accompanied us.

We had been invited to attend a pool party of one of the local residents with ties to Ms. Renee's work. Soon after our arrival, most of the people at the small party threw off their wraps and shirts and jumped into the pool. My mistress wiggled onto a floating lawn chair and pointed at her drink. It was only a tiny motion of her hand but it immediately put me in motion. Sitting beside the pool, I jumped up to retrieve her glass. As I knelt beside the pool and handed the drink to her, she playfully splashed me.

"Come on in!" she smiled.

Her hair lying damp across her shoulders and her wet swimsuit sweetly clinging to her were like a physical push toward the water. I wanted to accept her invitation but we both knew it was impossible. She laughed knowingly and called me silly for not getting in the pool. I wanted to but I could not take off my shirt.

Our friends knew me as a particularly attentive partner that our female friends wished their husbands would emulate. I was always quick to perform the small civilities one expects of a gentleman such as opening doors and helping her in and out of her coat. In addition, I was always pleasantly useful to whoever hosted a social gathering. Women often complimented my mistress concerning my polite, helpful manner. However, if I took off my shirt they would understand the reason for my demeanor. I was not her polite partner. Across my back were bruises and welts that she had placed there a few days earlier with a leather strap for a minor lapse in my service to her. No one who looked at my back could imagine I was anything other than a carefully and often harshly disciplined slave.

I had no doubt that she had timed my punishment a few days ago to coincide perfectly with this pool party. Normally she disciplines me by whipping my buttocks and the back of my thighs, but not this time. Instead, she had whipped me higher on my back. It was clear to me now that she looked forward to seeing me standing there embarrassed while making lame excuses about not wanting to swim.

I saw her looking up at me from the comfort of her floating chair. She twisted in it to display her curves and deliciously wet skin. She loved to tease me as much as she loved to discipline me. She had to be able to feel my desire wash over her like the water in the pool.

After a few moments of smiling and discreetly undulating her hips for me, her attitude shifted to sounding disappointed at not accepting her invitation.

"Phooey, if you are not going to swim then you can help our host clean up," she snapped as if she were slightly miffed at me for not entering the water. She turned away from me.

Lately, it seemed she felt more comfortable about asking me to perform small services for her and her friends in public. It had gone from embarrassing to become somewhat humiliating.

Was she drunk with wine or was she drunk with power? Did she know how she sounded? Was her response to me calculated or was she a bit out of control? When she spoke I could see a few eyebrows go up. I caught a smirk from one of her friends. Was it a knowing smirk? Had she told any of her friends the real nature of our relationship? I never knew how far she would go.

I did know what to do. I went looking for the hostess to offer my services. I knew if I were unsuccessful in charming her to allow me to help I would be looking forward to a fresh discipline session later that night.

While I was looking for the hostess I couldn't help but notice how much I lusted after the creative, cunning dominatrix who owned me. My life was an exciting adventure with her in control.

January 2013
Dear Renee,

I hate it when you go someplace warm without me. I love Florida in the winter. I know you invited me but work wouldn't allow it. I thought about being angry with you but then I decided to take it out on Butler when I get the chance. It's what he's there for isn't he?

Sometimes, I'm jealous of anyone spending time with you but me.

Feeling pea green,
Heather

Butler's Journal
Dressing Ms. Renee
February 2013

I began the day kneeling before a large picture of Ms. Renee that hangs on the wall of my tiny room. Dutifully, I began the mantra that my mistress had given me. "I am only a slave. It is a privilege to serve." She believes the continued verbal repeating of my place and my desire to serve her will engender deeper feelings of surrender. According to her this meditation will establish my priorities.

The picture is larger than life. It is black and white and slightly overexposed so her skin appears perfectly smooth and flawless. In the photo she is standing above the photographer, looking down so now it looks like she is hovering above me as I kneel in front of it.

When I started this practice I thought it was silly. I had no experience at meditation and I have never been religious. Nevertheless, as I continued to follow her suggestion I found that the quiet moments in the morning did help me to remember my priorities. In addition, taking the time to slow down for a few moments often allowed me to occasionally remember some small chore that I had forgotten but I would have been punished for forgetting.

Staring at her picture reminded me that I'm lucky to be living my dream of serving a woman like Ms. Renee. My life is my fantasy come true but it has its dangers. I often shiver at the quiet smile I see playing across her lips in the picture.

Despite the difficult training I was undergoing, I also recognized that in many ways my life had improved. Ms. Renee kept me on a healthy diet and demanded that I exercise daily. I had never been so fit. My piano playing had improved because she scheduled regular practice. Even my social skills were becoming more refined as she always gave me feedback after every social occasion. I was unable to spend money without her permission, so we had the funds to travel more often. I lived in a beautifully maintained home with a surrounding garden because she demanded it. Finally, she had involved me in her personal political passions. My service to her had meaning that went beyond our home. My retirement, instead of being boring, was filled with passion and activity. It was clear. Her domination was good for me. I had never felt so loved or in love.

After meditation, I dressed in what Ms. Renee calls my butler uniform of dark pants and white shirt.

Silently, I entered her room. I have grown to love the quiet moments waking her. If I'm very gentle, she often allows me to stoke her hair and kiss her before pushing me away. I always shudder when I remember the month of training she put me through at the beginning of my service when I was not allowed to touch her or see her unless she was fully clothed. How much this intimate moment would have meant to me then. Because of that training, these moments will always hold their magic.

Fully awake, she reached up toward my face and allowed me a lingering kiss. We are mistress and slave but our romantic lives remain very much alive. Keeping hold of my chin, she asked me, as she has several times the previous week, if I was willing to serve. This question unnerved me. I sensed things changing between us again. The previous week she had been more exacting concerning my work, with an unusual amount of physical discipline.

This morning she confirmed my feelings by asking, "Do you trust me?"

I answered, "Yes."

"Good," she replied. She looked at me intently and added, "I love you but you need to trust that I know what's best. We always have to move forward with our relationship to keep it alive."

I don't know what she meant but I knew not to question her.

After helping her dress, the day unwound in its usual rhythm of cleaning, errands, and attending to her personal needs. Complicating my day, Ms. Renee planned lunch with her friend Ms. Heather to be served in the garden room.

By long training and extensive practice things went well. Finishing the dishes, I could hear them still enjoying their dessert over the intercom that keeps me at her call.

Seizing a free moment, I began to set out the accoutrement I needed for her manicure and pedicure. Usually, I work on her nails in her bathroom. Today, however, she rang me from the garden room where she was still entertaining. I approached the table as she taught me. I kept my voice low, my hands folded in front of me, and my eyes lowered.

She informed me that she would prefer me to attend her there.

"Of course," I responded in a quiet tone.

"Also, you will treat Heather as well," she ordered.

Again, I murmured my acquiescence, but in fact I was in a bit of a panic. I didn't know how I was going to accomplish everything I needed to do and give the additional time to Heather. I suspect she knew exactly what she was doing. It's a frequent game she plays. She loves adding one more burden at the last minute to see how I will respond. I have also learned that the tiniest evidence of irritation from me in front of Ms. Heather would likely be punished. I quickly nodded and turned for my manicure kit. I knew that Ms. Renee and I were scheduled to attend a gala at a woman's shelter, her pet charity. I had a lot to do to get us both ready to attend.

Neither woman acknowledged my presence as I entered the dining area with my equipment. Both of them continued to sociably chat while receiving their pedicures and manicures. I noted that Heather still dressed like a retired fashion model. She's known in our circles as a man-eater and has been divorced twice. She has become so used to my service that I have faded into the background. I don't think she sees me as person anymore. I am merely part of Ms. Renee's home.

Toward the end of her pedicure, Ms. Heather reached over and took hold of Ms. Renee's hand to thank her. She has learned it is unnecessary to say anything to me. As she briefly held her hand, something passed between them that I sensed but did not understand. I continued to kneel as they both rose to say goodbye. They hugged in a brief friendly embrace. As Ms. Heather reached for her purse, she noticed that while they were saying goodbye Ms. Renee had been standing partly on my hand. These tiny, "by accident" cruelties have been a growing habit while my mistress is with her friend. Heather said nothing but I caught a fleeting smile cross her lips. I feared her relationship with Ms. Renee had even more for me to worry about in the future.

After her guest left, my mistress motioned with her finger for me to hurry after her. Inside, she turned to me in the living room with a raised brow and asked, "I hope you've been keeping your eye on the time. Do you have everything ready for tonight?"

I felt the first tingle of anxiety but I answered, "Yes, Mistress," and moved quickly upstairs. There was still much more to do.

Ms. Renee languidly reached for a book as she settled into her favorite chair. It had been a difficult week. My small mistakes during the week had earned me thirty strokes from her cane. This is the limit she would give me. If I earned just one more stroke, I would be denied the opportunity to make love to my mistress. To prevent me from pleasuring myself, I would spend the next week in my chastity cage. Consequently, I was determined not to make any more mistakes.

Her shoes were the first priority. I had received intense correction for improperly cared for shoes early in my training. Punishments were real from her hand and I worked hard to avoid those experiences.

Considering the dress I knew she was wearing, there could only be a dozen or so possible choices. Much would count on my knowledge of her sense of style. I passed through her private sitting area and into her dressing room. I vaguely remembered that it was once destined to be my bedroom. Before I moved in, Ms. Renee had remodeled her home by bumping her dressing room into most of what would have been my bedroom. Lining one wall of her dressing chamber was a honeycomb of wooden shelves reaching for floor to ceiling. Inside each section rested a different pair of shoes. They were logically arranged according to color and style. I knew she would wear black but there were a few pairs that had red highlights that might also be good choices.

After collecting my polishes and rags, I began in earnest, inspecting, cleaning, and polishing her heels. Although not as difficult as cleaning her lingerie, I had to concentrate on the task so that pain from my chastity belt did not slow me. The smell of leather and her lingering scent acted like twin traps for a mind broken to think constantly of her. Luckily, I had picked up her dress from the cleaners the day before. With these preparations I could finally focus on my usual activities.

Finally, at 6:00 p.m., with all of usual jobs finished it was time for her bath. Downstairs she was drinking a glass of wine and finishing her book. I entered her bathroom. It had taken me weeks of haggling with architects and builders to achieve a room I felt worthy of her. It had taken a good piece of my retirement savings to finish it. The tile was in earth tones and ocean blues. There was a large vanity and a shower at the back wall. Along one wall was a massage table. Along the opposite wall were shelves for scents, soaps, brushes, and oils. The room was lighted indirectly behind thin slices of marble. In the middle of the room was an antique claw-footed iron tub. I placed it in the middle of the room so that I could kneel behind her to massage her shoulders and comb her hair while she soaked. Allowing access to both sides of the tub enabled me to shave her legs without requiring awkward positions from her.

I started filling the tub. I had been whipped so often for not arriving at the perfect bath temperature that I no longer trusted my senses. I used a thermometer. I knew she would be coming soon.

I removed my clothes and knelt naked except for my chastity device. It was here in her bath that I always felt the most like her slave. In the years we had lived in the house, I could not remember a time she had so much as dried herself off except for the hellish month of my breaking when I was not allowed to see her naked. Although I had bathed her thousands of times, my hands trembled and my breath quickened at the thought of touching her skin.

I heard her steps on the stairs. I breathed deeply, reminding myself that I was only a slave and that sexual thoughts involving her would be instantly punished by the confines of my cock cage. Hearing the click of her heels crossing the floor made it clear as always that I would never achieve perfect surrender of self. I knew that the next hour would be torture for me but a relaxing, slippery pleasure for her.

I helped her undress, carefully putting some articles aside to be hung, others to be washed. I was careful not to touch her skin in a too familiar manner as if I had any right to do so. I struggled to maintain the attitude of a servant. Carefully, I helped her into the tub.

Over the years I have been instructed about each detail of her bath. I knew the different soaps to use on different parts of her body as my hands, encased in sponges and brushes, polished and cleaned her skin. The bath ended with her lying relaxed in the water as I massaged her feet. Just as the water started to cool, she stepped out of the bath, standing with her hands raised as I dried her.

Barely acknowledging my presence, she walked to the massage table, where my years of training have produced a careful and detailed knowledge of her pleasure centers. It was not unusual for a bath of thirty minutes to be followed by another thirty minutes of massage. She rarely spoke during these times. My back ached and my fingers cramped with fatigue as she sank into a blissful relaxed calm. I was wet with perspiration and my encased genitalia itched in its steel prison. Finished, I moved to her vanity to set out what she might need in preparation for the night. I returned and helped her into her robe and followed her to her large closet.

With her seated in the chair in her dressing room, I began combing her hair. She sat back with her eyes closed while I applied the brush. I have learned never to intrude on her silence. I wondered what she was thinking but I no longer felt free to ask. I knew that if I remained patient I would hear everything she meant for me to hear. I simply brushed until she motioned to the clothes I had ready.

I helped her on with her lingerie, stockings, and dress. She glanced over at the shoes I had placed in a row that I knew were prepared. There was a pause as she considered her options. To my relief, she pointed to black heels with the red soles I spent extra time cleaning.

"Did you guess these were the shoes I would choose?"

"Yes, Mistress," I replied.

"Hmmm," she responded, holding them in her hand. "It's not really a match, is it?" she asked.

She tapped the sole of the shoe with her nail to bring to my attention that the sole was a slightly different shade of red than her nails.

"If you knew, then why didn't you match my nail color?"

I felt a tremble go through me knowing I had displeased her. I waited for the ax to fall but she did not ask for my notebook to add to my punishment. I silently vowed to focus my entire being on trying to get through the rest of the evening with no more mistakes. It occurred to me that my mistress could count. She knew that I was holding exactly at thirty strokes, the limit she had imposed. She also knew that I was on fire to make love to her. I had frequently taken the limit and still been allowed to make love to her while at the same time avoiding the chastity cage. It was clear that sometimes she liked to position me so that I hovered at the limit. She knew precisely what she was doing. I could only do my best and wait to see what would happen.

Tonight, she motioned me back toward the vanity mirror. She made the hand signal that required that I kneel on my hands and knees. Feeling the weight of her firm bottom on my back only stimulated me further. Using me as furniture was simply part of my ongoing training.

Sometimes she is chatty during this time in front of her mirror. She talks about her day or the evening activity she is preparing to attend. I remembered that recently she frequently had left me at home when she went out. Tonight, she was silent as she expertly finished applying her makeup. It's my job to be perfectly still and stay sensitive to her mood. Satisfied with her preparations, she motioned me to follow her to the full-length mirror.

Immediately, I followed on my knees. Once at her feet in front of the mirror, I bowed my head. Lately, I had been instructed to kneel and kiss the toes of her shoes when she is looking at herself in the mirror. Thus, every image she has of herself now includes me humbling myself before her. It had taken all afternoon to bathe, polish, manicure, massage, and dress her but I was not allowed to lift my head while she inspected herself. Only when she stepped away from the mirror did I dare to gaze up at her.

She was, of course, darkly beautiful. Ms. Renee is a curvy brunette of medium height with perfect skin and brown eyes. There was something else hard to define about her looks. She had presence. In any room, if one were asked who might be a leader, she would be picked out as an obvious choice. I felt lucky to be near her. I longed to stand and crush her close to me. Instead, I remained motionless on my knees. It was obvious to her the effect she had on me. She wiggled and swayed her hips for a few seconds, teasing me. I gazed lovingly up at her, waiting for her to release me so that I could dress to attend the night's festivities.

She moved closely and cupped one hand under my chin, lifting my eyes toward hers. For a moment she held my gaze

"Slave, I was going to allow you to escort me tonight. You know that I'm being awarded Woman of the Year for my work at the women's shelter. I realize that it was your money that allowed me to do so much for them. I wanted to take you but there's a problem. First, you haven't really met my standards as a slave the last few days. I've been forced to write in your notebook multiple times." She paused for a minute. Then in a firm and serious tone, she continued. "I'm starting to consider the idea of not letting the world see you as my equal anymore. I don't know if I will ever allow you to escort me as an equal again. It feels inappropriate somehow. You and I know you are not really a man anymore. You are only a slave. I'm glad now that I kept our marriage a secret. I'm not sure what to do with you publicly. This is an important event. A lot of people will have their eyes on me tonight. I want to see if I like going to events like this without you. I've asked Heather to pick me up and to escort me to the party instead of you."

I felt my insides freeze at this announcement. I couldn't imagine what this meant for our relationship in the future.

She went on, "Don't pretend you didn't know this might be coming. We've been moving in this direction for the last year. Just look at yourself kneeling in what you thought was going to be your bedroom but is now my dressing room. These are the only clothes you've worn in months. Think about what you do all day. You clean and launder, chauffeur, and garden for me. It's all you do all day. Admit the obvious—you really are my slave. You may have to learn to accept it in public just as you do in private. If you can't accept who and what you've become, then you'll have to leave."

She stood over me with her hands on her hips, looking down at me.

The freezing sensation spread deeper into me. I was completely unable to see myself leaving. My mind has been so warped and molded over the last few years that she was most of what I thought about all day. What she said was true. All I did, all day, was take care of her needs.

In a firmer tone, she continued, "I can tell you are having problems with this, so I'm going to help you accept it. Spread your legs!" There was something very determined and cold in her voice.

I obeyed as I was trained to do, keeping my arms down by my side. I knew what was to come and tried to prepare myself for it. However, I was wrong. She didn't kick me. Instead she placed her shoe over my crotch and slowly started applying her weight. I couldn't move. I felt frozen.

"Look up at me," she demanded. "Be still!"

I could hear the coldness in her voice as I tilted my head upward. I saw her arm as it bent above me and in the next instant I felt her fist grab a handful of my hair. She continued to apply additional weight until I was squirming under her foot.

"I would have brought you to this point earlier but your slowness in becoming more submissive kept me putting this moment off. When you moved in I should never have introduced you to anyone again as an equal but I knew you weren't ready for such a deep level of submission. You could be coming with me tonight as my servant if you had submitted sooner. Now, I'm tired of waiting.

"Have you noticed how demanding I've been lately? It was to get you ready for tonight. After tonight, I'm thinking of raising the level of your servitude. To do that, I'm thinking of keeping you out of society for a few months, then slowly reintroducing you again but only as my servant."

She took a step away from me, turned, and looked over her shoulder. "I don't know yet if I will do it or not, but I do want you to be willing to accept such a change."

I was completely stunned. I felt numb and anxious all at the same time.

"I can tell you need more help processing all of this. Follow me!"

I followed on my knees through her dressing room and up the narrow stairs to her attic dungeon. Over the years it has been constantly improved to provide her with all of the equipment needed in a well-appointed dungeon.

Her heels clicked over to what she called the Horse. It's a rough-cut beam of wood set at an angle so that a sharp edge runs along the top about three feet high resting between two posts. She patted it with one manicured hand.

I knew what I had to do. I was too numb and frightened to protest even if I hadn't been trained to never complain. I swung one leg over the beam.

It is just high enough so that if I kept on my tiptoes I would avoid the rough, sharp corner of the beam from cutting painfully into my perineum. She locked on a pair of handcuffs through a chain hanging from the ceiling.

With the touch of a switch, an electric wench stretched my hands above my head. By pulling on the chain and standing on tiptoe I could avoid the edge of the beam but I knew from bitter experience that I would eventually tire. She strapped on a mouth gag that reaches deep between my jaws and buckled behind my head.

"I could tell you were having problems seeing yourself as I see you. This will help."

Helpless, I watch as she reached for her rattan cane. Its thin suppleness gave no hint of the amount of pain it would cause. Spinning on her heels, she stood slightly behind me. After a slight hesitation to allow me to anticipate its kiss, she brought it down wickedly across my buttocks. A searing agony raced across my ass. I could almost see the red stripe it left as she pulled back for another stroke. I couldn't twist or move in any way because of the fine edge of the beam pressing against the bottom of my scrotum. Six measured stokes fell, leaving me gasping and moaning. She began berating me harshly, punctuating her words with the stroke of the cane.

"You are not working (slash) hard (slash) enough (slash). From now on you will accept your place as my slave (slash). Look at what you'll put up with! You're nothing but a slave! Why should I share the spotlight with anyone tonight, especially a slave?"

Once more the cane snaked out, striking with force but it was not nearly as cutting as her words. I felt like I was being torn apart on the inside. After a pause, she moved forward to allow me to see her. She was perfectly coiffed, dressed in heels and an evening dress. Her complexion, slightly flushed from whipping me, added to her beauty. I sensed her usual excitement from causing me pain.

I struggled not to cry out through my gag. The mood shifted and she was suddenly beside me, touching my chest, speaking softly.

"Slave, you know how I feel about giving you too many strokes of the cane. If I give you too many strokes you'll be too sore to be of use as a servant. I'm never going to raise the limit I will give you each week."

I broke my training for a second and actually looked at her in utter surprise. Allowing me a brief moment of familiarity, she smiled.

"I know that leaving is really no longer an option for you and I can't physically increase your punishments. There is only one punishment left and that is further limiting the time you spend out of your cock cage."

She stopped and began touching me gently again. She tapped the top of my cock cage with a fingernail.

"You are a very attentive lover and I enjoy our sex life but I will give it up if you can't perform better as my servant. I didn't mention it at the time but it's only fair to give you at least one more stroke for not matching my nail color with the soles of my shoes. A good slave interested in details would have known to do that. That means your total for the week is thirty-one. You know what that means. You'll have to stay locked in your chastity cage."

With my gag, I could offer no argument. She stepped behind me and finished my caning. She stopped at thirty, leaving one on the books. It was just one over the limit but I knew it meant I would stay chaste.

"Of course, this means I can't have sex because you didn't perform adequately as my servant. Heather says I should take a lover. I don't agree—yet. I want to continue helping you become a better slave, but if you're locked up for weeks at a time what can I do?"

Something rolled deep in my guts. My knees turned to water but I barely felt the edge of the Horse slicing into me.

She began stroking and pulling gently on my nipples. It put me back on my toes.

"Don't you want to make love to me?" she whispered.

The waves of emotions crashed in one giant roar inside of my head. I moaned and nodded vigorously.

With an intake of breath, very tenderly she whispered, "Oh darling, I knew you cared. You're crying!"

Shocked, I suddenly felt the wetness on my face. She leaned in and gently kissed me below my eyes. I felt her lips burning on my skin. She stared straight into my eyes. Then, I saw her tongue touching her lips, tasting my tear. A slow smile spread across her lips. I could only shiver in response.

She stepped away, keeping her eyes on me. Twisting her body to show it off, she slipped back into a teasing voice.

"The party tonight will be full of men and women wanting to dance with me. I should keep my eyes open in case you can't do a better job as my slave."

I was frozen. It felt as if I had stopped breathing. I had no response. Suddenly, I heard the brassy honk from the Mercedes Roadster I recognized as Heather's car.

She looked at me quizzically as if I could respond with anything but moans. At the sound of the horn, she smiled triumphantly.

"Oh, I have to run! You don't want me late for my own awards ceremony, do you?"

She placed the cane on its rack and turned for the door. On the way out she turned to allow me one more look at her. She was radiant, happy, desirable, very much the goddess.

"Think about how you can improve your service to me. I'll see you in a few hours. I really don't know what I'm going to do with you. It doesn't feel right to be seen with a slave as if he was my equal. We may even have to move to another state so I can live the life that I want to live. I'll think about it more and let you know what I decide."

She leaned forward and blew a kiss in my direction.

"Goodnight, slave."

She switched off the light and closed the door, leaving me in darkness. I heard the enthusiastic greetings at the front door and listened for it to finally close. I heard the over-powered sports car drive off. I was alone. I felt the wetness on my face again. I wondered, was I still crying? I was frightened about the shift in our relationship but I knew she was right. I couldn't leave. I was hooked, body and soul. Living with this sexy, creative, dominant woman was the purpose of my life.

I shifted uncomfortably on the beam. I arched my back without relief. I would be trembling and exhausted before she returned but I had spent hours like this before. I tried not to picture her at the party without me but I couldn't help myself. Visions of her as the center of admirers filled my imagination. I saw her dancing, laughing, and enjoying the attention of her guests.

I cried out in the empty room but there is no one to hear. The Horse hurt more than usual. I replayed every missed opportunity I'd had in the last week to prove my submission. I desperately wanted to please her but hanging in the attic there was nothing I could do but suffer for her. I knew I would submit to anything she had planned for me.

Alone in the darkened shadows of her attic dungeon I waited and longed for her and wondered about the coming changes.

February 2013
Dear Heather,

Thank you for attending the awards dinner with me last week. I don't think we surprised too many people by showing up together. Your idea of leaving him at home was perfect.

While teasing him last week before the party, I told him that I might stop allowing him to be seen with me as an equal. I was only trying to mess with his head because I love our life here in Memphis. I love having him at my side. We have wonderful vanilla friends and I love my work. However, after I said it, I suddenly wanted it to be true. Well, I wanted it to be true part of the time. It's something to think about.

At this point, my domination of him has still allowed him to live a semi-normal life, but I'm certain that we both have the courage to go further.

I took your advice, so I have temporarily restricted him from leaving the house. For a while, I need him completely isolated and solely reliant on me for all human interaction. I think of this time as a rigorous slave boot camp that will last for several more weeks. This is necessary because the next stages of his enslavement will be increasingly difficult and very practical. I can't wait to tell you about it, especially if it works. If our life together has left him with the slightest shred of resistance to my complete rule, I intend to strip him of it over the next few weeks.

During this time, I want him to learn a new way to relate to all women and to me especially without outside influence. To increase his distress, I have not allowed him to see me naked. I want him to see me as impossibly out of reach. After all, I am his owner while he is only my slave.

I now control how he dresses, what he eats, and how he spends his day. I have kept him constantly busy attempting to avoid my punishments by providing a new level of service. For example, I have him clean something. Next, I find some tiny flaw. Then I whip him mercilessly for poor performance. I order him to clean it again. I find another flaw and whip him just as hard. I allow him to try again and again to please me with the same task, suffering additional punishments as long as it amuses me or until the task is finally perfect. I can tell that this is particularly difficult for him but I find this kind of discipline tremendously exciting.

I won't end his boot camp until I feel he sees himself differently. Time and pressure will finally produce the results we both want. When I'm done, he'll be eager to take the next very practical steps toward his complete enslavement.

I want this time to be a transformative experience for him because I don't want him to balk at the next step of his submission. I have discussed my plans with other friends who are into S&M and they have been worried that my ideas border on abuse. I can understand their concerns. It is true that I am skirting the edge of consensual practice but I think of my slave and myself as pioneers pushing the boundaries of a loving S&M relationship. My willingness to lead us into an intense experience is because I want so much for us.

For safety's sake I am always carefully monitoring Butler's response to my training. S&M practice, when executed correctly, should produce feelings of passion and adoration in the slave. My challenge will be to observe every tiny nuance of his response. While he strives to learn what pleases me, I must learn what creates a powerful sense of surrender in him.

Two people spending such enormous energy understanding each other will result in a growing intimacy. That's not abuse; it's love. It may not be everyone's definition but it is ours.

During his isolation, I have methodically burned his private life to the ground. When one of his friends who I don't approve of calls, I tell them, while he is listening, that he is too busy doing my housework for him to answer. Sometimes, I stand on him, digging my heels into his chest while listening to him explain that he is too busy scrubbing my floors to have any free time. How humiliating that must be for him! Just thinking about it makes me vibrate. As a bonus, his separation from his social life has made it easy for me to remove old friends who don't share my views of female supremacy. I have become his life.

While he is cut off from the rest of society, I will finish taking over his assets and emasculate him financially. In addition, I will take control of his retirement fund and his bank account. It's no longer enough for me that I've been added to his accounts as a co-owner. I want them all solely in my name. I want him totally dependent on me. I love the idea of him begging me for anything he needs.

Finally, I will force him to sign paperwork that puts him in debt to me for a large sum of money. At each stage I will remind him that he is doing this of his own free will. He must acknowledge that he craves his surrender as much as I do.

I agree with you that money is power, so he should have none. I can accomplish this because we have spent years preparing for this moment. In truth, I don't care about his money as much as I care about his willingness to surrender everything to me. Even with the increased level of pressure from me, I expect that he will attempt to wiggle out of this last step but I will mercilessly crush any opposition he shows.

Most men will acquiesce to any demand if they are placed in a chastity belt then removed every day to be teased and punished. After edging him almost to orgasm, I intend to return him to the belt day after day until he breaks. It might take weeks until I'm convinced that he is sincere in his desire to give me control. The idea of icing his swollen, aching testicles and then squishing his much-abused penis into a cruel chastity cage makes me weak in the knees. I can't wait to hear him begging to give me control of his finances. There are so many things to look forward to in the coming weeks.

When I think about everything I'll do to him and take from him in the next few months, I realize that there is nothing very unusual about any of it. The only difference is that this time it's happening to a man instead of a woman. I admit that "turning the tables" is part of the fun.

After gaining control, I will revel in the fact that he is financially powerless. He will have to come to me and beg on his knees for money to buy a new toothbrush. Of course, I would never take advantage of his helplessness. Ha! Oh yes, I would! I can't wait!

It will not be enough for him to change. I must change too. I must start seeing him differently. I hope that watching him submit will change my view of him. After all, only a true slave would agree to what I demand. If I can't start seeing him as my slave, I will mask him in a hood for days at a time so I can depersonalize him to the extent that he stops being someone I know. I must learn to see him as my property, a tool, a whipping boy, or a servant. Not being reminded of who he is by not seeing his face might help. I feel duty bound to experiment with different ideas. I need to steel myself not to show mercy.

I realize that both of us will have to work for our goal. At times I will need to harden my heart to his suffering. I know that he will weaken in his resolve to submit, so I must be strong for both of us. Also, it is my creativity that is called upon to lead him to surrender. That can be tiring.

He is not the only one who will be making sacrifices for our goal. I work very hard to stay in perfect hourglass shape to tantalize him. I also make it a point to dress in a way that stimulates his submissive leanings. I'm asking everything of him. I must match his commitment. After all, what would be the point of denying him something that he doesn't want with his whole being? After his boot camp and the surrender of his finances, I may allow him to see me naked again. Maybe, I'll even allow him to touch me. I want to see him cry in gratitude for that privilege.

You keep asking about love. Before we talk about love, we should define it. I think you can see that my definition of love is different from most people's.

Kisses,
Renee

March 2013
Dear Renee,

If Butler doesn't take ship to France to join the French Foreign Legion or if you aren't arrested or sued for spousal abuse, I think you have a marvelous plan. How long do you think "Boot Camp" will take?

You are on the right track when it concerns money. How else can I help other than encourage you?

I understand why it must be you who holds the whip. Surely, there is something I can do to help.

Be strong,
Heather

April 2013
Dear Heather,

I gave him a little break from his boot camp for the last couple of weeks so that we can both experience being in love again. It can't all be discipline or I'll lose him.

It's remarkable how tender we are to each other after a few weeks of intense training. During these times, I take special care to listen closely to all of his feelings. I reassure him repeatedly that even when things are hard, I still love him. Finally, I remind him of our promise to each other to make our dom/sub relationship real.

During this break, I reduced his discipline sessions but I never relax the rules. For example, I went to the movies last week with him. Butler loves movies and knows a lot about the history of film. He has a sophisticated appreciation for art and he is sensitive to nuance. I loved listening to him talk about the film because he frequently picks up on things that I miss. After seeing the movie, we sat comfortably in our living room with a glass of wine discussing it. The moment sounds like a typical vanilla couple. In some ways we are typical for two people in love. We are very affectionate and we are interested in each other's opinions and ideas. The difference is that as we talked I sat on the couch while Butler sat at my feet on the floor. He was following one of my many rules. He is not allowed on the furniture in the living room. (Actually, I think that was your idea!) The conversation was relaxed and loving but the rules remained in place. I can't always be standing over Butler with a riding crop. It's not how I want to relate to someone on a daily basis who is my life partner. However, to keep us both aware of our positions, we both continue to follow my rules.

During these gentler times, I also continue to require him to meditate in front of my picture each morning. In addition, I increase my practice of hypnosis. I spent a lot of time and trouble to learn hypnosis techniques. I think they are finally paying off. I can now put him into a deeply relaxed state in just a few minutes. While he is under, I insert my suggestions concerning his continued surrender. One can't make a subject of hypnosis do what he doesn't already want to do, but I know he wants this, so it's quite easy. Finally, I continue to insist that he play the music laced with subliminal messages suggesting his deeper submission while he sleeps. Even though I am not denying him or disciplining him during this gentler time, the work on his psyche continues. After a few weeks he will actually beg me to continue his training while not realizing that I have continued it all along.

Next month I think we'll be ready to finish with the goal I set for myself this year. I would ask you to help but I want him to know that the pressure is coming all from me. I'm nervous. I know I can accomplish my desire but I want him to want it also.

I've teased him a lot lately about his public role with me, but the truth is that I love him by my side in social situations. He's intelligent, funny, and obviously devoted to me. He's a terrific help with my fundraising. However, I don't want him to take his role by my side for granted.

I admit that I also wish I could introduce him as my slave but that day must to be put off until the world catches up with us. I have enjoyed treating him as an employee when we leave town. That has been tremendous fun and deeply satisfying. I don't know yet how to have both.

I like the additional twist you gave to my ideas when I'm keeping him chaste. I'll let you know how it goes.

Someday, I'd like to go somewhere warm with you and both of our subbies. Imagine how much fun we could have!

Renee

Butler's Journal
Banking
April 2013

The first part of the year was very difficult for me, but during the last month Ms. Renee and I had resumed our enthusiastic lovemaking. I was also deeply grateful to have a break from the chastity device. Of course, everything we did was to her rhythms and desires. I was simply grateful to be allowed to touch her again.

I love the times when things get easier for me but I know that we have not reached our goal of my complete surrender. After a while I start feeling anxious to begin again even though I know it will likely be hard. I never feel ready to continue for very long before Ms. Renee starts pushing me to the next level.

It started again on Sunday afternoon several weeks ago. I had performed adequately during the week, so I expected our usual bout of frenzied lovemaking after my weekly punishment. It was increasingly clear to me that normal foreplay for my mistress had become giving me a session with her cane. My discipline recently had been reduced to these weekly sessions but I could sense how excited she became when she whipped me.

Luckily, I only had five strokes coming to me for allowing dust to accumulate on her bookshelves in the living room. Five is about my limit to take with any stoicism. After that I'm reduced to twisting and yowling in discomfort. I work very hard to keep these sessions to a minimum number of strokes.

As usual, I was tied securely over the bench made for the purpose of my secure restraint. Ms. Renee, dressed in black heels with red soles and a black skirt with a red blouse, paced behind me as she chided me for poor performance as her housekeeper. Following a warm up of about fifty smacks with her paddle, Ms. Renee took the cane from its rack on the wall. I could hear it whistle as she tried a few practice swings. The anticipation of its kiss is almost as frightening as the actual contact.

"You have been an attentive slave this week but I did notice from your notebook that I gave you demerits for dust on the bookcase. You should know by now how to clean a room."

"Yes, Mistress," I stammered.

"Apparently you still need reminding."

With that, Ms. Renee gave me five vicious swipes across my buttocks. It felt like she was pouring lighted gasoline across my backsides. Before the last stroke had been delivered, I had broken out in a fearful sweat. She walked around to the front of me, running her fingers through my hair. She seemed on edge. I was ready for her to release me and allow me to begin pleasing her but something seemed to hold her back. She seemed unsatisfied.

I begged, "Please, Mistress, may we make love now?"

"No, I'm not ready," she replied irritably.

She stalked around me like a caged tiger. There was nothing else I could do. She was going to have her way no matter what I did. It would be better for me if I offered instead of allowing her irritation to grow.

I forced the words out. Each word seemed to weigh a thousand pounds on my tongue. "Would it please you to give me five more, Mistress?" I said in a thick voice.

She stopped pacing and held my head up to look into my eyes.

"Yes," she said in a quiet voice, "that's exactly what I need."

If I thought that offering such a gift would reduce the intensity of her strokes, I was in for a rude shock. They came with the same searing sting that the earlier strokes fell. Before they were over I was twisting ineffectually in my bonds trying to avoid them.

Afterward, we made love. For the next hour she rode my face and loins with her eyes closed oblivious to me while seeking her own pleasure. Finally, when she was satisfied she climbed on top of me and began twisting my nipples in her lacquered red nails.

Smiling down at me, her face partially obscured behind a curtain of dark hair, she whispered, "You pleased me tonight with your willingness to suffer for me, slave. We should always make ten strokes the new minimum. It's the least I need to give you to really get excited about whipping you."

I was too tormented and turned on with the need to orgasm to do anything but agree. It was a pattern of hers to wait until I was desperate for release before telling what new depths of submission she was about to lead me into.

She continued, "I appreciate your willingness to suffer for me; however, I think we have come as far as we can with physical discipline. I want to try something new. You're willing to go along with what I have planned aren't you, slave?" With that she gave my nipples another cruel twist.

"Yes, Mistress, anything!"

Still smiling, she cooed, "Oh, good slave. I love it when you are willing to please me. You want to come, don't you?"

I could only gasp.

Then she lowered her head a little closer to stare directly into my eyes. "Do you remember before we were married I talked about taking over your checking and savings accounts and you got a little nervous? I backed off because I don't like pushing you too far or too fast. I want you to want it too. Inviting me to whip you makes me think that are ready to go deeper but I want to be sure that you're ready. I care about you. I have a plan that will help you surrender your silly feelings of independence."

Again, she woke the nerve endings in my nipples.

Still smiling and speaking sweetly, she suggested, "I think you should really concentrate on how good this orgasm feels. It might be a while before you feel one again."

She squirmed around on top of me in an ecstatic motion. "I love you when you submit to me."

I was past all worry. My soul was in the present. I heard a quiet chuckle deep in her throat as she began moving in a way that gave me permission to release.

The next week unfolded as they usually do. I kept to the strict schedule that Ms. Renee has set out for me. Each day has its list of duties. Her house is divided into different sections so that each day I carefully clean a different set of rooms. In addition, there is laundry, errands, the yard, her car, and the garden. The proscribed list of chores does not limit my responsibilities. It is my special task to anticipate her needs. For example, if I drive her to a restaurant that is cold I'm expected to remember to bring her a sweater. If it rains I'm expected to magically produce an umbrella. It took me awhile to understand that her system was rigged for me to fail if she wished it.

She loves watching me stretch to please her. If I failed her expectations she asked for my notebook. After she had written ten in the notebook, it began to feel heavy in my pocket. It was a constant reminder to do everything possible to please her.

Ms. Renee loves pushing me as far as I can go and then a little farther. At times she has pushed until I showed signs of rebellion just so she could crush it out of me. Over the years I've had to rely on her superior knowledge of what I can endure.

That first week she was as gentle as I've seen her. She smiled and touched me affectionately more than usual. We kissed often each day.

Smiling sweetly, she also found enough wrong with my very best efforts to rack up over forty lashes. Again and again she asked for my notebook.

By Saturday I was a wreck. I was constantly checking everything. Had I watered her flowers? Was her bath the correct temperature? Was her car perfectly clean? Ms. Renee never wavers when it comes to my disciple. I was due thirty, with ten added to next week. I also knew that I wasn't going anywhere. I would say yes to her discipline no matter what the cost.

I was trembling as I helped her into her corset that evening. She seemed excited and energetic. Ms. Renee is shaped like a dominatrix from a dream. Poured into her leather corset she is enough to make me gasp and surrender without her discipline.

Once she was dressed, I crawled behind her to the attic space that has been remodeled over the years into a superbly well-equipped dungeon. I was already sweating. My mouth felt like it was stuffed with cotton. My fear was real. Thirty strokes from her cane would put me on the edge of my endurance. When she disciplines me, Ms. Renee puts me into a stock for a reason. It is simply impossible to stay still for that kind of pain.

I followed her up the stairs. Once there I draped myself over the bench and allowed Ms. Renee to secure the straps that keep me immobile. It only took a few seconds.

Now, I was at her mercy.

"Let's dispense with the usual warm up tonight, slave. You have thirty coming and I would hate it if you missed any work."

Again, I heard a brightness and happiness to her voice that made me shiver. I sensed her reaching for the cane and heard the first swish as she passed it through the air above me a few times. I heard her take out my notebook as she began reading in a cool, detached manner.

"Not opening the door for me in a timely manner, five. The skirt that I wanted to wear was not ironed properly, five. Forgetting to empty the trash in my office, that will be ten. I've had to remind you of that more than once. You almost disagreed with me in public. Ten. You know I expect you to be completely submissive in front of my friends. Not cleaning my hair brush, five.

Misplacing one of the towels. That was a towel for the downstairs bathroom, three. Missing one of my hand signals at lunch, two."

Then, in a more irritated voice, "That's forty, slave! You can't expect to stay my slave if you don't try harder to please me. Did you consider that I might like to have intercourse tonight? Now, I can hardly expect to reward you for such poor performance. What about my needs? I've warned you before about this! You should take me seriously! Will I be forced to find a lover because you can't be a better servant? How would that make you feel?"

I heard a roaring in my ears. I could feel my legs tremble. She had warned me before and I had failed her again.

She stopped and laughed out loud. "You really would be a slave then!"

She punctuated her laugh with a few swishes in the air with the cane.

Then, in a sterner voice, "I expect better service if you want to stay my lover."

She had not yet applied the cane but I was already on the edge of crumbling. Fear and humiliation crashed inside of my head, creating a whirlpool sapping my sense of self.

"You are lucky I'm still willing to train you. I could just kick you out. You'd still beg to come over and be my houseboy, wouldn't you?"

It was an appalling thought. I worked so hard for the honor of living with her.

"If I didn't do so much as kiss you, you'd still be here begging to be my slave. Well, wouldn't you?"

I knew the answer to the question even though my mind instinctively shied away from it. Trembling, I responded, "Yes, I would, Mistress. Please allow me to continue to live here."

"Then this is what it will cost you to stay."

With that she started applying the cane. The blows came as they always do, with just enough time between strokes for me to savor the pain of each lash. Before she was done I was begging for mercy. I had stopped using my safe word years ago. I never had used it unless something was happening that I thought she was unaware of, such as not being able to breathe. I knew she was aware of the shattering pain I was experiencing. I begged but I knew that there would be no mercy for me.

Finally, with a stifled moan, I accepted the last lash. I had grown accustomed to how a serious whipping stimulated her. I could feel the heat rising from her. She glided around me, touching me tenderly. I felt her nails raking my sweat-slick flanks. With a few deft turns of the clamps that held me immobile she released me. I immediately sank to my knees. She had stepped back across the room and into the thronelike chair we had positioned at one end of the dungeon. She was flushed and breathing rapidly. As I came nearer, she spread her legs, beckoning me to take my position. Every time I did this I was frightened all over again when I noticed how wet she became after whipping me. She always wanted immediate pleasure afterward.

I began licking her. I knew she was looking down at my buttocks and thighs. She could see the red stripes across my flesh. She could feel the heat as she placed her heels on my backside. Very soon I heard her moaning in joy.

Afterward, with my mistress relaxing from my administrations, I begged to be allowed a question.

Trying to sound as humble as possible I asked, "Is this your plan, Mistress? Will you keep making it impossible to earn a release until you think I'm ready for the next step? It's not necessary. I'm ready to give you what you want."

I had seen this pattern before of weekly punishments and denial. I knew I would eventually fold under the twin attacks. I didn't want to go through one of those times again if I could avoid it.

She cupped my face in her hands and said tenderly, "I know you think that what you've said is true but I know you're not really there yet." She kissed me tenderly. "But you will be, I promise."

She smiled mischievously. "And to answer your question, no, slave, that's only the first part of my plan. Since you asked so nicely, we might as well get started tonight. Go bring me the ice bucket and your chastity device."

I'm not normally required to be in forced chastity if we are routinely having sex, but when she denies me for any length of time she resorts to the CB6000. I brought the ice as she requested. Normally, she puts me in the tub in a few inches of icy water. This always makes me soft enough to cram myself into the device. I hate chastity. It's difficult to sleep and the device starts to rub painfully after only a few days.

This time was different. Instead of the matter-of-fact manner she normally uses when she locks me up, she was grinning wickedly.

"Put the bucket down and follow me."

She led me over to the metal hook that hangs from the ceiling. She quickly snapped handcuffs on me and brought them over my head. Of course I was still painfully hard after spending the last hour licking her. I try not to think of my pleasure when I know that I'm not going to orgasm, but it's impossible. She is so perfectly sexual and lovely.

Gently, she cupped her hand around my scrotum. I winced slightly. I never knew when she would painfully squeeze or when she meant me to feel pleasure. In a few seconds, it was obvious what she wanted me to feel. Using my own lubricant, she was slowly, luxuriously masturbating me. It felt wonderful. She brought herself close to kiss me. She was my goddess and she was taking her time to give me pleasure. Her skin was pressed warmly to my side. I could feel that wonderful pressure start to build.

"You're close, aren't you?" she whispered.

"Oh, yes," I murmured.

Suddenly her hand was gone. I gasped and arched my loins forward but there was nothing there. Finally, when she saw that she had timed it well, her hand came forward again but this time with just a tip of her finger she began making slow circles around the head of my penis. It was maddening. It stimulated me but there was not enough friction to finish. I tried again to push myself up into her hand but it only caused her to laugh quietly.

"You're so eager. Where was that eagerness when I wanted to take control of your checking account? No, I don't think you're ready."

I started to protest but was stopped when Ms. Renee gave me the signal for silence.

"No, you're not ready. I know you agreed to my request earlier but I don't feel your agreement was given with the right attitude. You should be grateful to me that I'm not willing to take you deeper than you are ready to go. I think we should work on your willingness."

Her hand reached out again and started slowly and gently stoking me once more. I have rarely tried to escape her punishment but I was tempted to try to escape that gentle touching that would lead me nowhere but frustration.

I was drenched in sweat when she finally stopped. She had brought me close twice more before stopping. She knew me too well. As soon as I was about to go over the edge, she stopped.

During this torture, she continued kissing me, telling me how much she loved having a slave to tease. She described in detail how her orgasm had felt and how much relief she experienced after I licked her.

"As your owner I get to come all over your face but you just get teased until I feel like you're truly interested in pleasing me."

Finally, when it was clear that I was only becoming sore from the continued stimulation, Ms. Renee brought over the ice and held it next to me until I was soft. I have always shuddered when she fastened my chastity device but this time it was like she was putting it around my neck. I doubted I would keep my sanity; I was so stimulated. It was only her matter-of-fact tone that brought me to my senses.

"Playtime is over. Prepare my bath, slave."

It was like I was awakening from another reality. I went through the rest of the evening in a daze. I bathed her and helped her into her gown. I brushed her hair as I always do each night. This night she seemed to glow with some inner light and strength that made me feel that she was indeed a goddess and I her lowly worshipful supplicant.

Finally, the evening was at an end. I was adjusting her covers. I usually sleep in a tiny room that she calls the servants quarters. She stopped me and motioned me closer. She kissed me tenderly and looked into my eyes.

"I love you," she said, her words a caress, "but you must learn to live only for my pleasure. Goodnight, slave."

***

The next week continued in the same manner. She made impossible demands and swiftly administered shocking punishments. I had survived times like that before, especially before moving in with her, but this was different because of what happened between the punishments. Every day she tied me securely and removed my chastity device to tease me mercilessly. Her own sexuality seemed to be in overdrive. She wanted endless orgasms that she described in great detail while offering a tender but wholly insincere sympathy that I was not allowed to come.

On Wednesday, Ms. Renee had me suspended in the attic dungeon with clothespins on my nipples for not sweeping the back porch. Of course I had swept it but it being very windy there was a constant addition of new debris every few minutes.

"I'm very disappointed in you, slave. I was thinking that you had suffered enough and had earned a release, but I can't do that now."

Then in a reasonable but irritated voice she added, "Why should I suffer because you can't do your chores? I like penetrative sex but I can't have it with you because you are still too interested in your own pleasure you'd probably lose control in the first minute. Weakling. You're very lucky I'm willing to try this. Actually, this looks like it might be fun. It's certainly bigger than you."

With that she placed a gag over my mouth that extended to a large dildo. I was unhooked and given the hand signal to lie on the floor. Ms. Renee was already excited from torturing me, so she directly placed herself over my face and pushed herself on to the dildo. I was utterly humiliated and helpless. I could feel internal psychological parts of me loosening and bending.

The week continued with Ms. Renee taking her pleasure whenever and however she pleased. The more crazed I became, the more she seemed to enjoy herself.

At the end of the following week I broke. At the time she was looking down at me, tapping the toe of her shoe over my chastity cage after a long session of cunnilingus. I suddenly heard myself moaning. The words came tumbling out of me unbidden. I heard myself begging her to please herself with anything that would make her happy concerning my finances. I told I would crawl to the bank if it would amuse her. I begged to be saddled and ridden there. I promised to wear my collar and be led there by a chain. Anything. Anything!

She stopped, and looking down at me, said sweetly, "Well, if it would make you happy then I guess I'm willing to give you what you want."

She went on, "I'm glad you finally feel free to give me everything. I don't feel it's appropriate to have your name besides my name as owners of property like your car title and your condo. It feels too much like we are equals."

"Oh yes," I begged. "Please, please!"

I was filled with relief and gratitude. I couldn't imagine why I had felt reluctant to give myself completely to this amazing woman. I was lucky that she had accepted my meager offerings. I was grateful that she continued to want to keep me as her slave. I knew that what financial arrangements I had made before our marriage, such as adding her as co-owner to my house, car, and bank accounts, were totally inadequate. I knew I should not just add her name but I had to take my name off all of my property. I needed to surrender everything.

I knelt to begin kissing the tips of her toes peeking out of her open-toed pumps. I could sense that she was pleased with me.

I was filled with relief until I heard her gently remind me, "Have you forgotten what day it is? Silly slave, this is Friday."

I started moaning again.

She continued, "Your bank is closed tomorrow. We also can't visit the title office or the lawyer's office until Monday. You should have told me all of this yesterday. Now, we'll have to wait. This should be a lesson to you to be more eager to give me whatever I want. Oh, there's no reason to cry, sweetie. I'll keep you in the right frame of mind until we get this all done. I promise."

May 2013
Dear Renee,

I just found your message. Did he do it? If so, you are my new hero. Damn, woman, if you were successful you should get some kind of medal or a statue in the park.

Of course I'll meet you for lunch. I can't wait to hear about it.

If you were successful, put him in his chauffeur uniform and have him stand outside and wait for us next to the car. I like the idea of leaving him hungry and standing while we eat lunch. I can't wait to hear what happened.

Café Society, noon?

Heather

Butler's Journal
Banking Completed
May 2013

I will always remember the day when she marched me into my bank and announced to a puzzled and slightly nervous bank clerk that my money now belonged solely to her. The morning had started at her lawyer's office to begin the process of turning over the ownership of my condo. A visit to the Department of Motor Vehicles took care of my car. My condo was being used as rental property but the rent check still came in my name. We changed that to her name.

I still shudder when I remember the state of mind she had brought me to before she would allow me to give her complete control of the remainder of my finances. Something in me had finally broken. Tearfully, I had begged her to ride me in with a whip and spurs if it had pleased her to do so. On that day all resistance to her will had been torn from me. Choosing a less theatrical approach, she dressed in a tight silk skirt, jacket, and elegant black heels.

She sat in the small, spare bank office impatiently tapping her foot as the nervous bank clerk filled out the required documents. This was the fourth office we had visited. I had been instructed to say as little as possible. In public, Ms. Renee has taught me to keep my head lowered when in the presence of other women who are not in our social circle. I'm never to look a woman in the eyes. She also requires me to use all possible honorifics when addressing other women. With most women I use ma'am. In this case I noticed that the young woman helping was unmarried so I used miss.

The clerk cautioned me, "This is a very unusual request. You understand that once you sign these papers you will no longer have access to your money?"

"Yes, Ms. Crenshaw," I quietly replied, dipping my head in deference.

Ms. Renee chuckled. "It's really my idea. I don't think men can be trusted with money of their own. He should only be concerned with pleasing me. I will make his financial decisions and every other decision for him from now on. Isn't that right?"

Again, I bowed my head slightly. "Yes, Ms. Renee."

I felt myself tremble. I was not afraid of what was happening so much as that there might be some bureaucratic hitch that prevented Ms. Renee from achieving her desire instantly. I couldn't imagine going home with this mission postponed for another day.

The interview continued with a series of questions, most of them answered by Ms. Renee. Apparently, it's not illegal to turn over your account to someone else. By the time we were done, Ms. Crenshaw was no longer bothering to speak to me at all. She knew that the power in the relationship belonged to Ms. Renee. Finally, she was ready to give Ms. Renee a password for the safety deposit box. Ms. Renee lifted her hand suddenly to stop her.

"Butler, wait by the car for me. The password is no longer any of your business."

"Yes, ma'am," I replied, once again dipping my head.

I glanced up at Ms. Crenshaw as I left. I didn't know what I would see. Would she feel pity or shock or worry? She barely looked at me. She dismissed me without a glance. Her focus was entirely on Ms. Renee. How could I disagree with her choice? I had rarely seen my mistress look more beautiful. She looked imperious as she adjusted the collar of her suit. I wanted to stay but I had my orders. I quietly stepped outside the office to wait at Ms. Renee's car door.

She was gone longer than I anticipated. This often happened when I was with my mistress. Other women want to befriend her. I often waited long periods as she chatted with a woman whom she has intrigued.

Standing there I realized that I had a wallet in my pocket but not one dollar in it. I was now totally dependent on my mistress for everything. My paycheck would continue to be deposited but I would have no more control over it than I would the weather. I felt lightheaded. I was frightened but not unhappy. I felt free. My worries had been reduced to only one concern: my mistress. Everything else dwindled and paled in comparison.

Finally, Ms. Renee stepped outside and allowed me to open her door. She looked radiant. I got behind the wheel and waited for instructions.

"Café Society," she said cheerfully.

I drove slowly as if she were fragile cargo. I didn't know what would happen next. I only knew that I would not be in control of it.

At the restaurant, Ms. Renee stood for a second in the car door that I had hurriedly opened. She glanced in my eyes and coolly told me to wait by the car. With another smile, she turned and walked away.

I was not told to wait in the car, so I assumed I should stand beside my car door. As I stood there, I heard the sounds of heels striking the pavement. I turned to see Heather striding confidently up the sidewalk. As usual I felt a wave of mistrust and fear as she approached. She actually stopped and looked at me standing beside the car.

"Interesting day, Butler?" she smirked.

She rarely speaks to me or acknowledges my presence, so I knew in an instance that she was fully informed of what had just happened. It was humiliating to see her and know that I had been lowered to a new level in her eyes. She only has respect for men with money. Even with money, she feels little respect, as two ex-husbands would quickly testify.

The parking lot faces the restaurant, so I was able to see the two women meet in the front window as they were shown to Ms. Renee's favorite table. It was clear that Heather was jubilant as she greeted my mistress. She hugged her and kissed her cheek. Just as she did so, I felt her glance of victorious scorn over Ms. Renee's shoulder.

The two women sat for an extended lunch. I stood the entire time watching them through the window. I had not eaten yet. My legs were raw from Ms. Renee's cane. I could feel my wool pants sticking to the fabric where my skin had been broken over the weekend. My chastity belt was itching so badly I was afraid I would go mad. I was hungry. There is a coffee shop across the street from Café Society. I had plenty of time to grab a sandwich while they enjoyed their lunch but I had no money. Once again the truth of my position was made plain. I was a servant.

Eventually, the lunch ended. Ms. Renee stepped out arm in arm with Ms. Heather. They affectionately kissed cheeks and Ms. Heather strutted by me with a look that went through me as if I was beneath her notice.

Ms. Renee, however, smiled at me when I handed her into the car and told me to take her home. We live only a short drive from the restaurant. I wanted to pepper her with a thousand questions about the future or how she felt but I knew to remain silent. This would only happen once in our lives. It was not my place to speak.

We finally arrived inside our home, or more accurately, Ms. Renee's home. I helped her off with her jacket.

"Meet me upstairs," she suggested.

This I knew was code for me to strip off my clothes and meet her on my knees in her attic dungeon. I waited there for what seemed an hour. I was trembling again. I seemed to do that a lot lately. It had been the most difficult month I had ever experienced with Ms. Renee. It seemed that in just a few short weeks everything had again changed. I had been beaten so often it seemed natural for me to kneel contemplating the skin on the front of my thighs. They were adorned with various layers of stripes that had been seared there by Ms. Renee's crop over the last few weeks. The stripes were turning rainbow colors as they healed. I hesitated to look in the mirror at my backside. Who was that in the mirror? My reflection disoriented me. How far had we gone?

I heard the click of Ms. Renee's heels as she ascended. Without volition, a moan escaped me. I waited for something but I did not know what. I had done everything she wanted. In fact, I eventually had begged to do everything she wanted. Now, she would tell me what was to come next. There it was again, the trembling. I focused on her footsteps and willed myself to stop.

Ms. Renee was a vision of every dominant dream I had ever imagined. She was dressed in an outfit I saw only rarely. It was the leather cat suit that I often longed for but feared because when she wore it there was usually a price to pay. She approached and stood over me with her hands on her hips swaying subtly from side to side, relishing my desire.

Finally, she spoke. "You did it. You gave me control."

"Yes, Mistress."

She approached and cradled my face in her hand. "I believe you wanted to do it . . . finally. What kind of man would do such a thing?"

I heard a sneer in her voice that surprised me.

"Your slave mistress," I replied.

"Yes, be still," she said icily. "Now you are only a slave." With that she slapped me hard against my face. "Only a man who was born to be a slave would do such a thing." Again her hand flashed hard against my face.

"I have no respect for you as a man anymore. I will use you anyway I see fit from now on. I will use you until I tire of you."

Again I felt her hand. I had done everything and still she was not pleased! I had no idea tears were so close to the surface but as her hand smacked against my face I realized that the leather glove would soon be slapping against wet skin.

She continued to berate me. She punctuated each comment by her gloved hand. My training kept me frozen but my heart was breaking. She continued to degrade me for doing exactly what she had told me to do. How could this be? I felt tears in my eyes now. What did this woman want? I was caught in a terrible vortex that would suck my soul from me. I had given everything. I would do anything.

"Yes, Mistress, do what you want with me! I am yours!" I cried.

Suddenly, I saw her pause. Several seconds went by. Was there tenderness in her expression? She looked down at me and slowly smiled. I looked up into the face of beauty.

"Anything? Then, I think you are ready."

I waited.

She smiled again, undid the clasp from the chain around her neck, and handed me the key to my chastity belt. In a warm voice she said, "Come downstairs and make love to me."

I stared at the key that I had longed for weeks to see. It felt hot and heavy in my hand. Awkwardly, I slipped it into the lock and felt the wonderful sensation of my first erection in weeks. I saw her slinking out of the room glancing over her shoulder with a challenging look. I hungrily followed her to her bed.

Downstairs in her bed we tore at each other. We had never known such passion. We both cried out again and again. I felt our love would grow until it filled the house. How could there be strife in a world when there was so much love? It seemed so simple. All a man had to do was give up everything to the woman he loved.

Afterward, I dreamed of flying.

May 3013
Dear Renee,

I admit I wanted to make love to you right on the table at the restaurant last week. Seeing Butler standing obediently next to your car with that torn expression on his face was so fucking hot. I wanted to rub it in.

Have I told you that you are my hero? Someone should write a headline article about you. You should be famous. The only thing wrong is that you can't tell everyone what you've accomplished. Well, maybe someday.

You have done the right thing. Once one starts talking about money one starts talking about real power. Domination cannot be real if he still controls his own money. I needed you years ago when I was married. Heck, I might still be married to the last one if I had put some of your ideas into practice.

I have to admit that I've been wrong about how long your relationship with Butler has lasted and how far you've been able to bring him. I think you might be a witch.

You are my hero.
Heather

Dear Heather,

I never could have done it without your help. You have always been there rooting for me. Also, as I've been trying to show you, part of the credit goes to Butler. His love and bravery make our life possible. He trusts me. Maybe too much!

It's all about love. I have been wondering about you. I didn't mean to pry during our last lunch. I know you have Suzy but it seems you are alone too much.

Worried about you,

Renee

Dear Renee,

I didn't feel you were prying. I did go out with the older guy who has been pursuing me. He's intelligent and rich but so full of himself I don't think he heard a word I said all evening. Somehow Suzy found out about my date with him. It caused quite a little revolution with her. Apparently, she hated the idea of me dating a man.

I'm very fond of her but life is short. Why should I be bound by the rules of someone who I'm supposed to be dominating? I love the sex with her but I don't want to be bound to the one I tie up.

Relationships are complicated.

I'm not telling Suzy what I am doing with my free time until I can get her to agree to let me be myself.

You mentioned that you were curious about my choice of dates. You called them old rich guys or pretty young ones. I date older and younger men because I find both of those ages biddable. I don't date men my own age because they want to get to know me. Shudders! I'm not what you would call an open person. Intimacy. I shy away from even the word.

You complained to me the last time we were together that I was less open to you than you needed me to be. What can I say? It's hard to open doors when I can't find the handle. You've always told me that you had a normal, loving childhood. Your childhood gives lie to the idea that people involved in the S&M scene are somehow damaged.

I'm glad for your nurturing family but mine was not so happy. You know that I suffered a period of molestation from a stepfather. I don't feel comfortable talking about it. All it seems to do is to dredge up old hurts. I'm not as healthy as you, but my relationship with you has been healing. I'm trying to combine my dominant inclinations with a desire for a loving relationship. Watching you has given me hope. I'm not there yet. Until then, the world will have to take me as I am.

I've seen how you discipline Butler, so I doubt he could complain about anything you might do but I've never seen you date anyone else. I see how men and women respond to you. Is it your secret marriage? Have you found it constraining?

While we are sharing intimate secrets, I admit to being curious about your sex life when I'm not there. I don't mean to be nosy. Feel free to tell me to fuck off.

Heather

PS

Now that you have his money, what's next?

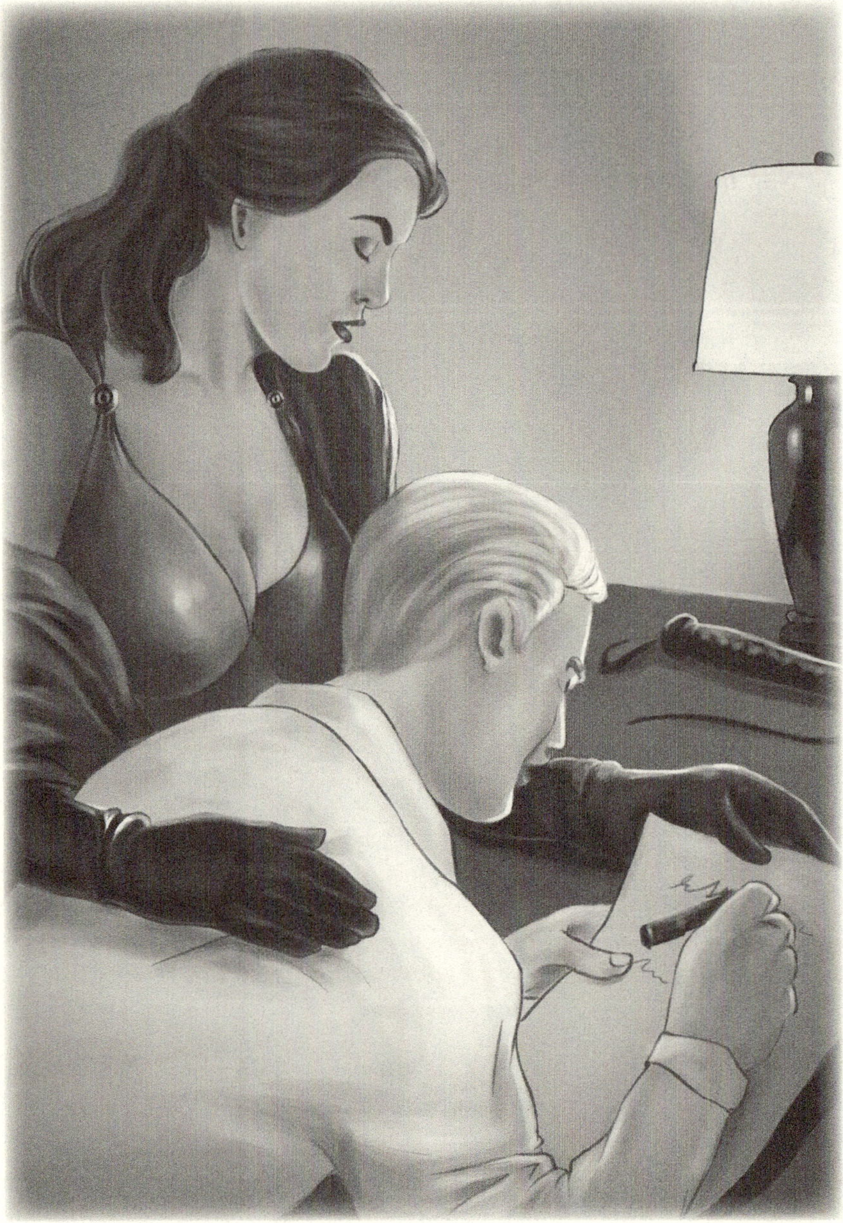

Chapter Eight

SEXUALITY

June 2013
Dear Heather,

I accept you. I didn't mean to critique your dating habits. I'm simply concerned for you.

I appreciate your delicacy about asking about my dating life. I usually don't encourage such questions. Nevertheless, with you, I'm glad to share everything. Other than you, I haven't been dating anyone.

It's not the marriage that keeps me monogamous! Who has the time for extracurricular activities? I have my job, this election, my friends, and my family. If I had more time, I don't know what my choices might be. Also, I don't have much anonymity in this town. Gossip travels quickly. With my job, I'm too much a public person. Finally, I have Butler's training, which I find completely absorbing.

What's next with Butler? I like to think that I have plans within plans. It is ironic that he entered into an S&M relationship with me because he wanted a sexual thrill when his relationship with me has necessarily led to his frequently being teased and denied. Such is the life of a slave. At least he hasn't found life with me boring.

After taking control of his money, his social life, and his time, I have extended my control to his sexuality. For example, I no longer allow him an orgasm without first disciplining and humbling him. I want him to associate my discipline with sexual pleasure. I'm not even sure if he is still able to get an erection unless I first hurt and humiliate him.

Of course, I'm controlling his orgasms with a chastity device a lot of the time. Increasing his denial elevates his desire for me. Every woman should have the experience of hearing a man break down and cry simply because he desires her. I feel strongly that I deserve it.

I've already announced to all of my kinky girlfriends that he wears a locked chastity device. While it may humiliate him, it made me a hero in the eyes of my special female friends. These women now think of him as a eunuch. I love seeing them tease him and make fun of him. I don't see how they could resist! If he ever feels a slight stirring in his loins for another woman I feel safe that his chastity belt will instantly punish those thoughts.

With him in a cage every woman in the world instantly became my ally. One day I will tell all of his male friends about his chastity. Some of them will scorn him but other, better men, will feel jealous.

Of the chastity devices I've tried I liked the Dream Lover the best because it allows me to administer electric shocks via my cell phone. Having the ability to spy on him by having cameras strategically placed in the house and punishing his genitals when I think he is shirking his duties has increased his awareness of his slavery. I have been deliciously cruel.

He frequently pleases me but his releases have been earned and humbling. Eventually, he will think of sex as the privilege of giving me an orgasm. My pleasure will be his. When this happens I know we will be on the right path. I love denying him while luxuriating in the intensity of his desire for me.

Chastity, humiliation, and denial are essential to achieve my goal. Of course I never plan on denying myself. Wickedly, I also use a penis extender that fits over his penis to increase my pleasure but denies him any sensation during coitus. I love humiliating him by telling him that his penis is too small while we have sex. I want him to feel inadequate. I can only imagine what my humiliation of his manhood is doing to his male pride, but the idea makes me giddy. It's prefect because he should receive all feelings of worth solely from his willingness to please and obey me.

I have discovered that there is an amazing freedom in knowing at the onset of a sexual encounter that I will be the only one having an orgasm. My orgasms are often more intense at those special times. I suspect that in some ways it also frees him in that he can forget about himself to concentrate solely on me.

Humiliating him is why I take him from behind with a strap-on dildo. How can Butler possibly feel macho when I'm pegging him? I want him to feel violated and powerless. I have a store of evil things I say to him while I rape his ass. I want him to feel reduced from a person to my sexual plaything.

In addition, there is something about invading his body that leads to invading his soul. I have already experimented with denying him an orgasm long enough that it was easy to stimulate his prostate digitally through his anus. I did this for the first time right after you spent a month with us. Having him on his hands and knees, watching his semen dribbling out of him through the bars of his chastity cage without the usual explosion of pleasure gave me a deep, happy feeling of accomplishment. At that moment, he knew that I was in complete control. I intend to do more of that.

I love that I am his only source of sexual gratification. I may at times allow another woman to punish him, but I doubt I will ever allow him to touch another woman intimately. I tingle all over when I think that I will be the last woman he will ever have the privilege of touching. Ever! The idea that I frequently deny him my touch when he has suffered so much for it sends a rush of pleasure through me.

Even when I am making him suffer I know enough about him to know that every denial, every humiliation, and every challenge I set up for him only turns him on. He wants me more because of my domination of him, not less. That is the way a submissive man's mind works. We are very lucky to have found each other. It makes me believe that there really might be a dark goddess who is working through dominant women for change in the world!

Much love,
Renee

June 2013
Dear Renee,

Your ideas are in line with mine, at least concerning male orgasm. Allow a man an orgasm and he'll instantly forget his manners. I love dangling a man on a string and denying him sex. I drove my first husband crazy. I see now what I also needed was a plan.

I have different problems with Suzy, as you well know. Alas, there is no effective device that can prevent female orgasm for very long. I often deny her after she performs cunnilingus on me by giving her a chore or putting her in bondage. I love seeing her writhe with need. I guess we are both built to enjoy a slave's discomfort. Lucky us.

How are you going to control your slave's sexuality other than removing the offending parts? Hmmm, the more I think about it, the better the idea sounds.

It's one way for a woman to rule a man.

Heather

July 2013
Dear Heather,

Now who's talking about fantasy? You are scary.

I am already leading a very different life from what Butler leads. After all, I am trying to prove to both of us that I am a superior woman and he is only my male slave.

One thing I've done is that I've started keeping more secrets from him. What better way to cement the ideal of my superiority than making him constantly aware of the difference between us?

Teasing him that he does not know every detail of my private life has only increased his desire for me. Most married women allow a strategic weapon in their arsenal to diminish by being too open. I have regained my aura of mystery that makes most men wild with passion for a woman when she is unknowable and possibly unobtainable. I don't have many secrets, but he doesn't know that. If this sounds like game playing, that's because it is. And it's a game I'm winning.

Unlike his very controlled sexuality, I have allowed myself to be promiscuous with you, and one day, with other men. When I go out with you, I always humiliate him about my sexual freedom and his slavery.

In fact, his opportunity to touch me depends on his being the perfect butler, maid, and gardener. Consequently, he has become even more of an expert at all of his domestic duties. If he is my slave, why would I allow him to touch me if he isn't willing to serve to the best of his ability? Only good service should be rewarded. Thus, when I briefly take another lover, I make it his fault. Why should I do without sex because he can't serve me properly? I love blaming him for my own adventurous spirit. His response has been to redouble his efforts to please me. Ha! Perfect.

For example, I loved making him prepare me for my dates with you. I make him iron my clothes, manicure my nails, bathe me, and dress me, all the while knowing that none of his careful preparation was for his benefit.

Cuckolding him with a woman has been fairly easy for him but I don't plan to limit my affairs to women. It is his job to surrender to my desires. When the time is ripe I will choose a man to use for his complete humiliation. I see it as my sacred responsibility to carefully use that moment to move him to a deeper surrender.

One day, I see myself standing in my dressing room after his careful preparations to ready me for a date and asking, "I know you are only a slave, but do you think the man who is taking me out tonight will like this dress?"

After humiliating him, I plan on squeezing his slave cock into the smallest chastity cage I can find. I will remind him in the most demeaning manner possible that only a man born to be a slave would humble himself to such an extent. I want him to burn for me.

I believe that a carefully calculated dose of jealously, denial, and humiliation comprise the perfect potion to transform him into a more surrendered servant. I know that men desire what they can't have. Therefore, I need to be occasionally unobtainable. Also, it's very important for him to see that I have sexual power that exists completely independent of our relationship. Oh, how I want to make him cry at that moment!

While I'm gone enjoying myself, I want him to be either chained in his cage or very busy doing some hopelessly dull domestic task. I want him suffering or working while I enjoy sexual pleasure. I want it to hurt his feelings. I want him to feel reduced. Maybe I'll purchase an especially uncomfortable cock cage with sharp spikes. I'll make him wear it each time I cuckold him.

My knees tremble at the thought of enjoying sex with a new lover while he stays at home in emotional, psychological, and physical torment. I'm certain I will enjoy an incredible orgasm, made more intense by the knowledge of his suffering. What a unique experience that will be! In that perfect moment, at last, I will feel that I truly own a slave.

To infuse him with the sense of utter subjugation that I he know he craves, I would invent imaginary lovers. I would go out in the evening only to tease him about someone who didn't even exist if I thought it would move us both forward to a deeper level of dominance and submission. I recall that according to our agreement it is perfectly within the rules to lie to him if it leads to his deeper surrender. I can let my imagination run wild!

One might see my harsh treatment of him as solely the fulfillment of my own selfish sadistic desires. This is not true. While I admit to a deep satisfaction in dominating him in this fashion, I'm also concerned that he experiences every sensation that he was looking for when he offered his submission. He wanted to be removed from his mundane world and transported to a more exciting life that left him raw with feeling. I want to give him that. I can't do any of this until I'm certain that my actions will bind him tighter to me. Until we are both ready, my plans must remain a dream. However, I know the direction I want to take. I plan on moving confidently forward until I reach my goal.

I have been reluctant to think about lending him or renting him to one of my dominant girlfriends other than you. I don't like the idea of him serving just anyone. However, I think keeping him securely locked in a chastity cage might alter my feelings about this. After all, what kind of trouble can he get in? He would serve and suffer knowing that there could be no reward for him other than being useful. I know it will make him feel like mere property. I think that might be a useful feeling to inculcate in him.

I want to change his view of all women. He should see them not as possible sex objects but as natural allies of mine in leading him to complete submission.

I also like the idea of him, while locked in his chastity cage, being babysat by a woman I trust while I am out of town. I never want him to have a break from being my slave. I have a fantasy that I develop a relationship with such a woman. She has no interest in him because she's in love with me. She becomes very strict with him to impress me and increase his usefulness to me.

Selfishly, she also wants to reduce him in my eyes to the extent that I no longer see him as someone I can be romantically attached to because of his lowly status as a servant.

I see his fear and helplessness increase as she crushes him. I sense her desire for me rise as she removes him as a competitor for my attention. Feeling his suffering and envy while she draws closer to me creates a tight triangle of sexual tension between the three of us. Does any of this sound familiar?

I hope that answers your questions about my view of marriage. Would you like to help?

Renee
July 2013

Dear Renee,

Would I like to help? Would I like to fucking help? Do you really feel you need to ask? Where and when can we start! Until I received this e-mail I thought I had lost you while you concentrated solely on your new marriage.
Of course I will help.
There is something that still bothers me. I'm not interested on putting on any kind of a show for him. What I liked about your honeymoon is that he was physically not there. We banished him to the servant's quarters. You used it as a tool to teach him his place but I liked it because he was not underfoot all the time.
When I kiss you it's for us or me but definitely not for him. I've learned to appreciate Butler in ways I never thought I would but I'm not interested in giving him a thrill by allowing him to watch us.
With that in mind, can I fit in with your plans?

Much love,
Heather

July 2013
Dear Heather,

I appreciate your honesty. You are right. I cannot be unaware that he is present, but anything that passes between us should be for us and us alone.

This next part of my plan may tell you how strongly I feel about us while also explaining what I intend for him.

At the beginning of our relationship, he gave me permission to ignore the rules of morality when I thought it was necessary to bring him into complete submission. One day I may want to take our sexual play to a completely different level. For a while I might want to make him sexless. I know that like most men he secretly considers himself a bit of a stud. I may want to strip him of that feeling. Simply keeping him locked in chastity won't accomplish this goal. He will always think that he could be capable as a man if I choose to unlock him. What I dream of doing to him pushes the edge of moral or safe practice. However, we both wanted to test the limits of what is possible in a dom/sub relationship. At least for a while, I want him to stop thinking of himself as a virile potent man. I want to take away something very precious to him so that I can return it later in my own way.

To accomplish this, I may secretly feed him hormones to the point that they make him impotent. Imagine his dismay when I unlock him and offer him sex but he fails to get an erection. Think of how desperate he will become! Of course, I will mock him and belittle his feeble efforts to maintain an erection. Then, I will lock him back up and tell him to accept that he has become merely my housekeeper and butler since he is no longer a man.

Oh, when I think of that moment my heart races! For a while he really will be my butler and only my butler. He will have to learn to serve simply for the honor of serving me. He will feel inadequate but lucky to be allowed to stay. I'm not interested in feminizing him. I want him male. However, I want him a broken, obedient, and humble male.

I have tried very hard not to care about his sexual excitement except in the context of making him more submissive.

I think you might feel more comfortable about a chemically neutered male in the house. What do you think? Would it feel like "putting on a show" if you knew that it was impossible for him to be physically turned on watching us? What if any feelings of arousal he experienced would only serve to remind him of his inadequacy? Would it release a hidden exhibitionist in you if you knew that watching us only tormented him and humbled him into a deeper surrender?

Curious,
Renee

July 2013
Dear Renee,

Now I know you are going to jail. Jeepers, girlfriend! You'd really screw with his hormones? Are there permanent problems with that? OK, I admit the idea is exciting but I would want a signed consent first.

Let's assume that we won't get in trouble. My first thought was that I still don't want to put on a show for any man. However, when I stopped to think about his suffering and what it would do to him, I started getting flooded with exciting ideas. Normally, a man watching me serves only to irritate me, but this would be completely different. The more he watched, the more it would hurt. Interesting.

I think you have done something I would have said was impossible. You actually thought of something kinky that I would enjoy that I have never even thought of before! Once again, you opened a door for me that I didn't know existed. I like you a lot right now.

Nothing like this would work on a woman. Women don't fear losing their femaleness. Men are so fragile. That's why we can enslave them. I have to think of something special for Suzy.

Heather

July 2013
Dear Heather,

Yes, Suzy will require a totally different kind of breaking. I think we should consider emphasizing your ownership of her. Have you considered lending her to me? It might make her feel more like your property if you lent her to another dominant woman. I could be talked into having her for the weekend if you bent my arm. OK, maybe it wouldn't take much bending. I'd do it as a favor for a friend because I'm so giving. Ha!

You'll be interested in this plan for Butler. There is a second part of chemically taking away his manhood. Consider what cuckolding him with another man would do to him while he is neutered. Imagine his utter humiliation! At least for a while I'd like to crush that macho streak in his nature. It's almost too delicious to think about. Later, I could back off of the hormones and decide in what scenario I would like him to physically regain the ability to maintain an erection. The possibilities are endless and inviting. Should I ever tell him what I had done to him?

Maybe I'll rethink this entire plan and actually tell him that I am chemically neutering him. I get weak in the knees imagining the moment when I tell him that I'm no longer interested in being his lover but I want him to stay my slave. Will my training hold? Will he surrender to my will? What would happen to him psychologically if he accepts my demand? That scenario also has many delightful sensations I would like to experience. Every option sounds like an incredible adventure.

Maybe I'll simply administer a placebo but tell him that they are hormones. I wonder, will he lose his ability to maintain an erection on a placebo? As his mistress, the truth is simply a tool. I'll have to wait and see what feels right to me. However, no matter what I do I want him to realize that his sexuality belongs to me!

I sincerely believe that my slave at some point will be physically impotent with other women even without hormonal alteration. He will treat other women with respect but he will deeply realize to whom he belongs.

Do you have any ideas along these lines?

I have no doubt that I will eventually return his sex drive to him. There is nothing like feeling his hot desire for me. Imagine what his first taste of sex will be like after his denial. Ha! He'll think I invented sex. Also, he will view his ability to have sex as a sacred gift from his loving mistress. He'll also remember that it can be taken from him again if he doesn't focus it completely on me. Perfect!

Disciplining him, blackmailing him, humbling him, stripping him of his manhood, and controlling his money are not what S&M aficionados talk about when they talk about consensual play. They are usually only talking about dress-up and erotic spankings. In contrast, the things he and I do will psychologically change him and how he thinks of himself. I realize that I am taking on a serious responsibility by dominating him to such an extent. I'm eager to do it because I care enough to want our life together to be real.

It is true that I hope that what happens between you and me helps to dive him deeper into submission, but what is ours is ours alone. You matter to me. I believe when he sees us together it only serves to reinforce his place as a servant.

I need you to get onboard with me about this. Let's continue to help each other with our slaves as we move ever closer.

Renee
July 2013

Dear Renee

I have discovered that Butler and I have something in common. Neither one of us can say no to you. Of course, I'll help. I already feel a part of your life.

I'll think about lending Suzy to you. It might be just what she needs. Maybe we should swap slaves for the weekend?

I'm ready to experiment with new sensations.

Heather

Butler's Journal
A Long Weekend
September 2013

If I had been paying more attention last Friday to my surroundings, I would have ducked behind a parked car. But as it was, I bumped into Ms. Renee's friend Ms. Heather while walking in a parking lot of a shopping mall. She was carrying several packages.

The instant she saw me, she snapped, "Come here!"

Drawing a step closer, I automatically held up my arms for her to unload the packages she was carrying. Following her was a well-dressed younger woman. After heaping my arms with packages, she continued her march to her car, followed by her young companion.

Ms. Heather owns a high-end shoe store close by. I could hear her offer several suggestions about the store's displays. When she got to her car, she resumed talking to who I now assumed was one of her employees. I continued to stand there silently for several minutes holding her packages. Occasionally, the employee would surreptitiously glance my way. I was becoming nervous about the time because I was due to pick up my mistress shortly. However, Ms. Heather continued to ignore me while she talked to her employee. I was never introduced.

I must have looked impatient, because her employee interrupted Ms. Heather by suggesting, "Why don't you unlock your car? I'm sure your friend might want to put your boxes down."

Ms. Heather turned to me in an angry flash.

"Did you say anything?" she spat.

"No, ma'am," I replied in what I hoped was a humble tone.

Ms. Heather held my gaze for another second, then turned and unhurriedly finished her conversation. After receiving several more instructions, her employee turned and mumbled to me an awkward, "Nice to meet you." She continued walking back, glancing back at her boss, and I assume, wondering who I was.

As soon as she was out of earshot, Ms. Heather turned to me and asked, "What were you doing back there tapping your foot impatiently or rolling your eyes?"

"No, ma'am, I'm sorry. Nothing, but I do have to pick up my mistress."

"Wait!" she said.

Instantly, she pulled out her phone and speed dialed Ms. Renee. After a few pleasantries, Ms. Heather said, "He's here and he knows he's late. Don't allow him to blame this on me. He was very rude in front of one of my employees and I was forced to have a conversation with him about the importance of good manners." She smiled sweetly at me while she said this.

As the conversation progressed, Ms. Heather wandered over to the other side of her car and turned away so I could not hear what she was saying. After a few exchanged sentences, I heard her brassy bark of a laugh. She was dressed as always in clothes that cost more than I made in a month. Ms. Heather looks like she was born rich but the truth is that she married well twice. There always seems to be a discordant note between how she looks and how she sounds. She looked like an educated businesswoman but I knew the cruder and rougher side to her. I heard her making kissing sounds on the phone.

She slipped her phone back into her purse and shot me a cold look. Her voice sneered, "Why the fuck are you still here? You're late!"

"Yes, Ms. Heather," I offered as I beat a hurried retreat.

My experience with Ms. Heather has all been unpleasant. I could never understand why my mistress found her interesting or why of all the women she knew it was Ms. Heather that she allowed to see the true nature of our relationship. It could simply be that it was the fact that anything Ms. Heather found out about us would not be shocking to her. Maybe my mistress simply needed someone she could tell the details of our life. I only wished it was someone other than her.

When I arrived to pick up Ms. Renee, I scurried around the car to open the door for her.

As she slid in she remarked, "You're late."

I knew a set up when I saw one, so I was careful to say nothing. As I pulled out of the drive, Ms. Renee asked for my notebook. I handed it to her and listened as she jotted down a note about my lateness and included the appropriate number that she would add to my punishment strokes on Sunday. I was deeply curious but knew not to look while I was driving.

After arriving home, I could not believe that she had added ten strokes. She knew it was not my fault. I vowed to say nothing knowing the number would only be increased if I tried to rebel.

Thirty-six hours later I was still trying to come to grips with the unfairness of it. I was lying over the bench in the attic. I had received the five I had "justly" earned by not vacuuming the floor of her car and the additional ten Ms. Heather's complaints had added. It was painful.

I was feeling hurt and frustrated but I had tried very hard to hide it. Of course my mistress could not be fooled.

"I know you are angry about the ten you just received," Ms. Renee stated, reading my mind.

"I'm trying hard not to be mad, Mistress."

"Yes, I can tell that or I would have given you twenty. Tell me why you are angry."

Honesty is a requirement in our relationship. She may lie but I must always tell the truth.

I replied, "It's hard to understand the point of working hard to avoid punishment if I am going to be punished no matter what I do."

She didn't answer. She calmly stepped back and gave me five more. I was shocked. I had done nothing but tell the truth. Instead of being merely physically hurt, this hurt my feelings. It was more than I could bear. I began twisting in the straps, trying instinctively to free myself.

"I'll answer your question, slave. Be still!"

She gave me another lash. I forced myself to stop struggling.

"There are two reasons. First, you work hard so I don't beat you even more! You only think you are at the limit of your pain threshold. You could take more if I thought you were ready for it. I could have given you twenty-five just for the car floor but I only gave you five. Am I wrong? Do you think you are ready to accept more?"

I felt I was at my limits. I was desperate. "No, please, mistress," I begged.

"Also, there is another reason. Did you ever think that I beat you for my own needs? Maybe you didn't earn that extra ten but maybe I needed to give it to you! This is not all about you! Do you ever think about anyone but yourself?"

I was utterly stumped. This was the one reason that I could not have foreseen nor could I answer. The idea that she needed this spoke deeply about our relationship. I saw my life unfold in front of me. It was without power or control over my own body, a toy or an object to punish for her pleasure.

My mistress moved closer, feeling my despair and desire. She traced her fingernails over my back, causing me to stir in response.

Gently she whispered, "Yes, I need it but I do try to control my urges when you serve me especially well. You still haven't had all I'd like to give you. There is much you still have to learn."

I shiver of fear passed through me. It was matched by the pang of lust that accompanied it. I wanted her despite and maybe because of everything I had suffered at her hands.

She continued, "When I spoke to Heather, she told me that she was having some painting done next week. I've invited her to stay with us for a few days."

I instantly lowered my eyes.

"Good, I can tell that you don't want her to come but you also want to please me. I love it when you struggle to obey me. This time when she comes I'm not going to ask you to be invisible. I'm not going to banish you to the attic. By now, I've trained you to be a better servant. I want you to discreetly hover like the well-trained slave you've become."

I knew I would not refuse her. I was deeply troubled by my urge to say yes to her again and again despite the shrill note of self-preservation I mentally heard in the distance. Relying on her mercy was a slender thread, but it was enough to clutch at in this moment of awareness. I would serve and hope in our love. She sensed my utter submission and opened the clamps that kept me restrained. I melted onto my knees.

"Now that you're in the mood to please me, follow me to my bed."

Enthusiastically, I crawled after her.

****

On Wednesday, I ran to the curb to open the door of Ms. Heather's black Mercedes sports car. She barely acknowledged me as she leapt into Ms. Renee's arms. I lugged the two large expensive bags Ms. Heather had brought for her visit upstairs to the guest bedroom. The room opens immediately to the right of Ms. Renee's bedroom. I have a tiny room to her left. I spent a few minutes unpacking Ms. Heather's things then I hurried downstairs. My mistress spent a lot of time with Ms. Heather but it was usually at Ms. Heather's home. I guessed it was because Ms. Heather preferred not to have me underfoot. She had visited us occasionally for dinner but she had not stayed with Ms. Renee since I had moved in.

I could hear them talking excitedly while I took the stairs to the kitchen. Earlier, I had completed most of the preparation for an afternoon tea. I served it in the garden room that Ms. Renee prefers when she has guests. I was careful to give Ms. Heather a wide berth remembering the last time I served her tea in that room. I caught her eyes following me as I detoured around her but I quickly averted my gaze.

After their tea, Ms. Renee took Ms. Heather on a tour of the house. Our house is smaller and much older than Ms. Heather's home, but in my opinion it offered more comfort and charm. Ms. Renee had purchased a few new pieces of art recently and had done quite a bit of remodeling. She pointed out the remodeled bathroom in the guest bedroom where Ms. Heather would stay.

Next, Ms. Mistress showed Ms. Heather what she called the servant's quarters. She smiled as she opened the door. I immediately saw that she had already told Ms. Heather about it.

After Ms. Renee had remodeled her closet, my room was now only a tiny space with just enough room to wedge a single bed in it. Along one wall were several pegs where my extra indoor service clothes hung beside my outdoor work clothes. Everything I owned could be seen, and if necessary, packed into a couple of cardboard boxes. I thought they would quickly pass over it as unimportant but Ms. Heather slowed the tour when she walked into the tiny space beside my bed and ran her red talons over the few clothes I possessed. It was embarrassing to see her smile agreeably at the scarcity of my possessions. Ms. Renee also pointed out the small hatch near the floor. On her side it opened through a panel on her bathroom wall.

Ms. Renee informed her guest, "I like it because when I ring for him he's already on his knees when he comes in."

Both of them had a nice laugh at my expense. Embarrassed, I could only stare down at the utilitarian black shoes Ms. Renee prefers I wear as part of my servant's uniform.

We stepped back into the hallway and my mistress led her friend into her bedroom. It is a beautiful well-proportioned room with a large bay window with window seats looking out over the garden. Her oversized bathroom was of particular interest to Ms. Heather, who loved the marble and the expensive accoutrements.

Finally, Ms. Renee showed off her expanded closet that had once been part of the room that I now slept in. Ms. Renee had her contractors push her closet out to allow a more commodious organization for her clothes and shoe closet. Her dressing area was now larger than my bedroom.

Ms. Heather paused in the middle of the dressing room. "This is a great space. I should do something just like it. This reminds me, while I'm here, may I have Butler dress me in the morning? I know you get up earlier than I do, so I won't be taking him from you."

"Of course, he's yours as long as you are here. He can also help you undress."

I continued to look down as they discussed my duties.

After the tour, I hurried to the kitchen, where I began dinner. The two women went outside to view the garden and linger beside the pool. Occasionally, I could hear their voices and laughter as I labored feverishly in the kitchen. Dinner, I knew, would be in the formal dining room.

The evening progressed without incident. Dinner went smoothly other than a slight wait while I finished preparing the dessert. After dinner, I served port in the living room and returned to the kitchen to wash the dishes and finish the ironing. Both women were having a quiet, relaxed evening. I kept busy until bedtime.

That night, I followed my usual routine of bathing my mistress and brushing her hair. She seemed to enjoy having a guest and made a few changes in the schedule for the following days. I wanted what I always want when I am serving her: to crush myself against her and begin making love. Instead, I docilely helped her out of her robe as she sat on the side of the bed.

"You did well tonight. It's taken years for you to learn the skills of a good house slave."

"Thank you, Mistress," I replied.

"Do you remember what it was like when you started? You couldn't boil an egg," she teased.

"Yes, Mistress. You were very patient," I answered, thinking of the innumerable cooking classes I had endured and the various disciplines that came with poor kitchen performance.

"Of course, there was the problem with the bread pudding this evening. We had to wait entirely too long. You should have been more organized. Give me your notebook," she gently reprimanded me.

Anxiously, I handed her my notebook and watched as she opened the pages that kept my weekly total of mistakes and the number of strokes with her crop she felt was necessary for me not to repeat the same blunder. She could be quite strict and capricious when she wanted. After jotting a note, she handed it back to me with the page still open so I could see the number.

It was "one." I had never been given only one stroke for anything. She was pleased with me.

Thankfully, I looked up into her lovely face. I felt her legs begin to spread and her hands behind my head guiding me to her center. I gratefully began teasing her with my tongue. My cage, which Ms. Renee insisted I wear when Ms. Heather visited, instantly caused the familiar cramped ache with my growing need. However, all I could really wanted was her touch, taste, and scent.

Later, as I left, she murmured, "Remember to check on Heather before you sleep."

Still a little elated and excited from being allowed to please my mistress, I knocked softly at Ms. Heather's door. I hoped that she was already asleep but I heard her order me into her room. She was reading in the chair next to her bed wearing an emerald-green Chinese robe that perfectly set off her red hair.

"Tidy up the room first," she said in a quiet, impersonal voice without looking up from her book.

I hung up the clothes she had flung on the bed and put her shoes in the closet. I straightened the towels in the bathroom and rearranged her cosmetics.

When I turned from the closet, Ms. Heather had opened her robe and was gently gliding her hand along the carefully trimmed red bush between her legs.

"Two," she said.

I knelt in front of her.

"Normally, I like an orgasm before I try to sleep. Do you think Ms. Renee would mind?"

Hypnotically, she kept stroking her softness with her lacquered fingertips. I was instantly on the alert. Ms. Renee had not given me any instructions about more intimate services I might provide Ms. Heather. I knew to err on the conservative side.

"I'm sorry, Ms. Heather, I would have to ask her. Would you like me to wake her?"

Ms. Heather snatched her robe back across her thighs and crossed her legs.

"Again?" she asked incredulously. "That's twice I have offered you the chance to serve me. And twice you have turned me down. On your back!" she snapped.

I reluctantly lay in a supine position. It was only my long training that kept me from scampering off in fear. She stood over me breathing heavily. I had been under the tutelage of her kicks in another encounter. I tensed but I could feel her gaining control of herself. She was a woman who never expected to be refused anything. I was frightened but also secretly proud that I had distressed her.

She placed her naked foot on my chest. I looked up into her flushed face. Changing the subject, she asked in a cool tone, "The house looked reasonably clean and the dinner was almost palatable tonight. Did she use the whip on you every day this week?"

"No, ma'am," I replied. "I try to please her without it."

She ground her foot harder into my chest. Icily she replied, "Then she doesn't understand you. I do. You need to feel a woman's lash every day. You are the kind of wimp who would be lost without it."

I saw her catlike eyes glitter at me with an avaricious gleam. I was a little shocked at her insight. I worked hard to avoid my mistress's punishments. However, I knew that if I went too long without feeling her whip I felt restless. The hold she had over me loosened slightly. After a punishment, I was more focused and calmer.

Everything she said was true. I suddenly knew I was wrong. In actuality, I was not at my limit with Ms. Renee. I also knew that Ms. Heather would take me there and beyond it. However, there was no choice. I didn't belong to myself anymore. I turned my head away.

"Please, Ms. Heather, is there anything else I can do for you tonight?"

Ms. Heather knelt down on my chest so close to my face that her short red pubic hairs tickled my chin. She grabbed my hair roughly to force me to look up into her cool green eyes.

"What I want to do is to beat you until you bleed, but you are not mine to do with as I please. Instead, let me tell you what I'm going to do. I'm going to break you but I'm going to let Renee do it for me." She smiled maliciously.

She continued. "Every chance I get I will encourage her to treat you like dirt beneath her feet. I want her to stop thinking of you as a person. You are only a slave. I'm going to make your life very different."

She stood up and turned from me. "You can leave . . . for now."

As I reached the door, she added. "When things begin changing, remember who did this to you."

*****

The next morning, I confessed everything to Ms. Renee. We have no secrets. Or it might be more accurate to say that I have no secrets from her. She listened intently to what I had to say, responding only that I had acted correctly. She reminded me that I never had permission to touch another woman. She ran her fingers through my hair as I knelt helping her into her shoes.

"No doubt, this week will be a little stressful for you but I'm sure that you'll manage. It's good to change things around a little. I don't want our relationship to get stale."

I shuddered slightly at what might be in store for me during the week. Even though I felt anxious, I couldn't leave. I knew I was where I was destined to be.

She sat at her vanity. "Now bring me some tea and go help Heather dress."

I carried Ms. Renee her tea on a breakfast tray. Afterward, with some apprehension I knocked on Ms. Heather's door. She was stepping out of the shower.

"It's 'bout time you showed up. I thought I would have to dress myself."

She turned away from me and bent over the bed, presenting me with her backside. I dutifully toweled her dry. Her skin was very pale with freckles. She is taller than my mistress, and in my taste, too slender.

I kept myself in neutral and methodically went about dressing her with as much passion as if she were a store manikin, which she somewhat resembled. She acted as if nothing had happened the previous night. Just as I was finishing, she suddenly reached between my legs and grabbed my cock cage tightly.

"Ha, no wonder you dress me like you're a eunuch. She's made you one, hasn't she? How long have you been in this without relief?"

"She put me in it after she knew you were visiting," I replied.

"Oh, she is so sweet to do that." She kept her hands on my cage. "I promise, before I leave you'll beg me to take you out of this."

She pressed me down to my knees. "Do you like wearing it?"

Cautiously, I replied, "If it makes my mistress happy, I'm glad to wear it."

"Ha, good answer. I will tell you something that you don't know. It was originally my idea that you wear one. I wanted you surgically neutered but she wouldn't agree to that. This was the next best thing. I want you to think about what I've done. Unknown to you, I reached into your life through Renee and caused you endless pain and embarrassment. I did this to you. If you ever really anger me, I'll do something even worse."

She smiled at me as if she knew much more about my future than I could guess. When she released me I hurried off to prepare breakfast. I'm not embarrassed to say that she frightened me.

The next few days flew by. I remembered the month I had served them during my testing. I had made myself almost invisible while she visited. In the intervening years, Ms. Heather had grown used to me. Now, my mistress expected me to be there for the service I provided. I wished for the opportunity to slink off to another part of the house. During this visit, when I had no other duties, I stood quietly in the rooms they occupied and awaited their pleasure.

I had been informed of their schedule. I knew what meals I had to prepare and which ones they would eat out. I never had any say concerning the day's activities. Often I had chores to do after they retired but I still had to be up in time to dress my mistress and prepare breakfast. Ms. Heather treated me with the same arrogance she had always treated me. My mistress allowed her to write in my notebook but not to decide on the number of strokes my lack of attention would cost me. Luckily, I was rarely alone with her, so she could not fabricate infractions. However, the few times when she had the opportunity, she privately pinched me or slapped my cage as she strutted by.

My mistress would not be outdone by anything Ms. Heather did. She too was very quick to notch up the pressure by instantly noting any tiny imperfections in my service. At times it felt like they were competing in how to be the perfect bitch goddess. They seemed to feed on each other's dominant nature. Alone they were a storm, but together they were a tornado. I was very glad that there were only a few days left in the week. In contrast, they seemed to be having a wonderful time.

Both women dressed to please a man with the most discriminating taste. Ms. Renee has a lovely shape and dresses with an understated elegance in classic-looking clothes. My financial surrender had allowed her to step up to a new level in her wardrobe. Men follow her with their eyes everywhere she goes. Ms. Heather also spends a fortune on clothes but in a trendier style. She has the model's shape to wear them well. Together, they can part a crowd of men simply by walking into a room. Each night I bathed my mistress, and each morning I helped them both dress. My cage had never felt tighter. I knew I was close to my limits as I lay each night in my bed writhing on sweaty sheets trying to think of anything but my aching need.

Finally, Saturday, the last night of Ms. Heather's stay had come. I prepared dinner but left the dishes to help Ms. Renee dress for a book group meeting at a friend's home. I was a little anxious about being left alone with Ms. Heather. I acknowledged my anxiety to her and asked if she had any special instructions. She looked stunning in a tight dark skirt, a cashmere sweater, and heels. It hurt to look at her but I couldn't keep my eyes off of her.

"No, I don't have any special instructions. I trust her not to do anything that would upset me and you should know by now what I want from you."

I protested gently, "Mistress, I never know what she is going to do or ask of me. Please be more specific with your instructions."

"No, I can't imagine every contingency that might arise. Just remember to whom you belong. I don't think that is going to be much of an issue. She told me she had a friend coming over, so I doubt she'll have much time for you."

I knelt and kissed the tops of her shoes. There was nothing more to say. I couldn't imagine what Heather's friends were like but I was sure that they couldn't be any worse.

I walked Ms. Renee to her car and opened the door for her. She kissed me lightly on the cheek and told me to enjoy my evening.

I had some doubts about how much I would enjoy my evening but I was encouraged this was the last night of Ms. Heather's stay. I was tired and the constant sexual stimulation of serving these two women had made me jumpy and twitchy.

Ms. Heather was seated in the living room when I returned. She saw me and smiled. "Two!" she snapped, pointing to a spot on the floor in front of her.

I complied instantly, not wanting her to be able to complain of anything while my mistress was away. She smiled down at me like a cat about to swallow the canary.

"I've invited a friend over to visit."

She was dressed in a black and white dress with touches of red that somehow did not clash with her coloring. As usual, she was in stiletto heels. Her hair was up in a complicated bun. She started lightly swinging one stocking-covered leg toward my crotch. I felt it make light contact with my cage. I was in such a state of swollen arousal that even a slight tap generated a catch in my breath.

Ms. Heather ignored my discomfort and kept talking while continuing to swing her leg lightly onto my cage.

"When my guest arrives, I want you to obey my instructions perfectly. I want you to serve dessert and wine, then I want you to go sit in the dining room. There is a chair waiting for you. I have closed the pocket doors so that only a tiny slit is showing. I want you to sit there and watch in case I need you. If I snap my fingers, I want you to instantly come into the living room. Do you understand?"

"Yes, Ms. Heather."

She swung her leg a little harder. "You always agree to everything, don't you? You really are nothing but a slave. I can't imagine why you allow Renee to do the things she does to you. No normal man would allow it."

"Yes, Ms. Heather."

"Go wait in the kitchen until I buzz you. I'll get the door."

A few minutes later I heard the bell chime and Ms. Heather open the door. I finished opening the wine and brought it to the living room. Ms. Heather was sitting on the couch smiling directly at me when I entered the room. Next to her was what appeared to be a large teenage boy. He was obviously an athlete. Taking a second look, I changed my mind and assumed she had invited a college student. I was utterly dumfounded for a second but I managed to set the wine and the dessert on the table in front of her. I avoided his eye contact although he was mostly looking at Heather.

Ms. Heather introduced me. "This is my friend's butler and gardener. He's such a good servant. And his name really is Butler!"

I mumbled a response, but the young man barely looked at me. I quickly excused myself and left before Ms. Heather came up with any other ways to humiliate me.

Nervously, I did as she bid and returned through the darkened dining room to take my place in a chair gazing through the tiny sliver of space left between the pocket doors that separated the living room from the dining room. I could see the room clearly.

Ms. Heather didn't waste much time with the wine. I had barely sat down when she slid over to his side of the couch and began to kiss him. She was almost twice his age but he was putty in her hands.

After a few minutes, Ms. Heather unzipped his trousers and pulled out one of the largest male members I have ever seen. Ms. Heather fished out a condom out of her purse. There was almost no foreplay. Ms. Heather slipped out of her dress and took him on the couch by sitting on him and grinding on his cock.

After a few minutes, she stood up and took his hand, leading him over to the chair opposite me. She knelt in front of the chair and positioned him behind her.

He knelt behind her and began to vigorously thrust into her. She was sweating and pushing back against him. After several minutes, she slowed the pace and looked directly into the crack between the door with a look of victory and contempt.

"Finish!" she huskily demanded.

With a groan, the young man stroked a few more times, shuddered, and collapsed out of her. With his collapse came my own. Watching what I had not been allowed to do for weeks was more than I could stand. I had constricted into a knot on the floor as silently as possible. My scrotum burned in agony. I could almost hear the cramped thudding pulse of my cock inside my chastity cage.

There were a few seconds of quiet while he recovered, but Ms. Heather didn't allow him to rest long. In minutes she had him clothed and out the door.

When she slid the pocket doors open, I was still curled next to the chair unable to move. She had slipped her heels back on and stood in front of me naked with her hands on her hips. Her red hair now hung loose and tangled across her small but firm breasts. Her skin glistened with the slight oil of sweat. I looked up at her, wanting to beg for mercy.

"I loved doing that in front of you, knowing you were in here suffering. You really are a wimp. That boy is more of a man than you are. He would never find himself locked in a chastity cage doing some woman's housework. No, you are only a slave. You were lucky to get to watch."

The burning was unbearable. I felt like rubbing my caged genitals across the floor. Anything to feel something other than the terrible cramped sensation.

"No doubt your mistress will start to cuckold you sooner or later. After all, you're just a slave. This is the next logical step. You better take what pleasure you can get from now on."

She placed a toe on my cage gently.

"Did you notice I haven't come yet? I never do with studs like that. I love the fucking but I need a slave's mouth on me to really get off. Of course, I could never offer you what he had but I would let you touch yourself after licking me. Wouldn't that be nice? Your balls have to be aching."

She smiled down at me and opened her fist. From her hand poured a thin stream of gold chain that landed with clink in front of me as the attached key hit the floor.

"Yes, it's the key to your cock cage. I noticed it hanging from Renee's bedpost. Go ahead. You need it after what you just saw. I know all about your limit on how many strokes of the whip she's willing to give you. Why do you think I found so many things wrong this week? You're not going to be out of that cage until next weekend. You better yank on your pathetic cock now while you have the chance."

Her hand strayed to her own triangle of red hair, anticipating her own orgasm. I was beaten. I knew it. I no longer had the will to resist. My body had betrayed me. I had to have some relief. I opened my mouth to say yes but what I heard was something completely different.

"Thank you, Ms. Heather, but I can't!" I sobbed. I was as surprised to hear myself say it as she was.

She bent over and pulled my chin up to look into her eyes.

"Are you going to say no to me again? Do you know what I'm going to do to you for refusing me?"

"I'm sorry," I croaked.

"Why? I'm not offering you sex, just a little relief. She doesn't even need to know. She doesn't beat you like she should. She hasn't broken you! Why are you so fucking obedient?"

The answer was right there. "I love her."

Ms. Heather went suddenly still. Her knowing sneer slowly melted. I saw her eyes widen. She raised her chin and quickly turned her head away. Had I seen tears there?

"Clean up this mess," she said as she left the room without turning back to me. Stiffly, she headed up the stairs toward the guest bedroom.

I stayed downstairs to await my mistress. It was a long and miserable wait. I was stranded between feeling sorry for myself and glad that I had passed a very severe test. If I had done what Ms. Heather wanted, then I would have been in her power. She would have been able to blackmail me. Even more importantly, I could never have faced my mistress with such a betrayal. It would have ruined years of trust that we had built.

When my mistress arrived, I needed to tell her everything. After taking one look at me, she suggested I undress and follow her to her attic dungeon. The only entrance to the third floor is through her dressing area. She knew that we needed to talk privately. Naked, I followed her up the narrow stairway. I had experienced some very painful lessons in that attic. Simply walking up the stairs put me in deep subspace. There is only one chair in the room. It is a large ornately carved wooden chair she used as her throne.

I was kneeling naked in front of it. Ms. Renee was still wearing the clothes she had worn to her book group.

She paused a long time after hearing my story.

Finally, she replied. "I won't tell you that I didn't expect something from her this week. Of course, she's a natural dominatrix but she's had no one to lead her into a loving relationship. Why do you think she went through two husbands so quickly? She was searching for someone. Unfortunately, those men weren't submissive. They were merely weak. She chewed them up and spit them out. You were different. You actually stood up to her."

"Barely," I said. "I was in danger."

"Yes, you were. What do you think I would have done if you had disappointed me?"

I knew the answer but couldn't say it out loud. I put my head between her feet on the floor knowing she would put her foot on my head. It was a gentle but profound act of submission and ownership.

"Yes, you are mine. But I love to put you to the test!"

I could only tremble in response. I saw this whole episode as coming from her hands. I knew she would do anything to complete my surrender.

"What will you do when you see her tomorrow?" I asked.

"I don't know," she replied.

****

The next morning, I woke at the regular time but neither my mistress nor Ms. Heather was in the house. I finally spotted them talking at the table on the patio. They both had cups of tea. I sensed that they didn't need me to interrupt.

A few chores later I looked outside to see the two women hugging. Apparently, they had agreed on something. I brought fresh pastries and orange juice.

As I placed the tray on the table, I couldn't help but notice that Ms. Heather had been crying but now they were both grinning like they had won the lottery.

Ms. Renee stopped me as I turned to go. "Butler, pack Ms. Heather's things. She's leaving this morning. Bring her car to the front."

Several minutes later I was standing in the driveway with the door to her sports car opened. Ms. Heather came down the steps alone, dressed as always like an older but still slender fashion model. She stopped before stepping into the car, fixing me with her eyes. She leaned in closely.

"You told her everything about last night, didn't you? I guess that's the way it works between you two. Total honesty. I can learn a lot from her about men and about love. I guess I've been a beast to you. I'm sorry."

I couldn't believe my ears. I looked at her and for the first time I thought I understood what my mistress saw in her.

"You see, I told her everything too. I don't think I've ever told anyone but her the truth about me. I understand why you love her so much. Also, I told her I wouldn't try to steal you or mess with you anymore. You know what she said?"

I nodded no dumbly.

"She said, 'Go for it!' Ha! I didn't believe it the first time I heard it either. I think I'm more than a little in love with her right now. She said you could use the pressure to expand your limits. Ha! So it seems I've been on the right track all along but for the all the wrong reasons. Now I want you to be the best slave you can be for her. I have a lot of great ideas to try on you. It's just going to get harder and harder for you until you are the perfect servant."

With that she kissed me on the cheek, stepped into the car, and was gone.

I was stunned. I had a sudden sense that my mistress had been pulling the strings all along. She knew something like this was going to happen. She was not only interested in my surrender but in Ms. Heather's healing. She allowed me to be tested to prove to Heather that some men could be trusted or at least properly trained. It had been a strategy to help her friend while at the same time put me through an experience that proved to me my rightful place. This had been a week of torture for me, but on the other hand, being the slave of a manipulative dominant woman was never dull.

Once again, I knew very deeply that belonging to Ms. Renee was my highest and best purpose in life. Suddenly, I remembered that Ms. Renee had not attributed a particular number of strokes with the whip to match Ms. Heather's complaints as she recorded them in my notebook. That meant that I might still have a chance to make love to my mistress if I accepted her correction with utter submission. Did I feel that way? I admitted to myself that I felt more completely hers than I did at the beginning of the week. She knew. She always knew.

I rushed to complete my tasks.

Chapter Nine

SPIRITUALITY

January 2014
Dear Heather,

We've made it through another Christmas season. I hate that we hardly see each other during the last quarter of the year. We are both too busy.

I know that this will likely not be your thing but we are have continued our meetings of the Temple of the Dark Goddess. I've worked with Candice for the last six months preparing the liturgy, prayers, and music. You met her here one night last summer at dinner. She was the short blonde intensely intelligent seminary student that you liked.

You know that I've spent years getting to know other dominant women in the area who are attempting a female-led relationship with their husbands. The Temple was organized for these women to come together to support each other. I always had you for help but many women have had no one to turn to for support.

You are such a natural dominatrix, you may not need any support. I needed your strength. I'm glad that you have finally accepted that no matter what happens between us, I love Butler and I'm going to keep him.

You and I were never going to live together full-time. We both agree that we each possess such strong personalities that it would be like having too much spice in one stew. But hasn't the occasional weekend been wonderful?

All of us have been through a real transformation in the past few years. I'm very happy that the conflict between you and Butler has abated. Finally, I think we are all on the same page. It was always about loving each other.

I don't say this to you enough but you have been a big help with him. Mostly you have done this because you have taken a keen interest that I receive everything I could from my relationship with him even when you didn't understand why I chose him. I appreciate that you have always been my advocate.

Tell me you'll come.

Renee

February 2014
Dear Renee,

I don't really understand what you hope to accomplish with the Temple. I don't believe in gods or goddesses. Well, except maybe you, of course.
    Will we beat on tambourines? Will there be a sermon?
    Yikes, first marriage, now church. Are you becoming a Republican? Tell me why you are doing this again.

Heather

February 2014
Dear Heather,

You make me laugh. No sermons, I promise. I'm not religious but spirituality remains important to many people. I see it as a tool.

Throughout the process of Butler's transformation from a worthless male to a useful slave I have had one powerful ally. I know that he wanted to experience true domination as much as I wanted to give it to him. Again and again I have asked him to agree to the next step, and repeatedly he has complied. There have been times when he felt unable to move forward. That is why he gave me permission to use blackmail and discipline to spur him on. When things got hard for him I knew what to do because I knew what he really wanted. My strength pushed us on. Heck, sometimes, it took my strength and your strength combined! Religious feelings are simply another tool to use to deepen his submission.

I am not a religious person, but I recognize that our lifestyle has been a spiritual journey for both of us. I'm certain that one of the reasons I rejected religion when I was young was because the only options to me were completely patriarchal. Perhaps if I had been introduced to the idea of the divine in a female incarnation I might have been more open to faith. Even though I cannot personally be religious, I know the power it has over some people. Butler is one of those people.

I happily intend to make use of his spiritual inclination by enthroning myself as his deity. At this point in his training, his carefully prepared psyche is open to suggestion. I want him to have a religious experience with me as his goddess! To encourage this, I have set time aside for a daily devotion when he kneels in front of my image and meditates on how best to worship me. I know it sounds silly but I believe that it might work. I've read that people often have deep religious experiences while under stress. I've supplied the object of worship: me. Together, you and I can supply the stress. Ha!

Ritual and sex magic have been an important part of culture for centuries. It is why I started the Temple dedicated to the Dark Goddess. Who knows, maybe if I practice a religion before I actually believe in it I might be surprised by a new spiritual awareness. What

I really want is for him to have a religious experience. That would be wonderful.

Blessings of the Goddess,
Priestess Renee

February 2014
Dear Renee,

OK, I'll come, but no fucking tambourines.

Heather

March 2014
Dear Heather,

I'm glad that you have decided to join us for our Temple meetings. I understand that it's not your thing. I am starting to really enjoy them. I love hearing from other women during the sharing portion of the meeting. I learn a lot from their challenges and I think that as a group we become better dominants than if we were alone. It's so easy to fall back into an equal relationship when you are alone with our submissive. Sisterhood empowers us.

Men aren't allowed into the service until the very end. We call that portion the Sacrifice. One man is chosen each month to be next month's sacrifice. That gives his dominant time to prepare him. At the end of each meeting the sacrifice is ritually whipped in an atmosphere of incense smoke, candles, and meditative chanting.

During the Sacrifice the men in the group look at each other and realize that complete surrender is what is normal for men. My female friends and I look at them kneeling before us and realize the same thing. There is power in the group. I know that I should not attempt Butler's continued submission alone. Being with others on this path has helped to make Butler and me feel more comfortable in our different roles.

The women have also started visiting each other in our homes. You should see how nervous their men are when we visit. They know very well that we are inspecting their housekeeping and how well they are serving their owners. I could never have journeyed this far with Butler without your help. It has been wonderful to see other women supporting each other.

With your help, I have become Butler's great love. He has become my living political statement, my example to other women, and my work of art. When he takes off his shirt other women see a perfectly toned torso adorned with old scars, bruises, and the newly applied whelps of recent punishments. He looks like what he is: a fit, loved, well-tended man who is also a carefully disciplined slave.

I admit it. I enjoy competing with other women concerning who has the most subjugated male.

It's been fun!

See you soon,
Renee

Butler's Journal
Dressing for the First Meeting of Temple of the Dark Goddess.
April 2014

I was told that all that would happen was that I would serve refreshments before the meeting. Afterward, I would excuse myself so that the women could have their meeting without the presence of a male.

I did not know what to think. This was obviously important to my mistress, because she had made sure that I was mentally in deep subspace before the meeting started. I cautioned myself concerning any mistakes. The women in the room would judge me. There would be no forgiveness from my mistress if I botched my role. Also, I wanted to be an example to the women in the group of the results of a loving, if sometimes difficult, female-led relationship.

I adjusted the harness under my clothes as best as I could. Once again I reflected about the thousands of individual choices and experiences that had brought me to this moment. Somehow, it didn't seem possible. How had it come this far? I was dressed in a white shirt with black pants and jacket, but that was not all. A casual observer would not be able to notice my predicament. I would be aware of it every second. Beneath my uniform, a wide leather belt was wrapped tightly around my waist. It was connected by an extension that pulled snugly between my legs. My testicles and my necessarily flaccid penis were squashed into a small metal cage attached to the leather extension that ran between my legs. Additionally, and if possible more uncomfortably, a butt plug extended up from the strap between my legs into my anus. The entire harness gripped me internally and externally. I could walk slowly but I would not be able to toilet myself without the key.

I finished dressing by brushing my hair. It seemed impossible to think about my hair but it was the last step to finish dressing. In three minutes I was due to open the door at the end of the hallway. I wanted to push against the time but the idea of being late filled me with dread. I slowly walked the length of the hallway, gripped the door handle, and pushed. It was more than just a door; it was a threshold that once crossed I could not return from.

April 2014
Dear Renee,

OK, it was fun. I didn't want to go but I forced myself.

I often find myself competing with other women. I loved that magically you have created an atmosphere of cooperation and support. I also appreciate that the meeting was women only. It meant we could have an adult conversation.

Who knew that there were a dozen women in Memphis practicing female domination?

Normally, I like to keep my kinks to myself but this seemed less about kinky sex and more about empowering the women in the group to take advantage of their husband's kinky desires. You have been on the right path all along. So yes, I plan on attending in the future.

I still hate it when you are right but I'm getting used to it.

Kisses,
Heather

Butler's Journal
Temple of the Dark Goddess, The Affirmation
October 2014

For over a year, Ms. Renee has brought together a group of women who dominate the men in their lives. Most of them are married, middle-aged, and for all practical purposes look like vanilla middle-class career women. Many of these women she met at our local S&M club. Others came to her by word of mouth.

Over time what started as a support group for dominant women has slowly evolved into a group of women seeking more spiritual answers. Her biggest fan of this approach has been a local seminary student. I remember the initial meeting concerning the start of the Temple because I served the two women dinner when Ms. Renee approached the student asking about goddess worship.

When I first heard about her idea, I was amused because I knew that Ms. Renee was a very practical person with no real religious leanings. I assumed that she was merely testing the waters for such an effort. However, Ms. Candice, a divinity student, encouraged her to move forward. Ms. Candice was an enthusiast of goddess worship. Together they carefully wrote a liturgy, prayers, and ritual forms of worship. Eventually, they combined ancient western rites with borrowed viewpoints from various religious traditions.

Of course, I was not invited to the meetings when they started. It was a women-only group. I'm sure that it was awkward at first but they persisted. It was always originally designed to eventually incorporate men, but for the first year men were not invited.

Finally, men were allowed to attend as supplicants toward the end of the service. I won't describe the order of worship here but the service ended in a ritual flogging of one of the men. The males were only brought in at the end of the meeting as a kind of climax to the service. At each meeting one of us would often go away quite sore.

Having heard some of the original conversations that started the Temple, I was not surprised by any of the rituals. However, what happened in this particular meeting was one of the most powerful experiences of my life. It was my turn to be brought in at the end of the meeting for the ritual scourging. It hurt as badly as I expected. There is something about a group of women together that makes whoever is handling the whip give it that extra zip so her sisters won't think she is weak.

I was standing at the altar recovering when Ms. Candice called the women together around me. That night there were about twelve women in the room. I expected something even worse to happen to me. Instead, Ms. Candice started talking about my commitment to my mistress. Ms. Renee confirmed her words, adding that I had recently become more open and obedient. This was true.

Ms. Candice asked the female congregation for an "affirmation." I had no idea what that meant. However, the women in the circle around me were prepared. I could hear them start to softly speak words of praise. Slowly, they moved in toward me. As they did so they continued to murmur encouragement.

They reached out their hands and caressed me, saying things like, "You have a loving heart to dedicate it to your mistress." They touched my back, my chest, and my thighs. As they gently touched me they continued to laud my qualities. "Your back has grown muscular in service to your love. Your hands are calloused from your loving work for your mistress."

Slowly they circled in a counterclockwise fashion. Dozens of hands stroked my flanks, my hips, even my genitals. With each caress came a compliment or a word of encouragement. There were dozens of hands on me. Often they would pause and kiss some part of my body. I felt an intense outpouring of love. I was surrounded in it. It only lasted for a few minutes but I have never felt anything like it. Twelve women touching you, kissing you, and praising you is a very exhilarating experience. I felt appreciated for every act of sacrifice. Also, I felt empowered to give more. Soon I found myself close to weeping. At the end I was left embracing my mistress in the center of the room. Reluctantly, I felt their hands leave me while their voices slowly stilled. I was left feeling loved, protected, and cherished.

From this moment I no longer saw their meetings as a church for women but saw it instead as a temple of love. The experience changed me. Was it magic? Were they a coven of witches? I was no longer sure. It no longer mattered. I entered into my relationship with Ms. Renee to experience life intensely. She had kept her promise. I vowed to keep my promises by renewing my commitment to her service.

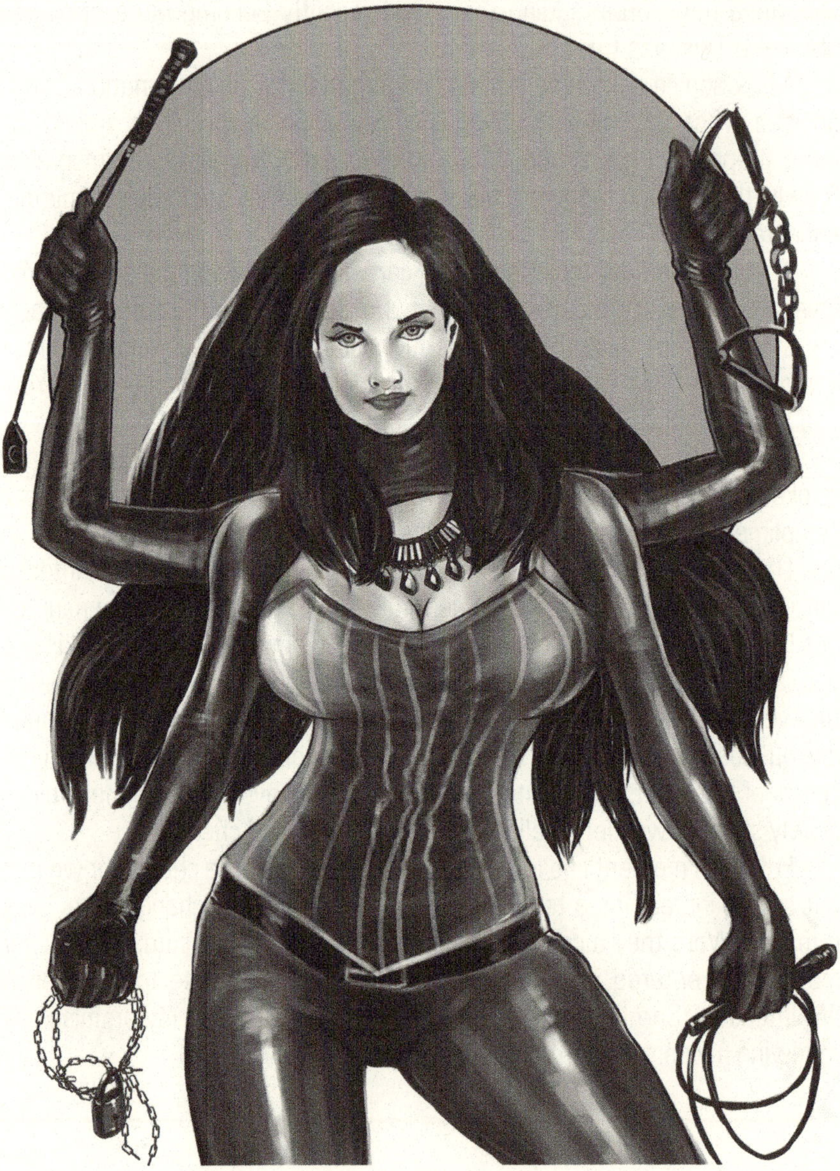

Chapter Ten

THE END GAME

January 2015
Dear Renee,

I was delighted to find you at the Watsons' party last night. I noticed you giving Butler hands signals. I loved watching how he had to pay close attention to you. That's one way to keep your slave focused. You looked radiant and happy. Marriage, even a secret marriage, seems to agree with both of you.

The store is breaking records. Apparently, women in Memphis needed stylish shoes.

I've seen a lot of Suzy lately. I've had her here often and I see her when I visit Atlanta to check my store there. We are making progress. I have some training ideas I'd like to talk to you about now that we have some time.

I love that we've been seeing each other more often. It's been fun but I feel we haven't done anything satisfyingly wicked together in months. Is there anything new and interesting lurking in your plans?

Heather

January 2015
Dear Heather,

I'm glad you're feeling ready for something new. It's ironic that you mentioned that we look like a happy married couple. I promise that this e-mail will satisfy any desires you have for something new and satisfyingly wicked. I feel fearful but tremendously excited about my next step.

I wanted to kiss you at the Watsons' party in front of everyone and tell you what I've decided about my marriage. One day my sexuality will get me kicked out of polite society. Or maybe invited more often. It's hard to know. Things are changing. Did you know that it's been over six years since we reconnected? Looking back over these years, I'm very glad that you moved back to Memphis.

We are so alike in so many ways. As two dominant women, we are not well matched for each other but the power struggles between us are often stimulating. You have been such a joy to have in my life.

Now, back to looking like a happy married couple. I feel very secure that I have taken Butler far enough down the road of submission that he is no longer buffeted by doubts about his role in my life. He takes great care of me and we have a wonderful love life. He's a gentleman in public and a slave in private. People see us like you did: as a happy couple, and I suppose we are.

At this stage I could stop pressing forward into deeper domination and submission. After all, I now control his money and his time. What can be better than a deeply submissive man trained to be the perfect partner? What could be more intimate? However, lately I've realized something about myself. He may have gone as far as his submissive desires would take him but deeper, darker needs torment me. After long consideration, I have decided to take an additional step toward his enslavement. Actually, I got the whole idea from you from an offhand comment you made about how crushed you left your last husband following your divorce. It started me thinking. Did I have the courage to keep going? Would I ruin what I already have? I am filled with anxiety but I am also filled with a sense of daring. I was about to call you because I need your feedback and your help with my plan.

I remember that I promised Butler more than he could imagine. I remember that he doubted me. However, my next move will come as a very surprising stroke to him. After years of suffering and work, just when he thinks he has surrendered everything to live with the mistress of his dreams, I intend to shock him.

I will begin as I always do when I want to introduce him to something new, by being more demanding than usual for several weeks. I will make it impossible for him to satisfy me. I will act disappointed in everything he does while increasing my physical discipline of him. This combination always creates in him an urgent need to please me. I will wait until he is squirming to obey me, then I will share what is bothering me.

I want to start the discussion with him securely bound on his knees. I will begin the conversation in a reasonable tone as I stand over him and explain that as a financially independent woman it doesn't seem appropriate that I am married to a mere slave. I will point out to him the differences in how we live, what we wear, and how we spend our time. I will remind him that only a man born to be a slave would agree to such an arrangement. I will explain that although I treasure him I can no longer feel any respect for him as a man or see him as an equal.

I am certain that he will feel anxious about the direction of the conversation. I'm also sure that he will attempt to suggest the advantages of being married to a submissive man. Nevertheless, as the conversation continues I will become increasingly colder and more adamant. I will explain that seeing him accept so many humiliating situations has changed my feelings for him. I will go on to explain that because I no longer view him as a man, it is beneath me to be married to him. At the tiniest disagreement from him, I will slap him repeatedly in the face. Finally, in as intimidating and humiliating manner as possible, I will announce my intention of making my feelings practical by divorcing him. Oh, how he will be stunned! After all his sacrifice and at the peak of his attempts to submit, he will find that I intend to cruelly reject him.

Our secret marriage has never meant much to me. However, I know our marriage meant a lot to him. I also know that he has always secretly hoped I would acknowledge our marriage publicly. Men are like that. Even after all my training, he still wants to put some kind of "owned" sign on me. I think that's one reason why I want to take it away from him.

Of course, divorce won't come as a shock to our friends or family because they never knew we were ever married. Butler will see our marriage and my plan to divorce him as nothing but a ploy of mine to take economic advantage over him. Well, he'll be right. I did want to take advantage of him.

I almost swoon when I think about the hurt look on his face! No matter how much he begs, I will go through with it. To increase his humiliation, I will make sure that he uses your attorney to do the necessary paperwork. Of course, I will get everything.

I tremble when I think of the court proceeding. I think about how he will be dressed in one of his old black Goodwill suits that makes him look like a waiter. I plan to dress in a brand-new outfit bought specifically for the occasion that will make him long for me. I imagine him sitting nervously in the courtroom unable to keep his eyes from me. No doubt, the judge will question him about the lopsided settlement but I know that my training will hold. He will agree to everything.

After the formalities, he will naturally assume that he will be coming home with me. Instead, while I watch, my attorney will hand him a protection order that demands he stay away from me. In addition, she will hand him a suitcase with one change of clothes and his toiletries. With these items, I will include a note.

"I told you I would take everything."

Imagine his dismay! I want to be sure to be in a good spot to watch his reaction.

Thinking about this I have been turning over several questions. Didn't I promise him complete domination? Have I really gone as far as our love and our desires can take us? Should I listen to my fears or my sense of adventure? I'm torn but I know that I will never be truly happy unless I continue to move forward.

After much soul-searching, I've deicided not to allow fear or convention to rule me. For me, this is the next logical step.

Any thoughts?

Renee

January 2015
Dear Renee,

I can't believe I'm saying this to you. You know how excited I get when it comes to dominating Butler, but are you sure you want to do this? I admit when you first introduced me to him all I wanted to do was to help you crush him. It was a new thrill for me to have a man like Butler under my thumb. Now, I'm starting to see that you both truly love each other. What do you hope to accomplish with this plan? Aren't you afraid that, finally, you will push him too far?

Don't get me wrong. You are my first concern. I will help any way you want.

Despite my worries, I'm always ready to be your partner in crime.

Heather

January 2015
Dear Heather,

I am shocked! You are suggesting mercy? How funny! This is one of the reasons I love you so much. We tend to balance each other.

Of course, I'm not getting rid of him. I love him. Even if I didn't love him, think about how much work I've put into making him such a good servant. It's been a huge investment of time and effort. I'd be crazy to let him leave.

Actually, I don't think I could get along without him now. I spilled something the other day while he was out running errands and I suddenly realized that I had no idea where he kept the broom. I had a good long laugh at myself. I've become useless without him!

Strangely, I feel free to do this monstrously wicked thing to him because I love him. I trust myself to bring him even closer to me by giving him experiences that lead to his complete submission. I know him well enough to understand that he craves surrender as much as I desire to dominate him. So even when he has been kicked to the curb, I intend to keep him safely in the palm of my hand. That's where you come in. I need you to keep an eye on him.

I'm doing this for him. I'm doing this for us. And yes, I admit that I'm also doing it for me.

I could rationalize this decision with a lot of talk about love, feminism, female superiority, or something about balancing the scales of justice so that at least one woman completely dominates one man. There are a lot of complex reasons that have pushed me toward this decision, but to you I can confide the one reason that gets me up in the dead of the night planning it: this will turn me on.

Of course, I'm not just talking about being turned on sexually, although the whole idea of divorcing him makes me slippery. No, I mean it turns me on intellectually, politically, and even spiritually. He and I are both on a mission of self-actualization. For me, being completely free while completely owning him is my image of my very best self. Conversely, I believe his complete surrender is his best purpose. Only you would understand my desire. We only live once. I want to experience life deeply, as does he.

In the weeks before our divorce, I want to secretly find a place for him to live. I want it to be close enough for him to be able for him to walk to what was our house but is now mine. I want to find the smallest, dirtiest, most humble dwelling possible. All I want to furnish it with is a used mattress.

By court decree, he will be unable to even speak to me. He will have nothing. In fact, he will still be financially in my debt. In addition, I will retain my blackmail portfolio I worked so hard to obtain should I want him jailed or embarrassed. Will he try to speak to me despite the restraining order?

What happens when a man is arrested while wearing a locked chastity device? I can't imagine. After the arrest, I assume that they would just leave it on. What a wonderful thing to think about. How would he explain it to the police and later to his cellmates?

If he avoids arrest, I plan on denying him my presence for a period of time. For weeks, I want him to be penniless, friendless, and still locked in my chastity belt.

This is where I need your help. You've mentioned to me that you were planning on using a different cleaning service to clean your store at night. Between different cleaners, could you hire him for a few weeks? I want to leave him broke but I don't want him to actually starve. Working for you would be perfect. He could hike to your store every night and clean it. You could pay him in cash each day. He'll take the job because he'll be desperate, and doing something for you will feel like he is still tied to me. I expect that he'll be available for about a month. I'm sure you can think of ways to make it interesting for both of you. Feel free to have some fun. All I ask is that you don't crop him. I want him to miss even the lash!

After a few weeks I will eventually send him instructions via a note explaining how he can enter my service again. I see him holding my note tearfully grateful for the chance to again obey me.

Eventually, I will instruct him to walk to my home each day and kneel at the driveway between 5:00 p.m. and 6:00 p.m. He will be fearful that I am asking him to do this so I can have him arrested for breaking the court order to stay away from me. He'll have to risk it. In my imagination, I see him each day walking to my home and risking arrest by kneeling at the foot of my driveway hoping that I will stop and speak to him as I drive into my carport.

I see myself stopping my car a block down the street to spy on him. Looking at his forlorn figure kneeling helplessly on the sidewalk will make me want to touch myself.

For days I will ignore him, but eventually I will stop and speak to him. After much pleading from him, I will reluctantly allow him to crawl on his hands and knees like a supplicant to my back door. Then, if he begs sincerely and agrees to my even more outrageous demands, I will allow him to serve me in some small way, perhaps as a yardman. Over time, if he continues to behave in a modest and obedient manner, I will slowly allow him to serve more frequently and more intimately. He will finally learn the privilege of serving without thought of reward.

Watching him bend and bow gratefully will give me such a deep satisfaction.

Finally, after much effort and tears we will have arrived at his ultimate surrender. He will own nothing. He will have no legal recourse to any form of justice other than my mercy. He will not be able to make a single demand of me. And finally, he will be begging to live again as my slave, subject to my whim while knowing what I am capable of. At long last, we will have arrived.

How I will crow in triumph! What joy! I will have conquered every selfish masculine part of him! Stripped of everything, he will know where he belongs. He will consider it a mercy to be my slave. I will have changed an independent but useless man into an eager and useful servant! That may be the day that I love him the most.

You are the only person I know who would understand why I would want to take a relationship this far down the path of dominance and submission. When I think about the shallowness and fragility of most marriages, I will look at all Butler and I have gone through and know that we will have forged a stronger bond than most couples will ever experience.

When I see him crawling back inside my house for the first time, I will remember that he is the man who has chosen to suffer physical torture, psychological torment, humiliation, sexual denial, poverty, and loss of self—all to open himself to allow me to wrap the tendrils of my love and control into every part of his body and his mind. I will feel more than loved. I will feel worshipped. In that moment, I will be completely in love with him because of his utter surrender.

This triumph will be worth every bit of the effort he and I put into it.

I have already experienced the delightful tenderness he offers me after I have put him through a particularly difficult experience. There seems to be a shell covering him that prevents a sweet free flow of affection. My dominance cracks that shell allowing me to bask in a flood of warmth and love. I can only imagine what he will be like after I've taken everything. Strangely, I know one of his strongest feelings will be gratitude. I will have freed him of every responsibility but love.

Renee

Dear Renee,

I think he is a lucky slave to be loved by you. However, I don't think you are doing all of this to improve your relationship or for a momentary thrill. If I know you, there is a part B to your plan. You are always looking farther down the road than anyone I know.
   Tell me everything. I won't judge you.

Heather

Dear Heather,

You know me so well. Yes, I'm fairly confident that I can get him through this divorce without losing him. In fact, I expect it to move us to whole new level. One of the reasons I'm doing this is that I selfishly want things he hasn't even thought of giving me. For example, I thought about moving to a different town so we can live openly as mistress and slave. I would do so today but my career and my life are here in Memphis.

One day I expect couples like us to be more accepted just as gay couples are now. Consensual female-led relationships will one day come out of the closet. I can't wait. Until then, I intend to live as close as possible to my ideal.

To help live out my dream, I've been thinking of buying a home in Florida. I want somewhere I can go during the winter. I can afford to buy one but I was thinking that together you and I could buy something special. I'm only interested in using it during the winter months. After working so hard during the Christmas shopping season it might also do you some good to get out of town for the first quarter.

We see each other often but I wish we had more time together. You have your store and I'm also terribly busy with an election coming up. I wanted you to be a part of what I consider an important decision.

My work for women's health and women's rights issues in Tennessee is an important part of my life. This is why I intend to spend most of the year in Memphis leading an outwardly conventional life. However, in Florida, for a few months every year, I will have the freedom I crave. I will able to see whom I wish as a lover or a friend without scandalizing society because in our winter home Butler will only be known as my employee. I want to stretch his horizons so that while he is in Florida he thinks of himself only as a servant. Remember how circumspect you and I are when we go out. It's not as if being a polyamorous, bisexual dominatrix is against the law, but I'm a private person. I don't want my sexuality to be the topic of discussion among my business associates, donors, and political contacts.

Freedom is why I want to spend part of the year out of Memphis. In Florida, I can lovingly keep Butler chaste, teased, punished, and anxious for every morsel of attention that I give him. At the same time, I can date you and anyone else I want without scandal. Finally, in Florida I can express a more public domination of Butler by introducing him as my houseman. Our public face will be limited to the relationship that can exist between an older houseman anxious to keep his job, and his well-heeled, demanding, and somewhat bitchy employer. I admit that I've grown to love playing that role. Maybe it's who I've really become.

I have a lovely dream of being invited to a social event and the hostess asking me if she could borrow Butler to park cars or serve drinks. That would be hysterically funny and deeply satisfying to me. There, away from people who know us, our difference in ages will help establish our public employer/employee relationship. No one will suspect that we are a lifelong couple. They will see him only as my houseman. Men and women will feel free to engage me again as a single woman, much to Butler's discomfort and my secret delight.

I know my plan sounds risky, but I'm sure he'll agree to everything if we are careful. However, if I go to all the trouble of divorce I want to get the maximum benefit for myself. My goal has always been to achieve intensity and passion in our relationship, but now it is also to give me something few women will ever enjoy. I want passion and freedom.

I believe I have the patience and the merciless will necessary to reach my goal, but I still need your help. You are the queen of good ideas. How can I make the potion I will force him to drink to be a more potent brew?

I need you to think like the conniving witch I know you can be.

We could have fun in Florida together each winter. I want this all done by this time next year.

What say you? Are you up for this?

Renee

February 2015
Dear Renee,

I don't know. I'm really busy. This seems like a lot of trouble. I have a lot of errands to run this week.

Oh, fuck me, of course I'll help! Only you could make divorce an erotic adventure!

You are who I want to be when I grow up! I want to kiss you. I started working on this last night as soon as I read your e-mail.

Your plan must be fate because I just found out about the perfect apartment for him. A customer of mine owns that huge ugly old apartment building on Poplar Avenue about six blocks from you. I know she has the perfect space because she was complaining to me last week that she recently lost her handyman who was living in the basement apartment. She told me that she is unable to rent it again because it would be a code violation.

After getting your e-mail last night, I called her. We went to see it this morning. It's a dump. Picture a single room on the basement level with one tiny window high on one wall at ground level looking out at the parking lot. That means one could look in and spy on the occupant. It's in the engine room with no more than a cot with an open bathroom at one end. It's just what you want.

A few weeks seems like such a short amount of time. We'll discuss this when I see you. You are correct. I am planning to change cleaners, so I can use him in the interim before I pick up the new service.

I am in a pout about the restriction you placed on me about the crop but I understand why. Even the whip can be a caress. Damn! I hate it when you are right.

I do have one important alteration to your plan. I think it is essential that you not stay home alone that month. He must see you out and about. He should see his life as empty but he should see your life as a rich, full one. It will not be enough for him to see me at your home. He's used to that. I think you should date. And although I hate to say it, I think you should date a man.

Luckily, I may have just the guy. He's been working in my store for about three months. He is gorgeous. I hired him for his looks. He's a slender guy from Costa Rica. I swear women will come into the store just to have this guy hold their feet. I saw one woman so besotted over him that she bought the same pair of shoes she bought the previous week.

We'll put him in the car a few times while you drive by Butler kneeling in front of your driveway. Eduardo will be happy to do it for me. He thinks he wants to date the boss but he really has no idea. Also, I've learned the hard way to not fuck the help. What you do with him once you get him inside is up to you but the important thing is that Butler sees him coming and going.

Of course, I wouldn't tease Butler about your new boyfriend while he's cleaning my store. Not me. I'm the soul of discretion. OK, maybe I would. Just a little. He-he! I want something special if I get him to cry.

The thought of sharing a house in Florida three months a year with our own domestic staff sounds like what I need. I can spare Suzy from the Atlanta store during the first quarter.

Of course, the whole plan may fall apart if Butler runs for it. However, I'm starting to trust that you know what you're doing.

If he survives, we shouldn't buy a place. We should build one. The stores are doing very well. I will pick up the extra cost. I have several ideas to incorporate into the design that will reflect our lifestyle. I haven't been this excited in years!

When do we start?

Heather

March 2015
Dear Heather,

I can't wait to see you to tell you how it felt this afternoon. The whole experience made we weak in the knees. The minute the judge pounded his gavel to finish the proceeding I had to grab your lawyer friend by the hand. I felt a little lightheaded. I might have sat there for a long time but I had to scurry to position myself so I could see her hand him his suitcase with his note. Oh, the look on his face! Now, I wish I had filmed it.

I spent the last few weeks getting him ready for this. I wanted him in deep subspace when he walked into the courtroom. After the month I gave him he was eager to do anything for me. The last thing I did was to put him in his chastity cage with instructions to never remove it without my permission no matter what happened. It all worked perfectly.

Even getting dressed today for my court appearance was tremendously exciting. I sent him there early on the bus so I could put on my new dress without him seeing it before the trial. I've always enjoyed dressing to entice him but this was different. It was like I was arming myself for battle. You and I picked the perfect outfit. I call the look "business bitch." The shoes you gave me were a dream. They are easily the highest pair of heels I own. They made me feel powerful. I could see him watching me and wanting me throughout the hearing. It was hard to keep my eyes averted.

I was excited this morning but it felt weird dressing myself. I haven't had to do that for a while. I hope I don't go very long without a servant.

I have lots to share. Meet me for drinks tonight downtown.

Renee

Butler's Journal
Cast Out
March 2015

I remember walking out of the courtroom in a daze. Ms. Renee walked out ahead of me protectively flanked by her two attorneys. I couldn't help but notice the new expensively cut dark blue business suit, dark hose, and especially high heels she wore for the occasion as she clicked out of my life. I shuffled out into the bitter grey afternoon with my cheap coat and one small ratty suitcase.

I had no money, a phone locked around my neck that had been turned off, and a metal chastity cage still locked on my genitals. I was not angry or sad. I was stunned.

She had gone through with it. Until the last minute, I thought the whole day was one of her elaborate scenarios meant to teach me a lesson. The divorce papers in my hand proved that she had been serious. She had taken everything. I stood blinking in the pale afternoon sun shivering but too stupid to take the next step.

Finally, feeling too cold to remain standing in front of the courthouse, I started walking the three miles to the address that her attorney had given me. I suppose I should have felt grateful for a place to sleep but even after I saw the divorce finalized I had still assumed that I would be going home with my mistress.

During the walk I reviewed the last few years of our lives together trying to understand what I could have done to prevent this outcome. Admittedly, I had not always tried my very best to provide a life of pleasure and leisure for her, but I had worked very hard in the house and had tried very hard to accept her discipline. I had repeatedly humbled myself. I had done everything I had promised. I tried not to think about the fact that she had also done what she had promised. Surely, she still needed me. Weirdly, even with what I had just experienced, I found myself worried about who would do her ironing this week. I'm not sure I was processing what had happened. Why was I walking down Poplar Avenue in the cold? Had I failed in some way to please her that I did not understand?

I had no answers when I arrived at my new home. It was a large timeworn apartment building several blocks from Ms. Renee's home. I let myself in the building with the key but had trouble finding my apartment. Finally, seeing one of the tenants, I asked for directions to the basement stairs. After descending one flight I trudged down a dark corridor of broken vinyl tile to a wooden door that had to be my apartment.

It was worse than I imagined. Obviously it had been part of the old engine room. There was a cot, a sink, and a toilet along the back wall. On the other side of the room was the giant boiler for the apartment building. There was no shower. I threw myself down on the cot. It was warm.

Several hours later I woke feeling dislocated from my surroundings. I had no money but I wasn't hungry. My mind felt dull. This feeling of not being alive would stay with me for the next week.

I opened the suitcase given to me outside of the courtroom. Inside I found my toiletries and a change of clothes. I was free, but free for what? I should have felt rage and sorrow but I was still too stunned.

I emptied the small suitcase. In one of the side pouches I found a cache of coins. I knew where they came from. Ms. Renee had a vase in which she placed loose change until there was enough to carry to the bank. No doubt, she had scooped it in the suitcase when she packed the bag. I counted it out to discover I had $34.04. If I were careful, I could eat for several days.

I didn't leave the room until the following afternoon. I could think of no reason to eat until huger required it of me. I wondered if Ms. Renee had sent out her embarrassing blackmail to my old friends to complete my isolation. I tried to care but couldn't.

March 2015
Dear Renee,

I'm planning to drop in on Butler tomorrow at the pit we found for him. Wish me luck.

Thank you for sharing everything. This is a dangerous plan but if anyone can make it happen it's us. I feel like an undercover secret agent. I love the excitement you bring to my life.

In return, I offer you Eduardo. I told him that you wanted to meet him. He's a perfect distraction for you. He's also perfect for your plans. Why should you do without while I have fun with your slave?

I won't let you down.

Heather

Butler's Journal
Lost
March 2015

The first few days I barely left the apartment. I had nowhere to go. The weather was freezing. I managed to stock my shelf with some cheap food from the local grocery store but I had no appetite. I had nothing to distract me, but all I wanted to do was to sleep. In my dream I kept crawling into a smaller and smaller diameter tunnel. I heard the cracking of the walls and realized that someone was knocking on the door.

I couldn't imagine who it was. They kept sharply rapping until I managed to struggle up from the cot and open the door.

Ms. Heather waited outside in the dark dirty passageway like an alien visitor from another world. She stood there silently staring at me without speaking. She wore black leggings, a sable fur coat, and ankle boots with fur around the tops. Her head was bundled in what appeared to be a black fur turban.

"Well? Are you going to ask me in?"

It came out automatically, "Yes, ma'am," I harshly whispered. I hadn't used my voice for several days.

She pushed past me to stand in the middle of the tiny squalor that was my room. She slipped off her leather gloves looking for a place to sit them down, but there wasn't one. No one could have looked more out of place than she. I wanted to ask her questions about my mistress but I could not bear to hear her scorn.

"Two," she said as she turned to me.

Instantly, a red-hot curtain dropped over my eyes. I felt myself tighten, readying myself to spring at her.

"Two, please," she gently repeated.

Her quiet request had its effect. I felt the storm of my burning rage subside as quickly as it had risen. Awkwardly, I looked around the room for a moment as if seeking advice. I still wanted to strangle her but I was just as angry with myself. Finally, the force of habit won. I sank sullenly to my knees.

"I did not come to gloat. You're past that. I don't kick dead dogs."

"Then, why did you come?" I was on my knees but if I was a dog, I was snarling.

"You want to kick me out. I understand, but I was the one who suggested to Renee that you could stay here. She would have abandoned you on the street. Kicking me out would not be a good idea. I know the owner of this building. She and I made an arrangement. It's cold outside, slave. This place is a dump but it's at least a warm dump."

I had wondered where the room came from and how I would pay for it. "Why did you come?" I repeated.

"To explain the new rules. You can stay here rent free for keeping the hallways clean. Each night you are to sweep and mop one of the floors. Start with the first floor tonight and work your way up through the rest of the week."

"There's more, there always is with you," I challenged her.

Ms. Heather paused and looked directly at me. I did not bend my head down as I had been trained. Once again I noticed the cool green ice she had for eyes.

"Yes, there is more. You are forbidden to return to your practice as an attorney. I now own the blackmail Renee kept on you. She was quite thorough. It will easily get you disbarred."

I felt the blade turn in my gut. "I have no money. I have to work"

"Yes, but for now it amuses me that you work for me. I need my store cleaned each night after hours. You will report tonight at 9:00 p.m. I will explain your duties. I will pay you what I think you are worth."

I had no more money and very little food. I had not had the heart to reach out to old friends. I didn't know if I still had any friends. Had Ms. Renee burned those bridges as badly as she burned me? Had they received her blackmail package? The fact that I had just been divorced made it clear that Ms. Renee did not bluff. What could I tell them? I needed time to think but I also needed food. I had no choice.

"OK," I said.

"No, no, no, Butler, we must keep the necessary civilities between us. Your response should be, 'Yes, Ms. Heather.'"

She looked down on me with complete confidence. I didn't answer. She was not my mistress but she was close to her. To be under Heather's rule was as close to my mistress as I could come. I realized surprisingly through my fog of depression and rage that I still wanted to be close to her.

She went on, "You've had a shock and you are not thinking clearly. Think carefully this time before you answer. The words you are looking for are 'Yes, thank you, Ms. Heather.'"

I looked up at her beautiful coat and her perfect angular face framed by her stylish turban. I heard the words grind out of me as if they each weighed more than my tongue could carry. "Yes, thank you, Ms. Heather."

As soon as I said it she smiled, patted me affectionately on the cheek, and swept out of the room. I knelt there on the concrete floor wondering if I had made a terrible mistake.

Would this all I would ever be? Would I end up as Heather's whipping boy? The idea gave me the shakes. I was Renee's. I had been her lover as well as her slave. What was left to me now?

April 2015
Dear Heather,

Thank you for your help with this. Keep him busy and fed. I know you will want to stand on him and grind in his misfortune but try to hold back somewhat. I don't want him to disappear. We are walking a tightrope. I want him to see how meaningless his life is without me but I don't want him jumping off the Memphis Bridge.

I'm not sending out my blackmail on him. If we are successful. I will still want him publicaly by my side.

If he is still wearing his chastity cage two weeks from now, I want you to move immediately to the next step. I know that your first urge will be to torment him for a while but two weeks is long enough to live without hope.

I think you are starting to understand that I love him. If you see this going sideways, I want you to step in and prop him up. I wanted to give him the experience of losing everything, only to be rescued by me in the end. I also want him to experience complete surrender. I made a serious promise to him that I intend to keep for both of our sakes.

We've talked about how I think you should handle the next phase. You are at your best when it comes to direct scorn and humiliation, but our next move will require finesse. This will be a challenge to you. Remember, at one point he may need you to be supportive. I know how excited you can get. OK, I admit to being excited too. We can do this.

I'm going to try to relax, trust Butler's training, and enjoy myself. I have complete trust in you.

Renee

April 2015
Dear Renee,

I admit that I didn't understand your relationship with Butler at first. You know why I have problems with men. I doubt I will ever learn to trust one. However, watching you and Butler continue to love each other through this journey has been a healing experience for me. You are my only real friend. If he is what you want, then I want to give him to you.

When you first suggested this idea, all I could think of was how much fun it would be if I caught him out of his belt. Your idea that I should take him home and treat him so cruelly that he came running home to you excited me. I had a thousand ideas I wanted to try. Yes, I admit I'm built that way but the more I thought about it the more, I want him to pass this test for your sake.

My goal is to land him on your doorstep wanting to serve you. I'll get him there one way or another.

Much love,
Heather

Butler's Journal
Alone
April 2015

There was nothing in my life. I slept, I ate, and I worked for Ms. Heather cleaning her store. I mopped the hallways in my apartment building. I stared at the walls until it was time to do the next thing. I tried very hard not to walk the six blocks to Renee's home. In the flurry of paperwork at the divorce I received a notice to keep at least 300 feet away from the house. I did not want to add an arrest to my problems.

The first night I worked for Ms. Heather, she showed me what she wanted done. If I worked quickly it would take me at least four hours to clean the store. Ms. Heather insisted that it should only take three hours. She paid me twenty dollars a night in cash. It was less than minimum wage, but it was enough money to allow me to eat.

As expected, on my second night she met me at the door. She was dressed, well, like Ms. Heather always dresses. For not liking men very much, she makes a point of turning their heads. She had on tan tights with low heeled but very tall above the knees brown boots, a tight coffee colored sweater, and wide studded leather belt that accented her small waist. She looked like a spoiled housewife who shopped for a living, but I knew her as a savvy businesswoman with a lot of street smarts. She looks like old money but she curses like trailer trash if aroused. I hadn't expected to please her.

She took me around to various spots in the store and berated me as only she could for my poor performance. I was too dead inside to feel much from her demanding bitchiness. I was warned that if I didn't improve I would be fired. Whatever tiny morsel of gentleness that I saw in my apartment was gone when she talked about her store.

I corrected the tiny mistakes she had pointed out. She continued to leave me a pittance in cash. I worked slowly and carefully to avoid mistakes. It took me five hours each night but I had nowhere else to go.

Two lonely soul-searching weeks later, I found her waiting at the store when I arrived and after everyone else had gone. She was obviously dressed to go out to a late dinner with someone. Her dress clung provocatively to her slender frame as she approached me. I didn't know what to expect. She was always unpredictable.

"Hello, Butler."

I was too tired to feel much. I was dimly aware of her but I knew I couldn't start again with another mistress. I couldn't be hers. This could not be any kind of beginning. Instead, I thought that this was probably where I lost my job and my apartment. As pathetic as they were, I needed both of them.

She stood still, allowing me to look at her. Most men would be attracted to her. She instinctively knew what clothes enhanced her slender frame. After a moment, she slinked closer into my personal space. She is used to getting a lot of attention from men for good reason. In her heels, she actually looked down on me. I could smell the expensive perfume she wore.

"You're doing a good job cleaning each night. You were always a good maid."

She gently placed one hand on my chest and slowly let it slide down to my belly. She took her time while she stepped around me, trailing her hand. I remained motionless, as I had been trained to do. Behind me her hand dropped below my belt and cupped one of my buttocks.

"You've always kept yourself in shape. I appreciate that in a man."

I said nothing. I felt like cattle being inspected. I had barely spoken to anyone in over two weeks. No one had touched me.

Standing behind me now with both hands on my waist, she leaned in to whisper in my ear, "Are you tired of the hole you live in yet?"

"It's warm," I offered. I could feel her hot breath on my neck.

"Yes, but are you ready to move on? Would you like to live somewhere else?"

I didn't know if this was an offer to live with her or not. I knew I had never been particularly drawn to her. I disliked her for a long time. Lately, I had begun to understand what Ms. Renee had seen in her. She was completely unconcerned with convention. She was brave enough to live exactly as she wished. That honesty translated into her personal relationships. One always knew what she thought and felt. Surprisingly, her shrewd, piercing mind could be trained inward. She had the ability to change that is very unusual in a person. I knew in my present poverty I would never be involved with another beautiful woman again. Here might be my last offer.

I could feel her hands slip around my waist. The mere human contact was a delicious feeling. Slowly her hands dropped to my groin. Suddenly, with a hiss, she jerked away as if she had been stung.

"What the fuck? Are you still wearing your cock cage?"

"Yes, ma'am," was all I could answer.

"You could have borrowed a bolt cutter and freed yourself. Why didn't you?"

I felt my knees weaken. I slowly slumped to the floor. I hadn't meant for her to know. Her touching me was unexpected. I was embarrassed. I felt like a fool but I had been unable to break Ms. Renee's hold on me. I didn't want to break it. Remaining faithful to her last command was my last tie to her.

Dejectedly I answered her, "She never gave me permission to take it off."

"You are a bigger fool than I thought! I can tell you haven't really accepted your situation yet. Maybe you need more time. Maybe you need to see something first. I want you to meet me at the coffee house near your apartment at noon tomorrow."

She stepped back and reached under her dress for a silver chain. Dangling from the chain were the keys to the phone around my neck and the chastity belt around my genitals. She looked down at me.

"I don't know if I have you yet where I want you. I think tomorrow should help."

She gave me a triumphant smile and strode from the room.

I felt like a fool. I should have realized that I was never going back to Ms. Renee. I should have taken the chastity belt off the first night. Now, Ms. Heather had the keys. Of course, I could still borrow a bolt cutter and remove them. Would Ms. Heather fire me and kick me out of the apartment if I did so? I didn't dare. I had nowhere else to go. Would she use the blackmail that she said now belonged to her? I knelt there thinking about my future but I soon stood up. No matter what happened I still had to clean if I wanted to eat. It was almost dawn before I crept back into my apartment.

April 2015
Dear Renee,

It's only been two weeks. I wanted to take him home at least for an evening to torment him a little, but when I saw he still had on your chastity belt it took the fun out of it. He's still very much yours.

I know it's what you predicted would happen. I know you love him. I know I promised, but damnation, I admit that I was tempted to torment him some more. However, I know how important this is to you. For once, I showed some restraint. He's ready. We'll be there tomorrow as planned.

It looks like we both love you.

Heather.

Butler's Journal
The Choice
March 2015

I only had one change of clothes. Each night I washed my shirt, socks, and underpants in the sink along with my body. After two weeks my suit began to stink but I had no money to get it dry cleaned. I never went anywhere but work and a nearby grocery store. No one came close enough to smell me. I made some effort the next day at brushing my suit. I placed my shirt under my mattress the night before in an attempt to press it. It looked like I felt. Worn, tattered, and thrown out.

The next day, I was there when Ms. Heather walked into the coffee shop. I stood up as she approached the table. The waiter hopped over to hold her chair. I wondered again what it was about a dominatrix that they often received better service than the rest of us mere mortals. Of course, it helped that Heather's simple-looking outfit cost more than the waiter made in a month. I had already ordered for her from memory when I saw her car drive up. I used the last of my money. Seconds later, her coffee arrived. She accepted it all as her due.

Uncomfortably, I sat down with her. I had known this woman for years. We had been on several vacations together, we had shared a home for a short time, but I had never sat at a table with her. She was also the woman who carried the keys to the two locks I still wore. She also owned blackmail information on me.

She smiled, no doubt guessing some of what I was thinking,

"You surprised me last night by still being in the cage. How are you doing?"

I looked up to see if she was teasing me but there it was again. She sounded solicitous. I remembered she has also spoken gently to me when she visited me at my apartment. It was out of character. I had to force myself against my training to look up and face her. I expected to read a victorious smirk. Instead, she simply stared at me with a benign and curious look.

If she had been the Ms. Heather I thought I knew I would have withdrawn. I mumbled some sort of reply but she continued to gently probe. She was the only person I had said more than three words to in weeks. Under her steady pressure I began telling her how I felt. I was not in good shape.

After listening to me for a while, she glanced at her watch and told me to follow her.

"Are you still locked?"
Reluctantly, I admitted I was.
"Then, I have something you should see."

Ms. Heather dropped five dollars on the table as a tip. I looked at the money as I left. Again, I was reminded why I could never belong to her. She had left the money carelessly, forgetting how broke I was. Ms. Renee would have done it intentionally to tease me. I remembered that even Ms. Renee's cruelest actions were thoughtful and were designed to bind me tighter to her.

Ms. Heater motioned me to climb into the passenger seat of her Roadster. I had been in her car before but then I was in the trunk.

She drove to Café Society. We parked across the street. From our parking spot we could discreetly see into the windows of the restaurant.

I knew before I looked what she had carried me to see. This was one of Ms. Renee's favorite restaurants. I wanted to get out of the car and walk away. Instead, I looked. Ms. Renee was sitting at her favorite table. She was not alone. A very good-looking younger Latino man was sitting across from her. From the way they were interacting, it was obvious that this was not their first date.

I heard Ms. Heather whisper into my ear, "Look at her. What do you see?"
I couldn't turn my head away.

"She's taken everything from you and tossed you out like trash. Now, look at her. It's obvious, isn't it? She's fucking someone else."

She pressed against me. "I wanted you to know that I suggested that she divorce you. I thought it was beneath her to be married to a slave. I suggested that she leave you locked up. Also, I'm the one who introduced her to the man at the table."

I looked up at her.

"I offered myself to you once but you turned me down. I told you then that I would ruin your life."

She leaned into me. Her hand slid between my thighs. She flicked a nail through my pants against the metal bars of cage.

"How does it feel? How does it feel knowing she left you in that cage while she's fucking someone else?"

Her hand slid back to her own side of the car, stroking the keys hanging from her neck. I looked down at my hands. I began clenching and unclenching my fists. Maybe I was wrong about everything.

"What are you going to do about it? You could cut the locks off." She touched me again. "Or you could come home with me." She paused. "You need to be with a woman like me. I've pried you loose from her. You can still follow your dream of belonging to a dominatrix. You know I'm strong enough. Look at what I've done to get you. Let's go home and use your keys. It's only fair after what she's done to you."

I heard the unspoken promise in her voice. I shook my head not trusting my voice. I knew that I was about to commit the unpardonable sin of refusing her again. Nevertheless, there was something in her voice that was not right. She was trying to seduce me but it felt half-hearted.

I shook my head again to indicate that I couldn't go home with her.

She nodded. I expected her to be angry but instead she said in an understanding voice, "I know that you find me attractive. I can tell. But once again you've turned me down. I guess I've come to expect it."

Did I detect a hint of relief? When she offered me herself I had sensed that she would not be offended if I refused. That was not like her.

She continued, "You won't come home with me. You haven't cut off your locks. Will you really go back to your hole in the ground and stay my cleaner but only my cleaner? Will you continue to hope for a miracle even after seeing her with another man?"

"Yes, I can't help it," I choked out. I was in an impossible situation but I could not see any alternatives.

I looked up at the restaurant. I thought briefly about confronting my mistress. I thought about smashing the windows. I was unable to move.

"I can tell you are angry at her."

Again, I nodded. Speech was almost impossible.

"Remember, all of this was your choice. All of your work and surrender has led you to this moment. You asked for this, didn't you? Now that you have nothing, what will you do? Will you throw away all of your effort by being angry? Will you deny your training? Or are you a man of your word?"

Heather pressed closer to me.

"There's a reason you never unlocked your cage. There's a reason you won't come home with me. What is it?"

I kept my head buried in my chest, still not trusting my voice. I refused to dissolve into tears.

"Look at her, really look. Does she look happy? Will you be like every other man and selfishly attempt to own or to stunt the pleasures of such a woman? Or can you be more?"

I looked. Ms. Renee was smiling at something her date had said. She looked beautiful beyond words.

"Now is your moment of truth. Ask yourself, are you still her servant?"

I had no answer.

"I believe that you are," she whispered.

I looked back down at my hands. I was unable to continue watching the window.

The female devil at my side continued to speak gently into my ear. "I'll tell you what you are going to do about it. You're going to do nothing. How can you? Look at her. She's having a good time. You can that see she is. Isn't that what's important to you? Isn't her happiness all that matters? I believe that you can step up to the next level. I want you to surrender to her even if it's hopeless. Surrender. Isn't that what you really want to do?"

I looked again at my mistress.

She paused then went on, "Think hard before you answer. Are you still her slave?"

I could have said a thousand different things. I had felt a thousand different things in the last few weeks. However, only one answer came from my lips.

"Yes."

I heard Ms. Heather release a long sigh. I could feel her relief. She reached in the small luggage compartment behind the seat of her convertible. She handed me a long cardboard cylinder.

"If you had said anything else you would not have been given this. She told me to wait until you had done or said something that proved to me that you were still hers. Remaining in your chastity cage proved yourself. If you had cut it off, this stage of your training might have taken months. Instead, your willingness to surrender saved you a lot of suffering. Now, get out of the car. Don't open this until you get back to your apartment. I expect you at work tomorrow night at the usual time."

"Wait!" She leaned in to me and gave me a quick chaste kiss. "You are a rare find, Butler," she whispered.

Thirty minutes later, after jogging home in the cold, I opened the cylinder in the privacy of my apartment. It was the poster of Renee I had on the wall of my room at her home. Scrawled across the bottom of the picture in Renee's handwriting were instructions.

"Meditate on this picture twice each day. Start when you rise and once again just before work. Concentrate on your complete surrender."

She was not done with me! This message was a lifeline. I felt an enormous surge of relief and love flood through me. My dark, empty life suddenly blossomed with meaning again. Nothing else mattered. She could have a hundred lovers. I could be punished or banished a hundred times as long as I belonged to her. No price was too high to be once more at her feet.

I immediately hung the poster on a nail on my grimy wall and started my own private meditation. I wept and hugged myself. I was alive again.

April 2015
Dear Renee,

I followed your advice about how to manipulate him. I wanted to take him home and play with him for a few days but I wanted even more to deliver him to your door in the right frame of mind. I still don't understand why he hadn't cut his cage off. You said it would still be there. What have you done to him?

When I showed him the two of you at the café I first felt only scorn. After all, what kind of man would allow you to do what's been done to him? Then we rubbed his nose in it. I almost felt pity. I was also a little afraid. I know he's physically fit. I thought for a second he might jump out of the car and strangle everyone in the restaurant.

I couldn't help myself. I put him to the test one more time. Once again, he passed. I admit I was proud of him. Afterward, I did what you told me to do. I encouraged him to overcome his jealousy. As I watched his reaction, I saw something rise from deep within him. I could see him breaking. I finally believe that he truly loves and worships you. He submitted.

As far as I'm concerned, I've seen a unicorn. He may be the only trustworthy man I've ever met. I understand that eventually he would have unlocked himself and I might have been able to snag him if I had kept trying. He is human. Nevertheless, for him to go as long as he did with no hope says something about his devotion to you. Of course, it also says something about your ability to weave a web of dark magic around him.

I followed him home just as you requested. I felt a little foolish standing in the parking lot spying on him through that dirty little window into his apartment. When he unrolled your picture and saw your note he acted like he had won the lottery. He immediately put the poster of you up on the wall and knelt in front of it just like you said he would. Incredible! I will never understand it, but you were right.

If I were you I'd go by and see him pray to your image before he goes to work tomorrow night. What does it feel like, to actually be someone's goddess?

I'll give him the rest of your instructions tomorrow night when he comes clean. I predict that he'll be camped on your driveway tomorrow just like you wanted. He's ready.

I think I may drive by to see him. Damn, girl, you've really got him tied up. I think you really might be a witch.

Bubble, bubble, toil and trouble,
Heather.

PS

I know Suzy is different and will require a different kind of experience but I want you to help me with her submission. I want her as bewitched as you've made him.

May 2015
Dear Heather,

Thank you for the last month. You have proved yourself to be a true friend. I could never have done this without you.

He's outside right now on his knees on my driveway. I admit to being very afraid the last few weeks. We took a chance but you landed him right on my doorstep just as you said you would.

It's hard to be patient right now. I want to go outside and kiss him but I want something else even more. I want him to belong to me. I want him to see himself and us differently. I want everything we promised each other when we started this journey.

I promised to use any means necessary. I think I kept that promise. He'll learn to swallow his jealous feelings about other men and women if it pleases me. His ability to do this is the ultimate symbol of his complete surrender. I actually care less about an occasional fling than I care that he accepts his place as my slave. This was his last hurdle.

We've left him no choice but to be grateful to serve me in whatever way I choose. It's all happening just as he and I envisioned it.

I plan on slowly bringing him back inside my life one step at a time. Of course, I'll make him work for each stage, but I know he's ready.

Certainly, I'm ready. The house is dirty despite the fact that I hired a temporary maid. I assume my standards have changed. My clothes are a wreck. I realized fumbling with the pump at the gas station that I have not filled up my own car with gas in almost ten years! It's almost comic how much I miss having a servant in my life. How did I ever do it?

Also, I miss him. I love having him in my life.

I owe you for your help with this.

We owe you.

Renee

Butler's Journal
Finding My Place
June 2015

I spent the last month slowly earning my place back into Ms. Renee's household. I was fearful at first approaching the house. I harbored suspicions that I was invited over so that I could be arrested for disobeying the court order to stay away. Anything was possible. That's one reason being her slave is so exciting. However, I knelt at her driveway for one hour each day as instructed.

Over the next week, during my vigil, I watched as different men and women arrived and left with her. It was clear that Ms. Renee was taking advantage of her newfound freedom and privacy. Despite the traffic of different people, I stayed there because I knew I was offering something completely different from what they could offer.

Finally, after several sharp humiliations and a reordering of our relationship, I again enjoy the privilege of living with my mistress. I occupy a different place than I did before the divorce. I still sleep in the same bed and I still have the same chores but now I know that I serve only at her pleasure.

My last test was to accept the task of preparing her for her dates. Emotionally, it's much harder to prepare her for a date with a man than when I prepared her for a date with a woman like Heather. There is the obvious bitter message that I'm not enough man for her. To complete my submission, she rubbed that fact in at every opportunity. Again and again, she teased and tormented me to distraction and tears. She often left me in my cage or restrained or kept me busy with some dull task while she was gone. But each night after a date, she returned to my narrow bed to snuggled with me, as her habit has been since we first started seeing each other.

Nevertheless, her message was clear. I belonged to her. She did not belong to me. She insisted that I recognize the difference in our sexual power. Her program to empower herself only made me want her more.

The first time I saw her drive off with a date I thought I would rage and tear out my hair. I thought it would crush me or destroy us. On some level I felt the normal righteous jealous wrath boiling in me, but on another deeper level a part of me felt exactly like I did the night I built a barge to row my mistress and Ms. Heather around the lake. It's true that sex was off the menu for me that night but I felt like I contributed to her pleasure by giving her something that only a well-trained submissive man could offer.

I looked at the impossible situation I live in today and think no man could be expected to put up with this. However, I am no longer a mere man. I am her deeply surrendered slave. The best looking young man in the world could not give her this freedom without years of arduous training. I am grateful that she has been strong enough to maneuver me carefully to this place, and I feel pride in my ability to surrender. In a strange way, at the moment it is the hardest I sense that I am more deeply and completely intimate with her than ever before.

Men are right to wonder why their woman stays with them. A woman might stay for a lot of reasons. Money, tradition, habit, and safety are obvious ones. I know that my mistress is completely free yet she stays with me. Between us, there is only love.

June 2015
Dear Heather,

My life with Butler has been everything I hoped it would be after I allowed him to move back in. It's like we are on the honeymoon that I never gave him. We have rarely been so passionate. I missed him.

Throughout our lives together, each time I put him through an experience to cement our relationship as mistress and slave I am afterward filled with tenderness toward him. Lately, the love between us has been especially sweet.

I love having him as my slave, and I love having him by my side in our vanilla life. Before our annual award banquet last month, I took him to a tailor and bought him a bespoke suit that I'm sure is the nicest suit he has ever owned. To go with it I bought a pair of English bench-made loafers and a Hermes tie. After all, his attire reflects on me. In public I want him to dress better than other men. Also, it was fun to dress him in something that I know he appreciates. Even in the midst of a powerful scene with him I remember that I am proud to stand beside him at a public gathering. He is literate, urbane, charming, and thoughtful. Knowing that he is also my dedicated slave makes me very happy.

You and I gave him a powerful experience with the divorce. He now understands what a privilege it is to serve me. I knew that if I went through with my plan that there would be benefits for both of us. Our love life is more passionate now than we first met.

Our interactions are so loving right now it would be easy to allow us to slip backward in our journey toward complete domination. I don't want to lose any ground. That's where I hope you can help. I continue to need your strength.

More firmly in control of my finances than ever before, I'm ready to help you with the cost of our vacation home. I love spending at least one weekend a month with you. Now I can look forward to winters in Florida. I also look forward to helping you with Suzy. Swapping out the two of them or one of us using both of them at the same time for short periods sounds like a lot of fun. I have a bunch of new ideas I want to share with you.

Eduardo was a lot of fun and useful for what I wanted. However, in retrospect, he was less satisfying than I thought he would be.

(Never mention this to Butler!) I'm used to receiving a lot of oral sex. I'm not remotely interested in giving it. It was exciting at first but having an untrained man in my bed soon irritated me. I let him go quickly. I understand that he moved to New York. He was beautiful but worthless. However, he was good-looking enough that I still have trouble believing that you never took advantage of him. Maybe we are both maturing.

Of course, I'm still a public figure because of my job. I still have to answer to clients, politicians, and donors. I try to remind myself that it's for a good cause. I've been out a few times but less than what Butler thinks I've been. This is Memphis, and more eyes than his are watching me. I recall clearly that in our original agreement I could lie about anything if it moved him closer to perfect submission. The stories I tell him about my dating life may be inflated but they only cause him to crave me more. Everything is fair in love and war.

Of course, I plan on being more adventuresome in Florida. Butler's position there publicly will only be as my employee. I'll feel freer. I also know that he will accept anything that increases my pleasure.

I've studied the plans of the house in Florida you sent over. What's the small building out by the pool? I know you have hatched some new diabolical scheme. Bless you for your every evil impulse.

Will it really be ready for this January? I can't wait.

I do have one problem with Butler that you could help me with. I really don't have enough work at home to keep him busy no matter how high I set my standards.

I was thinking of sending him to your home to clean, but I think he needs more stimulation. He doesn't need to be alone. I don't want to send him back to work. His job as an attorney might make him feel important again.

Do you have a position in the store for him? I want something menial that keeps him on his knees in front of women but in a job that no woman would respect him for having.

Love,
Renee

July 2105
Dear Renee,

You keep making me happy. Yes, I have just such a position. You knew that even if I didn't, I would find one. However, we really do need a runner or "shoe boy" to find the right size shoes from the stock room and then help our client into her new pair. He would not be salesman. In fact, I won't allow him to speak to our customers. We need him from 10:00 a.m. to 2:00 p.m. for the lunch rush.

I promise you that I will follow your process and training methods exactly. Having him under my thumb for a few hours each day will be a real pleasure.

Also, now that Eduardo has left, I have an all-female staff that could use a little fun. I like to keep them happy. How do you feel about me hinting to them what kind of man he's become? I'm sure that my staff could make his time with us more interesting. They are a very fun group of women. When we're done each day, I promise, he'll be glad to get back to you. I assume that's what you wanted?

Of course, I'll deposit his paycheck into your bank account. Let's get together to talk details. Lunch tomorrow?

Heather

December 2015
Dear Heather,

It's been a great year. I've been very fortunate with fundraising. We surpassed our goal.

You were right about the women at your store. I make Butler tell me everything about how they treat him. You have an imaginative group of women in your employ. It's been fun to tease him about how he earns his paychecks there.

I'm glad we are finished with this last quarter. I can't wait to see you in Florida. I don't think we've spent more than one night together for the last three months. Well, at least we are busy at the same time of year.

We will be there a little after you and Suzy arrive. Did you pick a uniform for Suzy to wear? I'm planning on keeping my servant in what I call his butler outfit. You mentioned that you wanted to make a couple of suggestions.

What did you have in mind?

Renee

December 2015
Dear Renee,

I'm so ready for this year to end. I loved spending the holidays in Atlanta with Suzy but I'm ready to head south.

A uniform for Suzy? Oh heck yeah, but I want it to be a surprise. Wait till you see her in it. You're going to love it. We're going to have a lot of fun with her. She'll love it too, of course.

I do have two requests. My first one is that I want to be able to help you discipline Butler. You've never really allowed me to do that except on your honeymoon. I now understand why but since then you and I have grown closer.

It was never much of a hardship to not have your permission to use the crop on him because I never felt a burning need to do it. However, after watching his response to his divorce, I suddenly wanted to take part in his training. There was something about his willingness to obey you that I found stimulating.

Over the years I've learned to believe in his desire to submit to you. One might think that his willingness would make me want to whip him less, but paradoxically I want to whip him more. I think it attracts me now because I feel that he is malleable clay, so I will not be wasting my time. You know I want only the best for you. I'm certain that I can help you with his training.

My second request I think will be much easier for you to agree to accept. I want there to be a hierarchy that clearly designates Butler as the bottom of our foursome. Suzy is my submissive but she should be considered a step above Butler, who is only a man. Also, I want Suzy to feel special.

What do you think?

Heather

December 2015
Dear Heather,

As always, great minds think alike. I was going to make the same exact suggestions.

At first, I wanted to be the only one who whipped Butler because I wanted him to understand who owned him. I always knew that hurting him excited you but I also wanted you to join me in doing it because you were trying to increase the amount of love. I'm glad to see that we are finally on the same page. Yes, I agree his recent submissiveness doesn't make me want to back down on his physical discipline. In fact, I only want to increase it now that I see its effectiveness. I am going to need all the help I can get.

You are also right that he has to take last place to all women, even submissive women. I'm sure that together we can find ways to teach him that important lesson. We are going to have a lot of fun over the next three months.

I can't wait to tell you about my new plan for our servants. I think you'll like it. We'll start the moment we arrive.

Renee

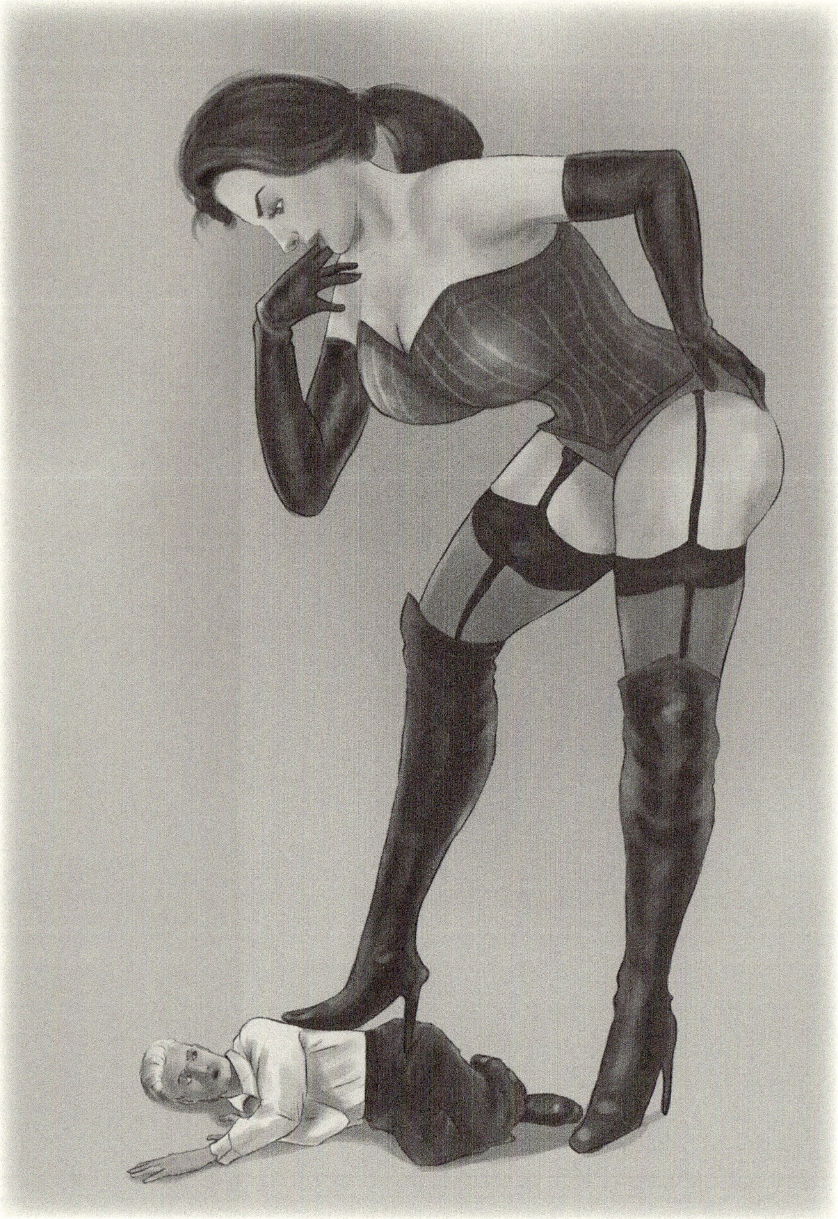

Denouement

Butler's Journal
Venice, Florida
March 2016

The first month of our stay in Florida was a transformative time for Suzy, Heather's submissive, and for me. Both Ms. Renee and Ms. Heather wanted us to see ourselves while we were in Florida as mere employees. There was an abundance of sexual play in private but in public we assumed the role of domestic staff. I acted as chauffeur, gardener, and butler. Suzy was used as an upstairs maid, cook, and beautician.

Both women dated other men and women. Both women also went out of their way to humble us in public and private. Ms. Heather finally had free rein to discipline me and to make use of me. It was very difficult for me to accept discipline from her at first, but as usual, Ms. Renee had her way. To my relief, Ms. Heather was actually more careful about going too far than my own beloved mistress. I assume that she still wanted to be careful with Ms. Renee's possessions.

I have had many humbling experiences with my mistress, but being under the thumb of two women at the same time was powerful. Being on the bottom of the pecking order among three women was mind altering. Suzy never attempted to dominate me, but unlike me she often ate with our owners and slept in the house. For the entire Florida winter I slept in a tiny structure next to the pool. Everything was arranged to inculcate the idea that I was a servant and they were nobility. Certainly, I began to think of myself, and them, in those terms.

Doubtless, many would view my relationship with Ms. Renee as unfair. That's not the way I felt. I was living in paradise with three beautiful women. I would never have been able to afford a vacation home without surrendering to my mistress and without the help of Ms. Heather. We even bought a tiny sailboat that I loved. I was cared for. I was required to stay in great physical shape.

Between bouts of discipline, we continued our varied interests. We continued to enjoy lively discussions on politics, literature, and film. I admit that I was usually sitting on the floor when we had those discussions, but maybe that's where men should sit. My idea of gender roles had undergone a complete transformation under Ms. Renee's gentle tutelage. When I am done with my duties, my mistress permitted me time to read and play the piano. I felt sincerely grateful to her for any free time she allowed me.

No matter what form of discipline she demanded or what configuration our lifestyle took, I was confident that my mistress knew how I felt about everything. In addition, I was convinced that how I felt mattered to her. In a deep way, I was known and understood. In a different manner, accepting her complete freedom and submitting to her discipline allowed me to know and understand her. It was always about love.

The terror and trials of the divorce were in the past. The first month in Florida had been very challenging for Suzy and me, but we had adapted to the demands imposed on us. As the first warm winter months passed, Suzy and I both fell even more under the sway of our goddesses. We both eagerly strived to please them.

At the end of the season and in celebration of Ms. Renee's birthday, our owners decided to throw a big party. Many women from Ms. Renee's temple came down from Memphis. Suzy and I worked overtime to get everything ready.

In the lull before the guests arrived, my mistress and I were standing beside the pool.

In the privacy of the backyard, my mistress slipped her hand around my waist and tipped her head up to be kissed. Everything was easier now that I had learned to trust her completely.

"Happy birthday," I whispered.

She kissed me again.

"I have nothing to give you but my love," I continued.

"Yes, we both have worked very hard for you to be able to say that," she answered. "I've taken everything from you but all I really wanted was your love."

My response rose up in me spontaneously. "I am only a slave. It is a privilege to serve." I meant every word.

She smiled at me for a moment and went on, "You have been so wonderful the last few years. You never hesitated no matter what I put in your way. I never thought I would ever be loved like you love me."

At the corner of my eye, I saw Ms. Heather trooping by with Suzy scurrying behind her with a tray of glasses for the party. I heard her bark in a phony voice of high dudgeon, "Renee, I'm appalled at how familiar you allow yourself to become with the hired help!"

Ms. Renee laughed and kissed me again. Ms. Heather had mellowed a lot in the warm embrace of our close-knit group during the last year. I knew she was happy when she saw my mistress happy.

This beautiful, dangerous, and exciting woman continued to lean into me and kiss me. "I love you," she murmured.

We continued to hold each other until she broke our embrace by stepping away and smiling.

"Come upstairs and dress me. It's time. Heather and I want both of you in complete harness for the party. You know that I love dancing and flirting with my guests as you serve drinks while your harness keeps you aware that you belong to me. Remember, I want you to be on your best behavior because some of our Temple members flew down from Memphis for this party."

I couldn't image why her Temple friends had come all the way to Florida. I should have worried more about it but I was too busy.

Complete harness for me meant a chastity cage with an attached butt plug combined in a heavy steel and leather harness I could, with proper adjustment, wear under my butler uniform. It was humiliating and uncomfortable. Also, it was awkward to walk in, much less stand for three hours carrying a tray. Suzy had a similar device to keep her mindful of her position as Ms. Heather's property. Our two owners might not be thinking about us as they enjoyed the party but we couldn't help but think about them every second. We would also both walk with a specific gate, which delighted both of our respective owners.

To the many locals at the party we were merely the maid and houseman of two very demanding employers. The Memphis visitors would never give away our real relationships. In public they would treat us as employees. However, our chafing harnesses constantly reminded us of our true positions.

Through trial and tears we had finally arrived at love. Both dominant women were happy. Suzy was excited to live with us. We had become family.

However, I was a little worried. I overheard while serving dinner the previous night some talk about a "branding ceremony." I recalled that there were a lot of guests from the Memphis Temple in town. I realized that they had to be talking about me. Ceremony? Branding? Hot metal? Skin? Really? Wasn't that finally going too far?

It reminded me of the saying, "When the gods would punish you, they give you your deepest desire."

Final words

If you are interested in commenting on the story of our lives, please e-mail me at MistressReneeLane@gmail.com

Or visit me at www.MistressReneeLane.com

Or you can find me on Facebook. I am Renee Lane in Memphis, Tennessee.

What you can do to further the rise of women:

- Vote for female candidates who want to empower women
- Hire and promote women to positions of authority
- Obey and love your spouse even if she won't dress in leather for you
- Honor and obey the women in your life

Finally, if you enjoyed our story you can help me promote this book by posting my website or a link to my book at any S&M blog, board, or site that you visit. Send my book to women you desire. Write me and tell me what you have done. I want to hear from you.

Thank you for your interest in our lives.

Ms. Renee Lane

Made in the USA
Monee, IL
03 May 2021